Moose Ridge: Ending to Beginning

CRAIG HASTINGS

CHAMPAGNE BOOK GROUP

Moose Ridge: Ending to Beginning

Published by Champagne Book Group
2373 NE Evergreen Avenue, Albany OR 97321 U.S.A.

~ ~ ~

First Edition 2021

pISBN: 978-1-77155-971-3

Cover Art by Melody Pond

www.champagnebooks.com

Version_1

To all the strong Christian women in my life:
My mother, Nancy.
My two sisters, Debra and Donna.
My wife, Rose.
Especially my Grandmother Josie who taught me,
"It's okay. God's in charge!"

Dear Reader

God has helped me through so many issues in my life and led me to want to share this with others. That led to this book, and the story of someone who has suffered multiple tragedies and reaches the point of thinking they have reached the ending and have no life, only an existence. But then they find someone who also has suffered tragedies, yet moves forward, encouraged and strengthened by their faith in God. How their sharing this faith leads this person to envision a beginning rather than an ending.

Nowhere are we promised life without tragedies, problems, or devastating events we have no control over, but God's word does promise, 'It's okay, God's in charge.'

Craig

Chapter One

My excitement builds as I rush down the jetway, trying not to bump into anyone. The four-hour flight from Boston was bad enough, but now everyone seems determined to get in my way. I struggle to remain calm, but knowing this is the start of the next chapter in Michael's and my life together doesn't help. It will be perfect, and I can't wait.

Michael moved here three months ago. After medical school, he accepted a neurosurgical residency in Wyoming. I stayed behind in Boston while he got things organized out here. We'd been inseparable for close to six years so it was a long three months, but I knew it would be worth it. This move is the start of something big.

As I reach the main terminal, I check my phone for the text Michael said he'd send telling me where to meet him. My heart flips as I see his message:

Can't be there to pick you up so sent Rick. He'll meet
you at baggage claim. He's tall and should have a dark
cowboy hat on.

I freeze and read it again. What could have happened? I push this thought aside realizing Michael's no doubt tied up at the hospital. I'll need to get used to the demanding life of a doctor. Now I only need to find a tall man in a dark cowboy hat. How difficult can that be? I race through the terminal, not really taking notice of the many people I dodge around.

At baggage claim, I find the carousel my bags should be at and, while waiting, I search for a tall man in a cowboy hat. This can't be right. Almost every man is wearing a cowboy hat, and most of them are dark. Right then, I hear a voice behind me. "Are you Miss Strake? Miss Jazmine Strake?"

I turn to find a tall, slender man, about mid-twenties, wearing the prescribed dark cowboy hat. "Yes, I am. Are you Rick, my ride?"

"Yes, ma'am. Are your bags here yet?"

Ma'am? I doubt I'm even a few years older than him. "Please, call me Jazmine. They should be coming soon." The carousel starts and bags are moving along in front of us. I spot one of mine and reach for it, pulling it off.

"I'll take that, ma'am," Rick says, taking it from my grasp. "Are there any more?"

"Just one more, and really, you can call me Jazmine." I spot my other bag and point to it. "Here it comes."

Before I can, he grabs it and, with my two bags in tow, turns and motions to the exits. "I'm parked across the way. It's not far."

We exit the terminal, and the cold hits me as he leads me across a large parking lot. I thought he said it wasn't far? After a long trek to the middle of the lot, he stops at a pickup parked among the rows of pickups. I stifle a laugh. I'm definitely not in Boston anymore.

He stows my bags as I climb into the passenger side. Not a simple task given my short dress. I saw it in a store window last week and knew it'd be perfect for seeing Michael for the first time in months. For reminding him what he'd been missing.

Once inside, the warmth from the truck's heater helps thaw out my legs. Maybe the dress is not the best for Wyoming? As Rick drives away from the airport, I watch the views passing, which further solidifies we're not in Boston anymore. That's okay. I'm here to start my new life with Michael.

As we park in the drive, I see the house for the first time. Depression threatens to overcome me, but I fight it back. Michael found this meager house in the country, wanting a place to relax from what promised to be grueling days ahead. I remind myself this is temporary. We will make do.

Rick helps me inside and sets my bags by the sofa as I scan the room. It's modest and contains a few pieces of drab furniture arranged on the speckled gray linoleum covered floor. There is a gray couch, a small, scarred coffee table, and an old chrome and Formica dinette table with two vinyl cushioned chairs.

On the far wall is an open metal cabinet which appears to have woodgrain contact paper covering it. Two more chairs are on each side, and an old TV is on top. A gray metal wardrobe sits by the front door in place of a closet. The room's distinct lack of color, thanks to the dull beige paint, and the musty smell speak volumes on its lack of attraction. The gray curtains covering the windows and a single frameless mirror above the TV are the extent of the decorations.

"It's not the Taj Mahal, but it should work for now," Rick says.

"It is rather basic," I agree while surveying the minute room.

He interrupts before more dread appears. "Dr. Stenson said your boxes are in the back bedroom."

"Oh, perfect. Did Michael say how long he'd be?" The title of doctor makes me smile, which helps since I'm seeing little reason to be positive.

"Ah, no, ma'am." Something in his voice causes me to break off my survey of the room and turn in his direction. He's holding out an envelope. "Dr. Stenson said to give you this. He said it will explain things."

"Explain what things?" Negative thoughts flood my brain.

"I'm not sure. He said to give it to you when we got here. I'm sorry, but I'm on the late shift and need to go to make it in time."

The sound of the door closing behind Rick intensifies my sensation of being alone. I stand in what they call a great room, but it doesn't appear great to me. I fight to keep the overwhelming dread from consuming me, trying to concentrate on the positive. I can do this. We can do this. It's temporary. The means to our future. All our hard work and sacrifice for his schooling is about to pay off. Yet here I stand, and no Michael.

The envelope Rick gave me doesn't help my thoughts to remain positive, and magnifies the silence closing in around me. Jazmine is written in bold letters on the front, mocking me. Fearing what it might hold, I'm reluctant to open it and eliminate any chance I'm wrong. Why do I jump to the negative? This could be anything. Maybe my worst fears are nothing but that. However, with my past life and its disappointments, I always expect my worst fears to come true. He could be working the late shift at the hospital? But why wouldn't he call? If there was an emergency and he's assisting surgery, he couldn't call. But a letter?

My pulse races as I stare at the envelope in my shaking hand. I know I must open it. Breathing is hard, and I'm sure I hear my heart pounding over the whooshing sound in my ears.

With a diminishing thread of hope, I open the envelope and remove the pages. I focus on the words while fighting to stay positive. As I read, tears fill my eyes.

Dear Jazmine,

I trust Rick found you. I'm sure you might be a little shocked and I'm sorry, but I have thrilling news.

About a month ago, the head surgeon, Dr. Williams, wanted to see me. He said he was impressed with me and that he'd been talking with a colleague about me.

To cut to the chase, there was a position for me in the residency program at UCLA Medical Center. He explained my talents demanded more than they could provide here and told me all about the program there. I couldn't let this pass.

The next few weeks were a blur. I wanted to tell you but didn't want to jinx it. Last week, all the details were finalized. The one issue was I needed to be there before you arrived. Not my choice, but I couldn't say no.

It was obvious this was fate since everything just fell into place. I have a place to live with Dr. Williams' daughter, Felicia, who is also going to UCLA for her psychiatric residency. We hit it off right away.

I needed to be there by Thursday, meaning yesterday, and it being a two-day drive, Felicia and I left Tuesday. Sorry I couldn't let you know sooner, but things snowballed and before I knew it, I had to leave. You'd already sent back the signed lease for the house, so I left it in your name. Now you're set. It's not much, but a year will go fast. You can find another place then. I was going to call to tell you not to come, but I knew how much you wanted to get out of Boston. Now you are. I used part of the money you sent for the first and last month's rent and to get the utilities started. The boxes are in the back bedroom, and I stocked a few groceries.

Jazmine, it's incredible how everything worked out for us. We're away from Boston and able to start our new lives. I appreciate all you've done and know you're thrilled with this fantastic opportunity for me. You're a special friend.

Now I leave you to start your quest for the perfect life. You deserve it. Take care, and with any luck, we'll meet down the road.

Michael

My heart creeps into my throat and warm, salty droplets spill down my cheeks. My legs weaken, and my knees buckle. The couch breaks my fall as I land on it. My eyes blur from tears as I read the letter over and over, hoping I'm missing something, but deep down I know I'm not. I thought ours was a close relationship, I thought we were about to start our perfect life. He makes it sound like this was nothing more than one friend helping another. I left everything behind in Boston to be with him, and now he wants me to start my quest? What happened to our quest?

My sobs rack my body, and while I wipe my eyes yet again with my already damp palms, I consider the possibility I'll never recover from this dark, desolate place.

The pages fall from my shaking hands, floating to the floor. I can't handle this. I've never felt so abandoned, so hopeless, so alone. Unable to stop, I slump to the side and end up lying on the couch in a ball. My arms hold on tight to everything I have, which is me, nothing but me.

~ * ~

I wake in a dark room. Somehow, I found my way to a bedroom. My coat is over me, but being cold and seeing my boxes in the moonlight, I stumble to reach them. After rummaging through, I drag out a blanket and wrap it around me, tumbling back on the bed. Once again, I'm all alone.

My head knows he's gone, but something has pulverized my insides. There's nothing left. How could he think we were nothing but friends hanging out? I thought what we shared was real. How did I not see this coming? The tears continue as my mind searches for answers. Was he biding time until a better offer came along? Someone he could upgrade to, like Felicia?

There's been a lot of sorrow in my life, but nothing like this. The pain in my chest is excruciating, and I hope it's a heart attack and I'm never able to leave this bed.

I wake again with the blanket wrapped around me, but it's little comfort. It's a struggle to rise, but I make my way out to the front room. In the pale moonlight it's even more depressing, and my gaze lights on the pages of Michael's letter spread out on the floor. My legs give way and I drop, but there's no couch to land on this time, nothing but the floor. With my legs against my chest, I pull the blanket tight. I should get up, but I have no energy.

While I lie, the tears flow again as thoughts of Michael fill my mind. The joy he brought back to my life. How he helped me to open myself to someone else. To concentrate on the positives. The fun we shared shopping for bargains and adding our own touches to our apartment. How for the first time since my father, I felt someone deeply cared about me. We shared everything and spent every moment together. Even when buried in our own school work we were together, across the table from each other. There was a home and someone to share it with, and that was all we needed. Now, there's no Michael. I'm alone.

I must have dozed off again, because the cold seeping through the blanket from the hard, worn linoleum wakes me. I struggle to get up, my stiff body refusing to cooperate. The realization there's dim light coming through the dingy windows gets through my stupor. Crawling to the couch, I gather my strength to stand behind it and gaze about the room. The dull light of the breaking morning does nothing to improve what is around me.

Not knowing where to go but needing to move, I take the few steps to walk past the couch. I trip on my bags and grab the couch to stay upright. My gaze again finds the pages of Michael's letter spread across the floor. Tears fill my eyes, and knowing I'm losing it, I stumble back to the bedroom, toppling into the bed.

~ * ~

When I wake again, sunlight fills the room. My phone shows it's close to noon, but the shock is it's Sunday. My flight here was on Friday, which means I slept through Saturday and most of this morning. I can't remember ever feeling like this, not when my mother died, or when my father left. Not even when I lost everything and moved into a foster home. This pain will never end.

It's not far, but stumbling to the meager bathroom adds to my misery. The hideous image in the flaking mirror startles me. My makeup is smeared, my hair's a mess, and my eyes are red and puffy. The revolting reflection matches how I feel.

There isn't much here. The small, worn sink below the mirror has visible cracks and two tatty faucets. The toilet crammed beside it has a seat but no lid, and there's a large tank mounted above it with a hanging chain. Across from these is what you could call a bathtub. It's miniscule, and there's not even a shower.

Maybe a bath will help? After turning on the water, I stagger to the bedroom to collect what's needed and return.

The water is getting warm, but I can't find the switch to shut the drain. There's a rubber stopper on a chain attached to the faucet. How old is this place? After plugging the drain, I undress. As I slip my dress off, I remember how excited I was seeing it in the store window, thinking Michael would be even more excited when he saw it on me. Now he never will. Not that he would care what I wore. It's only me, after all. The loser who sacrificed so much for him. The naïve little girl whose dreams will never be real. I want to toss the dress aside, but it's not its fault I can't attract anyone. That's all on me. I'm the one no one can stand to be around.

In the bedroom, I slide the thin, gray curtain covering the small closet open and hang the dress. It's a good thing I don't have a lot of clothes. Back in the bathroom, I step into the bath. While trying to lie back and let the heat soak into my body, its minute size becomes painfully obvious. As soon as I contort my body into a semi-comfortable position, I need to sit up to turn off the water. At least it's not a long reach.

I try not to think about my dismal life. My attempt fails and soon I'm crying again. Maybe I should end it all, let myself sink below the water and let go. No, that's not me.

The water is cooling, so I drain some and add more. The water coming out is colder than what is in the tub so I shut it off. With hardly any water left and my body shivering, I know my bath is over.

While drying off, I catch my reflection again. At least my face is no longer smeared with makeup. I brush my auburn hair the best I can, which takes time since it's well down my back. Michael bugged me about the time I wasted on my hair, but I prefer it long. After returning to the bedroom, I put on cut-offs and my favorite shirt. It was my father's and all I have left of his. It's old and several buttons are missing so it might reveal more than it should. Not that anyone is here to see. I could parade around nude.

Might have to, since my budget didn't allow much for clothes. While packing, I'd thought this would change since Michael would have an income here. Now, though, what I have must last even longer.

My suitcase is open where I left it, with the boxes from Boston off to the side. They contain everything I own. Might as well sort out my meager belongings. It's all on me, and will be from now on. What else do I have to fill my time? The tears start again.

Since there isn't much, it doesn't take long to unpack. It's a good thing I have so few clothes since there isn't much in the way of drawer space in the four-drawer scarred wooden dresser. In the kitchen, I find the basics, but knowing how to cook would help. Three frozen dinners are in the freezer, so I won't starve right away. When I discover there's coffee, I get my old coffee maker going and soon have a cup poured. I amble through to the living room, desperate not to let the drabness affect me.

With few choices, I flop on the musty couch and contemplate what is next. Michael's letter on the floor in front of me doesn't help. The tears are stinging my eyes again when I hear a knock. Before I can get up, there's another. After setting my cup on the bare coffee table, I hurry to the front door and open it. A man stands outside the porch door. He waves, smiling. The icy air making itself known makes me conscious of my missing buttons. I grab my coat and open the porch door, finding to my amazement a cowboy, complete with hat, boots, and a heavy coat I think they call a duster. I didn't know cowboys still exist.

I motion him into the enclosed porch and he steps in, removing his hat and releasing his mid-length light brown hair with its lighter blond highlights. He's s much taller than my five-six, and even though he's wearing a heavy coat, appears more than fit. "Afternoon. I'm Jason Withers. My grandmother sent brownies to welcome you to the neighborhood."

"Neighborhood? I have neighbors?"

He chuckles. "She's the closest and lives over the hill. She wanted to welcome you, but she's not real mobile and asked me to bring these by," he says, holding out a covered plate.

"Oh! Well, thank you. I'm Jazmine. Jazmine Strake," I tell him, taking the plate. "You say your grandmother lives nearby? Do you live with her?"

He smiles. "No! She'd think I was trying to take care of her."

"Well, it was nice of you to bring this by. I'll return the plate as soon as I can." That is a farewell. I'm hoping he'll leave.

"No hurry, take your time. I understand you're here alone?"

I'm not sure if he's trying to make conversation or what, but he seems nice. "Yes, the original plans didn't work out."

"I heard they offered your friend a better position."

How small is this community? Does everyone know? "Would you like some coffee and brownies?" Why did I ask that?

"No, I shouldn't come in, but thank you, I enjoyed meeting you. Let me give you this. It's my number, in case you need anything."

As I glance at the card, I'm startled by his title. "Doctor? You're a doctor?" I pause, appalled at my tone. "I'm sorry, I didn't mean it like it sounded."

"No problem. I'm not the type of doctor you're thinking. I'm a DVM, Doctor of Veterinarian Medicine. A large animal vet. You can still call me though, if you need something."

"Well, thank you. I might take you up on it."

"You should. Again, welcome."

He turns to leave and I half expect a horse to be close by, but no. Instead, there's a monstrosity of a truck out front. I've never seen a pickup that big. Not that I've seen that many. His name on the door with the words "Veterinarian Services" along with his phone number makes me snicker. I guess everyone has his number. He backs out and gives a wave before making the turn onto the road.

Not knowing why, I watch him disappear down the road toward who knows what. Fingers of depression crawl across my skin once again. Here I am, in the middle of nowhere, and I don't know which direction to go if I needed to go somewhere. Besides, I have no way to get there even if I did. How much more pathetic can my life be?

Back inside, I slip a brownie off the plate. It's rich and chewy and oh so tasty. I cram the entire thing in my mouth. Once in the kitchen, I set them on the worn, gray counter and leave before eating them all. Quite possible, considering my current mood. After taking the three steps to get to the living room, I stand still, thinking what to do. My image in the wall mirror is a fright as I realize my shirt reveals more than I thought. Why didn't I close my coat?

No wonder he didn't want to come inside the house. There's little left to the imagination. Might as well not even be wearing a shirt. I'm sure word will spread far and wide. In no time it'll be everywhere— how the big city harlot moved to town and flashed the local vet. Perfect, just what I need. As I collapse on the couch, the tears pooling behind my eyes pour unabated down my cheeks.

After more time wallowing in self-pity than I want known, I must do something. What is there to do? The memory of the brownies has me heading for the kitchen. Now I'm not a cook in any way, shape, or form, but I can make one thing well. Chocolate chip cookies are my forte. They were Michael's favorite, and I discover he bought everything I need to make them

While starting on the dough, my pathetic brain reminds me how he would sneak a cookie when they came out of the oven and was always asking for more. I tell myself to stop thinking about him, but I can't help thinking my life is over. I shake my head, trying to clear my thoughts, and concentrate on the cookies.

Not impressed by the grungy appearance of the old kitchen sink, I try scrubbing it while the cookies are in the archaic oven, but find what I thought was grime and dirt are marks of wear. Knowing the stains are permanent helps me feel better, and I decide the sink should work for washing my hair. After retrieving my shampoo and a towel from the bathroom, I do the best I can with what I have to work with while monitoring the cookies. Once they are done, and with my hair in a towel, I head for the bedroom and my hair dryer.

With the cookies finished and my hair dry, it's time to do something, anything. After removing the brownies and washing the plate, I place a generous portion of cookies on it and wrap it in foil. In the bedroom to change, I remember how cold my legs were when I arrived in the short dress. This time I opt for a cute pair of jeans, a nice blouse, and one of my favorite sweaters. Knowing boots will work best, I put on my knee-high black leather ones with the four-inch heels. It's time to venture out.

My mind screams: What are you thinking? Where will you go?

Why even try? Just stay here in your miserable existence. But that's not me. I must move forward. I must push through this. Regardless of how pitiful I am. My first adventure outside will be to meet my neighbor.

Once I leave the house, it's obvious my Boston coat might not be enough for the weather around here. Even being October, the cold is noticeable. While it's more for fashion than function, my coat has a hood of sorts and my scarf helps a little. I forge ahead, determined to accomplish my task.

At the road, I pause, not sure in which direction to turn. The road goes over a hill to my left and levels out to my right. Left it must be since Jason said it was over the hill. I start with a purposeful stride. He said she's my neighbor. How far can it be?

After what feels like miles, I reach a driveway. Like in western movies, there's a sign stretching across above it reading "MOOSE RIDGE" and a sizeable house set back from the road with two large barns visible in the distance. It's a large, rustic, western-style house built with stone and timber. This must be it, since there's no other house in sight. Pushed on by the cold, I hurry along the long driveway.

At the top of the porch steps, I can't find a doorbell so I knock on the frame. After a few moments, there's movement behind the curtained window, and the inside wooden door opens to reveal a mature lady. Once she sees me, she hurries out and ushers me into the enclosed porch. "Well, where did you come from?" Her cheery voice brings a smile.

"I'm Jazmine, your neighbor. Jason dropped off the brownies, and I wanted to return your plate."

"Oh, my dear, you didn't have to so soon." She takes the plate while glancing out toward the driveway. "Where's your vehicle? You didn't walk here, did you?"

"It's okay, I'm used to walking."

"Come inside, and we'll see what's on this plate." She heads in without giving me a chance to say I should leave. Tentative at first, I follow her through the front door, thinking it's a splendid idea to get warm before heading back. She calls out, "These cookies smell magnificent. We must try them. Would you like something to drink? Coffee or tea?"

"I should go," I say, walking the direction she went. As I walk through the front room, I notice how homey it feels. The braided rugs spread across the shiny wood floor have similar colors to the elegant drapes covering the many windows. The style carries on as I walk past the wide staircase and across the dining room with its massive two column dark wood dining table surrounded by matching chairs and a huge hutch filled with delicate china and crystal.

"Why? You have a hot date?" Right, like that will ever happen. "You can't leave until we sample these cookies. Did you make them?"

I find her in the large kitchen where she's setting the plate of cookies on the wooden table. "Well, yes. I didn't want to return an empty plate."

"Then your mother taught you proper. Many seem to overlook it nowadays. Which do you prefer? Coffee or tea?"

"Coffee is fine."

"Have a seat and I'll get it." She indicates a chair by the table and walks to the counter where a coffee maker sits.

The warmth of the room provides a cozy and comfortable atmosphere. I drape my coat on the back of the chair before sitting.

She returns to the table with the pot and two mugs. "I like your sweater. Did you make it?"

I chuckle. "No. I'm afraid the cookies are the total of my homemaking skills."

While pouring our coffee, she glances my way. "Well, the rosy color is picture-perfect for you. Highlights your blue eyes. Now, I must apologize for not introducing myself. Guess my manners are slacking. I'm Sadie, or Conswella Sandra Stephenson, but I prefer Sadie. Jazmine's a pleasant name. Is it a family name?"

"No, it was my mother's favorite flower. She used the z instead of the s."

"Well, it suits you. You're as pretty as any flower I've ever seen."

"Thank you." Not liking the subjects of my mother or me, I need to find another. "Is Conswella a family name?"

"No, it was the name of my mother's childhood friend. She vowed to use it for her first-born daughter. Sandra was my grandmother's name. I'm sure you don't want to hear all this."

"Honest, I don't mind. You were the first child, then?"

"Heavens, no. There were four boys before me." She places a mug in front of me. "I was the only girl, though. After me were three more boys. Do you want sugar or milk?"

"Sugar will work. My, eight children? Must have made for interesting times."

"Yes, we had our moments. However, my mother wished I was more like the original Conswella. I was too much of a tomboy. What did she expect? I grew up with seven boys on a ranch," she says, chuckling. "Glad you chose coffee. Afraid you'd be a tea drinker when I heard you were from Boston." Grinning, she slides the sugar my way.

"No, not me. Mind you, I didn't always live in Boston. I'm from New York City." Why do I feel so comfortable talking with her? "The coffee is delicious. Seems to have a pinch of something."

"A little cinnamon makes it special," she says, and I notice a slightly mischievous expression as she takes a bite of cookie.

"It does. I'll have to try it."

"A hint is all you need. I'm sure you'll get it right. Anyone who can make cookies like these will have no problem."

"Thank you, but these are the full extent of my baking expertise."

"I doubt that. These are excellent. Did your mother teach you to make them?"

"No, it was trial and error." I don't want to get into my past.

"Well, you hit on a winner. I hope I'm able to make them last. I might eat them all tonight."

"You go right ahead. There's more where these came from."

"If you're from New York City, why did you move to Boston?"

"I went to college there."

"There are fine schools in Boston. Which did you attend?"

"Harvard."

"Harvard's a wonderful school. Were you an undergrad?" I'm sure she's doesn't mean to be nosy.

"Yes, and continued to get my MBA and MSF." I enjoy sharing this, even if it may sound like bragging.

"An MBA is impressive, but what's an MSF?"

"It's a Master's of Science in Finance. It complements my MBA."

While we chat, I glance around. It's such a sizeable house, I can't believe she lives here alone. I wonder if she gets lonesome in such an enormous place. Even in my matchbox of a house, I feel alone.

"This was my parents' home," she says.

"It's nice. Large enough for eight children, for sure. Do your brothers live close by?"

"No, I'm the last of the family remaining. My two oldest brothers never came back from the war. One died at Pearl Harbor and the other in Europe during the Battle of the Bulge. Two other brothers died while serving. One in Korea, and the youngest in Vietnam."

"I'm sorry, I didn't mean to pry. That must have been heartbreaking to lose so many to war."

"They happened years apart, and war didn't take them all. Another died of influenza, the same as our mother, and another in a car accident. The brother before me died of cancer five years ago."

Knowing her thoughts are on her many losses, I feel the need to say something. "I'm sorry to cause you to remember them. I didn't realize."

"No, it's fine. I think of them often. They played an enormous part in making me who I am, and I'm ever so grateful they were in my life, even if for nothing more than a brief time."

She's a resilient woman. I wonder what her secret is?

We sit for a while before she asks what I'm sure she's been wanting to since I arrived. "Now, why are you here living down the road from me? Not the dream location for such a beautiful girl, not to mention a Harvard grad. Why Wyoming and why Cole Creek Road?"

"Not my first choice," I say with a giggle. "Things didn't follow the plan."

"I know part of the story. Not much goes unnoticed around here. I'm sorry things didn't work out. Remember, when one door closes, God opens another. It's what I've found. You wait. There is something delightful coming for you. Mark my words. In less than a year, you won't even recognize your old life."

"Well, I'll agree my old life didn't turn out how I thought it would."

"Don't worry, dear. God has a plan. You need to allow Him to work things out. You'll see." I guess she's one of those who believe in a god. With living all her life in such a rural area, I doubt there was much opportunity for an education or experience with the actual world. I'll overlook it. She's a sweet lady, and I don't want to offend her.

We sit, and she describes the surrounding area. It's obvious I'll need to figure out how I'll get places. With my cup empty, I let her know I should get back. It's getting dark out. She walks with me to the front and helps me with my coat. I thank her again for the brownies, coffee, and the visit.

Just before I leave, she hands me a flashlight. "Here, you'll need this. Don't want you wandering around in this cold. Now you be careful!"

"I can't take this," I say, holding it out.

"It's a loan. You'll bring it back tomorrow."

This catches me by surprise. "I'm coming back tomorrow?"

"Of course. You need to go shopping and don't know your way. In the morning we'll go shopping."

It's not a request per se, more an order, but in a nice way. She's lost me. "How? I don't have a car."

"Not a problem. You'll take my truck tonight. It's parked on the side. Keys are in it."

"What? I can't do that." Why would she do this for someone she just met?

"Why not? You drive, don't you? Now, you need a vehicle, and my old pickup is sitting there doing nothing. You take it tonight, be back in the morning at nine, and we'll have a beautiful day. Now drive careful."

Seems I have no choice in the matter. "Okay. I guess."

To my amazement, she hugs me. I've not gotten many hugs in my life and never one like she gives. It feels so enjoyable I'm close to tears. I'm quick to say thank you again and head out to find her old truck. She watches me through the bright gingham draped windows surrounding the porch as I walk to the driveway and give her a slight wave.

The pickup concerns me. My sum total of rides in a truck is one, and it was last Friday. There's one parked near the back of the house, but it doesn't appear old. Climbing in, one concern vanishes seeing it's an automatic. The keys are in the ignition, like she said, and I try it.

It starts right away. Why does this surprise me? The heater is on max, and the windshield is clear. Here goes nothing. Once it's in reverse, I back out with care.

The drive to my place is shorter than expected. Guess I didn't walk miles after all. I bundle tight and climb out, taking the keys. Once inside, I put the flashlight where I'll remember it. Not wanting to lie in bed letting my mind remind me of my pitiful state, I check out the TV.

There are more channels than expected. I come across the Hallmark Movie channel, which will do. I'm thrilled to find the small microwave on the kitchen counter works and put in one of my frozen dinners. One down, two to go. Maybe shopping tomorrow isn't a bad idea.

After the second movie finishes, I shut off the TV. Another day in my catastrophe of a life is complete. As my eyes close to sleep, I must admit there were delightful times today. Maybe tomorrow will be even better. Yeah, right. What are the odds?

Chapter Two

It's early when I wake, and I blame it on the time change, overlooking how much I slept this weekend. Why did I agree to go with Sadie? I lie staring at the ceiling, but I must be honest. What else is there to do? Plus, I need groceries.

While my gigantic washbasin of a tub fills, I select my clothes. An outfit appropriate for being in public. My one pair of designer jeans, a blouse and sweater, along with a cute pair of heels should work. Don't want a repeat of yesterday. I bathe fast since there's no point in stretching it out.

I was going to have the cereal Michael bought, but he failed to buy milk. Plus, corn flakes were his favorite, not mine. Especially not dry ones. I settle for coffee. I'm reminded of Sadie being glad I wasn't a tea drinker. Michael preferred tea and never drank coffee. Maybe that should have been a sign. Although I doubt coffee was to blame for his leaving. Did I drive him away? Did I not make him want to stay? This brings up the inevitable question: why didn't I see this coming?

The waterworks start again. I must get past this, must let Michael go and move on with my life. Of course, my mind has its say. Get past the man of your dreams tossing you away like day-old garbage? Sure, let him go. The man you sacrificed so much to help. Go ahead. Move on with your life. *That's a nice one since he is your life.*

Thankful it's time to leave, I redo my makeup, which was ruined during my self-pity session, and check the upper half of my appearance in the mirror. It will do. With my coat, scarf, and the flashlight, I head outside, not believing I'm driving a pickup.

It's one and a half miles to Sadie's driveway. My closest neighbor is more than a mile away. This makes me snicker. How many people lived within a mile of me in Boston? I already know Sadie better than any of the people there. I never even knew the names of the people next door.

After parking by the walkway, I make my way to the enclosed porch, knocking on the frame. Sadie hurries to open the door. I can't believe how cold I am after my brief time outside. "Come inside, coffee and rolls are ready. I hope you like pecans," Sadie says and heads to the back.

"I love pecans, but I thought we were going shopping?" I say, following her and the aroma of caramel and pecans into the kitchen.

"We are, but you don't want to go out without fortification. Have a seat, and I'll bring it to you."

"I can help."

"You can get our coffee, and I'll bring the rest," she says, motioning to the mugs beside the coffee maker. I fill two and go with her to the table. She sets the plates down, each containing a sticky pecan bun. They smell delicious.

We add sugar to our coffee, and after making sure it's right, I take a bite of the sticky bun. "These are fantastic, Sadie. Where did you get them?"

"Get them? Dear, I made them this morning."

"You're kidding. I've never known someone to make them from scratch."

"We always have around here. My mother taught me how. My husband used to joke these were the reason he married me."

"They are so delicious, I can believe it," I say, taking another bite.

"I enjoy cooking and baking, but I get little opportunity now. Jason and Tyler come for Sunday lunches and Wednesday dinners, so I get a chance then. Now with you nearby, maybe I'll have more."

"You'll have to watch it. If it's all this delightful, I might visit all the time," I say, holding out my roll.

"Wouldn't mind the company," she says, taking a sip of coffee.

"I met Jason, but who's Tyler?" I take a sip of my own.

"Tyler is Jason's son. He's four going on thirty," she says, chuckling.

"Son? I didn't realize he has a son. They visit, but not Tyler's mother?" I can't believe I asked that. "I...I'm sorry. It's none of my business."

"Not a problem. Carin, Jason's wife, passed away from cancer two years ago." Again, the hurt crosses her face. "She was a marvelous mother to Tyler and wife to Jason. It hit him hard."

"I can understand. Was it a lengthy illness?"

"No, the cancer was aggressive. Carin didn't live six months after the diagnosis."

I kick myself for mentioning that. We sit in silence, finishing our coffee and rolls. While Sadie stacks the dishes, I collect the cups and carry them to the sink.

"Let me get my things, and we'll get this show on the road. I'm sure you don't want to spend your entire day escorting me. Why don't you wait in the front room? I'll be right out." She leaves while I head for the front.

The room is neat and cozy, with carved wood and leather couches, matching chairs with cushions of brocade upholstery. There's a matching loveseat filling the area facing the enormous stone fireplace stretching across one wall. The furniture surrounds a large center rug in style with the house and the walls, mantle, and tables display many pictures. I recognize Jason in several. In a few, there's a woman with him. She must have been his wife. In one, she seems pregnant but appears to be outside in a rough setting.

"That picture was taken two months before Tyler was born," Sadie says, coming up behind me.

"It's a rugged area for someone seven months pregnant."

"They were on a rescue mission."

"A rescue mission? You mean overseas?"

"No, they were north of here rescuing trapped horses."

I'm not sure I understand. "Horses?"

"They'd gotten a call there were wild horses in trouble and worked with others to bring them to safety. Carin was a veterinarian too."

"Seems like an enormous risk for the sake of a few horses." I try not to sound harsh. We are talking horses.

"Yes, a few might agree, but if we can, we must help God's creatures when they need it." Her answer reminds me of her belief in this god. "Jason tried talking her out of it because of her being pregnant, but she'd have none of it. She was a strong, determined person and put others first."

A plaque gets my attention, and I move closer to read it. It's for a Doctor C. S. Stephenson for forty years of pediatric service. "Your husband was a pediatric doctor?"

"No, he was a banker. The plaque is mine."

"You were a doctor?" Too late I realize how bad that sounds.

"Still am. A pediatric cardiologist," she says with a slight smile.

I read where it's from. "You were at UCLA Medical Center?"

"Yes, was in the pediatric unit after med school at Stanford. Chief of pediatrics my last ten years."

I try to hide the surprise at this mild woman being a big city doctor. "You haven't always lived here?"

"Heavens no, I left for college. Then came medical school, where I met my husband. The Medical Center offered me a position, and he joined a bank in L.A. Now, we need to get going. We have a drive ahead of us," she says, turning for the doorway.

I hold her purse and help get her coat on. I do the same, and we're ready to head out to a place unknown to me.

Still not comfortable driving a pickup, I follow her directions and head south on Cole Creek Road. We stay on it for a distance. After crossing the North Platte River, we come to a crossroads, Highway 87. Sadie explains to the right is Casper and left is Glenrock.

As directed, I turn left, and Sadie guides me to the grocery store. Here, I get frozen dinners and other supplies. From her expression, I can tell Sadie doesn't like my selections, but I have no choice. I'm not a cook.

We stop for lunch at a small diner which provides an enjoyable meal. Sadie knows everyone, but most know of me too. There are a few inquisitive glances my way, but no mention of the big city hussy, to my relief.

As we return, I tell Sadie I'll stop and unload at my place before I take her home and walk back. She makes it clear that will not happen and tells me I'll need the truck for our trip to Casper tomorrow. This catches me off guard, but it seems I have no choice.

I help carry her items in and find out this means I must stay for coffee. I mention my groceries, but she chortles. "My dear, with the number of preservatives in frozen dinners and the cold outdoors, there's no problem leaving them in the truck. They'll be fine." Not able to argue, I help get the coffee on and put her groceries away. Afterward, we sit and chat.

She's a remarkable lady, and I enjoy talking with her, but I don't want to take up all her time. With my coffee finished, I thank her for the day and get ready to leave. She escorts me to the door and bids me goodbye, but that's not all.

"Now drive careful and mind the slick patches walking. Don't carry too much at a time."

"Okay, I'll try. Don't worry." I turn, but she catches me in another enormous hug.

"Tomorrow, we'll go to Casper and get you a warm coat and boots. Those high heels aren't suitable, and you'll freeze in this thin thing. Here we dress for function, not fashion."

I smile, knowing how out of fashion this coat is. "I'm okay."

"See, the cold is already impacting your thinking. We'll take care of it tomorrow. Now, be here at nine, and we'll have coffee first."

"Okay, I'll be here, but I'm not agreeing to the shopping."

"Nonsense. You need warmer clothing, and I know where to get it. It's simple logic. Tomorrow at nine, and you can bring more of your cookies." She checks that my scarf is tight to my chin. I guess I'm going to Casper tomorrow.

When I open my front door, I'm reminded how dreary my place is, but it's all I have for now. After putting my groceries away, which doesn't take long, I stand in the compact kitchen wondering what now.

In the past, I've been so busy with school and work, but now I have neither, and I feel lost. Then I remember Sadie mentioned cookies and occupy myself with those.

After dinner and with the cookies cooled and wrapped for tomorrow, I pass on TV and head for my minute bedroom. I'm picking out clothes for tomorrow when it hits me. There's no washing machine or dryer. I'm okay for a few more days, but I will need something soon. I'll ask Sadie tomorrow where to find the nearest laundromat.

With clothes laid out for the morning, I'm back to square one and at a loss for what is next. It's too soon for bed. I'd lie there, and the tears would flow again. The sight of my laptop bag gives me an idea, and I open it on the small table.

I'm not sure what I plan to accomplish since I don't have an internet connection. That will have to wait for an income. Which means I need to find a job first—that will be interesting, finding something fitting my MBA/MSF. As I stare at the blank screen, an idea pops into my head, and I grab my phone. I still have my unlimited data plan.

Now, my phone is not best for surfing, but I remember in college there was a shop favored for providing two things budget-weary students desired: bottomless cups of coffee and free Wi-Fi. One guy there would connect his laptop to his phone to access the internet. He said it was more secure and isolated him from everyone else. A total geek, but he knew computers. He told me once that to get to sleep he counted prime numbers backward from a thousand.

I search "How to use a smartphone to connect your laptop." A page appears with full instructions. It calls for a USB cord, which I plug in, and follow the steps. In no time, my laptop shows a connection, and my home page appears. I'm online.

With the browser window open, I wonder, now what? With limited free time in my previous life, I was never big on social networks. With plenty of time now, I search through several and create a login for one.

After filling in my details, I'm ready to go. The number of

groups, blogs, and pages covering many topics amazes me. On a lark, I type in "broken-hearted ladies," and an extensive list appears. I didn't realize there were so many of us. I wonder if any of them know Michael? Next, for fun, I search "broken-hearted men," but find no groups. Figures. I go back to the list of ladies' groups and select one claiming to be for women helping each other to heal their broken hearts.

The title page opens with a big red banner displayed at the top. The description says it's a group for women having difficulty dealing with the end of a relationship. Perfect for me. I click the "Join Group" button, and a notice shows for me to click another button to gain access. I follow the instructions and posts from women who seem to share in what I'm enduring appear.

The posts are compelling, with advice and comfort. I stay with my kindred spirits until the taskbar shows near midnight. Since I'm to be at Sadie's by nine, I tell my new friends I need to go but assure them I'll be back.

After changing into my nighttime attire and setting my alarm, I turn off the lamp on the minuscule nightstand and lie back. For the first time since I arrived, I feel ready to enjoy a decent night's rest. Of course, that does not happen. When my eyes close all I see is Michael, and when they're open all I do is cry. I don't know how much longer I can take this.

~ * ~

When my alarm sounds, I've been awake crying for a while. I pull on my old robe and force myself to get moving.

I arrive at Sadie's on time and she lets me in, leading me back to the kitchen. I'm carrying my offering of cookies, but I'm confused, sensing the aroma of cinnamon filling the house. The coffee is ready, and she's made a fresh batch of cinnamon rolls.

Setting my plate of cookies on the table, I turn to her. "What about the cookies I brought?"

"They're for later. Now have a seat," she says.

After fixing my coffee, I take a bite of my roll. "Sadie, these are something else. I don't think I've ever tasted anything like them."

"Thank you. These were another of my husband's favorites. I got the recipe from my grandmother."

"Was she a baker?"

"No, dear. She was a rancher," she says with pride.

"A rancher?"

"Yes, she came here with my grandfather in the mid-eighteen hundreds. The plan was to go further west, but when they saw this area, they stayed. The first morning they woke up, my grandfather pointed out a large moose standing on a ridge not far away. That was the start of Moose Ridge Ranch. They built it to be an enormous success. Others joined them and before long the town of Glenrock was born. Later rustlers killed my grandfather and, from then on, she managed it herself, right until the day she died."

"Wow, she must have been one resilient woman," I say, continuing to enjoy my roll.

"She was. She was also the local doctor. Her father was a doctor, and she worked with him before she married," she says, while taking a bite of hers.

"Your grandmother was a rancher and doctor, and you're a pediatrician. How about your parents?"

"My mother worked in the medical practice, which she took over. She met my father when he came to work on Moose Ridge. He became a veterinarian. They were happy here. Oh, look at the time. We best be getting on our way," she says, standing.

As she heads for the front door, she calls out, "Don't forget the cookies."

"You want me to bring them with us?"

"I have the perfect place for them." She's off before I can ask her to explain.

In the truck, Sadie tells me to take the right turn toward Casper. She has several places she wants to go and is insisting on my buying winter clothing. She doesn't direct me to the mall, but to several discount clothing stores instead. We find a nice parka and insulated boots at reasonable prices, so I get them.

We pop into another diner for lunch, and again, most know Sadie. She introduces me as her new neighbor. I follow her suggestion and order the vegetable soup. It's delicious and comes with fresh crusty bread. After lunch, Sadie says she needs to stop at a place in Glenrock. While making our way there, I mention my dilemma of needing a laundromat.

"Why would you need one of those?"

"I don't have a washer at home, and I'll need clean clothes before long."

"You'll use mine. Not a problem." She makes it sound like a foregone conclusion.

"No, Sadie, I couldn't use—"

"Why not? You need clean clothes, and I have the machines. Why wouldn't you use them? You can come Thursday. I do laundry on Wednesdays. Turn right at the next driveway."

It's not far, so I concentrate on slowing and making the turn into a parking lot without sliding. There's a sign saying "Community Center" and several parked vehicles. All seem to be trucks or large SUVs. Are there any actual cars here? I park where Sadie tells me. "What are we doing here?"

"It's my Women's Auxiliary Committee meeting. Bring the cookies." She's out the door before I can say anything.

"Sadie," I call, but she's walking away. With no choice, I grab my bag and the cookies and hurry to catch her as she disappears inside the building. "Sadie? The Women's Auxiliary? Are you sure?"

"Yes. It will be a chance to meet the ladies." She enters a sizeable room with chairs around several tables. Near one table, a group of ladies are talking and glance our way when we enter.

"Sadie, I wasn't expecting you with Jason busy today," one lady says, coming over to us.

"My new neighbor was kind enough to drive me. Jazmine, Jill Carmine, our chairperson. Jill, meet Jazmine. She makes delicious cookies."

"Welcome to our little group. We're glad to have you here, Jaycee." I'm not sure she is. "We appreciate you bringing Sadie."

"Thank you, and it's Jazmine," I say, setting my cookies with the other snacks.

"Sadie, you know where the drinks are. Be a dear and show Joyce. Then we'll get things going."

I doubt she heard anything I said.

I follow Sadie to get a drink and notice several women glancing our way, talking in hushed tones. When we return, everyone takes a seat, and Jill starts the meeting.

"Welcome, everyone, and thank you for coming. Let me introduce Sadie's new neighbor, Janice. She's the one who moved here from back East. Guess she realizes she's not in the Big Apple anymore." Jill chuckles.

Sadie speaks before I can. "Jazmine; her name is Jazmine. She arrived here last Friday from Boston, is a delightful neighbor, and has an MBA from Harvard. She's perfect for here. Nice to have someone with class."

This shocks Jill into several moments of silence before she speaks again. "Well, welcome. Anyway, ladies, we have serious work this afternoon. Sarah, the financial report, please?" It's obvious Jill enjoys being in charge.

When they take a break to get more drinks and snacks. Sadie announces, "Ladies, try the cookies Jazmine made. They are beyond delicious."

Several try them, and most have something nice to say. Jill, however, shrugs after taking a bite and puts the rest on her plate. Does she have a problem with me?

After a short break, the meeting continues. It ends with Jill making sure everyone has their assignments. Afterward, several welcome me, mentioning the cookies as an icebreaker. I'm sure they're being polite. Sadie visits while I get our coats and watch Jill put treats on a plate. About half of my cookies remain, so I wrap them and wait.

As the group breaks up, Sadie spots Jill with the plate of treats and motions to it. "Are you taking something home for later?"

"No, thought I'd take these by Jason's. I'm sure he skipped lunch," she says while slipping on a mink coat.

"I believe he's busy with a foal's birth. He's expecting it to be a difficult one. Best to leave him alone," Sadie says as we make our way to the parking lot.

"Oh? Too busy for even me?" Jill says as though that's impossible.

"Plus, I believe he's on a cleansing diet. I wouldn't take him anything," Sadie says with a shake of her head.

Jill stops by a Lexus, the lone actual car here. It's also taking two parking spaces. "I didn't know. How long is the diet for?"

"I believe a full week. It was in a magazine. You know how Jason is. You want us to drop them by the fire station? I know they'll appreciate them."

"Well, since Jason can't have them. Are you sure it's not too much trouble?"

"Not at all. We're going right past it."

"Well, it will help. The girls have choir practice after school then their dance class later. Never a moment to myself. Now you take care Sadie, and it was nice meeting you Jackie." Once in her Lexus, she's quick to leave.

We climb into Sadie's truck, and I turn her way. "Which way to the fire station?"

"Make your way back to the eighty-seven and toward home. It's right before we leave town."

"We can add the cookies so there's enough for the entire station."

"No, the cookies are for Jason. Don't worry, there's enough on Jill's plate. It's a volunteer station, so no more than two men are on duty."

I'm confused. "Isn't Jason on a cleansing diet?"

"Don't think so. Where did you hear that?" She's displaying an amazing act of innocence.

"Didn't you tell Jill he was?"

"Didn't want her bothering him. Jason would never try one of those new-fangled diets."

I give her a questioning glare. "Sadie, what are you up to?"

"Why would I be up to something? It's the next block on the right. Stop at the door and honk. One of them will come out."

I follow her directions. Soon the side door opens, and a man hurries out. Sadie lowers her window and holds out the plate. "Hey, George, meet my neighbor Jazmine. We had these left after our meeting and thought of you."

"Nice to meet you, miss. Miss Sadie, you are too nice. You tell the ladies thank you," he says, taking the plate. "Now drive careful and watch for ice."

"We will. Get inside before you catch cold. I can't believe you didn't put on a jacket."

"Yes, ma'am. I should have, but seeing it was you, I wanted to get here quick. Anyway, thanks again, and have a nice day, ladies."

Once on the street, we're on our way. "Head for home?"

"Of course not. We need to drop your cookies at Jason's."

"I thought you said he was too busy?"

"What? Where do you get these notions? He'll be fine with us stopping by. It's not like he's having the foal."

I take a quick peek her way. She seems innocent enough, but her looks might be deceiving. "And?"

"What?" she asks in the same innocent voice she used with Jill.

"What do you think will happen when we get there?"

"We'll say hi and drop off the cookies. Why, what do you want to happen?"

I can't believe this. "What? I didn't say I wanted anything to happen."

"Fine, then. We'll drop off the cookies and be on our way."

"If you say so, but I think you're up to something. Where should I go?"

"Stay on eighty-seven and take our normal turn. It's on the left after the river."

Chapter Three

I follow Sadie's directions, wondering why she wouldn't want Jill to visit Jason. After the river is the sign "MOOSE RIDGE ANIMAL CLINIC". Sadie has me park in the back behind a modern-looking clinic. There are several large buildings in the back with corral-like areas on the sides. Before I get out, Sadie's already heading for a door marked "Employees Only". She may be along in years, but you'd never know it by how she moves. I hurry to catch up and make it before the door closes behind her.

We're in an entryway, and Sadie pushes the inside door open and calls out for Jason. He responds, but it's not clear where he might be. Then I hear, "In the stalls."

Sadie leads me along a hallway which opens out into a section with multiple stalls. They are nicer than I expect for an animal clinic. There are five on each side and four across the back, with a gigantic table in the center space. While the area has the slight smell of animals, I'm astonished it's not heavier. It's more of an antiseptic smell, like a hospital.

A beautiful white horse is standing in the first stall on the right. A menacing snort from the stall next to it draws my attention to a bull—it's much larger than I imagined. While I glance in a stall containing several sheep, Jason appears from another. "What brings you here?"

"Jazmine wanted to bring you her cookies."

I can't believe Sadie said that. "In truth," I'm quick to add, "it was her idea. I hope we're not disturbing you?" I don't want to give him the wrong idea.

"No, not at all, gives me someone to talk with. These guys respond little, and they hate my jokes." Jason laughs and takes the plate of cookies.

Sadie walks over to the stall he was in. "How's the mare doing?"

"Not well. The foal's coming soon. We were hoping all would wait for Tom to return, but they got caught in a storm."

I can't help my curiosity. "Is Tom the owner?"

"Yes, they left for the Fall Championships in Montana. They were to return last Friday, but nasty weather came in, and they didn't want to risk it with the horses."

"Oh, they have others?"

"Several. They raise champion show-jumping horses. Two of theirs were in the championships, plus two others for show, so they needed to go. I'm glad we brought Cashmere here to watch her." Jason pours himself coffee. "Help yourself, it's fresh."

"Which means they made it this week," Sadie chortles. This doesn't deter her from filling two cups.

"One cup for you, Sadie," Jason says, giving her a glare. After trying one of my cookies, he turns my way. "Hey, these are excellent."

I smile. "They're nothing exceptional, and the only thing I can bake," I'm quick to point out.

"She doesn't know what she saying. They're more than excellent. This girl has talents she won't acknowledge," Sadie says.

"I doubt it, but thank you for the compliment." I follow her to a stall and peer beyond the gate to find the most beautiful buckskin colored horse I've ever seen in my life. "Wow, she's gorgeous. I see where the name Cashmere comes from."

"Yes, she's a looker, and knows it. Has a bit of an attitude," Jason says, entering the stall.

"I'm sure she isn't too bad. She appears so regal. Is she a show horse?"

"She was last year's Grand Prix Champion. The sire is this year's champion, so they have high hopes for this foal—which is why Tom is trying to fly back tonight."

My interest piques as I stroke Cashmere's neck. "We're talking valuable then?"

"You might say that. Cashmere herself is worth a healthy chunk, but the foal could be close to double. Even now, if all goes well with the birth, the value will run in the millions." He brushes Cashmere's neck, speaking in a soft, calm voice.

"Millions? As in dollars?"

"Yes, last year there was an offer of seven million for a champion horse. There's money in them, but also a lot of cost. It's not a business for the faint of heart."

"I can believe it, but seven million dollars? For a horse?"

"Which is why they brought her to Jason," Sadie says with a proud smile. "He takes care of all their horses because he's the best."

"Well, I have help. Mine and Carin's dads built this. The reputation is all their doing, and her dad is still here. I try to maintain it."

"Don't let him fool you, Jazmine. He's the best."

"Your fathers started all this?"

"First, it was my great-grandfather; he started the clinic. My dad was his assistant, along with Carin's dad while they were in school. They became partners after graduating. Once he retired, they ran with it. Now it's what you see around you, and the only large animal clinic in the area."

"Well, it's a nice clinic, very modern."

"Carin designed this building. We started construction a while back, but it took several years to finish."

Sadie is quick to clarify. "You were part of its design. Don't play like you weren't."

Right then, I hear a noise and turn as a plastic bottle rolls across the floor. A movement on the counter catches my eye, and I jump back, seeing a rather large lizard staring at me.

"Don't mind Stanley. He's my exterminator. He wants a drink." Jason goes to the counter and opens a bottle, filling a small dish. The lizard wastes no time in marching right over.

"Exterminator?" Not sure I like the sound of that.

"Yes, he keeps the place rid of most bugs and things, along with the occasional mouse or two. He's a bearded dragon and does an outstanding job."

A phone rings, and Jason answers it. I realize no one else is here. I'd have thought with the size of this place, there'd be an assistant, or at least a receptionist. He doesn't seem pleased. "No, I understand. I'll take care of things here. Maybe Tom will make it in time. Keep me posted."

Sadie turns to Jason. "Was that Stephen?"

"Yes. He's on an emergency call and won't return until late. The others are with him, so…I'm it. Cashmere and I will have to do this delivery. It would have to be a breech birth."

"Breech?" I didn't know horses had breech deliveries. "You mean it's backward?"

"Yes. The foal is not being presented, or positioned like it should be," Sadie says. "Don't worry, Jason, you're not alone. We'll help."

"We? I don't know how to deliver a baby. Horse or human."

"Doesn't matter," Sadie says, folding her arms across her chest. "You graduated from Harvard, so you're no dummy. Plus, Cashmere will do most of the work. Now, Jason, what do you need?"

He is busy getting instruments out of a bag, but glances at me. "You attended Harvard?"

"Yes, for a business degree. They never covered horses giving birth, even one worth what she is."

"Think of it as the end of a merger and acquisition." Snickering, he hands Sadie a long apron.

"What?"

"I'm kidding. Don't worry. Sadie and I will take care of the big stuff."

"The big stuff? Leaving what? What can I do?" I stare at the apron he hands me. Right then, the phone rings again.

"You can answer the phone. I need to get Cashmere settled. Take a note and tell whoever I'll call them back." With that, he's gone into Cashmere's stall with Sadie.

I hurry and answer the phone.

"Hello, this is Tom Jameson. Is Jason available?"

"He's with Cashmere, Mr. Jameson."

"Is the delivery getting close?"

"Yes, Jason said it appears like it."

"May I speak with him?"

"I'll get him." I call out, "Jason, it's Mr. Jameson. He wants to speak with you."

"I'll be right there," Jason says.

I relay this as he walks my way. I move aside, feeling like a third wheel.

"Jazmine, come give me a hand," Sadie calls.

Relieved to have something to do, I make my way back to the mare's stall. As I pass the counter, Stanley nudges his dish toward me. When I discover Jason had been pouring from a bottle of Mountain Dew, I'm dumbfounded. For a lizard? Shaking my head, I open the bottle and pour a little in the dish.

Another call from Sadie distracts me from my bewilderment. "Bring a bag of wood shavings with you. We need to make a place she can lie down."

"Wood shavings?" Not sure about this, I glance around.

"The white bags in the corner stall on the left," Jason calls out before returning to the phone.

I find the large stack of white plastic bags is where he said then lug one to Cashmere's stall.

"Grab the shovel. We'll clean the area first," Sadie says.

A cross between a rake and a shovel leans against the stall, and I get it before turning back to Sadie. "Now what?"

"Scoop up any manure, and we'll scatter fresh shavings."

"Manure? You want me to scoop up manure?"

"Either with the shovel or with your hands. I prefer the shovel."

She's serious. The shovel works well on the first pile.

Jason arrives at the stall opening with a cart. "You can put it in here."

While I concentrate on putting the first mound of poop in the cart, glad there isn't more of a smell, Sadie asks Jason what Tom had to say.

"He's stranded for now," Jason says. "The plane for his flight suffered mechanical problems. The airline is trying to work something out, but it's not looking good. Jazmine, I'd put an apron on before doing too much."

"Oh, okay." I go to the counter where I left the apron to find the lizard has made it into a bed. "Um, Jason, the lizard is on the apron…"

"Stanley, get off the apron," Jason calls out. Stanley turns toward the voice but doesn't move.

"He's still on it, Jason."

"Lift him off and set him aside, but be careful of his tail and don't hurt him."

Hurt him? That's the last thing I'm worried about. Stanley, with his barbed sides and spiky face, seems to dare me to touch him. I have an idea and grab the bottle of Mountain Dew, pouring a little in his dish. It works, and Stanley hurries off the apron to take another drink. Chalk one up for the Harvard grad. Then the phone rings.

"Can you answer it and take a message?" Jason says. "Tell whoever it is I'm busy delivering a foal."

"Is Jason there?" It's a female voice this time.

"Yes, he is, but he's delivering a foal right now. May I take a message?"

"You are?"

Is this his girlfriend, maybe? "I'm Jazmine, a neighbor of his grandmother."

"Oh, Jazmine from Boston? Welcome to our town. I'm Sharon from the *Glenrock Independent*, I wanted to see how everything was going with Cashmere."

"Thank you for the welcome. May I have Jason call you back later?"

"Sure, let him know I called, and I'm interested to hear how it goes."

"I will. I'm sure he'll call when he can."

"All right, then. Welcome again. Now you take care." She hangs up before I can respond.

I turn back to get my apron and see Stanley has again settled himself on top of it. I'm sure he's smiling, or grinning, or whatever lizards do. I can't believe what's happening. First, I'm scooping manure, and now I'm dealing with a stubborn lizard. I pour more Mountain Dew in his dish. How does a lizard drink so fast? Before I finish pouring, Stanley rushes back and curls his tongue into the bowl. I grab my apron and start back for the stall.

The phone rings again. I keep the apron this time and might get a dirty glare from Stanley. It's hard to tell—maybe that's his normal expression.

After the call, it's time to scoop manure. Trying to build—or maybe fake—excitement for my assigned task, I make it to the stall and start shoveling. There aren't many piles to shift, and afterward, Sadie helps put out the fresh wood shavings.

While Jason's busy checking Cashmere, Sadie is stroking her neck and whispering.

"It's coming soon. We need to get her down and get ready," he says, moving to Cashmere's head, holding the halter while stroking her neck. Soon, he has her lying on her side and listens again. "I'm afraid we're it. This foal is coming, whether or not we're ready. Jazmine, why don't you replace Sadie so she can assist me? You don't need to do much. We need Cashmere to stay calm."

I can't help myself. "Calm? She's having a baby. I'm not sure calm is even possible."

After taking her place beside Jason, Sadie explains, "Stroke her neck and whisper, but hold her harness so she doesn't lift her head or turn."

I take my position and follow her directions, but I'm not sure how this helps. How am I going to stop a horse from moving? I grip her harness tightly with my left hand while I stroke her neck with my right. "It will be okay, Cashmere. Jason won't let anything happen to your baby. Everything will be fine."

"Is it a breech?" Sadie asks.

Jason's eyebrows draw together in concern. "I'm afraid so."

"Is that a problem?" I ask as Cashmere tries to raise her head, and I'm not sure what to do.

Sadie gives me a reassuring smile and says, "Hold her head steady. If you need to, push with your other hand. Yes, a breech is dangerous. The umbilical cord could wrap around the foal or even break during the delivery."

"What happens if it breaks?"

"If it breaks," Jason says, "the foal won't get oxygen and will try to breathe while in the mother. Not useful. I can feel a hock, so it's breech. Once the foal comes, we'll have to move fast to get it out in case the cord breaks. We'll need to time our pulls with the contractions. Sadie, signal me when one is coming. I'll pull on the hind legs. Jazmine, you keep her calm."

"One is coming," Sadie warns, while stroking Cashmere's side.

He reaches inside with both arms. I can't believe it's happening, and I'm here watching. "Okay, I have the legs. Call it out, Sadie," he says while positioning himself.

Cashmere tenses as Sadie calls out, "One is starting."

Jason pulls, and soon small hooves are visible below the base of Cashmere's tail. He continues to pull, and the lower half of a pair of tiny legs appear. He takes a deep breath while waiting for the next contraction. I feel Cashmere tense again, and it takes all my strength to keep her head still.

When I look again, most of the rear legs are out, and Jason is ready for the next one. Cashmere is breathing deeply. I shush her and try to calm her. As soon as Sadie says another one is starting, Jason works to wiggle the rear legs free while keeping his weight leaning away from the mare. Soon, the upper thighs and back end of the foal are visible.

Jason resets his position, takes a deep breath, and pulls again. Sadie is stroking the horse's side, and I'm fighting to keep her head on the makeshift pillow of wood shavings. He raises his hand, and it feels like time stops while we wait for his instructions.

"The cord broke. I'll have to pull the foal out." He leans forward to get a better grip. His straining is obvious as he pulls back. He's wiggling the foal while tugging on its back legs and falls backward. Lying by his legs is the foal. Jason hurries to wipe the mucus and other bodily fluids from its nose and mouth and supports it, urging it to stand.

It does, surprising me. A minute old and already standing—on uncertain legs, but it's upright. "You did it, girl. You did it, and the foal is already standing. What an overachiever you have."

Jason and Sadie are busy cleaning the foal, and I watch in amazement, realizing it's trying to walk. Jason fights to keep it still while he cleans it. The foal escapes and stumbles around the stall, wanting to check everything out.

"It's a male. He appears well so far." Jason tries to catch our recent arrival pottering off behind its mom. The colt isn't cooperating though, and he struggles to cup an arm under its neck to keep it in place while placing a stethoscope to its side. "His breathing sounds excellent, and there's a strong heartbeat too. I think we're okay." The foal goes free and heads for Cashmere, nudging her belly. When she tries to stand, I panic and try to stop her. Jason laughs, "You can let her go now. The colt needs to eat."

"Eat? She just gave birth." I watch her stand, and the colt dives under her, searching for the right spot. "Well, not even a thank you."

I can't believe it. If you'd told me last week I'd see a horse giving birth, and also help, I'd have thought you were on drugs. Not the typical way for me to spend my spare time. Although I'm sure Jason and Sadie have been through this drama more times than they can remember, it doesn't diminish their obvious joy at the occasion. Both have enormous smiles.

He heads for the counter. "Better see if I can get Tom on the phone. He'll want to know."

"You did fantastic, girl. You're a natural," Sadie says while removing the soiled apron.

"Well, I don't know what I did, but watching was amazing. Jason is something else. He knew everything to do and what to expect."

"He's done a few of these. Maybe thousands, but not always horses or breeches. We can wash up at the sink."

When I remove my apron, I realize it's not the cleanest. She rinses them while I scrub my hands and arms and check if I missed any gunk. Sadie hangs the aprons to dry, followed by the long gloves they wore. I guess we're done.

"I caught him before he got on the plane," Jason says, returning and still smiling. "He's so thrilled he might fly here without one. Thank you, ladies, for your help. You've been magnificent. I couldn't have done it without you."

"Not without Sadie, I'm sure." I'm embarrassed at my lack of input. "I'll never forget it though."

"No, you were an enormous help. Couldn't have done it without you," he assures me.

Sadie checks her watch. "We better head home. Didn't expect to be out this late. You ready, Jazmine? Better bundle up, I'm sure it's cold out there." She gets her coat, and I get my belongings.

"Again, thank you both and assist me anytime." He walks us to the back door, holding it open.

"You and Tyler want to stop by later?" Sadie offers.

"Can't. I told Tom I'd stay here until he makes it in, and I need to wait for Stephen and the crew too. Tyler's staying at Dottie's tonight anyway, so I'll have to pass."

"Tomorrow night then? Six-thirty, okay?"

"By all means. Wouldn't miss it."

"Great. Dinner should be delicious. Jazmine's cooking."

I stop in my tracks while she walks to the pickup like my making dinner is an everyday occurrence. I can't say anything with Jason within earshot, so I smile, holding the door for Sadie, then hurry around to my side.

I fasten my seatbelt then turn to Sadie, who seems pleased with herself. "Who's cooking tomorrow's dinner, hmm?"

"You are," she says as if it should be obvious.

"I am. Yes, silly me. The microwave queen is cooking dinner. Are you serious? I can't cook."

"Your cookies prove otherwise. Don't worry; I'll be there. We'll keep it simple. A roast, potatoes, green beans, and rolls. Maybe a cake for dessert. You'll see, it will be fine."

"You better have a backup plan, and I'm serious."

The ride home is quiet. I'm trying to think of ways to avoid cooking dinner. I don't want to make a fool of myself. I know what Michael thought of my cooking. My gosh, another thought of Michael. Why can't I forget him?

"You coming in for coffee?" Sadie asks as I pull into her driveway.

"It's late. I should get home. I'll see you in and park the truck on the side."

"Why would you park it?"

"Because it's not mine. I appreciate the use, but I can't keep it all the time."

"It's not doing anyone any good here. Plus, you'll need it tomorrow. Might as well take it home. Be here at one, and we'll start dinner."

"You still think I'm cooking dinner?"

"Jason's expecting it. You don't want to disappoint him, do you?" Her expression is the polar opposite to mine.

"No, but he thinks I'm cooking because you said I was."

"Well, you don't want to make me out to be a liar, do you? Of course not. That's settled then. You'll take the truck home and be back at one to make dinner. Now, have an enjoyable evening, and I'll see you tomorrow." She's out before I can comment further.

I help her inside and bid her goodnight. She's watching me drive off and waving, and I realize I have no out for tomorrow. This will not end well.

At my house, the drabness hits me, causing all positive feelings to drain away like water from a leaky bucket.

After hanging my parka and removing my new boots, I strain to make the six feet to the couch. When I plop down, Michael's letter catches my eye. Why haven't I thrown it away? The tears start again. I don't want this. I don't want to spend any more time crying over him. I spot my laptop. Time to get online.

I feel a renewed energy while heading for the table. While my laptop is loading, I make the long trek to the kitchen to start the coffee. I return and open my group page. There are new posts, and it's perfect for filling my evening. I dive in with my sisters in heartbreak.

The stories and comments are compelling—a few helpful, a few not so much. Many are funny as several let off steam. One lady posts a picture of what she did with her man's belongings he said he'd be back for. It showed a smoldering pile of blackened rubbish with a sign reading: "Here's your junk. Time you clean your own mess."

This generates comments and suggestions of how to get rid of your ex's junk. Several are scary, but I hope meant to be funny. As I scroll, I feel I've found people who understand my plight. A lady posts explaining her current situation. From the comments, it must be a familiar story to many here. I offer my sympathies and mention my own circumstances.

The coffee is ready, and after filling a mug, I hurry back. Many comments have come in and most are supportive, but there is one I don't understand.

You should blog about your experience.

I know what a blog is, but I didn't think you could write one of a personal story. Why would someone want to read something like that? It's dreadful and full of problems, disappointments, tragedy, and heartbreak. I post my question to the forum, and the response intrigues me.

Which is why you need to blog about it. You're going through all of that and people will want to hear it, but more importantly, you need to tell it!

This hits me hard. Could she be right? Am I ready to share the story of my life? Would it help me put it behind me? Before I can answer, a post with a link appears with the words "Check this out."

I open the link in another window and start reading the introduction. It's in chapters, like a book. Each chapter appears to be a period in the writer's life: child, pre-teen, teenager, and such.

The blog is incredible, and I can't stop reading. The writer adds more each week and is working on the college years. She's open and honest about everything and covers her feelings and thoughts. It's amazing. Each week's entry has comments from other people.

They're spellbinding. Taking a sip of coffee, I can't believe my mug is empty again. I check the time, and I'm stunned to see it's after 2 AM.

I bookmark the site and close everything after posting a "Goodnight!" to the group. I set my mug in the kitchen sink on my way to the bedroom. The entire way there, and while undressing, the idea of a blog fills my mind.

Could I write one? Would people read it? Would it matter if they didn't? I ponder a multitude of questions while climbing into bed and turning off the lamp. I lie in darkness and wonder how to start it. My single memory of my mother is she always smelled like flowers.

This is my last thought as sleep overtakes my weary mind.

Chapter Four

Again, I wake before the alarm. It's not light out, but I don't care. I snatch my robe and hurry to my laptop. I'm going to start my blog. While the laptop is powering up, I get coffee started and grab a muffin I bought, much to Sadie's disapproval.

Once in my chair, I open the word processor. It displays a blank page glaring back, mocking me. Now what? With fingers poised above the keyboard, I stare at the screen for what feels like an eternity. It was all worked out last night, and I knew what to say. Where did it go? After spending goodness knows how long conjuring nothing, I realize my mug is empty. Glad for the distraction, I refill it and return. Now I have my coffee and another muffin. Time to write.

Still nothing. I want so much to tell how I felt when Michael left—how humiliated, how alone, and how scared. The words never come. I realize if I start with him leaving, it won't make any sense. Maybe I need to go back to when we met, but how to explain Harvard and my situation? This means going back to my time in foster care, which means reliving stories of my father.

I sit, frozen, staring at the screen. The blank page is unblinking as if daring me to write something. Me, this useless, unlovable, talentless joke of a person. But then my thought from right before going to sleep appears through the fog in my mind.

My Life

My mother always smelled like flowers. I was five when she died. I remember my father sitting on my bed and telling me there was an accident and she wouldn't be coming home.

The words flow from my soul as the tears spill from my eyes. I cover the funeral and how nice everyone was to me. I write about the dress and shoes my dad bought me for the occasion. About the nannies hired to take care of me and how he treated me like a princess, which was also his name for me. I share memories of how my mother named me after her favorite flower, and now this, along with jewelry, is all I have left of her. About life afterward. How my dad made everything so wonderful. He gave me whatever I wanted, and every year he'd replace all my clothes with the newest styles. My life was perfect.

I include how the girls at my private school were envious of me. My father and I were so close, and things were ideal in my eyes. I was the center of his life. I mention how I was the most popular girl in school. How all the boys fawned over me, and the girls all wanted to be my best friend. I was their queen, and they were my loyal subjects. What more could a girl ask for?

I reach a stopping point and review what I've written. After a few edits, I find it starts my future blog well. I doubt anyone will recognize who is writing it since I'll use a pen name. I think it's accurate and honest—even if it doesn't paint me in a positive light. Many might say I was spoiled, and others might prefer a word starting with a "B." That could even be closer to the truth.

I close my laptop and think of calling Sadie to say I don't feel well. But knowing her, she'd have Jason drive her here to nurse me. I resign myself to the coming humiliation. The last thing I attempted to cook was hot dogs, and I burned them. The saddest part is, I was boiling them. Okay, I got distracted, and the water boiled away. The next thing I knew, the apartment was full of smoke, and the smoke alarm was taking great delight in pointing out how useless I was at preparing even the simplest of dishes. I never tried again.

After a bath in my luxurious handbasin, I dry and style my dark auburn hair, pleased to see the deep red highlights gleaming through the brown. My roommates in college always complemented me on its color, and it took a while for them to believe it was natural.

I've decided not to be the grungy old Jazmine I've been since I got here and try to step up my game. One of my business suits I used for work will be perfect. With a new mindset, I want to dress for the occasion. With my parka on, I grab my purse. Yeah, I know, the coat doesn't go with my outfit, but it's cold here, and it's the closest thing I have to suitable outerwear.

I pull into Sadie's drive and hurry to the porch where she's already waiting to open the door. While I'm taking my parka off, she can't resist the urge to comment.

"Well, don't we look nice? Are we trying to impress someone special?" She's gone before I can answer. When I reach her, she's pouring coffee, acting like she never even spoke. Did I imagine it? I'm sure she said it. She looks at me, smiling. "Have you eaten lunch?"

"Yes, before coming, and I felt like wearing something besides jeans for a change."

"I'll grant you, it's a change. Now grab your coffee and let's see what you'll be making." She leads me to the dining room. By the time I'm seated, she already has a notebook open, filled with pages of hand-written instructions.

"I doubt any cookbook will help. I'm a businessperson, remember? The term cooking the books is closer to my talents."

"Nonsense. This is easy, and a roast is basic. You need to do nothing but season and sear it. Then put it in the roasting pan and in the oven. Simple."

"Care to repeat that, this time in English?" I say with a chuckle. Might as well have fun ahead of this inevitable disaster.

"Be serious, a five-year-old could do this." She spins the book around to face me.

I'm unable to stop myself. "In that case, do we have a five-year-old?" The recipe on the page she has open astounds me. "Are you kidding me? This is a rib roast. Do you know how expensive they are?"

"No, I never buy beef. We butcher several head a year for the family."

"This roast would be ninety dollars in Boston!"

"Good thing we're not there then. It's nothing but a cut of meat. No different from cooking a rump roast or an eye of round."

"Maybe not, but I haven't cooked one of those either. You might waste a fantastic roast."

"Don't be silly. I'd never let you ruin it. Now for the vegetables. I thought we'd have one of Jason's favorites with mashed potatoes and dinner rolls. That, my dear, is our menu." She says this like she's asking me to prepare a bowl of cereal.

"What are the vegetables? Asparagus in Hollandaise sauce?"

"I thought you didn't know about cooking."

"Cooking? No. Ordering? Yes. Not the same thing at all." With no way out, I resign myself to this ridiculous idea of hers. "What's first?"

"We'll start on the dinner rolls to give them time to rise." She gets up, taking the cookbook with her. I follow behind with our coffee. This must be what it feels like to walk the plank.

Time seems to fly as she walks me through step by step, starting with preparing the dough for the rolls, then the roast, and the cake. When the cake comes out of the oven, we take a seat at the kitchen table. "We'll wait for the oven to heat before putting in the roast."

"That's it?"

"For now. We still have the vegetables and the icing for the cake, but they can wait. The cake needs to cool, and the other bits take less than an hour."

"Are we making potatoes?"

"Yes, but they needed to soak in iced saltwater. I peeled and cut them earlier. They're in the pot in the refrigerator."

"You're soaking the potatoes in saltwater?"

"Look who's questioning me on cooking. Not even here two hours and thinks she's the expert."

"No, I've never heard of doing that. You said mashed potatoes, right?"

"Yes, and soaking them in saltwater helps remove the starch and makes them fluffier. You'll see."

The oven beeps to let us know it's at the desired temperature. I put the oven rack where she tells me and place the roast in while she sets the timer. "Thirty minutes? Are you sure?"

"Again, you're questioning me?" She's smiling. "At four-fifty. Then we'll set it to three hundred for the rest of the time. Should be perfect. Now we have time for another cup." She pours them and heads back to the chairs.

While we sip our coffee, she tells me about Jason's parents. They died in a car accident after he graduated vet school. I can relate to this, although my mother died when I was much younger.

We soon need to get back to work as Sadie says, "Now finish your coffee and let's see how things are going. We better get to it, or we'll have nothing but meat and rolls."

After rinsing the potatoes, I add enough water to cover them and put the pot on the stove. She sets several cans down and tells me to open them. "Cans? You're using something from a can?"

"Mind your manners, smarty. This is Jason's favorite. Green bean casserole. It's so easy, I doubt even you could ruin it."

"You never know. Where there's a will, there's a way."

"Open the cans, silly."

She walks me through the recipe, and I'll admit, it's easy. I could even make it on my own. But alone is how I'd have to eat it too. Next, I get started on the icing. True to a German chocolate cake, it's coconut pecan. It goes well enough for me to conclude the finished product even looks like coconut pecan frosting.

Now things are jumping. The potatoes are boiling, and she shows me how to check if they're done. Not yet, so I move to the next task. It's time to take the roast out, and the casserole goes in the oven.

She has me drain off what she calls the drippings to make a gravy, and the roast goes back in the oven. Soon, with potatoes mashed, the rolls baked, the casserole hot, the cake frosted, and the roast resting, we're set. The last thing to finish is the gravy, and now our meal is ready for the table.

I can't believe I made all this. I know I couldn't have done it or even attempted it without Sadie. Nevertheless, I did it. Of course, no one has tasted it yet. The jury is still out.

Jason and Tyler arrive right on time. "Something smells delicious," Jason says as he enters the kitchen. "I understand you're the chef this evening?"

"Chef is an exaggeration, and Sadie helped a lot."

"Not true, I did little," she says, coming in with a young boy. "Jazmine, meet Mr. Tyler Withers."

"Pleased to meet you ma'am," Tyler says holding out his hand. He's so cute I almost grab him in a hug.

"Thank you, Tyler. It's nice to meet you," I say, shaking his hand.

"Let's get this on the table," Sadie says. "Tyler, you take the rolls. Now be careful." She hands him the tray.

Jason takes the roast, and I'm right behind him with the gravy and potatoes. Sadie brings the casserole, and we're set.

She has a pitcher of iced tea waiting with glasses already poured. We take our seats, and I'm staggered when Jason mentions prayer. It must be the norm for them since even Tyler bows his head. While Jason prays, I sit waiting, not wanting to offend.

I don't get his prayer. He thanks this god for all their blessings, yet they've experienced so much tragedy in their lives. How could they ever see any blessings? I say nothing and wait for him to finish. He even adds thanks for bringing me into their lives.

He does the honors, slicing the roast while we pass around the other food. The platter of meat comes, followed by the gravy. My plate is full, so I have to be careful not to overflow with the gravy. With a small pool drizzled over the top, it's time to eat. Then it hits me. Everyone is about to taste my food. I hold my breath. Please let it be edible.

I hear Jason remark on the green bean casserole and how it's his favorite. Tyler chimes in, saying it's his too. I wait while they take their first bites. I'm too afraid to eat my first forkful—not that I could even if

I wanted to, what with my heart being stuck in my throat. Jason breaks the heavy silence. "You made this?" Was that a question or an accusation?

"Yes, she did. She's been cooking all afternoon," Sadie says.

"It's good." Tyler exclaims.

"Yes, quite good," Jason says. "I'd swear it tastes like Sadie's and I didn't think anyone could match her."

"Well, they were her instructions, but thank you. I can't tell you how it pleases me to hear that."

"Remember to save room for dessert. There's cake," Sadie adds.

Tyler has a hopeful expression. "Chocolate with coconut? That's my favorite."

"Yes, but you must clean your plate if you want any," she says.

In a second, he's concentrating on eating.

"Slow down, Tyler. The cake will be here when you're done," Jason tells him.

Here goes nothing. I take my first bite, and the delightful taste surprises me. Did I, the microwave queen, make this?

There's brief conversation while everyone eats. Then Sadie asks out of the blue, "Any luck on a replacement for Stephanie?"

"No, most aren't the take-charge type. You know how Steph was. She ran the place. Jill even stopped and asked about it, but has zero experience and was close to fainting when Stanley crawled past her on the counter."

"Jill? In an office? I'd pay to see that." Sadie laughs.

"My thoughts too, but it'd cost me a lot more than I'm willing to spend. Steph left two weeks ago, and already we can't find things. I don't know if we'll ever get the records right."

Now I understand why there was no one to answer the phone at the clinic. "This Stephanie was what? Your receptionist?"

Jason snickers. "I'd never say she was the receptionist. No, she ran the clinic. Doc Carson and I handle the patients. She did everything else, and I mean everything."

"Yes. Jason's father hired her twenty years ago straight out of business college. Been with them ever since," Sadie says.

My curiosity is piqued. "Why did she leave?"

"Her father suffered a stroke, and her mother isn't well," he says. "She moved to Arizona to take care of them. It came on quick. She wanted to stay until I found someone, but I told her to go. She needed to be there."

"It's nice of you to let her go, even with it putting you in a bind. Have you interviewed many?"

"Can I have my cake now?" Tyler's holding his empty plate for everyone to see.

"May I have my cake now?" Jason corrects him.

"May I have my cake now?" Tyler adds a gigantic smile to swing the decision in his favor.

"When we're finished," Jason tells him, which wipes the smile straight off Tyler's face.

"I don't know about them," Sadie says with a wink, "but I'm ready for mine too. Shall we get ours?"

He leaps from his chair then sprints to the kitchen.

"Slow down, no running in the house," Jason calls out before turning to me and rolling his eyes. "I've interviewed four so far. Most want to work around their children's schedules, but that level of flexibility isn't possible. Doc Carson and I have to be out often and need someone there."

"I can see how that might be problematic," I say as Sadie and a delighted Tyler return with enough cake for a small army.

"I thought it made sense to bring yours right away, rather than wait for you two gabby mouths to finish talking," she says, setting plates near us.

"He's explaining the difficulty he's having finding someone for the clinic."

"If he has any smarts at all, he'll hire you and be done with it." She sits and assumes an expression I've become familiar with—one of absolute innocence. As if she'd said nothing, she takes a bite of cake.

I stare at her, trying to find my voice. "What did you say Sadie?"

Jason speaks right after me. "Yeah, Sadie, what gave you that idea?"

She stares at us like we're the crazy ones. "You need someone; she needs a job. You need a business and finance person; she has MBA and MSF degrees. You need someone full-time; she's available full time. Could it be any clearer? Are you both educated beyond the ability of simple logic?"

Tyler clamps a hand over his cake-filled mouth to stifle a giggle.

Jason clears his throat. "I, um, don't think it's so simple. I'm sure she has options other than working at our clinic."

"Yeah, Sadie. I don't know the first thing about animals. I've never even owned a pet."

"He's not asking you to be a vet. He needs you to run the office. Believe me, veterinarians, like most doctors, meaning the male ones, are lousy at running an office. The poster children for unorganized. Anyway, what other options? This isn't Boston or New York City."

"Well, it never entered my mind." He turns to face me, appearing bewildered. "Would you even be interested? Do you have a resume?"

Splendid work, Sadie. What was she thinking?

Sadie, however, isn't one to back down. "A resume, Jason? She has an MBA from Harvard. What else do you need to know?"

Tyler looks like he's watching a tennis match as he tries to follow the debate. He seems amused by Sadie's persistence.

"Okay, but Steph did a lot of things with the computer," Jason says. "Someone will have to know the programs."

I doubt this will work out, but maybe I could do it until something else comes along. "What software do you use?"

"Software?"

I struggle not to giggle at his confused expression. "For running the business. Is it NetSuite, QuickBooks, or something else?"

"I'm not sure. NetSuite sounds familiar." He doesn't sound confident.

"Sounds like she knows this stuff better than you do," Sadie says. "Better grab her before someone else does. You don't even know where or when your next appointments are. I heard you missed two already this week." She pushes herself away from the table and gathers the plates, shaking her head all the while.

"Here, I can help," I say, keen to escape.

"No, you made dinner. I'll clear the table since no one else is offering."

"I'll help, Grandma," Tyler says, taking several of the dessert plates.

"Enough, I can take a hint." Jason sighs and stands. "You sit, Tyler, and I'll clear."

Sadie lowers herself back into her chair and smiles. "Well, if you insist. Bring the coffee on your way back." She gives me a wink.

"It's too late for you," he says from the kitchen. "You know what the doctor said."

"What does he know? Doctors nowadays never look up from those tablet things long enough to see you. What type of doctor is that?"

"The type who practice medicine the best they can, like you."

"I can take care of myself. Either bring me coffee or you'll not be taking any cake home."

Tyler turns to her with the cutest expression. "Do I get to take some, Grandma?"

"Of course, dear, but you can't share it with your father. He's being bad."

"Let me get it for you, Sadie," I say, rising.

Tyler has already vanished into the kitchen to rescue the last of the cake.

"I got it," Jason says, coming in with the coffee pot and mugs. "Half a cup for you, Sadie. That's the deal. Half a cup or none. Take it or leave it."

She watches with dismay as he pours two full cups and one half one. "You know it's illegal for a vet to treat a human."

"Not when the human is acting like a stubborn mule," he retorts.

I'm glad Tyler's still in the kitchen, but Jason winks at me.

"Mules can also kick, and you should know since you're acting like the back end of one." Sadie resumes her innocent face, and I can't help but laugh.

"Well, you know what they say. Better to act like one than—"

"I'd watch yourself, young man," Sadie says, shaking her finger. The twinkle in her eye suggests it's all in fun.

"Okay, I will, but you started it," he says, pointing back.

I can't stop myself. "What are you? Three years old?" This gets a startled look from him and cracks up Sadie.

"Oh, you're perfect. He needs someone to keep him on his toes," she says. Is she referring to more than working at the office?

"I thought that was your job," Jason says.

"Keep it up, young man, and see what it gets you. Now, what time you getting her tomorrow?"

"What?" He and I cry out.

"We haven't even discussed anything," he says.

"Are all young people so blind to the obvious? How do you ever get anything accomplished?" Poking her finger on the table, she glares at Jason. "Now, Jason, do you or do you not need an office manager?"

"Well, yes, I do. I—"

"No, you answered the question. Now, Jazmine, do you or do you not want a job?"

"Well, yeah, but—"

"That's enough from you too. Jason, you need someone qualified, trustworthy, self-motivated and capable. Is that right?"

"Well, yeah, but there—"

"Jazmine, do you feel qualified to manage an office the size of the clinic? Or is a Harvard education not what we're led to believe?"

How else can I answer a question like that? "No, I'm qualified."

"There you go. What more do you need? Now, what time will you pick her up?"

He sighs, shrugging in defeat. "I guess it wouldn't hurt for you to come in and talk." He turns to Sadie and adds, "Why do I have to pick her up? Can't she use your truck?"

That does make sense.

"Because she'll need to drive her truck home. If she has mine, she'll have to leave one there," Sadie says, shaking her head as though he should know better.

"Wait…my truck? I don't have a truck."

"Not yet. You'll get it tomorrow when you start work. Jason, you still have the clinic's truck Stephanie was using?"

"Yes, but again, aren't we getting ahead of ourselves? I already said she could come in and talk, you know, before—"

"Will eight-thirty in the morning work, Jazmine?" Sadie interrupts. "That will get you in with time to spare before the clinic opens."

"I guess, yeah, sure,"

"Great, Jason, you be at her place at eight-thirty tomorrow. Understand? And you'll take her home tonight. Let me get the cake for Tyler, and I guess you can have a piece too, Jason. Jazmine, do you want any?"

"No, I'm fine."

Sadie disappears into the kitchen.

Jason leans near and whispers, "We can talk more in the morning, but I want you to know you're under no obligation, okay?"

"Okay, and neither are you."

We both sit up straight when Sadie returns.

She holds out a cake container to Jason. "Here's the cake. I already told Tyler to get his jacket. You two do the same and leave so I can have a little peace. I'm an old lady, you know."

"I'm not sure your age has anything to do with it, but Tyler needs to get to bed," Jason says, smiling, and turns to me. "Jazmine, may I drive you home?"

"I guess you may, but I was going to help with the dishes. Do we have time?"

"Most are done, and the dishwasher is running, so you may go," Sadie says, helping Tyler.

With nothing else to do and knowing arguing further is fruitless, I get my coat and head for the door. Jason and Tyler soon join me, with Sadie following right behind.

"Now you drive careful. These roads are slick this time of night," she tells Jason while straightening his scarf.

"I know how to drive. Remember, no more coffee for you and get to bed on time. You hear me?"

"Go on, get," she says, grabbing his shoulders and pushing him toward the door. "I've been taking care of myself for eighty-two years. I don't need you telling me how to live now."

I hold back a giggle and say, "Thank you for dinner. It was a delightful time."

"You made the dinner," she says with genuine enthusiasm. "I should thank you, and so should two others."

"Let's be honest, I couldn't have even come close without your help."

"We are thankful," Jason says, ushering Tyler out through the front door. "It was an excellent meal and much better than we would have gotten at home."

"You can say that again. His cooking is awful," Tyler adds before running off in a fit of laughter.

"Well, thank you, but I still say it's Sadie you should thank."

Sadie wags her finger at me. "That's enough, all of you. Now go, you're letting in the frigid air. Jazmine, you take care and mind your step, it's slick out there. Jason, hold her arm so she doesn't slip. Wouldn't hurt you to at least act like a gentleman sometimes."

I can't help but think she's up to something.

Jason follows her instructions and holds my arm while we go down the steps and walk to his truck. He helps Tyler climb in the back, then assists me. This is helpful considering the height of this monstrosity. After one last wave to Sadie, we're set for the brief drive to my place.

I'm thankful it's not long before Jason pulls up to my house. After making sure I have everything, I thank him for the ride.

He glances at me. "Guess I'll see you at eight-thirty then?"

"You know you don't have to; I'll understand. You were pushed into this."

"No, I'm looking forward to it. Plus, if I didn't, Sadie would not be pleased. I'm sure you've learned—you never want to displease Sadie."

"Okay then. I'm willing if you are. I'll be ready when you arrive." I'm about to get out when Tyler dives from his seat in the back and hugs me.

With his arms wrapped around me tight, he squeals, "Goodnight, Jazmine."

This brings tears to my eyes. I return the hug and tell him goodnight, promising I'll see him soon. I tell Jason the same then slide to the ground, rushing for my front door before the tears start to fall. What's with me?

He waits for me to walk into the house. From the doorway, I watch him drive away. After putting my parka and scarf away, I turn back to face my living space, fighting off the depression that seeps into my skin when I enter my so-called home. I don't want any sadness tonight. It's been too enjoyable. There was laughter, joking, and so many smiles. Something I haven't experienced in a long time. I even skip working on the blog tonight, knowing it would cause more sorrow. I head straight for the bedroom. It's late, and I have a job interview in the morning.

I take time to pick out what I want to wear but decide not to go too dressy. After all, it's an animal clinic. Once satisfied with my selections, I slide between the sheets and snuggle my head into the cool pillow. In the dark, my last thoughts are full of what might be in store for tomorrow. Could this work?

Chapter Five

Excited, I wake before the alarm. I bathe as best I can in my lavish washtub, and do my hair and makeup. I want to present a business-like image, and maybe even go the extra mile.

Once dressed, I head for the kitchen. While I have my coffee and muffin, my brain goes into overdrive, covering everything I need for the day ahead. It seems like 8:30 will never get here. Why am I nervous? I don't even know if I'll take the job.

With a shake to clear my head, I put on my coat and scarf, wanting to be ready the moment Jason arrives. I have on an older pantsuit. What am I saying? Most of my clothes are older, but this one goes back several years. I don't know why, but I keep checking the mirror to make sure I look okay. Each time, I question why I'm nervous. It can't be the job. I doubt it's anything I can't handle. I have to live here for at least a year anyway, so I need a job, but I'm not locked in forever. Maybe it's seeing Jason again. I'm alarmed at this, but saved from further introspection when he arrives. Now we can get this whole rigmarole started.

After one last check in the mirror, this time with purse in hand to complete the ensemble, I head out. As I leave the house, a swarm of butterflies takes flight in my stomach.

He parks, and I reach the colossal vehicle before he can get out. I climb up—and I mean climb, since the seats are level with my shoulder when viewed from the ground. This has me wondering what Stephanie's might be like.

"Good morning," he greets me. "You all set?"

I attempt a confident smile. "I am. Let's go."

He pulls out, heading for Moose Ridge. "As you know, it's a quick trip."

"Yes, I do. How's Tyler this morning? Does he go to a babysitter while you work?"

"Sort of. He stays with my neighbor who has a son his age. She takes them to preschool and gets them when it's done. If I'm in the area and free, I'll get them to return the favor. It's working well."

"I'm glad. I'm sure it's hard on both of you."

"We make do. He also comes to the clinic and helps with the chores. It allows me extra time with him. He's a great kid."

"I'm sure he is, but I sense an ornery streak. Could it be he's following in his father's footsteps?"

"Who, me? Never. It's obvious he got it from his great-grandmother. The ornery gene appears every third generation." He's snickers as he pulls into the clinic parking lot. He drives around to the back and parks next to a large SUV. "Shall we see what trouble we can get into?"

I notice he leaves the keys in the ignition. I exit the vehicle in as much of a ladylike fashion as possible, which means sliding down the side of the truck until my boots touch the ground. He opens the clinic's door, and I'm astonished he used a key.

He holds the door for me to go in. "Do you need to feed any of the animals or anything?"

"No, Jake's crew takes care of the early morning feedings," he says, leading me along the hallway.

"Jake?"

"Yes, he's a retired rodeo cowboy. Now he takes care of the ranch's cattle and helps care for any animals we have. Most would call him the ranch foreman."

This is a revelation. "You have cattle too? I thought this was a clinic."

"It is, but the ranch has a few thousand head. This area is part of Moose Ridge Ranch. One of the largest working cattle ranches in the area. It works out well for when we need space to stable animals. Jake has a team of a dozen or so cowboys for handling the cattle, and can call more when needed. They are also available for help in the clinic."

"Makes sense." We reach a familiar area of the building. Cashmere's colt is standing at their stall's gate.

I hurry across to greet him and Cashmere, giving them both an enjoyable scratch on their necks.

"I'll start the coffee, and we can talk," Jason says, walking toward the office area. I hear him tell Stanley good morning.

After one last pat of the colt and Cashmere, I join him. When I reach the area, Jason is pouring water into the coffee maker. He motions toward a chair for me. Stanley is on the counter by his drink dish. He doesn't seem pleased to find water.

"No Mountain Dew this morning?"

"No. That's a special treat in the evening. He'll try to trick more out of you though. He's exceptional at being sly. Isn't that right, Stanley?" Jason strokes the top of Stanley's head. I swear Stanley glares at him. "Coffee will be ready soon. We keep it on hand for anyone. A pot or two a day is normal. Depends how busy we are."

I hang my things on a coat stand and take the seat offered. "What time does the clinic open?"

"Ten, today. We're open till six most days. Tuesdays, we're closed, and Doc Carson and I are out on calls. Steph would use Tuesdays for paperwork."

I can't help but wonder how something like this could function with so few people? Maybe this job is more than I want? "There were only the three of you and Jake?"

"Oh, no. We have two full-time assistants, Richard and Terri. Andi, who works part time and is a veterinarian student at Casper College, lives in an apartment upstairs and helps Jake's crew with the after-hours feedings."

"That still seems like a small group for a clinic this size."

"There's also our lab tech, Cindy, and her assistant Jimmy. We have another assistant starting next week, and a new doctor coming on board this summer. Also, we have students from vet schools in for short stints, and there are the ranch hands if we need them. It's quite a group."

This relieves a few of my fears. "Why weren't any of them here for the birth?"

"One of those perfect-storms. Doc Carson was called out on an emergency, and Richard and Terri were with him. Cindy and Jimmy work half days on Tuesday. Andi was in class, and Jake and his crew were at one of our barns a distance away, prepping for winter. You and Sadie stopping by was a helpful thing. Coffee's ready, you want a cup?"

"Yes, please. No other females other than Cindy?"

"No," he says, grinning while pouring the coffee. "Terri, Andi, and Cassie, the new assistant, are women."

"I guess the names threw me. I meant nothing by it, though. It's quite a crew."

He hands me a coffee mug. "Yes, and Steph kept us in sync. Since she left, it's been chaotic. Cream or sugar?" He's holding up the sugar dispenser.

"Sugar is fine," I say. "She took care of scheduling appointments and what else?" After he adds the sugar, I try the coffee. It's not bad.

"It'd be quicker to tell you what she didn't do. Steph wasn't keen on feeding the animals or cleaning their teeth or stalls, and refused to help with any animal larger than Stanley. Detested snakes and wouldn't even go in the kennel room if one was there. She's the one who got Stanley started on Mountain Dew. She drinks it more than coffee. Stanley knocked her bottle over once and lapped up what spilled. Since then, we have to watch him if there's an open bottle or can around. What can I say, she did everything but deal with the animals."

"Wow. I see how her absence would cause a vacuum."

"Yes, it has. Do you want the position or have I scared you off?"

"Do I want it? I thought this was an interview."

"I talked with Steph and Doc Carson last night, and they agree with Sadie. With your schooling and experience managing an office in Boston, you're perfect for what we need. If you want it, it's yours."

"Okay. It sounds interesting, but also a lot of work. What would the pay and benefits be?"

"Should have gone over those first," he says. "The basic stuff most places offer. Dental, vision, and health insurance, as well as a retirement fund. Three weeks personal time and six holidays, plus we close the clinic the week between Christmas and New Year."

"Are we talking salary?"

"Yes, but Steph kept it to forty hours a week. Doc Carson and I discussed the salary, and we doubt we can match your Boston rate, but we don't have Boston's economy either. How does sixty sound?"

It's more than I expected, but I don't tell him that. I also know better than to accept the first offer. "Seventy sounds better."

"I'd agree. Remember, the job comes with a vehicle, and we cover all costs associated with it."

"What type of vehicle is it, and can I use it for anything other than work?" I hope it's not like his F350 monstrosity.

"It's the black Excursion we parked beside, and you can use it for whatever you like, within reason."

"An Excursion? That's an SUV, isn't it? I thought you said a truck?"

"Around here we call them trucks. It's easier to say."

"Isn't it big though?" I'll never be able to call it a truck.

"Depends what's parked next to it, but it's four-wheel drive and works well all year 'round. Plus, you'll need to haul things from the feed store and other places. It runs well and has most every option you could want. What are your thoughts?"

I pause for a few moments, hoping it will worry him. When I gaze at him, his expression of concern delights me. "Let's meet in the middle? Sixty-five and the vehicle, plus the other benefits you mentioned."

"Sixty-five, huh." I don't think he's expecting an answer. After a few moments, he smiles. "Sounds reasonable. Steph sent me an offer letter for you to sign." He holds out a folder to me. "There's also a job description and a file on the computer covering her tasks."

"Why didn't you give me this when we began?" I open the folder. There's a page with "Offer Letter" typed in bold across the top, and I do a quick review. Two things stand out: it already has my name on it, and the salary reads "$65,000." Maybe my negotiating skills aren't what I thought. The job description is three pages and most of it covers what Jason said, but in a lot more detail. She even provides her phone number if I have questions.

"I guess we have a deal." I reach for my pen, but find Stanley is sitting on my purse.

"Here, use mine," Jason says, holding out a pen. "He's trying to get you to give him more Mountain Dew. Remember, I said he can be sneaky." With a stern glance at Stanley, Jason scolds him. "You have water, Stanley. You know the rules. No Mountain Dew. Now move on, we have work to do."

Stanley climbs off my purse, astonishing me, and slithers away to a lower counter shelf. His glances back at Jason are not pleasant.

"I'm sorry, didn't know there was a rule. Anyway, I signed the letter," I say, holding it out.

He takes the letter and adds his signature with a flourish before handing the original and copy back to me. "I guess you'll need to process this yourself. She said the forms and instructions are on the computer. Do you have questions for me?"

"Well, first, where is this computer? I don't see one out here?"

"It's in the office," he says, standing. "All the offices are through here. There's mine and Doc Carson's, and one for the new doctor. The first one on the left is yours." He waves for me to follow.

"It's in the office?" This is oh so wrong. "You don't use a computer for your appointments?"

"We've always used an appointment book. Steph mentioned doing it on the computer, but most of us aren't into the hi-tech stuff."

Through the door is a hallway with several doors on either side. He motions to one on the left, but I first notice the junk room across from it. I'm hoping that door can be closed.

"That's my office," Jason says, noticing my interest. "Doc Carson's is the one past mine, and across from him is the spare. Farther on are two storage rooms, the bathroom, and entry to what we call the warehouse."

It takes a moment before my utter astonishment diminishes and I can speak. "That's your office? Sadie's description of your organization skills was correct. Is there even a desk in there?"

I'm laughing while entering my new domain. It's well laid out. Quite a contrast to what's four feet away. There's a desk and filing cabinet. Both appear old but functional. An old-style monitor sits on the desk, with an even older style computer tower sitting beside it.

I notice it even has a slot for a floppy disk. "A little dated, but this should work."

"Consider it yours. Questions?"

"Not right now. I'll get on the system and check out her files and get back to you if I need anything." The computer is on already, so I click the mouse to bring it to life. I'm startled by what shows on the screen. "I guess you're correct on the hi-tech. This is Windows XP, and it's not even set for a login. You don't secure them?"

"Never thought about it. Is this a problem?"

"Well, the login I can take care of, but Windows XP hasn't been supported in years. You should upgrade." While talking, I'm using the mouse to check things.

"Steph was always saying that, but it works fine."

"You realize XP came out in 2001. How old are your computers?"

"Steph would know. She put together a plan for upgrading before she found out she needed to leave. It should be there somewhere."

"Okay. I'll let you know what I find."

"Well, if you have questions, I'll be checking on our patients." He appears to be thinking for a few moments. "I'll leave you to it. I'm sure the others will come meet you when they arrive. You know where the coffee is. Shout if you need anything." He smiles, waves, then walks out.

"Thanks, Jason." I sit back for a moment. I can't believe it. I got a well-paying job and a vehicle—albeit a huge one. Time to get to work.

Stephanie's notes even include a task calendar for each day. I'm reviewing Thursday when I hear a light knock. I turn to find a lady in a lab coat.

"Hello. I hear you're the new Steph. I'm Cindy, the lab tech."

"I guess I am. I'm Jazmine. Nice to meet you, Cindy."

"I'm sure you'll meet the rest of the crew later. If you have questions, call out or come get me. You should find me in the lab. I understand you're new to our town?"

"Yes, I am. Haven't even been here a week."

"Steph will die hearing it took a Harvard grad to replace her," Cindy says, giggling.

"Not sure I'll be able to replace her, but I'll try."

"I'm sure you'll be on top of things in no time. Anyway, I'll leave you to it. Remember, shout if you need something." As she turns to leave, another young lady appears.

"Jazmine, is it? Hi. I'm Terri. Boy, it's great you're here. I thought the docs would lose it if someone didn't show soon. How are things going? Did you find Steph's notes? Have you met everyone?" She rattles off an endless list of questions.

"Calm down, Terri," a young man behind her says. His face peeks over her shoulder. "Hello. I'm Richard. As you heard, Terri, can get a little excited. It's nice to meet you, Jazmine."

"Nice to meet you both. I understand you are assistants?"

"Yes," he says. "Terri worked the front desk for several years and now is an assistant. I've been here three years. I hear you helped deliver Cashmere's foal?"

"I'm not sure—"

"You got to help?" Terri is off again. "I so wanted to be here. What was it like? Did she have a hard time? Was it a breech? Did anyone have to pull the colt out? Did he stand right away? How was Cashmere?" Richard places a hand on Terri's arm to silence her and rolls his eyes.

A third person, an older man, arrives in the doorway. "That's enough, Terri. Remember, you're limiting your questions to three at a time. Hello, I'm Stephen Carson. I'm glad you took the job. We sure need someone to take charge of this place."

"Doc, did you hear? She delivered Cashmere's colt, and it was breech." Terri says.

This time, I raise my voice to get her attention. "Jason delivered the colt. I tried to keep Cashmere calm. Plus, Sadie was here. Nice to meet you, Doctor Carson."

I'm astounded I get it in without interruptions.

"Please, call me Stephen, or Doc Carson if you must. We're informal around here."

"Doc Carson it will be."

"Well, knowing Steph, I'm sure you have a lot of reading to do. There's plenty of work for us to get on with too. Nice meeting you, Jazmine. Shout if you need anything." Before he leaves he adds, "Okay, people leave her alone. We all have things to do."

"Bye, Jazmine," Terri calls out, as does Richard.

Once again, I'm alone in my office. I return to my seat and back to reading. Doc Carson is correct, there is quite a lot here. As I work my way through, it becomes obvious this Steph was an organized person. The arrangement of folders and files is easy to follow.

I find a document describing a plan for upgrading the PCs. It's using laptops and docking stations for most. That might work, but I also wonder if including tablets would help.

She's gotten a quote for the equipment and gives a detailed list. She even references emails she received with the doctor's approvals. It appears to be complete.

After a few hours reviewing everything, I go back to the schedule of her daily tasks, which also has detailed instructions.

Being Thursday, this is the day she submits the supply list via email to what she calls the Feed Store and CO-OP. According to the notes, Richard fills out a form and should give it to me by 2:00 PM. She mentions reminding him is an excellent idea.

This might be the perfect time for a walk around my new workplace. I can speak with him on the way. With my system in screen lock, I venture out.

When I find him, Richard is manning the front counter and several people are sitting in the chairs with their pets. Looks like a dog and a cat with their respective owners. Stanley is lounging on the counter. When he sees me, he hurries to his drink dish, gazing at me. This lizard is something else.

"You can have water, but Jason said no Mountain Dew," I tell him while pouring water in his dish. Seeing it's not what he wanted, he returns to where he was. The admonishing expression on his face shows I'm not his friend anymore. "Richard, Stephanie has in her notes you're responsible for doing the supply list?"

"Yep, that's me. I'll have it for you this afternoon. Did she tell you how to send it?"

"Yes, she did," I say as Terri comes in from the back.

"Richard, Doc Carson said to remember the wood shavings when you do the supply order. Also, Cindy says to make sure you see her before you give it to Jazmine."

"I know, I'll get it," he snaps in a huff before heading to the back.

Terry turns to me, whispering, "What got into him?"

"I mentioned the list before you got here. Maybe he felt we were ganging up on him."

"He'll get over it." She shrugs. "Mrs. Stapleton, you want to bring Maestro back?" She's motioning toward one of the exam rooms.

A woman with a rather gigantic dog stands and follows close behind. Terri talks to the dog while taking the leash, and they disappear into the exam room.

Behind me, I hear a noise and turn. Stanley is pushing his water dish again. "You have water. Now behave," I tell him. Inspired by Stanley's thinking, I pour myself a cup of coffee.

"Great minds think alike," Jason says, coming in from the back and pouring one for himself. He then greets the gentleman holding the cat. "Mr. Wilson, how is Sassy?"

"She's being fussy. Like something's wrong with her stomach." He's almost whispering, and I struggle to hear him.

"Why don't you come back, and we'll see what we can find?"

While the gentleman stands and follows Jason to an exam room, I take my coffee back to my office. My one task left for today is sending the order for supplies, so I review the schedule for tomorrow. I'm partway done when Richard arrives.

"Nothing unusual this week," he says, handing me the list. "What do you think of our town?"

"Casper is a little more than a town," I say, chuckling.

"No, Glenrock. I try to avoid Casper. Too many people for me."

"Oh, well, seems like a pleasant place. Everyone I've met so far has been nice."

"Most are, but they can be nosy."

"I haven't noticed."

"That's because you were with Sadie, and most people have already heard of the lady from Boston. Don't worry, they'll be sticking their noses in your business soon enough."

"I think you're giving them a bad rap. Anyway, why would they have heard of me?"

"You're joking, right? Any change in this town is instant news. There are only two hotels and four churches, so everyone knows everyone else's business. Wait till it gets out you're working with Doc Withers. Tongues will wag for sure. Hey, you two aren't dating, are you?"

"What? No! What gave you that idea?"

"I heard you made dinner for him, and he was at your place Sunday. I thought maybe…"

"No. We're not dating. Sadie was giving me a cooking lesson, and he and Tyler came to eat. Sunday, he dropped off brownies Sadie made for a welcome gift, that's all. How did you even know about Sunday?"

"Told you, small town. Not much goes unnoticed. Plus, there aren't many women like you around these parts."

This catches me off guard. "What do you mean, women like me?"

"You know. Smart, sophisticated, and a knock-out." With that, he winks and spins on his heel, heading out to the hallway.

I can't believe how he described me. Shaking my head, I get back on task and do the orders. Once I'm done, I review the plans. Seems tomorrow is the day for payroll. I know the software they use for finances well. I read the notes she has for the task, and it seems straightforward. Next, I move on to the permits. I'm immersed in this when Jason arrives.

"I realized we didn't discuss your hours this morning," he says, standing in my doorway.

"No, we didn't. I thought I'd stay until closing."

"Your choice. Steph came in at nine and left around five. The earlier start allowed her to get things done before the staff got here. You do what works for you. Oh, there's something else we need to talk about," he says, seeming a little tentative.

"Okay, I'm all yours." Too late it hits me how this might sound. "I mean, what do you need?" I hope I'm not blushing.

"We need someone to man the front desk. You know, check people in and answer the phones. Richard and Terri used to manage it, but not so much anymore."

I was afraid this was coming. "I'm not sure how that would work. I don't know how much time I'd have to handle being the receptionist too."

"Oh, sorry, no. We weren't thinking you would do it. We need you to hire and train someone. We're thinking two people, each part time working half days. What do you think?"

"Knowing little of the clinic operation yet, I'm not sure I'm the right person."

"It's more an administration role. They won't be dealing with the animals. This way, you can make sure you can work with whoever you hire, and I'm sure you know more about what the position requires than anyone else."

"Okay. Do I need to place an ad to get things rolling?"

"It's running in tomorrow's paper. I forgot we scheduled it. Your desk phone is the number listed. You'll need to do the interviews, and Terri can help with a job description."

"Okay, I'll check with her. You want two people for twenty hours a week. Do you have a minimum age? The high school might have a work program."

"I'd like to hire someone from there. You think it through and keep me informed."

"Okay, I'll call the school tomorrow and see what we can do. Anything else?"

"Yes, Sadie said to remind you tonight is laundry night, and she has dinner covered. She's expecting you around six. You better get out of here or you'll be late—and you don't want to be late," he finishes with a slight snicker.

"Yes, she said Thursdays are best, but since I got this job, I thought I'd find a laundromat close by. Can you tell her thank you for me?"

"Are you kidding? I'll not be the one to tell her you're not coming. If you're smart, you won't either. With Sadie, it's best to say 'Yes, ma'am' and follow her wishes. Believe me, you'll be happier, she'll be happier, and by extension, I'll be happier."

"Okay. I guess I will for now."

"If you'll excuse me, I have a pony with an attitude waiting. You have an enjoyable evening with Sadie, and I'll see you tomorrow." He turns to leave.

"Wait," I call after him. "What about the Excursion?"

"What about it?"

"I'll need the keys." Why isn't this obvious?

"Yes. I would think so."

"Where would I get them?"

"Ah, where else? In the Excursion."

"You leave the keys in it?"

"Sure. If they're not in the ignition, check the sun visor. Kind of depends who drove it last. Oh, if it needs gas, make certain you use premium, and you'll need a company credit card." He's gone before I can say anything else.

"Thanks!" I call after him. Now it's time to get my laundry. I'm sure he's correct, and I don't want to be late.

~ * ~

It's after ten when I return to my place. Once the clothes are put away, I get my laptop to check out my Heartbreak Group. The splendid news is, I can do this from bed. I check recent posts and notice several ladies I've replied to before are online. I mention the job, and they're thrilled for me. But I must call it a night since I'm a working girl again. I post a comment telling everyone goodnight, but before I can shut the laptop, a message appears.

You never mentioned what's-his-name tonight.

You're on your way, girl!

I realize she's right. In fact, I don't think I thought about "what's-his-name" today at all. Maybe there's hope for me, but the weekend is coming, and with it, few distractions to occupy my mind.

Chapter Six

One month later

I finish transferring the data from the old computer to my new laptop. Everyone is excited about the new systems. Well, except Jason, Mister non-hi-tech. The offices have laptops with docking stations running Windows 10 and two twenty-four-inch wide-screen monitors. Most people also have tablets and their cellphones synced to their laptops. Everything is on a wireless network, and communicating is much easier.

We also hired two people for the front desk, Georgia and Jennifer. Man, was Jill stunned when she came in to apply for the vacancy to find I was the one interviewing. She couldn't put together a coherent sentence for several minutes. I'm ashamed to admit, I might have enjoyed it.

On the personal front, I've settled into a flow. Thursday nights I spend with Sadie doing laundry, and she's started giving me cooking lessons. I'm not sure why since I'm single, but it's fun and I'm learning. The other nights, I have dinner, spend time with the Heartbreak Group, and work on my blog.

I named it "The Rich Girl's Poor Life" by Tiffany Waldensmyth. It has a magnificent ring to it. It took time to get it set up, but it's going well. The ladies from my group have been spreading the word, and I'm getting new followers daily. I post a new section every Sunday and reply to comments throughout the week. I spend Friday evenings and Saturdays getting the next one ready to publish. It's not like I have anything else to do on the weekend.

The first two weeks of my writing covered my younger years. I shared about my mother and her death and how that changed my life. How close my relationship with my father became and how everything was more than perfect. I ended with my twelfth birthday, when he took me to Tavern on the Green and to the *Phantom of the Opera.*

Our seats were in one of the private boxes, and he even let me have a glass of Champagne to toast my birthday. I'll never forget it. It's the last cheerful memory I have of him.

This week, I'll be dealing with his leaving and how my life changed again, but I put it aside for now. Sadie has asked me to drive her to the Women's Auxiliary meetings since the clinic is closed on Tuesdays.

They meet the first Tuesday each month; the other Tuesdays are committee meetings. Her fundraising committee met this past week. Jill was not pleased to see me again.

Sadie even raised an idea I shared for a fundraiser. I don't know what bothered Jill more—the fact I suggested it or the other women liked it. Now I need to provide a marketing plan for the next meeting. That and the blog fill my free time, which is fine.

The busier, the better, since it leaves little time for thoughts concerning he who will remain nameless. It's working. Maybe not well, but I'm doing better.

I also purchased clothes for the office. Sadie was after me to buy jeans, so I took her advice and got a few since it can get messy at the clinic. But as a rule, I prefer to keep things more professional. I found several adorable outfits. One is Gaucho pants with a cute vest and blouse. To go with the jeans were what Sadie calls "work shirts." Never dreamed I'd wear a flannel shirt, but they're comfortable and became my norm at the house.

On a whim, I got an XL men's one to wear to bed. It's unbelievable how the flannel envelops me in its softness and is getting softer with each wash. It keeps me warm and feels like someone wrapping their arms around me.

I find comfort in knowing it could never be you know who. He'd never wear flannel shirts. Jason does. No! That thought did not come into my mind.

Boots work better with the weather, so I found several stylish knee-high pairs, with nice size heels. I'm in love with the snake skin ones I got. They're so cute with the Gaucho pants. I also found a more fashionable coat than the parka. I'm set until spring. However, I've found I enjoy shopping, and in particular for clothes. Never had much time or funds before. You might say I'm making up for lost time. I even found a few magnificent sites online.

The ding of my computer system snaps me out of my daydream. Time to get back to work.

It's the supply order from Richard. I review it and add things the docs need. There are a few things I must get at a store in Casper. I order everything else online and have it shipped here.

I fill the rest of my afternoon with scanning old records into the system. At this rate, I should have everything scanned and organized by Thanksgiving. Not sure which Thanksgiving, though. The best news is, any records for current patients go straight into the system, and there's a hard copy made later for the files. Both doctors feel it helps to keep these. Despite their lack of trust in modern technology, I'm not giving up and will change their minds.

Before I know it, it's after five and I need to go since Sadie expects me at six-thirty. I power off my computer and get my bag and purse. I leave my door open because Stanley has taken a liking to the bottom shelf of my bookcase. There are a few areas I need to check before leaving. This is my standard procedure since the clinic is still open, and one reason I'm not out of here until after five-thirty.

I find Jennifer, the high school student who's our afternoon receptionist, in the usual place, and she says everything is fine. Then I go to the kennel room and find Terri with the patients. The variety of animals we have amazes me. Terri's holding a snake when I walk in. I'm not thrilled with those and stay far away.

There is one other group I need to see. Someone brought in a stray they found who was in terrible shape. When Jason examined her, he found she was pregnant and due any moment. He tried his best, but he couldn't save her. However, he saved three of the pups, and they are the cutest things I've ever seen. The mother was a miniature Long Haired Dachshund, and who knows what the father was. The pups are taking after their mother. It's hard to tell one from the other because they like to scooch close to each other in the box. That is, until feeding time. Then it's every puppy for itself.

Jason warned me not to name them or get too attached, but I couldn't help myself. They are too cute, and their names are Mindy, Lindy, and Bob. What can I say—Tyler named the boy. The girls have golden highlights in their reddish coats, but Bob's are darker. All three can raise a ruckus, but Bob is the worst. We must feed them with a bottle for now, and I try to help with this. I lift each tiny ball of fur one at a time and hold them close, their tongues licking my nose. They're two weeks old and small enough to fit in the palm of my hand.

"We all know you'll be taking one of them home once they're weaned," Terri says. I'm glad she's already put the snake back.

"What? No. I wouldn't know what to do with a pet." I place Lindy back beside Mindy and lift Bob. Dare I say he's my favorite? I hold him against me and hear his soft whimper of contentment. He is beyond cute.

"Yeah, right. You'll have no problem watching someone walk out of here with him, no problem at all." Terri gets Mindy. I notice she holds her close for a sneaky cuddle.

"Says you." Laughing, I snuggle my nose into the plump folds of Bob's stumpy neck, but I must go. I place him in his bed next to Lindy and turn to leave, but I'm not quick enough and hear him whimper and cry. It breaks my heart every time. I lean down and stroke his tummy.

"Sure, okay," she says, her voice laced with sarcasm. "You can't leave him now, even knowing you'll be back tomorrow. No, I can tell. He'll be going home with you. You'll see." She gives Mindy a kiss on the head and lays her back in the box.

I ignore her while I continue to pet Bob. Soon his little eyes have closed, and he's sound asleep. I back out with care and leave before he wakes.

I find Richard in the stalls room. He reports all is fine and, after checking with Cindy in the lab, I make my way out to my SUV. I can't bring myself to call it a truck.

Once home, I change into casual clothes and make the two trips required to transport my laundry. I need one last trip to grab my purse and the cookies I promised Sadie.

After the brief drive to Moose Ridge, I park by the rear steps. Sadie is waiting at the door. This brings a warmth to my heart, since few times in my life has anyone been waiting for my arrival. I climb the steps and hand her my purse and the plate of cookies before going back to get my laundry.

With all my belongings inside the house, I shuttle the laundry to the utility room, and get the first load started. Sadie is waiting at the kitchen table with two mugs of coffee by the time I return.

"Perfect, thank you." I slump into the seat across from her.

"How was your day?" We share how things have been going since I saw her on Tuesday. It's so nice to sit and discuss my day with someone who's interested. What's-his-name never was, and I don't think he even listened, but Sadie does.

After finishing our coffee, I move the first load to the dryer and put in the next. When I get back, she's already laid our plates on the table and started making dinner. I help with what I can, following her instructions, of course. Tonight's fare is a roasted stuffed chicken breast with macaroni and cheese and green beans.

She says her prayer, and it amazes me how she talks to this god of hers like they have a personal relationship. It's not something I'm used to hearing. Once she finishes, I take a bite, and it's better than I imagined.

We put the world to rights while we eat, although I let her steer the conversation. I'm sure she gets lonesome out here all by herself, and I wish I could visit her more. The ding goes off for the washer, and I go check on it.

I hang my blouses to dry and start my last load. When I get back, Sadie has already cleared the table and poured me more coffee. Since she's behaving tonight and only having the one, I'll make this one last.

"I was sorry to read about your mother. You were so young. It must have been hard on you."

"What? Where did you read about my mother?"

"On your blog."

I stare at her for several seconds. "You read my blog?"

"What do you think I do all day, sit around waiting for someone to stop by?"

Then it hits me. "How did you know it was mine? It's still about my younger life."

"Obvious to me. Maybe not to most, but I know you well. I can't wait for the next segment. Will it be up this weekend?"

"Wait. How can you know me so well? It hasn't even been two months since we met. And yes, the next segment will be posted Sunday."

"Time is not what allows someone to know you. It's desire."

"Okay, if you say so." I pause for a few moments. "I started it on a fluke. I wanted to write something about my recent breakup to help work through it, but there were too many holes and questions, so I started earlier to fill in the background."

"You write well. It's a fascinating read."

"Thank you. Please don't let anyone else know it's mine."

"Oh, I'd never dream of it, but others may put two and two together."

"They may, but it's not like everyone around here will read it. I don't even mention the state, let alone the city or town I'm in. Nothing but New York so far."

"I understand, but it's hard to hide facts when you're sharing your life. You continue, though. It's useful for you, and I'm learning more. Seeing *Phantom of the Opera* in New York has been a dream of mine. It must have been a special night."

"Everything was perfect." The blissful remembrance floods my mind. "We even took a carriage ride in Central Park."

"It sounds like a splendid memory. You hold on to it."

"Yes, I'll never forget it. I still have the program."

The dryer's buzzer sounds. After moving the last load from the washer, I bring the dry load back to fold. While I'm doing this, we continue our conversation.

"There's something you should understand concerning Jill," Sadie says. "I know you think she dislikes you, but it's not because of anything you've done. There've been a few setbacks over the years, and she's never gotten over them."

"Setbacks? What kind?"

"It started a while ago. Remember I mentioned my mother's friend, Conswella? Her parents owned the ranch across from here. The area hit on hard times, and trying to keep things intact, Conswella's dad made several deals he shouldn't have. Things got worse, and they involved a rather shady character. In the end, he owned most of what they had, and they moved away."

"Was Jill related to the shady character?" Not sure why I thought of this.

"She was. His nephew, who became Jill's grandfather, was the young lawyer who ran the entire thing. He made a name for himself and opened a law firm in Casper. It grew to be so large most forgot how they got their start. He received an enormous part of the land across the road and hired people to run the ranch. The house you're in was for the ranch foreman."

I can't help but laugh. "Must have been a no-frills guy."

"Jill's father returned from school with a wife and joined the firm. His prime area was finance. He became the senior partner when his father died from a hunting accident. The firm grew, and the family became local royalty. Jill came along and became the princess. The girl everyone wanted to be. Sort of like the young woman in your blog—the most popular girl in school. Head cheerleader, homecoming queen, you name it. She attended college and got what many call her MRS degree and married a young lawyer. He joined the firm, and everything was going well. She became pregnant with a baby girl, soon followed by another."

Taking a sip of coffee, I glance over the mug. "When did the setbacks start?"

"Years back, her father convinced a large group of people to invest in several financial deals he showed were paying well. He kept bringing in new investors and would keep moving the money around promising better and better returns. But then everything caught up with him, and right after Jill's last daughter was born, everything fell apart.

"They sold what they could, but most of their holdings were real estate. With the local economy being so bad, the market wasn't positive. Many people sued him, and the judgments caused him to file for bankruptcy. The court took everything, except for the few places Jill's father already gifted her. Her parents couldn't face seeing the local people every day, so one night, they packed up and left."

"That's terrible. Jill stayed here though?"

"Yes, but she needed to move out of her house in Casper because her father owned it. Her husband was swift to distance himself from the firm. It forced Jill to move to a rental property she owned in Glenrock. Turns out, her husband was seeing a lady at the firm on the side since he got here, and they took off together. The divorce was quick. Her lifestyle changed drastically, though. She now has two primary tasks: taking care of her girls and bringing back the glory of her family's past. For this, she needs a husband. Not any man will suffice though, she requires one who is a pillar of society. Someone who'll allow her to get back on the pedestal. This is where you come in," she says, taking the empty mugs to rinse and put in the dishwasher.

"Me? What do you mean where I come in?" How could I have any part in this? The dryer buzzes and I need to get the clothes. "I'll be right back, and you can explain how I became involved." I hurry to collect my clothes, and she continues while I fold.

"Well, Glenrock isn't huge, and Jill concentrated on climbing the social ladder. She's on every committee possible. Her girls are at the age where they're getting involved in dance and music, those types of things. The ultimate thing she's missing is a husband. She has no one to escort her to any of her social events, which restricts expanding her influence outside of Glenrock. The size of Glenrock limits the number of eligible men suited for what she needs."

"You mean like Jason," I say, nodding.

"Yes. She's been trying to get close for a while. She's even asked him to escort her to events. Jason feels bad for her and goes with reluctance. He has no plans for anything further though."

I continue stacking my folded clothes. "What does this have to do with me?"

She chuckles. "You're kidding, right? Jill thought she was making headway with him, then you arrived."

I freeze, staring at her. "Why would my arrival matter?"

"What matters is Jill sees a beautiful, talented, well-educated and classy lady who is around Jason daily. Which she's not been able to accomplish. In her eyes, you are the enemy."

"What? I work with him. I don't want to date him, or anything else."

"Doesn't matter. In her mind, you're the competition when she felt there was none. I bet even the wedding plans were in motion. She might even have plans for Moose Ridge itself."

"What? Why would she have plans for the clinic?" I say, sliding into my seat.

"You are naïve. I mean all of Moose Ridge. The ranch, the livestock, the clinic, and everything they entail. The land itself is worth quite a chunk and Jason and I own it all. He inherited his share when his parents died. When I'm gone, it will be his. This is Jill's ultimate aim—to once again 'be someone,' not only here but statewide or even further. She doesn't care how it happens. To her, the end justifies the means, and Moose Ridge was to be that means."

I don't know what to say. On the one hand, I feel sorry for Jill, having experienced something similar. I can't believe anyone's so calculating as to want a man because of what he owns or will own. "Are you certain? Jason doesn't seem to think she's trying anything. Sure, he jokes about her stopping by the clinic, and I'll admit, her reasons seem contrived since she doesn't even own a pet. Wouldn't he know if she was trying to box him in?"

"Dear, my grandson is a noble and intelligent man with a kind heart. He sees Jill as someone who's suffered tough times, and he'll help any way he can. He sees the positive in people and looks past any bad. It's the way he is, and he has this idea everyone is like him and wants to help others. He doesn't realize many might have other motives."

"Are you sure? Maybe Jill's trying the best she can with what life's thrown her way. She stayed, even after her parents left. Maybe she's not what you think?"

"No, dear. Her mother trained her well and was the driving force behind Jill's father. There were even political aspirations. Jill took over after her mom left. The desire was to build a dynasty, and she regards what happened as a minor bump in the road. She'll continue this quest nevertheless, and Jason is the man to make it possible. Believe me, she's planning each step, and everything was going well until this beautiful lady from Harvard arrived. Unattached, desirable and, more importantly, available. Not a mere enemy, but a tremendous threat."

"A threat? How? I'm not after Jason. He's my boss. Nothing's going on with us."

"No one said there is, but you've spent time with him and Tyler. Now I know you're trying to be helpful, but it's what she'd do to build a close relationship with him. Therefore, in her eyes, you're doing it for the same reason."

I sit thinking for a few minutes before saying with resolve, "I can't believe this. I'll tell her I have no interest in Jason and make it clear I'm no threat."

"It won't help. She'll never believe you're not motivated by personal desires like her. She'd never admit people don't see others as nothing more than a means to get what they want. If she did, she'd have to concede she's not perfect, and that will never happen," she says. "She eliminates it as a possibility, and thus everyone is like her. However, she's better at it. Her training was from one of the best."

"Wow, I mean, this is unreal." I sit in wonder. "What should I do?"

"Don't fret. There's nothing you can do. You go ahead being the best person you can be. Remember, you're not responsible for other people's actions. Forget about her. I wanted to tell you so you'd know why she treats you the way she does. Don't let it concern you. God has a plan, and He's in control. You concentrate on yourself and helping others." Her faith in this god of hers hits me again.

In spite of this tremendous revelation about Jill, I know it's getting late, and I need to go. "If you say so. If this god of yours has a plan for me, I'd like to know what it might be. My life hasn't been what I'd call something someone would plan."

"Don't worry. You keep doing your best. You'll see, it will work out. I have faith in you and in Him." She seems to believe this. I hope she's not betting on a lame horse in my case.

She helps me carry my things to the back porch, and I make the trips out to the SUV to pile my clean laundry inside. I return one last time for my purse, "Thank you for everything tonight. I enjoy our talks and your home-cooked meals. You take it easy, and I'll be by Saturday to take you shopping."

"Oh, posh. Dinner wasn't much, and you did your laundry while I sat and gabbed. Thank you for listening to an old woman gossip, and I can't wait for Saturday." She gives me one of her massive hugs. I realize she wasn't gossiping, and a thought comes to mind.

"Should I mention any of this to Jason?"

"I wouldn't bother. I know what she's doing, and I'm taking care of it. Jason will be fine." She's busy fixing the scarf around my neck.

"I thought God was in charge? Why are you involved and taking care of it?"

"He is in charge. Remember, He works in mysterious ways. Now, drive careful and have a fantastic day tomorrow. I'll see you Saturday morning around eight with the rolls ready."

I'm halfway to the SUV before I realize she never answered my question of her involvement. Shaking my head, I drive away as she waves one last time.

I make it to my place and unload. It doesn't take long to put my clean clothes away and pick out an outfit for tomorrow. It's late, but I want to check on my blog and the group. After getting ready for bed, I boot my laptop.

There are several sad posts, many ladies sharing how devastated they are. Then one post appears, and the thread goes quiet.

Ladies, you will never move forward with your life if you continue living in the past!

This is harsh and feel I must say something in our defense.

But he was my life!

I hope she'll understands how lost we feel, but her response is not what I expect.

Notice your word in the middle. "Was." He "was" your life. Not anymore. Your life is today, tomorrow, and the future. He's yesterday's garbage gone off to the dump, never to be seen again. Time for you to live!!!! :-)

I stare at the screen. Sure enough, I wrote "was" and not "is." Does this mean I've moved on? Do I see Michael in my past? No longer a part of me? These thoughts shake me, and the thrill of being able to answer "Yes" makes me smile and brings relief to my soul. I can't help but post my next thought.

Thank you for your comment. Brutal, yet what I needed. Now I have one thing to say. Michael has left the building! Never to return!

I hit the enter key, and it's like I'm punching Michael himself. I can't believe the release I feel. The screen fills with posts of support.

You go, girl!

You got it.

The camaraderie is amazing but, being a working girl again, I need to call it a night, and I let them know I'll be back soon. After powering off my laptop and turning off the light, I'm asleep in no time, without a thought about him. Okay, a few, but I ignore them. Okay, I try to ignore them.

Chapter Seven

Arriving at the clinic the following morning, I unlock the back door and head for my office. Several of our patients look my way as I walk past their stalls, and I bid them good morning. I drop my bags on the floor and make sure Stanley has water. This does not thrill him, but he knows the rules.

After consoling him, I start the coffee, then make my way to the kennels to check on the pups and I find Andi feeding Mindy. "Good morning. Don't you have class?" The bottles are ready, and I lift a whining Bob. He's quick to latch on to one.

"I have time. Wanted to give these guys their breakfast. Lindy ate, but she'll tell you she didn't," she says, grinning at me.

"I know. You have to watch out for those two."

Soon, Mindy finishes, and Andi spends a few minutes with her before putting her back. "Well, I'm off to class. Catch ya later."

I feed Bob while petting the other two. They seem content with my fingertips ruffling through their soft fur. That is until Bob finishes, then he demands my full attention.

The door opening startles Bob, which causes a grumble, and Cindy comes in. "Good morning. How are they?"

While trying to calm Bob down, I answer, "They're fine, and they've already finished their morning feed. Why are you in so early?"

"Samples are coming from Guernsey and Doc Withers asked me to rush them. Should be here anytime now."

"What's Guernsey?"

"It's a town southeast of here. Part way to Fort Laramie. There's a herd of wild horses needing testing." We both hear knocking at the front door and she goes to check on it.

I need to get on with my work, but can't drag myself away from these pups. Every time I put Bob in his box he whines. Having an idea, I put him in the pups' box and carry it to my office. I set it on my spare chair where I can reach them. Now I can get to work. Stanley is glaring at me from his spot. Guess he doesn't approve of his area being invaded.

Soon, Terri comes in and laughs at my new nursery. "I should have known. You know this will bother Doc Withers. It was bad enough when he found out you'd named them, but this, well, I'm not sure what he'll do." She winks at me and lifts Mindy while petting Lindy. Bob is on my lap, sleeping.

"Jason's not here," I say, like that matters.

"Well, I'm out of it, it's all on you," she says. "Has someone fed them?"

"Yes, before Andi left. No doubt they'll soon be ready for the next one."

"True. I'll mix the bottles and bring them here. I should remind you not to get too attached, not that you'll take any notice," she says, putting Mindy back.

"Don't you have work to do? We're fine here and don't need any comments from cold-hearted people."

She sticks her tongue out at me as she leaves. The sound of the door closing startles Bob, so I lay my warm hand on his back to settle him. He's asleep in no time, oblivious to anything around him.

Just before 11:00 AM, Terri brings the bottles. I let her know I'll take care of feeding them so she can get back to work. However, she insists on staying and feeding Mindy. Bob lies on my lap while feeding, and I hold the bottle for Lindy, who's also decided my lap is an excellent place for meals.

Once they're done, Terri takes the bottles back to clean before the process starts again. After the 2:30 feed I have training to do with Jennifer, so I'm forced to take the puppies back. My heart breaks hearing Bob's whines as the door closes behind me, but I must be firm. When I reach the lobby, Stanley has come out and is standing by his bowl waiting for me. Well, it's close enough to evening. I pour a shallow helping of Mountain Dew into his dish. He might even smile as he heads for it.

"Don't tell Jason," I whisper to Jennifer.

"Never. Your secret's safe with me," she says, giggling.

With this, we start. Today, we're training on the customer database. She catches on fast, and I enjoy teaching her. We continue in between the patients who come in, and she's doing an excellent job with greeting them and taking care of their needs.

We're almost done when the front door opens, and Jill, of all people, enters.

"Good afternoon, Jill," I say, trying to sound cheerful.

"Oh…you're here," she says and turns to Jennifer. "Is Jason available?"

"No, he's out on calls," I answer.

She gives a slight huff, still glancing at Jennifer. "I was hoping to catch him. We have a date tomorrow night. He's escorting me to the charity dinner. I wanted to let him know the girls are spending the night with friends." She looks at me for the first time. "We'll have the house to ourselves and can make a late night of it, or maybe even something better," she says, smiling. It's more information than I want or need. She shifts back to Jennifer. "He needs to be at my house at six forty-five sharp. At least we can take my car and not his old junky work truck." She shakes her head while gazing up and sighing. "Can you imagine me wearing one of my designer gowns while riding in that monstrosity?"

"Six forty-five. I'll remind him," I say.

"Well, seems I have no choice. I hope you get it right. At least write it down so you can keep it straight." She gives another huff and rolls her eyes. "I hope he remembers it's black tie and doesn't wear jeans or worse." She points at me. "Make sure you give him my message. Six forty-five and not a minute later," she says and leaves without saying goodbye.

Jennifer fights to hold back a cackle. "She doesn't seem pleased. Can you imagine the doc in a tux?"

"He has one. I got it from the cleaners on Tuesday. He's set."

"You should have told her. I'm sure it'd help ease her mind." Now she can't stop giggling.

Cindy comes in from the back. "Was that Jill?"

"Yes, she wanted to talk with Jason. I told her he was out on a call."

"She made sure we knew he's taking her to a charity dinner," Jennifer says.

"Sounds exhilarating," Cindy deadpans, joining in the humor.

"I think you mean excruciating," Jennifer says.

"Now, you two, settle. I'm sure it will be a delightful occasion."

"If you like funerals," Cindy mutters, heading back to the lab.

With Jennifer's training done for the day, I go back to my office to tie up a few loose ends before the next feeding.

Soon after five, Jason comes to my office.

"Great, you're still here. Any issues today?" He seems glad to see me. What's with that?

"No. I'm leaving right after I help Terri feed the puppies. Jill stopped by to remind you about your date tomorrow. Said you need to be at her place at six forty-five, and to be prompt," I say and pause, glancing at him. "She also mentioned you could make it a late night since her girls won't be home."

"It's not a date. She doesn't have anyone to take her to this charity dinner, and when she asked, I had nothing scheduled." He's silent for a few moments before continuing, "It's bad for appearances when she has to go to these things alone."

Why does he feel the need to explain himself? Plus, he made no comment about the late night and corrected it being a date.

"Well, it's nice of you to do this. I'm sure she appreciates it."

"Seems to, but I'll be glad when she finds someone else to take her. For now, I guess I'm her designated other," he says with a slight snicker. "Better than her significant other."

I think Jill sees things in a different light. "Any plans for tonight?"

"I'm surprising Tyler and taking him to the Pizza and Classic Arcade in Casper."

"Sounds like the perfect father-son outing."

"You bet. They have all the great classic games, like Donkey Kong, Frogger, Duck Hunt, and even Space Invaders." His excitement is obvious.

"Seems it's true—men never mature."

"Okay, okay. I dare to share something, and you get all adult on me. I've half a mind not to even tell you about it when we get back," he says, turning to leave, but I'm right behind him.

"Well, at least you realize you only have half a mind." I'm heading in the other direction and through to the lobby before he can respond.

It's fun feeding the puppies, but I need to go. Since I'm taking Sadie shopping tomorrow, I need to get a start on my writing for the weekend.

Once at the house, I'm hit again with how depressing and lonesome the place is. Being at the clinic helps me escape it for short times, but when I return, I'm reminded how dismal my life is. I should pick up a few things tomorrow, like drapes—something with color. A bright tablecloth for the table and something for the couch. Maybe even new bed linen.

The possibilities help me move past the dreariness this time. Not having what's-his-name's school bills anymore, I can afford it. Then, who knows, in less than a year I can find myself a new place. This gets me going. I'm even smiling.

Like most days, dinner is eaten alone, but I'm also checking my group, which provides the illusion I'm with others. There are several new postings to peruse. Reading their stories reminds me I need to write the next part of my blog. I say goodnight to everyone, close the browser, and open the file for my next segment.

The Rich Girl's Poor Life
Where did he go?

Right before my twelfth birthday, things change around the house. My father is not himself and works long hours. Even after work, people stay late in my father's study. Many nights I go to bed without him even telling me goodnight. It's obvious something is happening. Maybe he's planning an enormous surprise for me. I need to give him space until he's ready to spring it.

This continues for several months, but now, I have my own things keeping me busy. Next week is the vote for class president, and I'm bound to win. There's this spaz running against me, but he's no competition. My posse, as I call them, tells me most of the students don't even know who he is. I know I'll win by a landslide, but I want it to be the most devastating defeat ever. That will make running for office easier next year.

My driver drops me off at the regular time after school. The girls are so jealous I have a chauffeur. I get out, telling him I'll see him in the morning, and walk up the steps.

Inside, I notice a coat on the hall rack I don't recognize, and my dad is walking toward me. He's smiling, but not his normal smile. Maybe he's springing the enormous surprise?

"Princess, can you come into my study? There's something we need to discuss."

"I'll be right there, Daddy," I say, not letting on I know.

I put my things away and hurry to his study. My father is behind the beautiful oversize mahogany desk my mother picked out. Mr. Mackey is in a chair off to the side. He's my father's friend and lawyer. I wonder why he'd be here.

My father tells me to have a seat and starts to

explain, but he's having difficulty talking and keeps starting over. Then Mr. Mackey speaks. "Maybe I should explain?"

"Yes, maybe it's best. I can't."

"Tiffany, there's been a problem at your father's business. We've been dealing with it for a while, and we were hoping for a better outcome. I'm afraid I have terrible news." I stare at my father, who can't seem to face me. Mr. Mackey continues. "Your father was involved in a financial project. Things were going well, maybe too well, and they discovered it to be a scam. Since he was a principal involved, they found him guilty of securities fraud. I'm afraid he must surrender to the court first thing in the morning. We thought it might turn out better, but the judge sentenced your father to ten years," he says. "Do you understand?"

"Ten years? You mean jail. No! This can't happen! Not to me!" I stammer, realizing what this means. "What will everyone at school say? I'll be the laughingstock, the girl whose father's in jail. This can't be happening to me."

Mr. Mackey affirms it is. I find out it's not even the worst part. He explains that with my father in jail, there's no one to take care of me and the court is confiscating everything my father owns. Even the house. All is being sold to repay the money people lost. Even with selling all, it won't cover everything.

He says he'll take care of any legal issues I have and will find a place for me to live while my father is away. They're hoping, that with good behavior, he might be out in three to five years. For now, I need to pack my clothes. He has a place for me until something more permanent is available.

"I'm moving? What about school? I'll still be going to my school, won't I? I'm going to be class president!"

"I'm afraid not, Tiffany. You'll attend a public school closer to where you'll live."

"Public school? I'm not going to any public school! What will my friends think?" I can't believe what is happening. My entire world is crashing around me. I'm losing everything. My room, my house, my

school, my posse, my father, everything! I glance at my father, but he still won't look at me. I have so many questions, but no one has any answers. This can't be happening. Not to me. Not to Tiffany Waldensmyth. It can't be!

"Tiffany, you need to pack," Mr. Mackey says. "Ms. Davis is upstairs sorting clothes. You need to select what you want. The things you can keep, at least. Now, hurry, we must be there by six."

What does he mean by "there"? Where am I going?

I cover going to my room and Ms. Davis, my nanny, helping me pack. She's crying but trying not to show it. We pack three bags. She hopes that will give me enough for now. I still don't understand why I can't stay here with her. When I ask, she explains she can't stay because my father can't pay her. Plus, the house is being sold so I can't live here anymore.

I share how I don't even know where I'm going and how she hugs me and says she understands and wishes she could help, but it's not possible. There's the long drive with Mr. Mackey and his stopping in front of a building, with a sign saying, "Children's Home."

I try to convey my distress and how I'm going through the motions without thinking. We walk inside, with Mr. Mackey carrying two of my suitcases. I have the other and my school bag. He introduces me to a lady who takes one suitcase and heads for a massive flight of stairs while explaining I'll be staying in the girls' ward. I struggle with my other two cases, having to stop every few steps. She stands waiting at the top, checking her watch and tapping her toe. As I make the last step, she whirls, walking down the hall. While catching my breath, I glance back and see Mr. Mackey has left.

I end it by telling how lost I felt seeing the empty landing below me. How devastated I was discovering what she called a "ward" was a room with lots of beds and I wouldn't even have my own room. I write about the next few days, which became weeks, then months, with no word from anyone. There was nothing and no one. I was alone.

I feel I'm at a suitable place to end it. I can proof it tomorrow and be ready to post it on Sunday. Everything should go according to plan. I turn out the light and close my eyes. Tomorrow, I'm going shopping and can start making this place my own. However, when I close my eyes, my mind has to have its say. Why bother? No one is ever going to see it. You're all alone like the loser you are.

Chapter Eight

My alarm sounds, but it can't be time. I lie motionless, trying to think of a reason to stay in bed. But the thought of Sadie making cinnamon rolls changes my mind. In an instant, I'm moving. Her rolls are worth losing sleep.

I'm ready on time, fueled by the prospect of livening up this place. Between this enthusiasm and the expectation of Sadie's rolls, I'm all but floating out the door. I don't even mind the cold biting at my fingers while I make the brief drive.

I pull in, and she's at the porch door before I even get out. After hurrying up the steps, I follow her inside, where I trace the sweet aroma of cinnamon through to the kitchen.

She already has the coffee poured and the rolls on plates. All that's left to do is enjoy. While we eat, Sadie shares plans on where she's hoping to go, and I mention my ideas for the house. This causes even more excitement, and we're soon discussing various ideas. We're almost finished when Jason's truck rushes past the window, heading around the back.

"What's he doing here?" Sadie rises to investigate. I'm right behind as we hurry to the back door. "It's rare for him to pull around back."

The door bursts open before we get there, and Jason hurries in carrying Tyler. "I got a call and need to inoculate several wild horses near Guernsey. When I woke Tyler, I realized he's running a slight fever. He says his stomach hurts. I'd take him with me but can't with him feeling like this. Can you watch him while I'm gone?"

"Take him to the front room, and I'll get blankets for him," Sadie says, heading off.

"Thank you. There's little time, and I must take care of this today. Plus, I can't be late for the charity dinner," he says while putting Tyler on the couch.

It's obvious our plans have changed. "How many horses are there?"

"Forty, they're corralled in an area northeast of Hartville. Once I get there, it shouldn't take long."

Sadie rushes back into the room with an armful of blankets and pillows. "Who's going with you?"

"Everyone is out, and I don't have time to find them," Jason says while covering Tyler with a blanket and tucking the pillow under his head.

"Jazmine will go," Sadie says.

"Who, me?" Is she doing this for real? She's avoiding eye contact with either of us while checking Tyler's temperature.

"I'm fine going by myself. I'm sure Jazmine has her day planned," he says, shaking his head while tending to Tyler.

Sadie continues. "We were going shopping, but we'll do it another day. I can't go out with Tyler sick, and there's no use in Jazmine staying here with me. She can keep you company." Seems it's not up for discussion. "Besides, I have an order in Guernsey. They'd ship it, but if you're there anyway, you can get it for me."

"I doubt I'll have time," Jason says. "I need to be at Jill's at six forty-five, and will need to shower and change. Can I go next weekend for you?"

"Jazmine can drop you off and get my order while you prepare everything for the horses. When she returns, you'll be ready to start. Now, you have little time, so no arguing. I'll get the address for where my order is." She's off before we can stop her.

"But, Sadie, I can go by myself," he calls after her.

"No time," she says as she disappears.

He turns to me. "You don't mind coming along?"

"Do you not know this lady? I doubt we have a choice."

"Here's the address," she says, returning in a hurry and handing it to me. "Jazmine, you need to change. Put on work clothes and your parka, and don't forget your scarf, gloves, and a hat."

"Sadie, I need to leave," Jason reminds her.

"You have time. Jazmine, go change and Jason will get you at your place. In the meantime, I'll pack food and coffee for you."

"I still think I should go alone—" he starts.

"You want to waste time arguing? I thought you were in a hurry," she says, shaking her head. "Jazmine, go change. Jason, come with me." She marches out of the room again.

"I'm sorry, Jazmine, I—"

"You don't have time to chat," Sadie shouts from the hallway. "Now move. Both of you."

With no alternative, I leave for my place.

Once there, I toss off my clothes and put on work jeans. After buttoning one of my flannel shirts over a T-shirt, I add my insulated vest I use out in the barns at Moose Ridge. That, with my parka, should be warm enough.

With one last check that I have everything, I spot my laptop bag and grab it, thinking I can work on my blog while I'm gone. It seems like it might be a lengthy trip. Collecting my parka, scarf, and hat on the way out, I lock the door behind me. Jason will be in a hurry and I don't want him waiting.

By the time he stops out front, I'm at the truck. I hand him my bag and climb into my seat. Once I'm settled with my seatbelt on, he heads out. We're on our way.

"I'm sorry she roped you into this," he says.

"Well, I doubt there was a choice, but I'm excited. I hear wild horses are something to see, and how many chances does one have?" The truck is warm, so I slip off my parka and vest for now. "Did she get anything packed?"

"Anything? She packed the entire kitchen. There're two thermoses of coffee, bottles of water, a loaf of bread, and what appears to be slices of half a roast for sandwiches. Plus, all the extras, and even cookies, which I understand are yours. I think we're set for days."

"Sounds like Sadie. Did you think you'd talk her out of me coming? Tell the truth now."

"Moment of weakness. I was concentrating on getting Tyler settled and hitting the road."

"That's your story?" My voice dripping with sarcasm, I glare at him.

"Yes, and I'm sticking to it. Oh, she also sent a few of her rolls along. I could go for one, if you wouldn't mind getting it?"

"That's why I'm here." I undo my seatbelt and reach for the large basket behind him on the rear seat. It's a stretch, and realizing how close my chest is to his face concerns me. "Don't have an accident now. I'd hate to explain how I ended sitting partway through the windshield."

Somehow, I laugh my way through the awkwardness of my current position. Being the gentleman he is, he leans toward his door as much as possible. My distress increases as I need to lean even further to reach everything, causing me to press even more against him. Why didn't I keep my vest on? After grabbing what I need, I throw myself back into my half of the truck and pull my seatbelt in place. The clicking noise brings a welcome end to the embarrassment.

Wanting to put the memory of the past few moments behind me, I turn to him. "Okay, we have cinnamon rolls and coffee. I didn't see sugar, so I take it she already added it."

"Yes, she prepared travel mugs for each of us."

"Of course, she did," I say, rolling my eyes. "How long is this drive?"

"About two hours to Whalen Canyon Road, providing there are no delays. We'll turn off there and meet folks from the Bureau of Land Management. They'll lead us out."

"Looks like I need to get her order on South Guernsey Road," I say, checking the address.

"That's right before you get to the river. After you drop me off, you can double back. I'll have someone wait to bring you out to where the horses are. It shouldn't take you long. By the time you return, I should be ready to start the inoculations."

"You mean shots?"

"Yes, there's a killer virus and the ranchers' concern is the wild horses passing it on to their herds. BLM heard someone corralled this herd and were planning on selling them. They expressed blood samples to us yesterday morning to check if they're carriers. Cindy did a rush job, and they're negative."

"So why don't they let them go?"

"Since they're already corralled, it gives us an opportunity to give them the vaccine and treat them for several other things too. Plus, a few are pregnant, and I can give them an additional shot. Also, someone got permission to auction them off because they aren't vaccinated. That's the driving push to get this done today. They convinced a judge this herd's a threat."

"Can't you treat them once the new owners have them?"

"Not so easy. The usual buyers for wild horses are the dog food companies."

My jaw drops in shock. "You mean they'll butcher them?"

"Yep, unless I have them treated before tomorrow morning. If I do, their approval is void and they must get another. In the meantime, the BLM can drive them off into the hills."

"That's why this must be done today? To save forty horses from being killed?"

"You got it. For now, I guess you can sit back and enjoy the ride."

While we drive, we enjoy the rolls and coffee. Jason talks about his parents and what living in Wyoming was like as a kid. The highway bypasses a town named Douglas, and he mentions several of his dad's friends live there. He shares stories of the times they'd go fishing at the Glendo Reservoir, which it seems we'll soon reach.

He chuckles while telling me about the time his mother drove his dad's pickup into the lake during an ice-fishing trip. She was driving from their ice shanty to the cabin and didn't see the sign warning of thin ice. It was fortunate she was near shore, and the water didn't reach to the doors. Seems his dad's truck was like Jason's beast and you needed a step ladder to get in it. He shares it was a lot of work to get it out, plus his dad was having to fight hard not to laugh. Jason mentions how quiet it was in the cabin afterward.

As we pass the lake, there's a sign for the state park, and Jason recounts how Carin and he spent their honeymoon there. He smiles when he tells me he doubted it stunned anyone when they got engaged.

"I dated no one but her," he says after several minutes.

Should I say something to this? What could I say? I stay silent and watch while we drive along the reservoir he mentioned earlier.

"We dated throughout high school and even college. It seems like we were together much longer than the three years of marriage."

Neither one of us says anything for a while, and I get the thermos to refresh our coffee. Breaking the silence, he reverts to something which must have been bothering him since we started. "I still can't figure out what Sadie needs us to pick up."

"It doesn't say on the sheet."

"This place is a wholesale nursery. What could she need from them this time of year? It's November. What could she be planting now?"

"I don't know. Maybe it's something for the house to get ready for spring?"

"She can't start anything like that until late February. It makes no sense to get anything now," he says, shaking his head.

"Well, we'll know once I get there. No sense worrying now." When I glance over, he seems to be deep in thought.

A few minutes pass before he speaks again. "You don't think she did it to get us together, do you?" He's glancing my way.

I'm close to choking on my coffee. "What do you mean together? We're together at the clinic all the time," I struggle to say, but a thought I had earlier shoots through my brain again. "You don't think she's thinking something more, do you?"

"Something more? You mean with us? We're co-workers and friends. What more could she want?"

"I know. You've got Tyler, and I'm fine the way things are. I need nothing more," I say, wanting my genuine feelings to be clear.

"I agree, but there's something going on with her. I can feel it. You know, she can be sneaky and even a little underhanded when she wants to be."

"She is adept at making things go her way. She told me the other night God's in charge. If so, He might get His orders from her."

"Maybe she's one of His most trusted advisers."

"I think she's better at bossing than advising."

His laughter suggests he agrees with me.

At the signs for Guernsey, we take an exit onto a side street. It's a short distance before we reach the city and Jason drives straight through. I notice the road I must take, and this gets me wondering again if Sadie is up to something.

A few miles outside of the city, we reach the next turn onto Whalen Canyon Road. It's a lot like mine. We pass several ranches on our right, with nothing but hills and open land on our left. Soon, we come upon two parked trucks, and Jason stops behind them.

"These are the BLM folks. Let's see what they have planned," he says, opening his door.

Slipping on my parka, I take my hat, scarf, and gloves, and follow him.

"Jazmine, meet Jeff Ketchell, John Watson, and Jerri Collins," Jason introduces us. "Jeff says we have around twenty miles to the corral."

I'm startled one of the BLM folks is a female, even though she's dressed for the part, complete with cowboy hat and boots. While we shake hands, Jason discusses my errand and asks if someone can wait for my return.

"Should be fine," Jeff says. "You can ride with me and John. We'll set up the other corral and be ready to go. Jerri can wait here. Is that okay with everyone?" After nods all round, Jason goes with Jeff and John while I head back to the humongous monstrosity Jason calls a truck.

It's a heavy-duty, four-door, four-wheel-drive pickup with a full-size bed and something they call a dully. Not sure what that means, but it has four wheels in the rear and two stick out from the sides, making it even wider. This will be something. I hope I don't make a fool of myself.

I start it and wait for Jeff to pull out. At least there's only one person here if I make a mess of it. I maneuver the beast to the direction I need, and I'm on my way. The width of the freakish vehicle in relation to the narrow road makes me hope no one comes in the other direction.

Retracing our route back to Guernsey, I reach a road that is a little wider. Not much, though. Plus, there's traffic. Don't let me run over anyone.

After an eternity of maneuvering the beast around many impediments, which seem to appear out of nowhere, the sign for the place appears. I stop right in the middle of the parking lot where there are no other vehicles. Not sure this is even a parking space, but then this behemoth wouldn't fit in a normal sized one, anyway.

Once through the main doors, I see it's a garden center, as Jason said.

"May I help you, miss?" A tall gentleman greets me.

"I hope so. I'm here for Sadie's order."

"You must be Jazmine. I'm Ben. Sadie said you were coming. Is your truck out front?"

"Yes, right outside. But I can carry it out. I don't mind."

He chuckles. "Better to load it in one trip. Go on out and open the tailgate. I'll bring it to you. It will be easier and quicker."

What on earth would Sadie order requiring loading? I do as instructed, and a few minutes later, a forklift appears with a pallet stacked high with large bags. After positioning the load inside the truck, he reverses a short distance and climbs out. The clipboard he holds out for me to sign lists sixteen bags of sphagnum. Not knowing what that is, I check the pallet and count sixteen. One bag has peat moss on the label, so now I know what sphagnum is. I sign the paper and hand it and the pen back to Ben.

"Kind of surprised Sadie wanted this now." He's tearing a sheet off and handing it to me. "She usually waits until late February."

"Well, you know Sadie. She always has a plan."

"Oh, I agree. You never question Sadie. When she called this morning, I told her, 'Yes, ma'am.' It's the best answer when dealing with her."

"She called this morning?"

"To place the order. She said you'd be coming to get it. Is there a problem?"

"No, no problem. Sadie being Sadie." I don't believe this. What was she thinking might happen?

"Okay, then. You tell her hello from Ben and not to be a stranger. She's a special lady."

"Unless she's trying to run your life," I mutter under my breath.

"What was that?"

"Yes, she is special. Thanks for loading it, I might see you again sometime." After climbing in, I start the titanic. Thankful it's a straight exit onto the street, I pull out but notice it's low on gas.

There's a station out near the main road. I'll fill up now to save time. The pump area is empty so there's no one to watch me park. I come to a stop and get out, relieved to find the gas opening is right by the driver's door and nearest the pumps. I'm also grateful to discover my effort to keep the wide rear wheels from crashing into the pumps still allows the hose to reach. Not much slack, but it works.

Once I start, I'm surprised it doesn't run long considering the size of the beast. Checking the pump's screen, I see it took less than twelve gallons. Must not be an enormous tank. I put the hose back and print out the receipt.

As I leave, the gauge still shows the same amount—not even a fourth. Maybe the gauge isn't working? That would explain why it didn't even take twelve gallons and why Jason said nothing. Either way, we're set now.

The return trip is as harrowing as before, with vehicles seeming to pull out in front of me on purpose. Can't they see this massive hunk of metal? Not to mention why they would put signs so close to the corners. I almost run over several making turns. Jerri's truck is sitting where I left it. As I approach, she waves out the window and starts moving. The road isn't the best so it isn't a smooth ride, but I manage. At least I have someone as a blocker in front.

After around twenty miles, she turns off onto a path of sorts. I thought Jason said it was a road? Progress is slow going because of the various bumps and holes. I'm amazed when we enter a clearing and see horses in a metal corral off to the side.

Jerri stops, and I park beside her. I don't have to worry about getting the behemoth out since Jason will do that later. Jerri leads me to the corral where the three men are.

Jason motions to me. "Any problems?"

"No, it was fine." I want to tell him the one problem is his grandmother and her meddling ways, but now is not the time.

"Well, we're ready to start. I'll get my things." While he heads for the beast, I observe the horses—they're beautiful, even with their thick winter coats. One seems to watch us with intent from the back of the corral and appears on high alert.

"That's the stallion. He's the herd's leader," Jerri says, standing beside me. "Aren't they something?"

"Yes, they are. He's magnificent, but seems like he could be trouble."

"I'm sure he is. You don't become the leader without proving yourself first. He's waiting for us to make a mistake, then he'll bolt. We need to be careful around him."

Jason approaches, carrying his medical case and something like an electric guitar case. He sets them by a narrow chute leading to a second corral. Jerri explains they'll drive a horse into the chute with the end closed. Then he can give the shots required before they open the other end and let the horse run into the other corral.

"Then thirty-nine more to go." She makes it sound simple.

He motions me over. "All she ordered was sphagnum?"

"Yes, sixteen bags of it."

"That makes no sense. She can't use it until March."

"Ben, the man there, said the same thing. He also said, 'You know Sadie.' I'm sure she has a plan."

"That's what I'm afraid of. Her plans can get folks in trouble."

He opens the guitar-like case, and I see there's a rifle in it. "What's that for?"

"For the leader. We need to control him so the herd stays calm. Otherwise, he'll keep them riled, hoping for a break." He attaches a scope to the rifle, while I watch in disbelief.

"You're going to shoot him?"

"Yes, it's best," he says, and even seems calm.

I am not. "Are you serious? Killing him is best?" How could he even think such a thing?

He glares at me. "I'm not killing him. It's a tranquilizer gun. I'm drugging him, so he'll stay quiet while we treat the others. We'll treat him last and wait for the effects of the drugs to subside. I'd never kill a horse for no reason."

"Oh, sorry." I hope my embarrassment isn't obvious. "Wasn't sure what was happening."

Soon, Jason's set, and Jeff has moved his truck closer and facing the corral. Jason climbs to the front of the bed. Using the roof to rest the rifle on, he takes aim. Jeff and John walk along the corral waving ropes. They have the stallion's full attention.

Once he's standing broadside to Jason, I hear a noise, but it's not loud like I expected. The horse spooks and glances around, but the drug is already acting. It takes a few moments, but he's soon going down. The other horses watch their leader fall to the ground. A few walk near, sniffing him. He can still move somewhat and takes a swipe with one of his rear legs when another gets too close.

Jerri calls for me to join her, and we climb on the metal rails by the chute to the other corral. "You can man the second gate."

"What do I need to do?"

"Haven't you done this before? As a vet's assistant, I'd have thought you'd be a pro by now."

"Oh, I'm not an assistant. I'm the office manager. I deal with the computers, not the animals."

"Now it makes sense," she says. "Still, you'll be fine. Have a handful of hay and hold it out so the horse sees it. When one comes in the chute, let it have the hay. Once Jason says so, open the gate and let the horse go into the other corral. Then shut the gate again." She makes it sound like it will be a breeze.

"You mean a handful of hay will get them to come into the chute?"

"Kind of. We'll be moving them in this direction. Plus, they've eaten little for most of the day, so the hay will draw them. There's plenty of it in the other corral when they get there. It should be fine."

"Okay, if you say so."

"Just follow my instructions, and there shouldn't be any problems." She and Jason join Jeff and John by the corral gate, and I hang onto my spot by the other gate.

Jason gets several syringes ready. Now I understand what they mean by a horse needle. Once everything is prepared, he climbs the rails by the other gate. He flicks something, and the gate opens. All I can do is hold the handful of hay out for the horses to see.

There isn't much room in the corral with forty horses, but the closest one to the chute seems to spot the hay. Jeff is coaxing it forward with a coiled rope. The others are behind him, keeping the other horses away.

The horse moves forward with caution, and I wave the hay. He takes several steps until his full body is in the chute. Jason closes the gate behind him.

The horse jumps a little and flicks his ears, but his attention is soon back to the hay in my hand. I let it fall to the ground, and the horse lowers its head and starts munching on the hay—I can tell he hasn't eaten in a while. Jason uses this time to administer the shot. He's terrific and finishes in a second. He calls out, "Let him go."

After I open the gate, the horse trots off into the other corral with the help of a swat by Jason. We go through this process for all thirty-nine horses. He gives the pregnant ones a second shot. I lose track of time, and I'm stunned it's been over two hours since we started as the last one moves to the other corral. He assures me we're on schedule, though. Now for the leader.

He's a beautiful horse. Jason mentions he's an Appaloosa stallion and points out the unusual markings on his hindquarters. He gets everything ready and climbs into the corral. Several horses stretch their necks across the corral sides to see what's happening. While kneeling beside the stallion, he strokes the neck several times and gives it the shot. There's no reaction from the horse.

As Jason gets to his feet, he continues stroking the horse while inspecting the rest of its body. He gives him a second shot, near where the mane is at the base of the neck. After a few more minutes of stroking and soothing words, he comes to the rails and climbs out.

"Well, that's all of them. They should be set to go in the morning." He looks at Jeff. "Do you expect any problems with their release?"

"No, the word's out we're giving them the shots, and we'll drive them off in the morning. Everyone seems to be fine with it. You sticking around?"

"Until the stallion is standing. It shouldn't be more than a few hours. I want to make sure he's okay. We'll leave the chute open so they can have more space between the two corrals. They should be fine until morning."

"Okay, we'll set hay in the corral with the stallion. Once he's up, you can open the gate for the others. That way, they don't bother him until he's awake."

"Sounds like a plan. You heading out?"

"Yeah, not much else for us to do. We'll be back at first light with horses to drive them off a distance. Were you able to tag him?"

"Yeah, the wire is in deep under his mane, so it should give solid readings."

"Great. We'll see how it works tomorrow. Thank you for coming. I know it was a drive, and on a Saturday," Jeff says.

"All part of the job. I'm glad to know they'll be running the range." Jason shakes Jeff's hand, then John's and Jerri's. They do the same with me and, after their last goodbyes, they head for their trucks. As they drive out of sight, it hits me: Jason and I are alone, and I have no idea where we are. He doesn't seem concerned, so I try to put my fears aside.

"Ready for lunch?" he asks.

"Sounds perfect. Do we eat in the truck?"

"Yeah, it'll be a little warmer. Let me stow these cases, and I'll meet you there."

I climb into the goliath on wheels, and he jumps in the driver's side a few moments later. Before I can say anything, he moves the pickup to where we can watch the stallion lying on the ground. He shuts the engine off and sits back with a sigh. "Now, we wait."

There are various items for sandwiches in the basket, and I get them out, setting them on the console between the seats. While I'm doing this, Jason grabs the cooler with the water in it.

"I think I'll start the engine and run the heater a spell," he says. "Don't let me forget to stop for fuel on the way out."

"Oh, I wouldn't worry. The gauge isn't working, but it's full," I say, taking out the bread.

He snaps his head my way. "What? Why do you think the gauge is broke?"

"While I was out I filled up, but the gauge never moved. It didn't even take twelve gallons though, so the gauge must be off," I say while spreading the mayonnaise on my bread, followed by slices of roast beef and cheese. I realize he's silent and look up to find him staring at me. "What?"

"Which tank did you fill?" His voice is close to a whisper.

"What do you mean, which tank? The one by the driver's door. How many tanks are there?" Then I realize why he's concerned. "Oh, don't worry. I put in premium since it's what the Excursion takes. It's fine." My explanation doesn't calm him.

"Two." He sounds disgusted. "This truck has two tanks. By premium, you don't mean you put in gasoline?"

I pause while opening a bag of chips. That can't be right. "Two tanks? Where's the other one? And of course gasoline. What else would I use?" Why is he so troubled? We needed gas, and I got it. What's the big deal?

He sits, taking a few deep breaths like he's trying to control himself. "Oh, I don't know, maybe diesel, since it's a diesel engine, in a diesel truck. With diesel written in several places...including on the flap for the fuel cap."

"Diesel? You mean like semis use? Why wouldn't you use gasoline?"

He turns to face out the front window, squeezing the steering wheel with both hands. He stares straight ahead for several long, silent moments. "Yes, diesel, and you use it because diesel engines perform better in a truck like this. Like the semis that need the extra power. Do you know what happens if you run gasoline in a diesel engine?" He's talking in a quiet, steady tone while continuing to stare straight ahead. The skin on his knuckles is turning white from his forceful grip on the wheel.

"No, but why does it matter? Isn't all fuel the same? If it burns, what's the problem?" Shrugging, I take a bite of sandwich. Sadie also included a jar of pickles. Perfect. I glance over at Jason again, but his smoky gray eyes are still staring straight ahead. He's motionless. "Aren't you going to finish making your sandwich?"

In a slow and distinct voice, he responds. "I guess they didn't cover internal combustion engines at Harvard. No, not all fuel is the same. If you run gasoline in a diesel engine, it will ruin it." He's silent again and shuts off the engine. I thought he was going to run the heater.

"You mean I ruined the engine?" The guilt and fear building in me cause me to ignore the Harvard comment.

"If it ran using the gasoline, you did, but you say the gauge didn't move after filling the tank?"

"Correct, it continued to move lower while I drove here, but it never moved after I filled it."

"You're sure you used the opening by the driver's door?"

"Yes, the one right by the door. Why?"

"If you filled that one, and you never switched tanks, the engine is still using the one with diesel. Not the one you contaminated."

"That's perfect then, isn't it? No harm, no foul. Isn't this what they say? Everything is fine. Now finish making your sandwich so we can have the cookies." My jovial voice does a splendid job at concealing the wave of relief flooding through my veins.

Jason appears calmer, but he doesn't say a word while we have our sandwiches. We eat in the eerie silence, and I'm not sure what to do. Any question I ask is met with a single word answer or maybe two at the most. Why is he still disturbed? I thought he said everything was okay. Should I ask him what's wrong or should I leave him be? He'll work it out. I busy myself with putting everything away so we'll be ready to go.

We sit in silence for I don't know how long. This is irrational; what is he still distressed about? That's it. I've had enough of his silent treatment. He's going to talk to me.

When I turn to speak, Jason's sitting forward and watching something outside with great interest. "He's moving."

I follow his line of sight. The stallion's legs and head are moving, albeit not much. Mesmerized, I watch the stallion fight to stand. He struggles to lift his head then heaves himself upward so he's resting on his stomach with his legs underneath his body. After a couple more moments, he props his forelegs out in front and uses them for leverage to haul the rest of his body off the ground. Once he's standing, I breathe a sigh of relief and laugh, seeing him shake and wobble from the tip of his nose right down to his tail. This sends a cloud of dust into the air. After peering around the corral, he takes tentative steps on unsteady legs. He finds the hay and eats, but all the while, he continues to scan the area.

"We'll let him eat before I open the chute gates. He should be a hundred percent by then," Jason says, sitting back with a smile.

"Great, we can head home after that."

He gives a sort of snort and turns to me. "Are you forgetting something?"

"I don't think so. You said we needed to wait until the stallion is awake and eating. You can open the gates, and we can start back. Can't we?"

"Are you forgetting we're low on fuel?"

"Not at all. You said it was fine since it never used the gas. We're okay, right?"

"Not quite. Yes, you never used the gasoline, but we're thirty miles from anyone who might have diesel and at least forty miles from a fuel station."

"Okay, what's the problem?"

"The tank with the diesel has less than an eighth. I doubt we'd get ten miles with this rough terrain. The engine might be fine, but we have no fuel to get anywhere. The diesel in the other is mixed with gasoline so it's useless."

"Wait...you mean we're stuck out here?" I almost scream. This can't be. "There's nowhere to get gas?"

"Except we don't need gas, we need diesel. We have plenty of gas. Twelve gallons of the stuff, wasn't it?" He must think his smirk is cute.

"Hold it. I've got my cell. I'll call someone and have them bring us diesel."

"That would be great."

Is he snickering? With a glare his way, I select the phone app.

"You might want to check for a connection before you bother dialing," he says with obvious sarcasm.

I check, and there's nothing. Not even one bar. "There's no connection! How can this be?"

"Might be because the closest cell tower is, oh, I don't know, forty miles from here." Again, with his snicker. He sits watching the horses like there's nothing to worry about.

"You're not concerned we're in the middle of nowhere with no phone connection and no gas?"

"Again, we have plenty of gas." He sits back and pulls his hat down over his eyes. Why is he so smug?

"Fine, no diesel! Happy now?" I huff. "What are you going to do?" I demand.

"Well, I could walk to the nearest ranch and hope they're home and have diesel. That could take several hours."

"You mean leave me here alone in this wilderness?" I shake my head vehemently. "Not on your life, buster."

"You go then. Take the trail back to the road. Hang a right and follow it until you reach a ranch. Can't be much over thirty miles. I'd stay on the road and go soon, because we're losing daylight." His hat is still covering his eyes.

"Are you crazy?" I'm on the edge of panic when I get an idea. "You can ride a horse to the ranch and they can drive you back." I know there's always a solution. You must remain calm and consider your options—like they teach so well at Harvard.

"One of those horses?" He's pointing to the corral.

"Yes, they appear sturdy enough. They run wild all the time. I bet they're in excellent shape."

"I'm sure they are. For wild horses—emphasis on *wild*. As in, they've never been ridden. They've never even seen a saddle or a bridle, let alone worn them, which matters little since we have neither. Believe me, no one is riding one of those horses tonight."

With his comedy routine complete, we revert to sitting in silence. Two can play the silent treatment game. After a while, Jason gets out and opens both gates. Several of the horses are quick moving to the other corral. He hurries back to the truck.

"Shut the door!" I tell him. "You're letting in the cold air."

"Wow, for someone who caused all this, you sure are bossy."

I can't believe he said that. "You're saying this is my fault?"

"Um, yeah. You put in the gasoline."

"And who let me take a truck low on gas...I mean diesel?" How can he blame this on me?

"The one who knew he had half a tank of diesel."

"Right, half a tank. In a truck getting ten miles per gallon. Not even enough for a hundred miles when we're close to a hundred fifty miles from home." The audacity of him accusing me.

"Yes, a hundred miles' worth, and we're forty miles from the fuel station. We could make it twice, but someone put gasoline in the tank, so now it's worthless except for starting forest fires."

"You mean the extra tank you never mentioned, or that the truck needed diesel, I might add. No, sir, this is not my fault. It's all on you." This ends the conversation.

"I'm sorry, I thought they covered reading at Harvard." Seems he didn't get the hint. "It says it on the flap you opened to get to the cap, beside the cap you removed to pump the fuel, and believe it or not, even on the cap itself. We should write Ford and let them know about their lack of explicit markings."

"Great, you agree, it wasn't my fault. Now we're getting somewhere." I'm glad he's coming to his senses. "Now, how are you getting us out of here?" When I glance over, he's snickering—again—which gets louder, and soon, he's in borderline hysterics. "You find this funny?"

"It's nothing." Drawing a lungful of air helps calm him, but after a few moments he starts again.

"What is it now?"

"There's no way I can make it to Jill's in time. Nor call to let her know."

"Oh, you're right. This will devastate her."

"She'll be waiting for me and might call, but I'm out of range, and she'll get voicemail."

"What do you think she'll do?"

"I don't know. I hope she'll realize something happened and drive herself. She can say they called me for an emergency to cover for being alone. You know, she might call Sadie to check if she knows where I'm at. Sadie will tell her I came here, and there must have been a delay." He seems delighted with this conclusion. Thinking it through causes me to giggle. "What? What is it?"

"You better hope she doesn't call Sadie."

"Why not?"

I wonder how well he knows his grandmother. "Because she'll tell her I'm with you. That's why."

"Why would she need to tell Jill you're here?"

"Because she set it up for me to be here. This was all in her plan, I bet."

"Yes, maybe for the trip here and back. It should have been a half-day trip though. How could she plan on us being stranded? Did she tell you to put in gas or something?"

"No, but Ben at the garden center told me she didn't call the order in until this morning, around the time we left my place. Who knows how she managed the rest, but you know what she's like. She said a prayer or something. No, this has Sadie written all over it, and she'll be thrilled to break it to Jill we're spending the day together."

"More than the day I'm afraid." He sits back again, but seems lost in thought.

"What are you thinking about?"

"Tyler. I wasn't expecting to be gone so long. I hope he's okay."

"You said it was a fever, do you think it could be something serious?"

"Not likely. His fever was just a slight one, so probably only a bug he picked up at pre-school. His only complaint was a slight stomachache."

"Didn't you go to the arcade last night? What did he eat while he was there?"

"Not much. We had a pizza, some sodas, corn dogs, popcorn, funnel cakes—oh, and they had these awesome deep-fried Oreos."

I stare at him in disbelief. "What, no deep-fried Snickers available? Are you serious? No wonder he has a stomach ache."

"It wasn't that bad, and he was fine when we got home."

"Well, Sadie should be able to take care of him. She is a pediatrician."

"Yeah, I know. He's in excellent hands. I'd just prefer to be there for him."

"I understand, but I'm sure he'll be fine once all the junk you fed him gets through his system."

"That's enough out of you," he says, laughing.

Chapter Nine

We've been sitting in silence for a while when Jason starts shaking his head and laughing.

"What? What is it? Do you know how we can get out of here?" That must be it. He's thought of something obvious he overlooked.

"Did Sadie ever tell you about my proposal to Carin?"

I wasn't expecting this. "No," I say, confused. "Why would she mention that to me?"

"Believe me, it relates to today."

"Sounds intriguing, so tell me more."

"Carin's the only girl I ever dated. It seems everyone knew we'd get married. Well, except me. I planned on graduating and helping my dad build Moose Ridge into something like it's become now. Once it was going well, I'd get around to marriage and family. Figured there was plenty of time."

Sounds like a person who will remain nameless. "Was Carin okay with your plan?"

"In truth, we never discussed it. We'd always been together. In my eyes, we always would be."

"Okay, so a typical male. What happened?"

"What? No," he says, scowling at me. "Anyway, we were home for Christmas break. Mom had a box of decorations for Sadie, so Carin and I drove to her place. While we were there she asked if we could do her a favor. She told me Dad hadn't gotten the turkeys for Christmas yet, and she was hoping I could pick them up and Carin could go along to keep me company. Sound familiar?"

"Sort of…continue."

"She packed us a basket with snacks for the trip. When we arrived at the farm, Mister Vickers says he'd been expecting us.

"He asked if we were going somewhere for the holidays, and I told him we were staying at home. He was surprised because Sadie never gets her birds until the week of Christmas. When she called to tell him we were coming, he figured we were celebrating early."

"What? I thought she said your dad was supposed to get them but hadn't yet?"

"Yes, she did. Seeing the pattern here?"

"You mean she lied? Like she did with the order today?"

"It seemed like it, but I said nothing. We loaded the turkeys and headed back. It's around a three-hour drive on a desolate stretch of road. A lot of range land and few houses, or people. Still, I felt we'd make it home at a decent time.

"Carin opened the basket, and there were sandwiches, chips, and a lot more. Even two thermoses of hot coffee. We ate while I drove. Things were going well, and it was dark by then. We were halfway home and hadn't seen another car for a while.

"Without warning, something big came from the field on our right. It was on us before I could do anything. I hit it square. We both felt the impact. Hitting the brakes caused the truck to slide on the icy road. We spun, and I fought and pulled out, but over-corrected. We slid into the ditch, hit hard on something, and came to a stop. I was thankful we were still upright and the truck seemed to be running okay. All the gauges were showing normal. Making sure it was in gear, I pushed the throttle, but nothing. It didn't seem like the wheels were even spinning."

"Oh, my gosh. What did you hit?"

"I wasn't sure. I got the flashlight from the glove box and checked the truck. It was sitting at a slant, and I could see underneath. The transfer case was hanging loose. Whatever we hit did a lot of damage. I knew we were stuck, and there was no way I could repair it, even with the right tools."

"Okay, what happened?"

"I didn't think we were in any immediate danger. We had plenty of fuel, and I could keep the truck running to keep us warm. We had no cell reception, so no way to call anyone. We decided to wait for someone to come by."

"You mean you stayed there, in the truck?"

"Had little choice. We were off the road, but I could see someone coming and could turn on the lights. There was plenty of food, and with the low temp outside, it made little sense to leave. At worst, my dad would come searching in the morning, and if someone came before, we could get word home. Plus, Sadie knew where we went, she could tell them our location. With no other option, we settled in for the night. We listened to the radio and talked while eating."

"Okay. So, what then?"

"We talked about our hopes for the future, and I realized how aligned they were. It was getting late, and I laid back against the door, and she rested against my side, with the emergency blanket covering us. Around one by the dash clock, I was still thinking about our talk and asked if she was awake. She said yes, but she was getting cold, so I started the engine."

"Didn't you say this was when you proposed?"

"Yes, I'm getting to it. We stayed this way while the heater was running, and I thought, why not? Then I wondered how to approach it."

"What? You're joking, right? You're sitting there with thoughts of proposing and all you can think is why not? Not how much you love her or how much a part of your life she is or, I don't know, a million other things? Just, why not?"

"Well, yeah, but it wasn't like what you're implying. It made sense, is all. I said, 'You know what? We should get married. Don't you think?' She—"

"Wait. Hold on. You said 'We should get married.' Those were your exact words? You didn't even ask her to marry you or anything. Nothing but, 'We should get married.' Is that right?"

"Yeah, but I asked her if she thought so too."

"Wow! Mr. Romantic. What a way to sweep a girl off her feet! What happened?"

"We decided to have the wedding after graduation in late June. That's pretty much how it was."

"That is how you proposed to the love of your life?"

"Well, yeah." He shrugs. "We spent the rest of the night talking about it, like where to have it and all. Later, when it was getting light, I saw a pickup heading our way. I turned on the flashers, but as it got closer, I could tell it was my dad. After getting the truck on the trailer he'd brought, we drove home. We waited until Christmas to tell everyone. By then, we'd picked out the rings. That Christmas was one for the books."

I'm still in disbelief. "That was it? I'm glad it worked out for you, but it's a little anticlimactic, don't you think?"

"Maybe so, but I doubt it was as bad as it sounded. I'm not a superb storyteller. Ask Tyler. There was something that happened afterward though I never figured out."

"Well, what was it? You can't stop there."

"With our current situation being what it is, I doubt you want to hear more."

"Why not? Come on, you must tell me now. What happened?"

"Okay, but don't get mad or anything. Remember, I had nothing to do with this—"

"I understand."

"We got back to town and drove Carin home. We went to Sadie's to drop off her turkey, and I told her about the farmer wondering about us getting them so early. She explained that she thought it'd be an excellent idea to get them in case another storm came in and we couldn't get there."

"I can believe it. She's said something similar to me in the past. Is that it?"

"No, then she said, 'Sometimes, you need to give things a push,' When I looked at her, she acted like she said nothing. I thought maybe I imagined it. As I was leaving I heard, 'I'm sure you and Carin can't wait to share your news.' When I glanced back, the door was already closed."

"Wait, are you saying she knew you proposed? You think she set the entire thing up? How could she cause the truck to break down and arrange for you to hit an animal or whatever? There's no way!"

"All I can say is one of her favorite sayings is, 'All things are possible for God.' She says it all the time."

"What? You think...you think Sadie sent you on that errand hoping you'd get stranded and ask Carin to marry you?"

"Well, yeah. It explains everything. I think she arranged the entire thing."

I sit for awhile. "No...it can't be. There has to be another explanation."

"Okay, believe what you want. I know what I know, and it's so similar to what happened today. That's all I'm saying."

"You mean she wanted this to happen? How could she know we'd need fuel or I'd put in gasoline? Sure, she facilitated me coming along, but that's where her influence ended. What could she hope to accomplish? It's not like you're going to say, 'Hey, we should get married.' Right?" He's silent for several moments. I glance his way. "I said—"

"Well, I don't know. We should think this through."

I stare at him, eyes wide and mouth open. I doubt I even take a breath.

Then he laughs. "Gotcha. You should have seen your face. Priceless."

"You can't blame me, considering your track record. Back to my question, what could she hope to accomplish by getting us out here together?"

"Help us get to know each other, maybe? Who knows, we're talking about Sadie here. What can I say?"

"I think you're crazy and maybe she is too," I say, staring straight ahead. The sun is setting behind the hills in front of us, past the makeshift corral. I can't believe the colors as it sinks below the horizon. "Wow, I don't think I've ever seen anything like it."

"Yes, God is an amazing artist," he says.

I expect him to laugh, but he's not joking. Not wanting to spoil the moment, I let it go and immerse myself in nature's show.

As the sun disappears and the last light fades away, I realize it's becoming quite dark, to the point where it's hard to make things out. After sitting a while, Jason searches for something in the back seat. "What are you doing?"

"I'm checking to see what we have. You know, there's more room back here. Maybe we should move."

"You want me to climb in the rear seat with you? Do we know each other well enough for such a gigantic step?"

"Oh! Ah, I meant nothing by it. Thought it might be more comfortable is all."

"Comfortable? Is that what you call it in Wyoming?" I'm glad it's dark as I try not to laugh.

"What? Oh, no, I wasn't implying…I mean, I wasn't thinking…" His pleading voice is becoming more high-pitched by the second. "Nothing like…well, there's more room is all."

"Gotcha back," I say, giggling. "Calm down, I know what you meant. I'm giving you a hard time, but it sounds like a marvelous idea." The flashlight illuminates his face, and I'm sure his expression is more priceless than mine was earlier. "How shall we do it? I'm not getting out for anything."

"Let me get situated, and I'll hold the basket on my lap while you climb back."

"Okay, let me know when you're ready."

Once he's in the rear he says, "Hand me the travel mugs and come on back." He's holding the light for me.

It's a struggle, but I climb to my side of the seat with most of my dignity intact. He places the basket between us. "This is better. I guess you were right," I say before I can catch myself.

"Would I steer you wrong?"

"I'm guessing that's a rhetorical question?"

"When have I ever given you poor advice?"

"Are you serious? What about when you told me not to get close to the puppies? That was terrible advice."

"You didn't listen to me, anyway. I heard they were even in your office most of yesterday."

"You're right, I didn't listen, which is what you knew would happen and why you said it. It's all your fault, and there's no arguing with that."

"What kind of logic is that? Did they teach you that at your expensive Ivy League school?"

"What's the deal with you and my school? No one needed to teach it to me. It's undeniable to more than half the population and easy to understand if you're a female—which is why you have a hard time grasping it. The Y chromosome of yours makes you keep asking 'why?'"

"Yeah, figured it was something like that. Your go-to card whenever you can't explain something. It's a female thing. Female logic and men can't understand it. I think that's getting old, don't you?"

"You do understand. Perfect. I'm so proud of you. It's old because it makes sense—i.e., logic. See, there's hope for you yet," I say, winking.

"What? I never said I understood. Didn't even imply it. You're twisting my words."

"I'd never. You said yourself it was logical. I was hoping you'd made a breakthrough."

"When did I say it was logical?"

"Just now. You said, and I quote, 'It's a female thing. Female logic and men can't understand it.' End quote. You agree it's logical. Now, I'm having something else to eat. You want anything?"

"Wait. That's not what I meant, and you know it. You're twisting my words again. Besides, you changed the subject because you know you can't win."

"I twisted nothing. Those were your exact words. Their meaning was so obvious there's no need to elaborate on them, and I didn't change the subject because I can't win. I did it before you embarrassed yourself further. You can thank me later," I add, smiling. "Now, do you want a sandwich?"

"Thank you? No, never mind. Why do I even try? Yes, let me have a sandwich."

"What? Now I have to make it for you? Sorry, I didn't realize that was one of my duties. What would his lordship like on it?" I can't help snickering.

"I didn't mean…I was answering your question. Do you have to take everything the wrong way?"

"No, I've got it. Boy, you sure can't take a joke, can you? Do you want mayo on both slices of bread? I think it makes it better."

"I can take a joke, but can't tell when you're joking and when you're not, and no, no mayo on either slice. The meat and cheese are fine on their own."

"Are you saying my dry Eastern humor is not discernible enough for you? Is this an East versus West thing?" I hand him his sandwich, dying from laughter inside. "How can you even eat this without mayo?"

"Maybe I just don't know you well enough. And the sandwich is fine this way."

"Well, we have time to get to know each other. What do you want to know? My political views? The style of panties I prefer? It's thongs, by the way. Do I believe in men from outer space? Do I wear anything to bed? Varies. What are my views on climate change? Maybe my breast size or sexual preferences? Come on, ask me." This is the polar opposite to what he meant, but I can't help it.

"What? I wasn't asking...I mean, I wouldn't...I'd never...I didn't mean any of that. I was pointing out a reason for not seeing when you're joking. Is everything so literal with you?"

"Boy, you really can't tell when I'm joking. Can we run the heater? It's getting cold."

"I guess it won't hurt for a short while." He shifts places with the basket and struggles to reach past the console. The engine comes to life, and after adjusting the heater controls, he moves back to the rear seat. "We'll let it run for a few minutes."

"Thank you, kind sir. Now, any chance you can hand me my bag with the laptop? It's on the floor in front of my seat." Why didn't I ask when he was there?

He hands me his food, frowning, "Sure. Is there anything else you need while I'm there this time?"

"No, the bag will be fine. Unless there's a heating pad there somewhere?" I'm trying not to laugh, watching him struggle to get back across the console and reach my bag. After he hands it to me, I place it against the door. Once he's settled, I pass him his sandwich and continue eating mine.

"Aren't you going to get something out?"

"No, I don't need anything right now. It's entertaining watching you climb up there."

"Entertaining, huh? I should have known. I might keep this blanket all to myself now."

"What? Where did you get a blanket?"

"From the console when I was entertaining her ladyship. You learn to keep one of these around this time of year." He's busy unfolding the blanket over himself.

"You're not going to share?"

"No."

"I can't believe this. Why not?"

In the glow of the dash lights, I see his mischievous grin. "Hold your horses. I'm getting it spread out. Now who doesn't understand humor?" He positions the blanket so it's covering both of us.

"Well, you're forgiven for now." I'm enjoying poking him.

"Forgiven for what?" He holds his hand up. "Never mind. I don't even want to know, but thank you, I guess. Now are you going to hog the chips, or do you know how to share?"

"I was holding them while you were laying out the blanket. Here, have the bag."

"Thank you for your sacrifice."

"Wanted no more, anyway. Are there any cookies left?"

"I think so. Is there anything else her highness would like while I'm getting them?"

"No, I'm fine. You're the one who left the basket over there when you came back. It's not my fault. I think you wanted to sit next to me."

"No, I meant nothing by it. I didn't bother to move it back yet. Here, hold this, I'll move it."

"I was joking. Are you always this literal? Stay where you are, and you can share my blanket."

"Your blanket? This is your blanket? No, never mind. Don't answer. I'm sure you have a so-called logical explanation only a female could understand. We'll leave it at that."

"See, you're learning so much during this trip. I'm proud of you. What shall we discuss next?"

"I think I've talked enough for a while. I'm going to sit back and stay out of trouble."

"Well, one can hope."

"Ha, you're hilarious."

"Should you check on the horses?"

"I'm sure they're fine. They are wild horses."

"That's not a pleasant bedside manner."

"I don't need one. Animals don't have bedsides. Don't you have work to do on your laptop? Maybe there's someone else you can torment?" He sits back, lowering his cap over his face.

"Yes, I have something to do, and it will be more stimulating than watching you sleep." I take out my laptop and get busy with things for work and reviewing my blog. After a while, I check the time and I'm surprised at how long I'd been working. Jason seems to be asleep, and I decide not to bother him. I close the laptop before putting everything away, place the bag on the floor beneath my legs, and settle back, pulling the blanket to my chin. The cold is seeping in, but there's not much we can do. I try to bundle tighter.

"Here, sit up a little," Jason says, startling me. Was he not asleep?

"Sorry, didn't mean to wake you. Why should I sit up?"

"Do you have to know everything?" He moves around, but it's dark so I'm not sure what he's doing. "Now move back."

Not knowing what else to do, I move back to where I was. He's moved, and his arm is now around my shoulders. He spreads the blanket out again and repositions his coat to cover both of us. I'm astonished by this, but already sense the improvement. I turn to face him a little, allowing my head to rest on his chest.

"Better?"

"Much better. Thank you. You come in handy at times."

"Brother, I can't catch a break." He gives a slight chuckle though.

I never go to sleep because of the cold, but enjoy the warmth under his coat and blanket. We lie this way for a while.

"You awake?" His voice cutting through the silence startles me.

"Yes. It's hard to sleep in this cold, and I don't want to hear anything you think we should do." I can't help but chuckle.

"What?" It takes a second before he gets it. I let him stew in the awkwardness until he starts again. "That's enough, I wanted to say I was sorry for what happened with your dad. I'm sure it was hard on you being so young."

"You read my story?"

"Well, yeah. You weren't hiding it or anything. I'm sorry if you meant to keep it private."

"No, it's okay, I guess." It is on the internet.

"Is this like a diary or something?"

"A blog. It's a long story, but several friends on a social network told me I should write about what happened to me. They said it might help. Another mentioned I should write a blog which might even help others. I realized my story was hard to explain without telling what happened earlier. Now it's turned into my life story. I was working on the next section, which I'll post tomorrow."

"A blog? Has it helped?"

"In a way. It's allowed me to see several positive things that happened while reviewing the bad. It's also opened my eyes to how others might have seen me. Not always a pleasurable thing."

"That's good, I guess. I can't imagine someone having to tell me something like that concerning my dad."

He holds me a little tighter. It feels nice. "It embarrassed my dad. He wouldn't even glance at me while his lawyer explained. I can still envision him behind his desk, where he once seemed bigger than life itself. Then, sitting there as his lawyer explained things, he was a shell of his normal self. Ashamed by what happened. Couldn't even tell me goodbye." The memory floods my mind.

"I'm sorry anyone would have to experience that, but even more sorry you did."

He cares. It's obvious by his tone. I tell him everything. I'm not sure why, but it comes out. I struggle and need to stop at times to let the tears flow. The darkness helps me open up. He holds me and allows me to talk at my pace. I describe our enormous house in Scarsdale, and tell him about spending summers at our house in the Hamptons and holidays at our place in Martha's Vineyard.

I cover my time as a foster child and what it was like taking care of and watching the girls grow. This brings back fond memories, like taking them to the carnival that came every spring and Saturday afternoons at the park. I smile, explaining how they were twins but nothing alike.

This leads to what being the single foster kid in the neighborhood was like. I share how several boys grabbed me, dragging me into the boy's locker room. I was lucky and someone came in before they could do much and they ran out. I explain how they got off saying I wanted it and it wasn't the first time. Which was a lie, but I was a foster kid and it was my word against theirs. How the rumors about it kept being repeated until I graduated high school. I've told no one this in years, but sitting here beside him, it seems I need to share it, and he doesn't mind. I spend little time on Michael, but otherwise cover my years at Harvard. When I reach the day he appeared at my door, I go quiet. We sit wrapped in his coat and blanket.

It's late, but I don't want to disturb our already limited warmth to find out the exact time. He speaks for the first time since I started sharing. "I can't imagine what it was like to live through something like that on your own. I've been through hard times, but there were people there to comfort and support me. People I could trust, and there was my faith in the promise from God that He's in charge. I know I could never have gotten through any of it without those things, yet you went through so much more all on your own. Sadie is right. You're one special lady."

"Jason, if your god is so loving, why did you and Sadie—two people who have such a great faith—have to endure such tragedies in your lives? All the heartache and pain. How could that be?"

I stay quiet while he holds me, and I listen to his story as he listened to mine. His first statement impacts me. "I don't have a great faith in God. I have faith in a great God!" He explains how his parents died and how Carin helped him through the hard times, and how much raising Tyler, who was a few months old then, gave him something else to concentrate on. He covers Carin's illness and death, and how much support he got. How even to this day, he misses her. What strikes me most is, despite these hardships and tragedies in his life, he's still close to this god of his. He even shares a few verses from the Bible, which he says helps him, even now, when he's feeling low and wondering the "why" of all of it.

> *"Psalms 34: 17-19. The righteous cry out, and the Lord hears them; he delivers them from all their troubles. The Lord is close to the brokenhearted and saves those who are crushed in spirit. The righteous person may have many troubles, but the Lord delivers him from them all."*

In the children's home, we attended chapel every week, but the God Jason's describing is not the one I remember. I say little while he talks and let him tell it his way, like he allowed me. Maybe this will help heal his wounds too? It also causes my thoughts to turn to this god of his. A phrase from one verse stays in my mind. "The Lord is close to the brokenhearted." I wonder if it's true. In Jason's case, it appears so. I might have to think this through more. However, I don't want to discuss it right now, so I remain silent.

We stay wrapped in his coat and blanket. His arm is holding me while I rest my head on his chest. After a while, it strikes me how safe I feel, even though we're stranded here—alone in the wilderness on a cold, dreary night. I feel safer than I have in a long time. With this thought, I drift off to sleep. Today has been a magnificent day.

Chapter Ten

I wake to find the first glimmers of dawn appearing. I'm not sure if Jason is awake and lift my head to check.

"You awake?" he whispers.

"Yeah, I guess. Stiff and a little groggy."

"Stiff I understand. You want to get out and stretch?"

"In the cold? I don't think so."

"Suit yourself, I need to check on the horses."

He moves the basket to the front and slides out from under the blanket, taking his coat with him.

The stallion is suspicious of Jason and watches his every move as he throws hay over the rails. The horses swarm around in no time, appreciative for their breakfast. He grabs an armful and carries it back to where the stallion is. The leader continues to observe Jason as he puts the hay into the corral.

He studies the other horses and, after several minutes, turns toward the truck. Once he is a harmless distance away, the stallion makes his way to the hay. Although the other horses are oblivious to their surroundings and tucking into their food, the stallion remains uneasy. He lifts his head to scan the area and flicks his ears back and forth to take in the minutest of sounds—he's serious about his job.

"Care for lukewarm coffee?" Jason asks once he's back.

"I'll pass. Water will do."

He gives a slight bow of his head and hands me a bottle. "Whatever her highness desires."

I glare at him. "When do you think someone might be here?"

"Should be soon if they want to cover any distance today."

We continue to view the horses while having our drinks. Everything seems so peaceful. After a while the horses turn to our left.

A truck towing a horse trailer stops next to the corral. I've never been so glad to see a pickup and trailer in my life. Jason and I hurry out.

The biting cold hits me, but it matters little since we should be heading home soon. Jerri is walking our way, and the two men are right behind her.

"I thought you were heading home last night," Jeff says, holding out his hand to Jason.

"That was the plan, but an issue arose and we needed to stay," Jason says.

John appears concerned. "What happened?"

"After you left, I found I couldn't change to the second tank. The other is close to empty," he says. I'm glad he's not telling them the full reason. "Since I knew you were coming back this morning, we stayed here."

"Could be the switch. Maybe we can check it," John says.

"No, it's not anything we can fix here, but I could use a lift to get diesel."

"Are you sure? Might be worth a gander," Jeff says, walking toward Jason's truck.

I can't let Jason squirm any longer. "What he's trying not to tell you is I put gasoline in the second tank by accident, and we can't use it."

"You put gas in a diesel truck?" John asks, like how could anyone ever do anything so stupid?

"Yes, I didn't know it was diesel. My SUV is a Ford too, but it uses gasoline so that's what I got."

Jeff is trying not to laugh, but failing.

"Hey, it can happen!" Jerri says, coming to my rescue. "I'm sure she wanted to be helpful. Right, Jazmine?"

"Yes. I knew we were under a time constraint, so when I saw we were low, I stopped. When the gauge didn't change, I thought it wasn't working. Jason explained about the two tanks. I am sorry. I didn't realize."

"It's fine, Jeff," he says. "The gasoline never got to the engine, but I need to get diesel. Can you give me a ride?"

"I can do you one better. I've got five gallons right here. Will that get you far enough?"

"Yeah, but won't it leave you without? What if something happens and you need it?" It's amazing how he always thinks of others first.

"Shouldn't be a problem. We'll unhook the trailer, and I'll follow you back to the first station while Jerri and John get the horses ready to go. That way, I can refill my spare can while making certain you make it to the station."

"Well, if you're sure. We'd be mighty grateful."

"No problem," Jeff says, and the three head for his truck.

Jason goes with them and returns with the five-gallon can. He pours it in after he opens the flap in the rear by the tailgate. Good thing I never noticed it. By the time he's emptied the can, they unhook the trailer, and Jeff climbs into his truck. He turns it around while Jason and I tell John and Jerri goodbye and climb into ours.

Jason turns the ignition and I give a brief shout, seeing the gauge rise to above a fourth. "Will this be enough?"

"Should be. There's a station in town, so we're set."

I check the gauge again after about ten miles. It's showing a little below a fourth now. Jason still says we should make it to the station. While we drive, I try my phone. No connection yet. With nothing else to do, I sit back and hope. We make it back to the main road and head south for Guernsey. As we pass the sign for the city limits, I spot the fuel station, and he stops beside the pump. I'm sure my relief is clear. When he turns off the engine, the gauge doesn't move much.

Jason gets out and starts filling Jeff's fuel can first as Jeff approaches. While they're doing this, I check my phone. Much to my relief, I see bars. I call Sadie. This should be interesting. I listen to several rings before she answers.

"Jazmine, it's so nice to hear from you. Are you two on your way back?"

I can't believe her calm tone. It's like this was a planned trip and nothing out of the ordinary happened. "Don't you dare act innocent with me. Do you know what we've been through?"

"No, dear. How would I know that? Was there trouble?"

She still sounds like the harmless lady she claims to be, but I know better. "Trouble? Indeed, there was. We ran low on fuel and spent the night in the truck waiting for the BLM folks to return this morning before we could drive home."

"Oh dear. Well, things are okay now, I suppose. Did you get my order?"

How dare she dismiss this out of hand. "Did you hear me? We spent the night in the truck."

"Yes dear, I heard you. Did you get my order?"

"Yes, but I have questions. Ben at the nursery said you called yesterday morning."

"Yes, dear. I called to tell him you were coming. I wanted it ready so not to delay Jason."

"He said you hadn't even placed the order before then."

"Well, Ben never was the sharpest tool in the box. He didn't bother checking and assumed I hadn't placed the order before, but it's fine now. You've got my order and are heading home. We'll see you when you get here. I'll have lunch ready."

She's acting like we were out on a Sunday drive. "Well, we'll be home soon, and you'll need to explain this to Jason. I can't believe you did this."

"Explain what, dear? Everything here is fine. Oh, I got a call last evening from Jill asking about Jason. I explained they called him out of town on an emergency and a delay must have kept him from returning right away. I let her know he was someplace remote and probably didn't have cell service, so he couldn't call her. Told her not to worry though, you were with him and you'd take care of him. You'd both be fine spending the night together. I guess she understood because the call ended. Now don't worry. Everything here is splendid. We'll see you when you get back."

I shake my head, stunned beyond belief. Wanting to move on, I ask, "How is Tyler?"

"Oh, he's fine. It was a small stomachache. He had soup last night and fell asleep. Woke this morning right back to his old self. Tell Jason and we'll talk more when you get here. Take care." She hangs up before I can say another word. Jason comes back and sees me holding my phone.

"Did you get a hold of Sadie?"

"Yes, I did."

"How's Tyler doing?"

"She says he's fine. He had soup last night and fell asleep, and woke this morning his old self. She thinks it was a stomachache."

"Glad to hear. I was hoping it wasn't something worse."

"I didn't tell her what you fed him the night before."

"That's enough. Did she say anything else?"

"She said there's no reason to hurry, and she'll have lunch ready for us."

"Okay, I guess. Anything else?"

"Oh, she was full of news. When I mentioned her calling in the order after we left, she put it down to this Ben person forgetting she placed it earlier. She also mentioned Jill called her, and she explained you were called out of town for an emergency and were delayed."

"Great, so Jill understands why I couldn't show."

"Oh, she knows. I'm not sure understanding is correct though. Seems Sadie thought to mention I was with you somewhere without cell service, and we'd be fine spending the night together."

"I doubt it's an issue," he says, driving out.

"Well, Jill's your problem, not mine."

He turns to me with a questioning gaze but doesn't say anything.

The drive is long but goes well. We pull into Sadie's when expected, and Jason parks by the barn behind the house. "You can go in the house. I'll unload."

"I can help," I offer, grabbing my parka.

"Suit yourself, but I can get it," he says, opening the barn before climbing into the truck bed.

"No, I'll help. It will go faster." I'm exuberant to prove my worth after the diesel incident. "What should I do?"

"Carry this bag inside and to the left. There's a pallet you can set it on." He holds out a bag of peat moss for me to grab. I wrap my arms around it, and as he lets go the weight startles me. Taking a moment to get my balance, I turn to go inside the barn.

"You got it?" he calls out and might even laugh.

"I think so. To the left?" I struggle to ask.

"Yeah, to the left."

I spot a pallet on the floor while peering over the top of the bag I'm carrying. When I reach it, I let the bag fall where it will. I'm glad to see it land in its designated place. Why did I agree to help with this? I head back for the next one, but my eagerness has somewhat dissipated.

Jason has several ready. I strain to get one in a bear hug and follow my steps back to the pallet, drop this one beside the first, and head back. Fourteen more to go. Jason is setting the last one on top of the others and jumps down. He grabs two, lifts them over his shoulder like they're nothing more than feather pillows, and turns toward the barn.

"Show off!" I shout, grappling to lift the next one. By the time I get a solid grip, Jason is already back. He stands aside to let me pass, albeit with a sarcastic smile, and I trudge back to the barn. I set it on top of the others and stand back to catch my breath. Jason stifles a chuckle, passes me, and lays down two more.

When we place the last of the bags on top of the pallet, I breathe a tremendous sigh of relief, reminding myself never to volunteer for any such task ever again. Jason heads back to the truck and returns with the pallet. He stands it beside the stack of bags and turns to me. "Ready to go in?"

"I guess. Is this all we need out here?"

"For now. She'll let me know where she wants it next spring when it's time to put it out." He snickers while heading for the truck. "Hop in and I'll drive to the walkway in front."

Once he parks, I help put the rest of our food in the basket and check one last time to make sure we have everything. With my normal slide down from the beast, I turn to grab the basket, but Jason already has it. I join him, walking to the porch where he opens the door for me. He does the same at the front door, following behind.

"Anyone home?" he yells out, and we hear the stampede of tiny feet approaching.

"Jazmine, you're here!" Tyler squeals, running in and wrapping his arms around my legs. "I got to see Bob and the girls today and even got to feed them. They were awesome."

Sadie arrives after him. "It's all he's talked about since we got back. Couldn't wait to tell Jazmine. Now, what are you waiting for? Lunch is ready. We're hungry, aren't we, Tyler? Don't you two dilly dally around. Get your coats off and let's eat." She takes the basket from Jason and heads toward the rear of the house. "Let's go. No one moves as slow as you two."

"I guess we have our orders," Jason says, removing his coat. He helps me too since Tyler hasn't let go. "Tyler, we need to eat."

"Come on, Jazmine, you can sit by me," Tyler says, grabbing my hand and pulling me toward the dining room. I shrug, glancing back at Jason, unsure of what to say.

He follows behind us, shaking his head. At the dining table, Sadie has everything set, and she arrives carrying a large bowl. "I thought chili would work for now. There are onions, cheese, and crackers," she says while setting the bowl in the middle of the table.

Jason uses the ladle to fill Tyler's bowl before doing the same for Sadie. "Do you want me to dish yours out?"

"Sure, I guess," I say, taking my seat next to Tyler. He hands me a full bowl, which smells delicious. I pass on the onions and crackers but take cheese. The others have theirs ready, and I start to eat when Jason mentions prayer.

I lower my head while he prays for the meal. He thanks his god for all the blessings, for watching over Tyler while we were away, and for watching over us. He says a few more thanks and ends with, "In the name of Jesus, amen."

"Jazmine, you should have seen Bob," Tyler says, his eyes brimming with excitement. "He was running all over the place. The girls were too. Andi covered them with a blanket, and they couldn't get out. When she took it off, Bob ran and jumped in my lap. It was awesome."

"Tyler, eat your lunch. You can tell us about the puppies later," Jason says. "Now, would someone like to explain how he got to the clinic? You didn't drive him there, did you, Sadie?"

"No, I didn't drive. Andi came and got us for church since you weren't here, and we stopped off on the way home, knowing you'd be a little longer."

"Okay, I guess. I wanted to make sure you didn't drive."

"Where did you put the peat moss?"

"In the barn by the lawn tractor."

"What? I need it in the greenhouse out by the garden. We'll have to move it."

"We will, in four months when you're ready for it. For now, it's fine in the barn."

"It would have been less trouble to put it where it goes, but you're the one who'll have to move it, so it doesn't matter. Remember this, I don't want to hear any complaints or questions about why it's not where it needs to be."

Jason is shaking his head but says nothing. I do the same. Once we finish with lunch, I know I'm wiped out. "Thank you for lunch, Sadie. Amazing as usual, but it's been a long two days. I'm going home to take a nap. Any chance of a ride, Jason?"

"No, Jazmine. We need to go see Bob. He told me he misses you," Tyler says with the cutest expression.

Jason places a hand on his son's arm to calm him. "Tyler, Jazmine doesn't want to see Bob right now. Her weekend has been hectic, and she's tired. You get your things ready while I take her home."

"Why do we have to leave?" Tyler gazes up, pouting.

"No arguments, please. We're heading home, so get your things ready for when I get back." Jason gets up, stacks everyone's bowls, and heads for the kitchen before Tyler can say anything further.

"It's okay, Tyler," I say, feeling sorry for him. "I'll see Bob tomorrow, and he can tell me what the two of you did, okay?" I hope this resolves the problem.

"I guess, but Bob won't like it." Tyler's face shows his utter disappointment.

When Jason returns from the kitchen, he glances at me. "You ready?"

"Maybe we should stop by the clinic to make sure Bob's okay," I say.

"He's fine. Andi is there with several others handy. I'm sure he'll be able to make it until tomorrow," Jason answers, rolling his eyes. "Now, are you ready to go?"

"Yes, I guess. Sadie, I'll see you Tuesday for your meeting."

"Okay, you go relax, and I'll see you Tuesday."

With this, Jason and I walk down the steps. He holds my door open and helps me climb into the beast for what I hope is the last time. I put on my seat belt while he goes around to his side. We're at my place in no time, and I know I'm done for the day.

"Well, thank you for an unforgettable experience," I say, gathering my things.

"Yes, a genuine experience," he says, laughing.

"I'll see you in the morning. Take care." I perform my usual slide to the ground and drag myself to the front door. Once inside, I turn back and see he's waving through his window. I return the wave, letting him know all is fine, and watch him back out before closing the door.

With little energy left to do anything too exciting, I decide a soak in my magnificent washbowl of a tub would be perfect. I begin the arduous walk to the bathroom, dropping my bag off on the small coffee table as I pass. I hope I make it.

Chapter Eleven

I can't believe it's Monday morning already. The weekend flew by, and the only planned thing accomplished was posting my blog. Now another work week begins.

After parking in my normal spot, I drop my bags in my office and head for the kennel room. It's been two days since I saw the puppies, and I'm surprised how much I miss them. When I open the door, their whimpering is unmistakable. By the time I get to them, they're already standing on their hind legs, trying to climb out. There's also a note from Andi.

I fed them at 8:00 AM, no matter what they say!

Giggling, I pull a chair close to them. I get Bob first and hold him to my neck. His little tongue is going a mile a minute, but I can't ignore the girls and need to put them on my lap as well. This necessitates moving Bob to get everyone arranged before they settle into perfect positions for me to scratch their bellies. It's not long before they're asleep, but the door opens, causing them to stir and turn toward it, wanting to know who dares disturb them. I want to know myself.

"Knew you'd be in here," Cindy says, rushing in. "I came early to find out if it's true."

"If what's true? That I spend time with the puppies each morning?"

"No, everyone knows that," she says, waving her hand. "I mean this weekend. You know? You and Doc Withers spending the night together? It's all over town. I can't believe it. Tell me you did. You did, right?" Her eyes are wide in anticipation.

"What? No. Where did you hear this?"

"You were all the talk on Sunday. More people than I can count asked me. Even Sharon from the local paper called to ask. We're all friends from school. Come on, you can trust me. Tell me everything."

"Nothing like that happened. I can't believe you'd think anything would."

"Why not? He needs someone, and I can't think of anyone better than you. It thrilled me when I heard it. Now you're saying it didn't happen! I'm bummed to be honest. So you didn't spend the weekend together?"

How can I answer this? "Well, yes, we did, kinda, but before you get excited, let me explain. They called Jason out on an emergency, and Sadie needed someone to pick up her order in the area. I went along to get Sadie's order and help Jason. There was trouble with the truck, and we couldn't get back until Sunday afternoon. That's all there was to it."

Her eyes open wide. "You were together! You should have seen Jill's face when she heard you didn't come back until Sunday. So where did you stay Saturday night?"

I doubt I can avoid explaining, and we need to get the facts out before this made-up version goes viral anyway. "Well, we were out a distance from any town, where the wild horses Jason inoculated were. Three people from BLM were with us. Once we finished, we waited for the lead stallion to recover from the tranquilizer Jason gave him to keep the herd calm. It took time before he could stand and started eating. When we were ready to leave, we discovered there was a problem with the truck, and we couldn't drive back. We were far out, and it being too cold to walk anywhere and knowing the BLM people were returning in the morning, Jason thought it best to stay there and wait for them. That's all it was. They returned, and we got the problem rectified and drove back. End of story."

"Not on your life. You're saying you and Jason spent the entire night together?"

"In a way, I guess. Didn't have any option. There was food Sadie packed for us, and we could run the engine for brief times to get warm. We were fine."

"Then you did sleep together."

I can't believe she said this. "What? No…Well, I guess…in a way. We went to sleep, but we didn't like, sleep together. We slept."

"You slept together the whole night? Did you snuggle or kiss?"

"Cindy! No, why would we kiss? It was nothing. We were two people stranded in the wilderness, doing what we needed until help came. That's all."

"Sounds like the plot of every romance I've ever read. Two people meet, are stranded and forced to spend time together, then they fall in love. It's textbook, and I notice you didn't deny the snuggling."

"It was implied, and I've read horror stories with a similar starting plot. I'd be careful," I say, giving her a sarcastic scowl. "I don't know what textbook you're referring to. We're friends, and I was helping him out while getting Sadie's order."

"Yeah, well, you can try to fake it all you want, but I see the two of you daily. You might fool others by putting on this friend act of yours, but I know better." She turns to leave.

"What do you mean? We are friends."

"Right, sure you are. Friends. Like anyone believes that," she calls out as the door closes.

This could be a problem. I can't believe it's all over town already, but with less than three thousand people, I guess it wouldn't take long. What if by town, she meant Casper? That would be a whole other problem. No, she had to mean Glenrock. We need to control this and get the truth out, but how?

The puppies begin to whimper as soon as I put them back in their box. I can't leave them. I take the box and head for my office. If I hurry, I can get there before anyone else sees me. I take the route through the lobby as a precaution. This allows me to avoid the gigantic room where the stalls are. Stanley, who is lying on the counter, turns when he sees me, so I put the box down and freshen his water. I notice he's glaring at me—a judgmental glare at that.

"You behave yourself, we only slept," I tell him, grabbing the box, then march on to my office.

Once inside, I put all this behind me and get to work. How could anyone believe this story? It's ludicrous. Even beyond ludicrous. With the box of puppies on a chair near mine, I open my laptop. Of course, I must get Bob out and place him on my lap before I can do anything else. The girls are fine where they are for now. I busy myself with work and try to put everything else out of my mind. Easier said than done.

About mid-morning, I hear a knock and figure it's Jason. He usually sticks his head in when he gets here. Still, it's later than normal. "Come in, Jason."

"Well, I'm not Doc Withers, but I'll come in," Terri says, opening the door. She has the bottles for the puppies' next feed. "Thought I'd find these guys in here." She sets the box on the floor and sits in its place. After handing me a bottle for Bob, she lifts Mindy, who is now wide awake. Lindy seems to prefer continuing to sleep.

"Sorry, I didn't realize the time. Have you seen Jason? He hasn't stopped by this morning. Not the norm for him."

"I hear you're better at knowing where Doc Withers is than me. I guess we can excuse him after your exciting weekend."

"What? Oh, you mean our being stranded?"

"Stranded? Is that what they're calling it now?" She's smiling.

"Terri, it was nothing. We needed to stay with the truck until someone came. That's all there was to it. Now mind your thoughts."

"Sure it was. Spent the entire night together in the wilderness in a cozy little truck."

My shaken reaction to Terri's pokes causes me to move Bob's bottle away from his mouth. He makes it clear he's disappointed with me.

"Believe me, there's nothing cozy concerning that beast," I say, moving the bottle back to Bob's lips.

She exchanges Mindy for Lindy, who is not happy—at least until she sees the bottle, then all is well. "Are you referring to Doc Withers or his truck?"

"Terri!" I can't believe she asked that. "The truck of course. Anyway, do you know where he is?"

"I heard Doc Carson left to get him at the garage. Seems his truck has something wrong with it. I'd hate to think what it could be…suspension, maybe?"

"Enough, Terri. I'm sure he's having them check the problem we had—with the fuel tank, I might add. I'm certain he'll be in soon."

"I'm sure he will, which means I better get these guys back to their proper place or he'll have a fit. Look who I'm talking to though."

"What do you mean?"

"You, of course. He'd never complain to you concerning this. If anything, I'd get the blame. Either way, we'd better go." She's putting Lindy back and reaching for Bob.

"Why wouldn't he complain to me? I'll have you know he gave me a hard time about having them in here Friday. Don't think I get a pass."

"I see you ignored anything he said. Now, when did this happen? Was it this weekend when you were all cozy?" She grabs the box and turns to leave.

"I didn't ignore him. I chose not to follow his suggestions, and we were never cozy." I call out as the door closes behind her. How could anyone be cozy in that truck, out in the wilderness, when it's so cold? It's beyond imaginable. However, it felt nice having his arm around me, with the blanket and his coat wrapped around us. I guess it was cozy.

"Stop it." I say out loud, even though I'm alone. I catch my euphoric expression in the mirror on my desk. "Traitor." This is getting nuts.

I leave my office, not wanting to spend any more time with

myself and my traitorous thoughts, and make my way to the lobby. "Good morning, Georgia," I say.

"Thank you, but I understand there's no need to wish you one?" she says, smiling.

"Um, no, I guess not. No, wait. What do you mean?"

"About you having a good morning. From what I hear, you enjoyed one heck of a weekend. I figure you're still on cloud nine."

"Georgia! You don't think these rumors are true, do you?"

"Well, I know my husband and I used to get mighty cozy in his old pickup before the kids came along." She winks.

"I can assure you nothing happened. There was trouble with the truck, and we needed to wait for someone to come. That's all it was. Nothing else. No getting cozy or anything. What is it with you people?" I turn to leave, wanting to end this conversation, but I'm not fast enough.

"Okay, if you say so. Your secret is safe with me."

I spin back. "What secret? I told you nothing happened. How did you hear, anyway?"

"Are you kidding? There's been nothing this exciting around here since Jill's husband ran off with that lawyer. You were all anyone could discuss at the fundraiser yesterday."

"Fundraiser?" I can't believe this. "What fundraiser?"

"For the school music program. Most of the families with school-age children were there. Quite a group."

"They were talking about Jason and me?"

"You were the talk of the town. Not that you weren't a lot before, but you sure are now. Cindy and I were the most popular people there since they know we work for you. Boy, a few questions were stunning. Is it true you were topless the first time you met Jason?"

"No!" Did she ask that for real? "I wasn't expecting anyone and was wearing an old shirt I use around the house. When he knocked, I put on my coat before going out. I swear, I was wearing a shirt."

"Nothing but a shirt?" She has a sly smile.

"No, I was wearing shorts too. Did someone tell you I met him topless?"

"It was everywhere the first week you were here. It even got my neighbors across the street talking to each other. That hasn't happened for fifteen years, when one of June's trees fell and took out Agatha's porch. I thought nothing could get them talking again. Don't worry, Sadie and Jason clarified it for everyone and most forgot about it."

Not having a clue what I needed to do, I ask Georgia, who seems to have her finger on the pulse of this community.

"I wouldn't worry. Before long, something else will come along, and this will be old news." This helps me feel better. "After all, this knocked Jill's divorce out of the limelight."

"Wasn't that years ago?"

"Yeah, but it was an enormous deal for a long time. Well, until you got here. Now it's all but forgotten."

At that moment the front door opens, and my nightmare continues.

"Good morning, Jill. What brings you by?" I'm smiling and try to sound cheerful.

"Oh, you…I forgot you work here," she says, glancing in my direction before turning to Georgia. "I was on my way to the Appreciation of the Arts' committee meeting and needed to drop this off for Jason. Hearing about his awful weekend, I wanted to do something special for him. I know how much he likes my cherry pie. Georgia, is he here?"

Is she dismissing me out of hand? I can't stand for this.

I answer her with a sweet smile. "I'm sorry, Jason is out, but if you leave the pie, I'm sure he'll be ever so grateful."

She scowls at me before turning to face Georgia again. "When will he be back?"

I answer before Georgia can. "We're not sure. He's out with Doc Carson."

There's a lengthy pause while she stares at me.

"I heard of your little, ah, misadventure. Seems I wasn't the only one who suffered a dreadful weekend. I had to attend the dinner unescorted." She sounds like this was the ultimate embarrassment.

I can't help myself. "Oh, that's too bad. It troubled Jason he couldn't make it or even call. However, our weekend wasn't terrible. In fact, we had a magnificent time. I mean, how could we not enjoy being out in the fresh air, beautiful countryside, no one but the two of us? It was so cozy, and I can't begin to describe the picturesque sunset, then the moon and all the stars shining so bright. Oh, and the sunrise? It was, well…" I pause, glancing off in the distance, and then back at Jill. "What can I say, delightful. How could anyone not enjoy it?" I'll pay for this, but can't stop myself.

"I see," she says, locking her disdainful glare on me.

Two can play this game. I hold her gaze, but with my pleasant smile. The long period of silence stretches out, enveloping the room, before she spins and stalks out without even a goodbye. Georgia is dying, trying not to laugh. Once we hear the front door close, she lets it out.

"Oh, my gosh. I thought she might explode. No one has ever stared her down. Plus, she took the pie with her."

"I shouldn't have done that," I say, concerned. "But she pushes my buttons somehow."

"No, lady. You should have. It's time someone stood up to her," Cindy says, entering.

"You heard?" I still don't believe what I did.

"We all did. We saw her pull in and listened at the door. I thought Doc Carson would fall over, he was laughing so hard."

Georgia adds, "You should have seen her face when Jazmine said, 'It was so cozy.' I'm certain steam came out of her ears."

This causes me even more distress. "Doc Carson? You don't mean Jason heard it too?"

"No, he dropped the doc off and went on a call. Doc Carson said when they saw Jill's car pull in, Doc Withers couldn't get out of here quick enough."

"Well, I apologize to all of you. I shouldn't have done it. It was unprofessional and cruel. Please forgive me. I didn't mean it," I say, hoping they don't hate me. Jill is one of them. I'm the outsider.

"Don't you dare apologize," Cindy says. "She's been needing someone to stand up to her for a long time. She was the same when we were in school."

"You got that right," Georgia adds. "She treated everyone like we were her subjects and she was our queen. Does my heart good to see someone put her in her place."

"You attended school together? Didn't she live in Casper then?"

"No, her parents had a huge house in the country, so she went here," Cindy says.

"She treated everyone like dirt and didn't care. She used to enjoy stealing girls' boyfriends and tossing them aside. Had a fresh one every month," Georgia says.

"Oh!" Cindy says, pointing at Georgia. "Remember when Misty ran against her for homecoming queen, and Misty's purse fell off the platform during the assembly? Then the principal picked it up, and a bunch of condoms fell out. All these little foil packets scattered across the floor. There must have been a dozen of them. Then he pulled out a vibrator sticking out of the purse, and Misty was close to fainting. I can still hear Jill in her oh-so-sweet voice saying, 'Oh my. Are those yours, Misty? How embarrassing for you.' The principal stood there holding the vibrator out like he'd never seen one."

"I know, it was unreal," Georgia says, fighting laughter. "Misty grabbed her purse and ran off crying, and the principal ran behind her, holding out the vibrator and calling her name. She locked herself in the janitor's closet and wouldn't come out until everyone left for the day. It devastated her, and she even moved to her grandmother's in Colorado to finish school."

"Well, it doesn't mean I can act horrible. I still don't know why I did it. I'm sure Jason will be livid when he hears."

"He'll laugh it off like he does most things," Cindy says with a wave of her hand. "It's not like you put gasoline in his diesel truck." She saunters off through the back door, giggling as she disappears.

Georgia glances at me. "What'd she say?"

"Not sure, um…oh, look at the time. I have reports. 'Bye for now." I head for my office.

"I'll find out. You'll see," I hear as the door closes behind me.

I stay in my office, trying to concentrate on work, but it's hard. I can't believe what I said to Jill. I never act that way. Even when kids in school made fun of my clothes and all, I never lashed out at them. Why this time? Why does she bother me so much? It makes little sense. I know she's not the most pleasant person to be around, but that doesn't give me the right to antagonize her. It's close to 2:30 and the puppies' feeding time.

Terri comes in right on cue carrying their box and sets it on the floor. She also has the three bottles for them. "Thought you might want to feed them in here." Bob is struggling to get to me, and she grabs him, handing him over.

"I guess you heard I wasn't nice to Jill?" Bob is on the bottle in an instant.

"I wouldn't worry. She can take care of herself. Plus, if she didn't want to run into you, why come in even with the doc's truck not here? She'd have known he wasn't here."

"You mean you think she came in here to confront me?"

"Seems obvious to me. She didn't even leave the pie. I wouldn't sweat it any." She's now feeding both girls on her lap. They're still so tiny.

"Well, I guess you might be right, but I shouldn't have acted the way I did. Anyway, I can't change it now. I hope Jason doesn't get mad."

"With you? Yeah, right." She rolls her eyes. "Like that's ever gonna happen."

"What do you mean? He's gotten mad at me. Why wouldn't he?"

"Like when you filled his tank with gasoline instead of diesel? Sure, he was so mad he wouldn't even tell anyone what happened. He must have been livid."

Things keep getting worse. "Well, if he didn't tell anyone, how do you know?" I demand.

"My dad owns the garage the docs use. Doc Withers needed to

explain what happened so they could fix it. Dad said the guys in the shop got a hoot over it. Doc Withers still wouldn't tell them who did it. My dad called to make sure it wasn't me. Don't worry. I only told Cindy because she heard me on the phone."

"Yeah, I figured. I guess I can still show my face around town. Except for all the other rumors. For what it's worth, I can assure you Jason was distraught when he heard about the gasoline. He squeezed the steering wheel so hard I thought it might break. Wouldn't even glance my way."

"Yet, never raised his voice, I bet. Talked slow and even," she says, smiling.

"Yeah. How did you know?"

"Because that's how he talked to Doc Carin the time she did it."

"What? Carin did the same thing? How? Wasn't she raised around trucks?"

"She drove the Excursion you drive now. One day, she needed to leave in a hurry and another truck was blocking hers, so she took Doc Wither's. When she saw it was low on fuel, she stopped to fill it, forgetting it took diesel. Like you, she filled the one, but unlike when you did it, the truck was using the tank she filled. The engine blew after a few miles."

"What happened?"

"She called Doc Withers, and I heard him ask her in a steady voice, 'You did what?' Then he got quiet for a long time before he told her he was sending help. He put the phone away, took a deep breath, and stood silent for several minutes. When I asked what happened, he turned and told me, in a quiet tone, to call my dad and tell him to send a tow truck to Carin, five miles the other side of Glenrock on highway twenty-five. Then he went in his office, closing the door."

"What happened?"

"Nothing. When Doc Carin got back, he asked her, again in a quiet voice I might add, if she was okay and finished what she needed to do. Then he left to check on the truck."

"Were they able to fix it?"

"In a way. Once he talked with my dad, he called the dealer in Casper and bought a new one. That's what he's driving now. To be honest, the other one was old with a lot of miles on it."

"So that's why he was laughing so hard," I say, but more to myself.

"What do you mean?" She's setting the girls in their box. There's no way Bob is going back in yet, so I leave him on my lap.

"After he found out what happened, he was quiet, but then

started snickering a little and laughing. When I asked him what was funny, he stopped and told me it was nothing, but after a few minutes, he started again. When I asked a second time, he said it was because he realized he couldn't meet Jill. I bet he was remembering the time with Carin."

"I'm sure he was." Terri struggles to speak, she's laughing so hard. After a few moments, she settles. "However, the best part was, once he got back with the new truck, he wanted to discuss with her how it happened. He couldn't understand how she didn't see all the markings that said 'Diesel Only.' I remember him listing off where they were. He even suggested writing Ford, explaining their oversight to them. I'll never forget what Doc Carin replied. She turned to him and said, 'Great, you agree, it wasn't my fault. Now we're getting somewhere.' Without another word, she turned and left. He stood there, shaking his head."

"You're kidding?" I'm able to get out through my laughter. "I told him the same thing."

"No way? I bet it threw him for a loop."

"It might have even been the same words. No wonder he started laughing so hard. I didn't think he'd ever stop."

"That's crazy. It must have been like déjà vu. I can't even imagine it."

Right then, there's a knock on the door. It opens to reveal Jason standing in the doorway. "What are they doing in here?" He doesn't seem pleased. "Terri? Aren't they supposed to be in the kennels?"

This causes me to give a huff worthy of Bob. "I asked her to bring them in here for their feeding. It's easier with two people, and I needed to get something done online. It's my fault, so yell at me if you must."

"I'm not yelling at anyone. I know in a few weeks when we find homes for them, you might have a hard time letting them go is all. Have they finished?"

"Ah, yes. All finished," Terri answers and takes Bob from me before putting him back in the box. He makes a point of making his displeasure known. She takes the box and heads for the doorway where Jason is standing. "I'll take them back." I can't believe how quick she disappears.

He closes the door, glaring at me. "What did I tell you about getting attached to those puppies?"

"I know, but they're so cute, and I'm not cold-hearted like other people. I'll be okay when they leave, I promise. In the meantime, they need to know they're loved. They don't have a mommy or a daddy to take care of them, remember?"

"Shush, I don't know why I bother. Guess we'll see. It will be bad enough with Tyler letting them go. Don't need another softy making it even harder." He pauses for a few moments, avoiding eye contact with me. "Do you have a minute?"

"Sure, what do you need? Oh, first though, how's the truck?"

"The garage is working on it. It will take a few days to make sure the system is void of any gasoline, but they're confident there was no damage."

"Oh, that's splendid news. I feel better now. What did you need?"

"I'm glad too." Not sure he is. "I thought we might need to talk."

"About what?"

"About what happened."

"What happened when?"

"This weekend."

"Concerning what?" I can't help but think this might be fun.

"We were stranded in the wilderness, remember?"

"Yes, I remember. So?"

"An overnight stranding, with the two of us, alone."

"I was there, you know." I'm trying to keep an innocent expression.

"We were stranded alone, overnight, the two of us, together with no one else."

"That's all true. So?"

"Well, people might get the wrong idea and think something happened."

"Something did happen."

The panicked expression on his face is priceless. "What? No, nothing happened. Nothing at all."

I state with emphasis, "I beg to differ." It's hard to keep from smiling.

"No, it didn't. What do you think happened?"

"We were stranded together alone in the wilderness overnight. Isn't that what you said?"

"Well, yes, but nothing, you know...happened."

"I don't know about you, but in my mind our overnight stranding was something. Is there anything else?"

"What? No, I mean nothing else happened."

"We talked, we ate, we talked more, we watched the horses. I think a lot happened."

"Yeah, but besides all those things. Nothing else, you know, happened." It's clear he doesn't want to be any more specific. This is hilarious. "I don't want people to get the wrong idea."

"Correct, nothing else happened...other than us sleeping together. How could they get the wrong idea?" I present the sweetest innocent smile.

His stunned expression is perfect. "See! That's what I mean. You make it sound like something other than what it was."

"How?"

"By saying we slept together. People might take it wrong."

"How? It was nighttime, and we slept. End of story."

"Yes. That's all it was. We slept." He's calming a little. Too soon for that.

"Together..."

"What?"

"We slept together. Like, beside each other. Didn't we?" I could keep doing this all day. What fabulous entertainment.

"No!"

"We didn't? Weren't we together and didn't we sleep? How else would you say it other than we slept together?"

His frustration level appears near its peak. "Why do I even try? Fine. Whatever. Have it your way." He stands to go.

"Oh, by the way, do you want me to write the letter?"

He appears confused. "What letter?"

"The one to Ford on their oversight in the 'Diesel Only' markings?" How I don't burst out laughing, I'll never know. He freezes, peering at me in disbelief. "Well? Do you want me to write it?"

He shakes his head, raises his arms, and turns to leave, saying, "You're nuts. You're all nuts."

"That's a no on the letter then?"

Chapter Twelve

The rest of the afternoon goes by quickly. I'm still basking from my talk with Jason when I notice it's after 5:00. Close to the puppies' feeding time. Not wanting anyone to get in trouble for bringing them to me, I head for the kennel room.

When I arrive, Richard and Cassie, the new assistant, are feeding the other animals. I take my regular seat while getting Bob and wait for them to finish. Cassie gets the pups' bottles ready, and Richard grabs his bag, He heads for the door while I get Bob started and Cassie feeds Lindy and Mindy. All are comfortable.

Cassie states out of the blue, "I hear you and the doc are a couple now."

"What? No! Who told you that?"

"No one, but you spent the weekend with him in Guernsey," she says with a sly smile.

I start to correct her when Jason arrives. "Great, you're still here," he says. "Can I get a ride to Sadie's?"

"Sure, but why do you need to go there?"

"To get her truck. Mine will be in the shop for a few days, so I'm borrowing hers."

"Oh, okay. When do you want to leave?"

"Once you finish pampering the royal freeloaders, I guess. Meet you at the truck." He heads out.

"It's an SUV, not a truck, and they're not freeloaders," I get out before the door closes.

"You sure sound like a couple to me," Cassie says, putting the girls back into the box.

"We're not a couple."

"No, not at all." Her voice drips with sarcasm. "I need to help

Richard feed the others so better hurry. Anyway, you don't want to keep your other half waiting." She's gone before I can reply. Guess I deserved it after what I put Jason through.

I make sure the puppies are resting before going out to meet Jason. Once outside, I see he's standing beside my SUV with his arms crossed. After I double click the unlock button, he opens his door while glaring my way. After storing my belongings inside, I take my seat.

"I can't believe you locked it." He's shaking his head.

"Hey, you can take the girl out of the city…"

"I know, I know, but you can't take the city out of the girl. Ha. Do you not trust anyone?"

"Locked doors keep honest people honest. I'm helping my fellow man." I pull out and notice he's still shaking his head.

We're soon on Cole Creek Road. Jason's quiet during the drive. Maybe I took things a little too far. At Sadie's, I drive 'round to the back, parking next to her truck so he doesn't have far to walk.

I watch him get his bags together. "You okay?"

"Yeah, fine." He never even glances my way.

"You sure? You're being quiet."

"Tired, I guess. I'll see you tomorrow." He gets out and shuts the door. Right then, Sadie appears in the doorway, saying something but I can't hear her exact words. Jason motions for me to wait and comes back. "She says she has questions about her computer and needs your help." Without another word, he walks to Sadie's truck.

I give her a wave and turn the engine off before jumping out. As I reach the back door, I notice Jason backing farther than he needs to until he's right beside me, then he opens the passenger window. "By the way, the diesel markings are noticeable all over the truck, and we slept in the truck together. Not together in the truck," he says before speeding away.

"What got into him?" It's Sadie, and I'm chuckling at his bizarre behavior.

"Oh, nothing. Maybe in a hurry to get Tyler. Now, I believe you have questions?"

"Yes, I do," she says, leading me inside.

I follow her to the computer. "About what?"

I help her and am about to leave when she tells me I must stay for dinner. Knowing arguing with her is useless, I stay. We have a delightful meal and conversation, but it's getting late.

"Sadie, dinner was superb, but I need to go. I have work to do before bed," I say while clearing the dishes.

"I'll get those, dear. You're my company."

"As you say, the cook never clears. Have a seat, and I'll put these in the dishwasher."

"Okay, but I'll put the leftovers away. You don't know where to put them."

"Like in the refrigerator? You're right, I'd never be able to figure out such a complicated appliance. It's like magic."

"Keep it up, young lady, and you might find yourself not invited to dinner again," she says, wagging a finger my direction.

"Yes, ma'am."

"That's better." She smiles, but it quickly fades. "I read your blog from this week. It must have been terrible having to experience something like that. I'm sorry for what you went through."

"Well, I survived, and it's in the past. I came to grips with it years ago. It's funny though, sharing it this way has me remembering the pleasant times too. Most of which I'd forgotten. I feel like they'll stay with me now." After rinsing the last plate, I place it in the dishwasher, and make one last check of the kitchen to make sure I've missed nothing, I add a detergent packet from under the sink and close the door. "You want me to start it?"

"Yes, that's fine. It will finish by the time I go to bed then."

I push the start button. "Okay. It's running. You need me to do anything else before I leave?"

"What am I? A helpless old person?"

I know she's joking. I'd never dare imply she's old. At least not where she might hear me.

"Well, you're not young, that's for sure." I can't help but giggle.

"All right. That's enough from you, missy. What time you getting me tomorrow?"

"Do you want to go for lunch before the meeting?"

"Splendid idea. The Paisley Shawl in Glenrock okay?"

"Works for me. I'll swing by around noon. How does that sound?"

"Perfect." She helps me with my coat, checks to make sure my scarf is correct, and hands me my purse and bag. Once I'm set, she gives me an enormous hug. "You drive careful and watch out for the slick spots."

"I will. You take care, and I'll see you tomorrow. We'll have a delightful afternoon."

She holds the door open and watches me start down the steps. "It should be after your run-in with Jill today. Wouldn't miss it for the world."

I spin back, mouth agape, but she already has the storm door shut and is smiling like she said nothing. Still in disbelief, I drive home. I'd like to know how she heard.

Again, the dreariness of the place hits me as I enter, and I remember my idea of buying things to brighten it. Maybe we can tick a few items off the list tomorrow?

I'm soon changed, and my soft, oversized flannel shirt is enveloping my body. I open the laptop while getting my phone set. Once it's up, I review the comments on my blog. There are more than usual. I read through them and try to answer what I can. This keeps me busy until I feel my eyelids drooping. I need to get to bed. Time to call it a night.

With the lights off, I fall into bed, closing my eyes. I'm ready for a decent night's sleep, but the shrill ringing of my phone causes me to bolt upright. With my heart hammering from the jolt, I grab it, squinting against the bright light. I can't believe who's calling. It's he who will remain nameless.

I let it ring, unable to tear my gaze away from the name displayed. Why on earth is he calling me now? I'm sure he didn't even think about the time—not that he'd care, anyway. I let it ring. He can leave a message. I lie back and drift into a peaceful sleep. What's-his-name is already long forgotten. Yeah, right!

~ * ~

My alarm sounds, and I silence it. With phone in hand, I notice a voicemail icon sitting in the notifications. I delete it without even listening. Boy, that felt great. Next, I go to my contacts and delete the entry. Last, I block the number. Now I'm ready for my day.

After soaking in my luxurious miniaturized tub, I wash my hair, taking extra time afterward to style it. Not sure why? My normal for the clinic is to tie it back, but I feel like doing something different today. I select an outfit I bought as a gift to myself when I received my graduate degrees. It's a Ralph Lauren suit and cost more than most of my other clothes combined. It's a dark blue jacket and skirt with silver threads for highlights, and the skirt has a split to mid-thigh, showing the silver lining underneath. I pair it with a silver silk blouse and matching blue stiletto heels with silver trim. For now—despite how ridiculous they seem—I have on boots. I'll change to the heels at work.

The knee-length coat I put on gives my outfit an elegant yet professional finish. Yes, this will work. Of course, my mind has to have its say. Who is it supposed to work for? Shaking my head, I make sure I have everything and head for the office.

Once there, I change into the heels straight away. Now for the puppies. As I pass through the lobby, I start the coffee and Stanley appears. Is that a judgmental expression? "It's nothing. Wanted to do something different," I say while checking he has water. Making my way to the kennel room, I feel his hypercritical eyes following me.

Andi has Mindy when I arrive. "You better hurry with Bob, he's having a fit," she says while spinning her chair around to face me. "Wow. What's the occasion?"

"What? Oh, you mean the suit. It's Tuesday, so I'm taking Sadie to the women's meeting and we're having lunch first. I wanted something I hadn't worn in a while. It's nothing special." I hope this sounds convincing enough. I drape a towel across my lap as a precaution. Bob can get excited.

"Nothing special, huh? Hanging in the back of your closet. Yeah, right." She's smirking. "You may fool a few people with that, but I know a designer outfit when I see one. Come on now, whose is it?"

"It's a Ralph Lauren, if you must know."

"Did you get it in Boston?" She feels the material. "It's so soft, and those shoes. I don't think I could even walk in those."

"No, I got it in New York when I finished college. I needed something for going on interviews."

"Bet those were excellent interviews. Did you get it at Bloomingdale's? I so want to go there."

"No. It wasn't Bloomingdale's. Anyway, don't you have class?" I'm hoping to change the subject.

"Nope, it's labs today. All my projects are complete, no need to go. Where did you buy it?"

"I'm not sure I remember."

"Don't give me that. You know. Now where was it?" she demands.

"Okay, it was Saks Fifth Avenue."

"You're kidding? Wait till Doc Withers sees you. He'll flip."

"I doubt it. Besides, Jason's doing house calls today. I won't even see him."

She stares at me, wide-eyed. "You knew the doc wouldn't be here and you wore it anyway?"

"Why not? I'm not wearing it because of him. I thought it would be nice for lunch with Sadie." Be quiet mind. It's the truth.

Andi finishes with Lindy and puts her back in the box before going to feed our other residents. I return Bob to his box, making sure I don't wake him. Putting the towel back on the counter, I turn to leave. As I go out, I hear Andi behind me gasp.

"I got it. You're wearing it because Jill will be at the meeting. You're going to show her up, aren't you? Come on, I'm right, aren't I?"

"Don't be ridiculous." Busted! "I wanted to wear something

different is all," I say and turn to leave.

"Sure, and you styled your hair for the same reason." She's still snickering after the door closes.

With as much conviction as possible, I remind myself I didn't wear this to impress Jill. Well, I didn't.

I busy myself pouring coffee while trying to push these thoughts away. I notice Stanley is glaring at me. "I wanted to wear something different. That's all there is to it," I tell him, heading for my office.

My major task is to sort through the old files I still need to transfer. After what feels like five minutes later—although it's been several hours—it's time to get Sadie. I stop in the restroom to check my hair and straighten several creases in my skirt before heading out. Thanks to the parking area being kept clear of snow, the heels don't cause any problems as I walk to the SUV.

Sadie is waiting when I turn into her drive.

"Good morning." she says, getting into her seat.

"Good morning to you!"

"I like your hair. The style frames your face well."

I'm amazed how happy this makes me. "Thought I'd do it a little different."

"I'll admit, it's different. Now, Paisley Shawl?"

"Is there any other place?"

"I can already taste the Portobello fries."

"We're on the way."

We chat while I drive and find ourselves in Glenrock in no time. I stop in front of the hotel where the restaurant is. I don't usually use the valet parking, but I make an exception. The valet helps Sadie out, and I hand him the keys. Once inside, I help her remove her coat and hang it on the rack, then do the same with mine. Now we're ready for lunch.

She motions to my outfit. "Oh, my. Is that new?"

"No, I got it when I finished college."

"Well, it's perfect on you. Even beyond perfect."

"Thank you. I like it."

"Those heels complement the outfit. You chose an excellent day for it." She turns to the server who's appeared to greet us. "Sam, my usual table please."

"What do you mean? Why is this an excellent day?"

"Because we're here. Why else?"

I'm not sure that is what she meant. The server hands us our menus, and another is filling our water glasses while we choose what we want to eat. The menus are on the large side, but I enjoy perusing the offerings. The sound of a familiar female voice makes me realize not being able to see over the top of one's menu isn't always an outstanding thing.

"Sadie, I didn't expect to see you today. Did you come with Jason?" The insincere words belong to Jill. I feel her gaze burning through my menu, desperate to get a glimpse of the person behind it. As I lower my menu, her hopeful expression changes when she recognizes my eyes are peering over the top, not Jason's.

"No, I'm with Jazmine. We're making an afternoon of it. Are you expecting Jason?"

Jill looks at me. "Well, yes, Jason and I have a lunch date. We're discussing plans for the Spring Rodeo Days with the mayor. Have you seen him?" She breaks her glare at me and turns to Sadie, smiling.

Sadie glances at her with an innocent expression. "Seen whom? The mayor?"

Even I know Jill didn't mean the mayor.

"No, Sadie. Have you seen Jason? I hope something dreadful doesn't keep him from coming like the last time. We so enjoy our times together." It's slight, but I'm sure she curled her upper lip at me. "You have a pleasant lunch, Sadie," she says. Turning on her heel and with her chin in the air, Jill struts off to the far side of the room.

"Did you know she would be here?" I ask.

"Now, dear, how would I know?"

She has her ever-innocent expression, which I've learned is anything but. "Sadie, what are you up to?"

"Lunch, dear. Didn't we come here for lunch?"

"Yes, and you better hope it's nothing more."

"You're the one who invited me. What else could it be?"

Again, I recognize her innocent smile.

We order what I expected. She has the steak stir fry, and I have the chicken parmesan. For starters, Sadie has her Portobello fries, and I have chilled shrimp. With the house salads, this will be all I need today.

I don't know where Jill is sitting, but I feel her glaring at me from somewhere inside the restaurant. I need to put her out of my mind. A gentleman enters dressed in a nice suit with a western cut. It goes well with the Stetson he's carrying.

"Sadie," he says, approaching our table. "I can't believe it. I knew this would be a magnificent day when I woke this morning."

"Oh, Mayor, you're always the perfect politician." She stands and shakes his hand, and I follow suit. "This is my neighbor, Jazmine. She works with Jason and was nice enough to have lunch with me."

"Oh, yes, the young lady from Harvard. Welcome to our town."

"Thank you, sir." I'm thinking of something else to say when a shrill voice cuts across the room.

"Mayor, we're over here," it squeals. Jill is rising from her table, waving her hands in the mayor's direction.

In her excitement, she bumps her glass of red wine and tries to catch it before it hits the table. Amidst her panic to catch the glass, she knocks over the bottle. Jill stares in horror at the mass of red stains covering her beautiful cream dress. It's not a pretty sight.

"Noooo!" she screams, and two servers hurry across with towels and start dabbing her dress, much to Jill's apparent frustration. "Stop it! You're making it worse. I can't believe you'd furnish this place with such rickety tables. I thought this was an upmarket venue," she says, shooing them away.

"Ms. Carmine, I'm sure it was an accident," the mayor says, rushing over.

"Accident? You call this an accident? With this wonky table and the server filling the glasses so full, it was a disaster waiting to happen. Look at my dress. It's ruined. The owners will hear from me before the day is out."

Using her purse to cover what she can of her stained dress, she storms out of the dining room, all the while promising to lodge a serious complaint. I hide my smile, noticing the trail of wine drops she leaves in her wake.

"Well, that didn't go so well," says the mayor, returning to our table. "At least not in her case. For me, to be honest, it's worked out excellent. May I join you ladies?"

"We would cherish the opportunity," Sadie says while motioning to a server. "Sam, bring two more place settings, please. Jason should be here soon, and he and the mayor will join us for lunch," she tells him.

"Right away, ma'am."

Jason walks in, and our eyes meet. He smiles and makes his way to our table. "Hello, Jazmine, Sadie, Mayor. Did I see Jill rushing out?"

"Yes, she suffered a slight altercation with a bottle of wine and needed to leave, so the mayor joined us. You sit by Jazmine," Sadie says.

Somehow, I know she knew they were meeting here today.

"Okay." While sitting, Jason gazes at me questioningly. "Did you do something different with your hair?"

I can't believe he noticed. "Yes, wanted to add a little curl."

"Doesn't she look nice, Jason? You should see her suit. Don't you think it lights up her face?"

Sadie is pushing, and I give her a glare, but she averts it. The servers bring the extra place settings, organizing the cutlery in front of

Jason and the mayor. They must come here often since they order "the usual."

Everyone soon forgets Jill's minor incident, and the mayor turns to me. "What do you think of our fair town, Ms. Strake?"

I'm stunned he knows my last name. Sadie didn't use it when she introduced us. "Oh, please, Jazmine is fine. It's delightful. I've met several marvelous people."

"Well, Sadie here is one of our best. You can't go wrong being friends with her. I hear you're doing a fantastic job at the clinic."

"Thank you, sir. I'm trying my best, but Stephanie left a huge void to fill."

"You keep doing what you're doing, and Moose Ridge might even join the twenty-first century."

"That's enough, thank you," Jason says as our starters arrive.

Both men tuck into jalapeno poppers and seem to enjoy them. The three of them talk while I listen to their discussion concerning the town. The mayor is gracious while Sadie explains things he needs to get done. Soon, our salads arrive, followed by our main courses. The men both have rib-eye steaks. Should have known.

It's an enjoyable lunch, and the mayor is engaging and sociable, but then again, he is a politician.

"Well, I can't remember the last time I had lunch with such charming company," the mayor says once we've finished eating. "However, I have a full afternoon and must go. Miss Jazmine, welcome again, and I hope to see more of you. Sadie, always a pleasure and wish it was more often. Now, you all have a magnificent afternoon. Jason, I'm sure we'll reschedule once Ms. Carmine lets us know when she's available."

When the mayor stands to leave, Jason gets to his feet and shakes his hand. Once he's gone, Jason retakes his seat, and we continue our conversation.

When the check arrives on a small silver tray, he insists on paying. I try to argue, but Sadie will have none of it. After leaving enough money to cover the bill, plus a generous tip, he helps her with her chair and hurries around to assist me with mine. Before I can explain I can manage well on my own, I get a glare from Sadie. Smiling, I tell him thank you.

"Now you can see her suit better. Isn't she charming?"

"Yes, she is," Jason says. What else could he answer?

"Thank you, sir, and thank you for lunch too. Sadie, we better get going, or we'll be late for your meeting." I accompany my statement with a stern glare of my own, but she ignores it.

The valet takes my ticket and leaves to get the SUV while we get our coats. Jason holds Sadie's for her, then mine for me. "Are you going back on calls?" I'm determined to break the tension before we leave.

"You know I am. You know my schedule better than I do."

Sadie can't resist. "Well, she's being an excellent helper. That's what she's here for, isn't it?"

Why did she phrase it like she did? The SUV arrives, and Jason assists Sadie in while I go to my side.

"Be careful on the road, and I'll see you tomorrow morning," he says, glancing toward me.

"Tomorrow afternoon, you mean. You're seeing the Jeffersons in the morning."

"See what I mean?" he says, smiling.

"You get on now," Sadie says. "You have work to do. Don't forget, dinner tomorrow."

"Yes, ma'am. We'll be there."

I start the engine and head for the community center. What will Jill wear since her previous outfit fell victim to an attack of clumsy behavior?

It turns out I didn't have to wonder. Jill is absent from today's gathering. The vice chair handles the meeting and tells everyone Jill could not attend. This is a blessing. The meeting goes so well, I'm staggered when it's announced we're done for the day, but it's right on time. I chat with the others, several of whom comment on my outfit. Sadie must share it's a Ralph Lauren I got for finishing my graduate degrees. I notice she enunciates "degrees" in its plural form and never explains I bought it myself. What am I going to do with her?

After the meeting we head off for our afternoon of shopping. A wave of unexpected excitement fills me at the thought of buying a few items to enhance my place.

Chapter Thirteen

After a long day, I return to the house, but the drab dullness no longer hits me. It's still small and not decorated, but I have items to make improvements.

I pass through the kitchen to start the coffee and on to my soon-to-be gorgeous bedroom to change into my writing uniform: my luscious warm flannel shirt and a pair of thick socks. In my defense, my flannel shirt is by far the most comfortable piece of clothing I own. I even bought two more today.

Once changed, I unpack my purchases. I throw a quilted spread across the couch, with matching pillows. The drapes, sheers, and tablecloth for the small table share the same bright color scheme. I also got a few rugs—one big one for in front of the couch, and three others for by the front door and along the hallway.

However, the best is the bed linen. What's-his-name was never into stylish things, so my old ones were rather plain. Not now. It's burgundy and cream with a lot of lace trimming. There's a bed ruffle, pillow shams, sheets in each color, and a reversible comforter. Now this is a lady's room.

Last night, while reviewing my blog, I couldn't believe how many people were already following it. There were a lot of requests for the next section, and I decide to post twice a week—my usual one on Sunday and another on Wednesday. That means I have two nights to write the next installment. I'd better get started.

The Rich Girl's Poor Life
Foster Care or Foster Slave?

One day after school, as I enter the children's

home, Ms. Willows calls out my name and says to follow her. When we reach the office, there's another lady there I've never met.

"Tiffany, Ms. Erickson with Social Services is here. She'll be taking you to a different place to live," Ms. Willows says.

This catches me by surprise. "I'm moving?" It's been six months since I arrived, and no one mentioned moving elsewhere.

"Yes, dear," Ms. Erickson says. "I've found a foster home willing to take you. They have two small daughters but feel they have room for a girl your age. Go pack your things, and I'll take you there."

"Now? I'm moving right now?"

"Yes. Now be quick. We have little time."

With no other option, I hurry to retrieve my suitcases from the storage room but only find two. I know I came with three but can't find the third. The other kids are outside, so I'm alone when I get to the ward. With my suitcases open on my bed I pack my things from the dresser I share with three others. This fills two-thirds of one suitcase. I add the two pairs of shoes I still have and go to the closet for my hanging clothes. The two suitcases are more than enough because a lot of my clothes have gone missing since I arrived.

My toiletries are last, and I load my books and other things into my backpack. I start to cry, realizing everything I have in the world fits in two suitcases and a backpack, but I fight back the tears. I learned soon after my arrival tears waste energy and solve nothing.

With my backpack on, I grab my suitcases, knowing there's no one to help, and head downstairs. I don't say goodbye to anyone, since there's no one who cares I'm leaving.

"There you are. I thought I told you we're in a hurry?" Ms. Erickson says as I reach the bottom of the steps. "My car's out front. The blue one." She's motioning toward the door. "Helen, I'll see you next time," she tells Ms. Willows.

I put a suitcase down to open the door and struggle to get my belongings outside and to the parking area. A blue car is across the lot, and I keep walking toward it.

"Put those in the trunk," she calls out, and the trunk lid opens a little.

I place my suitcases in the trunk, but hold on to my backpack; it contains the things most dear to me. Ms. Erickson arrives and tells me I can ride in front. Once in the passenger side, I fasten my seat belt. She wastes no time driving for the exit.

After six months, I'm leaving, and no one bothers to say goodbye. I wonder if anyone will even notice I'm gone.

We drive in silence for a long time before reaching a residential area. The streets are similar, with identical rows of houses along each side. Ms. Erickson stops in front of one. "Here we are. Your foster parents are Sid and Martha Kingston. They're agreeable people, and I'm sure you'll like it here. I'll be by to check on you. Now, get your things and go meet them."

I climb out of the car as a gentleman exits the front door. A lady is standing inside the screen door with two small girls peeking out around her legs. When I reach the trunk, Ms. Erickson has already hit the release to open it. By this time, the man is beside me and grabbing the suitcases.

"I'll get these. You go meet my wife, Martha," he tells me. I follow his instructions. He stays back and talks with Ms. Erickson, but she's driving off at speed before I reach the front door.

The lady opens the screen door so I can enter, and her husband is right behind me. "Two suitcases," she says. "I wasn't expecting so much, but it helps. What we get for you living here won't pay for many clothes. Your bed's in the basement. Sid, show her the way and get her situated. Hurry back, it's late, and dinner is ready." She turns her back on me and walks into the house.

This is my welcome.

The man leads me to an unfinished basement. There's a washing machine and dryer on one wall with a large sink beside them. He holds back a curtain hanging in the doorway. This must be my door. I enter, examining my room. It's a small, gray cell, from the cold cement floor to the bare cinder block walls. Exposed floor joists decorate the ceiling. A wooden crate on its side serves as a nightstand beside a cot, with a makeshift desk and chair on the other side. An old dresser sits on the opposite side of the room, with a cord stretched across the length of the wall behind it.

"We put this together so you'll have a little privacy. You can hang any clothes on the cord. There's the dresser for anything else. A toilet and shower are in the bathroom next to the washer. It should be fine. Don't unpack now. Martha has dinner ready. Leave your bags, and we'll eat." After this, he leaves.

I wish I could say it got better, but it didn't.

From here, I explain what my duties were while living with the Kingstons. I was there to take care of the two girls. Each morning, after getting myself ready, I'd get them up, dressed, and fed, before Martha took them to daycare, or later on to school. After I got home from school, I'd watch them and do any chores the Kingstons gave me. At nighttime, I'd help the girls change and put them to bed. On Saturdays, I did the laundry for everyone while also watching the girls when needed. Sundays were my own, but I couldn't leave the house or have any visitors without permission. Many times, I'd watch the girls if their parents went out.

I write how I understood I was there to take care of the girls for food and a place to sleep. It was room and board in place of pay. I explain how much I enjoyed watching the girls grow and spending time with them at Christmas and birthdays. They were the one bright spot in my life. Lying in my makeshift room each night, with nothing but the sounds of the heater turning on and off to distract me, I knew I was the outsider. They weren't my family, and this wasn't my home. I was the hired help.

I describe how the next few years went and cover Mr. Mackey stopping by during my fourth year. I was excited, thinking he's there to share my father was being paroled. Instead, he told me my father was injured trying to break up a fight and died earlier in the week. The next day he drove me to the cemetery for the small service beside my mother's grave. On the return drive, Mr. Mackey explained there were funds available to me after my eighteenth birthday. They were to be used for college, but included restrictions, and he needed to review these before explaining more. While dropping me off, he promised to get back to me soon.

I write about how I couldn't sleep that night. My mind was full of thoughts of college. Of having a life I controlled. Did I dare dream of a life where I was free to make my own choices? To wake each morning knowing I was in charge of my decisions? I remember being surprised when the alarm went off, but I didn't care I hadn't slept. There was a future for me. Something to look forward to. A month went by, and then another, and no Mr. Mackey. I settled back in, knowing I was foolish to dream of any life beyond what I had.

I explain how, in the spring of my last year with the Kingstons, Mr. Mackey came back. He'd been ill and apologized for being away so long. He also shared he had everything set for me. He told me my mother's father made a trust fund for my college, but the funds were only for one of two colleges. Yale, where my father went, or Harvard, where my grandfather and Mr. Mackey went. This caused me concern since neither was easy to get into. He told me there was an issue with Yale because of my father's criminal history, leaving Harvard. Luckily, with my grades and scores being excellent, and with my grandfather's name and Mr. Mackey's connections, they accepted me for the fall semester.

From there, he explained how the finances would work. He would pay tuition and books directly to the school, along with the cost of my dorm and meals. I'd also get an allowance for other expenses, but he warned me I couldn't get any advances and I'd have to budget. After I completed two years, I could move off campus. If I left before completing a four-year degree, the remaining funds would go to the school. If I left after finishing my bachelor's, seventy percent of the remaining funds would go to the college. If I completed a master's, any remaining funds would be mine.

I write how his announcement was beyond anything I imagined. Also, how Mr. Mackey planned to drive me to Harvard in late August and he'd be controlling the funds. Ending this section, I mention asking the Kingstons if I could stay through the summer. It thrilled them to keep me for another few months.

Delighted with what I've written tonight, I decide to review it again tomorrow. For now, since I have work in the morning, its bedtime. I power off my laptop, excited at the thought of spending my first night in my fresh bedding, and I'm soon wrapped in my fancy sheets and comforter.

As I lay my head on my pillow, I remember what it felt like learning I was going to Harvard. All the excitement fills me again. The anticipation of knowing my dream life would be within my grasp. The exhilaration of knowing I would decide what my future would be. The euphoria of knowing I would now be the priority in my own life. One of the few positive times I remember in my life. The overwhelming joy I experienced resurfaces and overtakes my body as I succumb to my exhaustion from the day. However, it's not long until my thoughts turn to how depressing my life turned out. The tears aren't far behind.

~ * ~

My week is normal from here. I post my latest section of the blog on Wednesday and spend Thursday with Sadie doing laundry. Friday is the typical workday with no surprises. I'm getting better at driving the Excursion. I also named it Boris—it suits him. The win of the week is my normal depressing Friday evening is canceled when Cindy calls to invite me to the movies at the Casper Mall with her and Terri. We have dinner and do a little window shopping. Okay, okay, actual shopping, but they made me.

I find two outfits for work. They have both skirts and slacks with the jacket. It's like getting four outfits instead of two, and with the different blouses I bought there are even more options. Then I spot a dress and fall in love. It's a breathtaking cocktail dress in glittering black lace. They talk me into trying it on, but the three they have on the rack aren't my size. The clerk is quick to get a smaller size from the window. As I stand before the mirror, scrutinizing the dress, I know it's perfect. Even with boots.

The ladies love it and I decide to buy it so I don't disappoint them. While waiting to pay, I wonder what I'm doing. It's not like I have anyplace to wear such a dress, but it's so beautiful, and it's been such a long time since I treated myself to anything like this. Leaving the store, I take everything straight out to Boris, making sure not to glance in any other windows on the way. Well, okay, except for the shoe store, but it's not my fault. They have the cutest heels on display. They're perfect for the dress. I have no choice. It would be sacrilege not to get them.

The movie and the rest of the evening are brilliant, and I enjoy spending time with Terri and Cindy outside of work. Are we becoming friends? Something new for me.

~ * ~

With it being Saturday morning and having little planned, I sleep late. Once awake, I don't even change out of my flannel shirt to work on my blog. Adding my thick socks, I'm ready to go.

With the coffee brewing, I get a bowl of cereal and boot the laptop to check out my group. There are new members and mentions of my blog. After commenting on a few, I chat with several regulars. I still haven't shared about the night I spent with Jason or the events following. Not sure why?

After draining what I realize is my second mug of coffee, I know

I need to stop wasting time with the group and move on to my blog. I post a quick message saying I'll catch them later, refill my coffee, and get set. This might be an emotional rollercoaster ride as I write about how I met he who will remain nameless.

The Rich Girl's Poor Life
College Bound

My first semester at Harvard flies by. I'm enjoying myself and share a room with three girls. Two are pre-law, and the other is a literature major. Meaning, not a lot in common other than we're freshman and committed to our studies. I'm glad for this. We spend most of our time in class, in our room studying, or in the library, with stops at the cafeteria.

There's another student who seems to spend as much time in the library as I do. He normally sits a few tables away, and we'll say hi sometimes. We've shared names, and I jokingly think of him as my study buddy.

It's hard work, but I'm able to maintain my grades. My three roommates go home for the holidays, but I stay on campus. It's vacant, and I spend most days at the library preparing for the next semester. My study buddy is about the only other student here besides me. After the usual greeting, we find our isolated spots.

One day, we both arrive to find the doors locked. This seems strange to me since it's still the day before Christmas. I'm about to leave when he says, "Looks like it's the two of us again. Café Pamplona is over on Harvard Square, want a ride?" Not seeing any harm in it and needing coffee anyway, I go with him.

He leads the way to a typical college student's car. I'm not sure of the year, but it's seen better days. There's even tape holding pieces of trim in place. However, I can't complain since I'm carless.

The drive isn't long, and with most students spending the break elsewhere, the shop is empty. We put our backpacks on a corner table and place our orders.

I notice he gets tea and wonder who comes to a coffee shop for tea? Shaking it off, I order my standard dark roast. After adding sugar, I go to the table and get set for studying. We say nothing else until several hours later, when he asks when I'll be ready to leave. I let him know I'm ready whenever he is.

Before we leave, I get two of their pre-made sandwiches for dinner tonight and tomorrow. The drive back is like the one there, with the exception he asks which dorm is mine. He drives me right to it, and I let him know I appreciate everything.

As I'm getting out, he says he'll catch me later. I climb the stairs to my floor and settle in for the night with my books and sandwich. Even though it's Christmas Eve, it's nothing but another night for me. I go to bed right on schedule.

In the morning, I'm awake at my usual time. This is my first Christmas without the girls, and I'm amazed how much I miss them. I sent each a card, but have heard nothing back. I'm starting in on my studying when there's a knock. Looking through the peephole, I see it's my study buddy and open the door.

"Since the cafeteria's closed today, I thought we might get breakfast. There's a Waffle House on Massachusetts Avenue. It will be open if you want to go?" Not having much else to do and thinking a hot meal would be nice, I agree. "I doubt they're swamped today, so we can hang out and study."

I pack what I need and walk out with him to his car. There are few other customers, and we spend most of the day there. The server tells us not to worry and keeps filling our cups. I buy lunch since he drove.

I cover how my year progressed and how the boy and I often studied together. I share my memories of the next year, how it followed the same pattern, and we spent the holidays together. I'd taken classes through the summer, so I was a semester ahead by this time. Meaning, the second semester was the start of my third year, and this finished my second calendar year. I explain how every month Mr. Mackey called to check how I was doing and what my plans were. He liked me moving at a faster pace and reminded me I could move off campus after the second year was complete.

I also cover how things were going with my study buddy. How he'd completed pre-med and continued on to med school. How we spent time together and went out. This was something new for me. I've never dated before, but I enjoyed being with him. I never realized how much I missed having someone around I could talk with. Someone who chose to be with me. We kept to our studies and even helped each other. The semester flew by, and it was summer break before I knew it. To prepare for moving off campus, Mr. Mackey told me what he thought was an acceptable amount to pay for renting an apartment, and I began searching.

I describe how difficult finding an accommodation within my budget and near campus was. How I thought about staying in the dorm, but wanted something that gave me more freedom and allowed visitors—which was needed because I was spending a lot of time with my study buddy and was thinking of him more as my boyfriend. Unless in class, we were pretty much always together. I write about how while checking out a place that ended not being one that would work, he mentioned his lease was up the next month. He planned on crashing at a friend's place for a few months to save money. Which meant it would be available. It was a sparsely furnished studio apartment and close to campus. Perfect. I signed the lease and moved in the next month.

Writing about how his moving in with me sort of happened, I try to explain how we were together all the time anyway. About how magnificent it was to have someone else in my life. How this brought me so much joy. I had closed off others for so long, and now there was someone to share things with. My likes, my desires, and my day. He was quieter than I was and would joke I talked too much, but even the long quiet hours we sat buried in our studies were special knowing he was there. Since the rent was within my budget, I covered it and most other living expenses. This allowed him to put his money toward tuition and kept him from having to take time off to earn money. Everyone thought we were a couple anyway, so it didn't matter.

I explain how we lived this way for the next year, and until I completed my graduate degrees. It was during this time he started his four-year medical school. He had two years left when I finished my graduate degrees, and by then, we'd grown close. I write how I couldn't remember what it was like before he came into my life. We were a genuine couple, and he was so nice to me.

I include that, for the first time, I got red roses for Valentine's Day. He was busy, so asked me to order them, and in a roundabout way I paid for them, since I split my spending allowance with him while also covering our other expenses. However, the thought was what counted to me.

There's the part on how Mr. Mackey learned of my other half and was disturbed with the arrangement when he realized I was covering most of our expenses. I never told him I was providing for all our outgoings, not to mention part of his tuition. I write how much Mr. Mackey being at my graduation meant to me and how it felt to hear how proud he was of me. He said he knew my parents would be too. He was also my sole guest. My significant other was studying for finals.

Next is about how, after completing my graduate degrees, I was hired as the office manager for an insurance firm. We moved into a one-bedroom apartment closer to the hospital while he continued his schooling. Since I'd finished school, I was no longer receiving money from my fund, but was earning a decent salary, and we made do. I didn't mind covering the bills because I knew once he finished, we'd be doing well. There was money left in the fund after graduation. Mr. Mackey recommended I open an investment account, thinking it would provide me with a start on retirement.

I write about Mr. Mackey calling me every month until he passed away right before the boy finished medical school. I attended the funeral and met his daughter and family. He was the closest thing to a parent in my life, and now he left me too. Then how, when I returned from the funeral, there was news. He who will remain nameless was accepted for a neurosurgical residency at a hospital in Casper, Wyoming. Not my first choice, but he explained how perfect it was. We started making plans for what would be a six-year program.

I follow this with how he needed to be in Casper by July, soon after medical school ended. This presented a minor problem. I was in the middle of an essential task at work and couldn't tell them I was leaving. However, he thought my staying behind for now would be better. He could get everything set for my arrival. We both knew he'd be busy at first anyway, so this was the best solution.

This section ends with me sharing how the last week before he left was special. How excited I was for this new chapter in our lives to begin, how I took the week off to spend with him and get his things packed for the move. About my giving him a check to open a bank account for us. This was one of the best weeks I ever remember having. I then cover the several months after he leaves while I counted the days. Our plan was working out, and this was only the beginning. Our life would be perfect.

I'm so absorbed in what I'm writing it's mid-afternoon when I finish. I didn't even notice the time. The memory of the last week with him and the following months of anticipation has left me, once again, feeling depressed. To remember how happy I was, how much I cared, and how I thought he cared too. How our individual dreams soon melded into one dream, with a joint goal for a life and a future for which few could even dare to hope.

I need a change. Need to get away for a little while. It's close to feeding time for the puppies, which is perfect. I grab my jeans, brush my hair, and I'm in Boris before I know it.

At the clinic, I don't see Jason's beast in the parking lot. Perfect, since I'm not what you would call presentable. I shake my head to clear this thought. I'm here for the puppies, not Jason.

Once in the kennel room, I find Andi prepping the bottles.

She has an amused smirk as I get Bob. "I knew you couldn't stay away."

"Oh, I was driving by and realized it was feeding time so thought I'd help."

"Sure you were. How fortunate for me," she says with a little sarcasm while handing me a bottle. "You're so thoughtful."

"Think what you want, but I was. How are things going here?" I want to move on to another subject, while Bob is concentrating on the bottle I'm holding.

"It's been quiet. Richard's taking care of the patients this afternoon with Doc Carson, and your doc is out on a call for a sick horse. He doesn't expect to be back until late."

"He's not my doc. You need to stop talking that way." I glance around for a few moments. "He's out on a call, huh?"

"Yes, and you know he's afraid you're getting too attached to these guys, Bob in particular. They'll be ready for adoption in a week or two. You realize that, don't you?"

"I don't know what you're going on about. I'm helping feed them. Not attached in the least." As if on cue, Bob finishes his bottle and rolls on his back so I can scratch his chest and stomach.

"Sure, not attached at all. I guess we'll see." She puts the girls back in the box. I can tell they aren't ready to be there yet, so I pet them. "Like I said, no attachment."

"Don't you have something to do?"

"No. I'm here to feed the patients."

I watch her preparing various bowls of food before putting them one by one in the cages.

Once she's done and ready to go, I know I should leave too. Putting the now sleeping Bob into his box, I tiptoe out of the room behind Andi.

"Heard you went shopping for clothes," she says as we enter the stalls area.

"Yes, at the mall last night. I wasn't planning on it, but I found a gorgeous dress. The others kept going on about how perfect it was and how it was made for me. I think I bought it to make them stop. It's not like I have any place to wear it." Right then, Stanley scampers to his drink bowl, having heard my voice.

"I meant the new suits for work, but you bought a dress too? Is it a party dress?"

I grumble to myself at the question while pouring Mountain Dew for Stanley. "Oh, the suits. Yeah, I got two, but they both have slacks and a skirt, so it's more like four," I say as Stanley is pleased to find his favorite.

"The dress?"

She will not drop it. "Well, yes, it's a party dress, and that's why it was a waste. When am I ever going to a party?"

"You never know; we're entering the holiday season. Lots of parties during the next several weeks. I bet you get invited to one. You'll see."

"Well, you can dream all you want, but I doubt it." I get my coat. "I'm heading out. You have an enjoyable weekend. See you Monday morning." I'm about to leave, but she has to make one more comment.

"I'll have the puppies' bottles ready for you tomorrow. You doing one, two, or maybe all four?" she calls while I'm making my way through the back room. She's pushing it. I have no intentions of coming here tomorrow. It would give me something to do though, and it's not like it's a lengthy drive.

Boris and I make the return without incident. Sitting at my laptop, I review what I typed and consider the possibility of splitting it into two sections.

I work through last night's writing, editing, and splitting it while I pick at my dinner. I add more about campus life and living in the dorm to balance it out. Having settled on this split format, I ponder a title for the second part. After a while, the perfect heading makes its way onto the page: *Mr. Right!*

It explains well how I felt being with him. The elation of having someone in my life. The euphoria of sharing this life with him. The joy of knowing someone cared about me. The excitement I held in my heart boarding my flight. I include everything, right until I leave for Wyoming.

There are comments on the blog itself, so I respond to those until the clock on my laptop shows it's close to eleven and time for bed.

~ * ~

Sunday morning, I lie in bed enjoying my new sheets. They're soft and warm, and I contemplate staying for the rest of the day. The thought of going to feed the puppies their breakfast crosses my mind more than once, but Andi would never let me live it down, so I stay put. That will teach her.

Knowing I won't sleep tonight if I stay much longer, I peel myself out of bed. After shuffling to the kitchen to start the coffee, I return to the bedroom. Although diving straight back between the sheets is appealing, I decide on house cleaning instead. After brushing and tying my hair back, I pull on an old pair of jeans and leave on my large shirt. This won't take long since the house isn't a mansion. In fact, I remember several mansions with porches larger than this place.

However, as the puppies' feeding time approaches, I'm finding it hard to ignore the possibility of popping in on them. Could I get away with going there in what I'm wearing? I'm sure no one will be there except Andi. No need to sweat.

Deliberation complete, I slip on my boots and parka, and grab my scarf. I arrive a few minutes later and, sure enough, Andi's truck is in its usual spot, alone. I park Boris around back so no one will know I'm here and head straight for the puppies. When I get in, Bob is trying to hoist himself out of his box. Giggling, I rush to grab him before he hurts himself. Then I spot Andi's note.

Jazmine, the bottles are in the fridge. Call me if you need
me. Now, whatever you do, don't give Stanley any Mt.
Dew. He drove me nuts last night with his dish. He kept
pushing it off the counter and making a racket. I'm glad
it's made of metal. I told him he gets no more until he
learns to behave. No Mt. Dew!

She is one hard taskmaster. I get the bottles out and start the feeding. Bob's done so fast it's comical. He settles while I rub his stomach and finish with Mindy. I trade her for Lindy, who latches onto the bottle like no one has fed her for days.

Once she finishes, I rub her tummy for a few minutes. As I put her in the box, I hear a noise from elsewhere in the clinic. Thinking it's Andi or Jake, I turn my attention back to the sleeping puppies.

Seconds later, I hear Jason's voice. "You can play with them for a few minutes. I've got to check a few things, then we need to leave."

I remember how I'm dressed. This must be a cruel nightmare. What did he mean by "we" anyway? I get my answer when the door opens, and Tyler pops his head through.

"Jazmine? Hey, Dad, Jazmine's here!" he calls out before I can stop him.

"What? Why would she be here?" Jason says, walking through the door. All I can do is smile. "I should have known. You know that's Andi's job?" He ushers Tyler to the box and gives him silent permission to pet the puppies. Tyler's face is a picture.

"I was free, so I came to help. It turns out it's a great thing I did.

Andi got little sleep last night thanks to your exterminator."

"What was Stanley doing?" Before I can answer, Jason raises his hand. "No, let me guess. He was knocking his water dish onto the floor, trying to get her attention. Am I right? It seems he's started this ever since a certain someone started giving him extra Mountain Dew. Care to guess who?"

"I don't have the foggiest idea. I'm sure whoever is doing that is only compensating for how terrible others treat him."

"You always seem to have an answer." He shakes his head and lifts Bob by the scruff of his neck. This does not go over well with Bob, and I hear a growl of protest—well, more of a loud squeak.

"He doesn't enjoy being lifted by the scruff. He prefers cuddling."

"I think I know how to lift a dog."

"Terri said they're not dogs," Tyler states. "She said they're Dachshunds and don't enjoy being called dogs."

"You're all going to be the death of me. I need to check the test results. Tyler, stay here. I'll be right back." Jason hands Bob to me. Delighted to be away from the nasty man, Bob crawls under my hand and rolls on his back.

Tyler and I busy ourselves with the puppies until Jason returns. After he tells him it's time to go, Tyler is off like a shot, leaving Jason to put the girls back in their box. He tells me goodbye and reminds me not to stay long.

As he leaves, I breathe a sigh of relief, thankful I could stay seated the entire time so he couldn't see what I was wearing. Jason cracks the door open, popping his head through. "I like your grunge look. Kind of reminds me of the first time we met. This shirt has too many buttons though." It's obvious he's pleased with himself, and he chuckles, closing the door.

With Bob on my lap, I can't run after him. Besides, it would make things worse. I stay seated and try to think how to get even.

Andi comes in and is laughing before the door shuts. "I was right. You came. I knew it. Did I hear someone else?"

"Jason was here to check something, and he let Tyler play with the puppies."

"How long you going to hang out?"

This sparks an idea. "Depends. What do you have going on today?"

"Nothing for now. I have studying to do, but it can wait. Why?"

"Care to help me with something?" I know I have a mischievous grin.

"Something I can get in trouble for?"

"Maybe, but not much. You'll never know until you try."

"Sounds fun."

After I explain what I have in mind, she's excited, and we struggle to contain our enthusiasm. I tell her to bring the box, and she's right behind me while I carry Bob.

It takes hours to get everything set how I want, but it's worth it. Andi is an enormous help and has excellent ideas. We take a break for the puppies' evening feed and order a pizza for us, then are back at it. It's late when I complete the finishing touches and carry the puppies to the kennel room.

Time to leave and let Andi get on with her studies and for me to get back to my blog. I say goodbye and cuddle Bob one last time before putting him in the box with his sisters. He's fast asleep and lets me leave with no complaints.

Heading straight for home, I shed my coat, scarf, and boots on arrival. Jeans go off next and after pulling on the thick socks, I'm in my comfortable state dressed in my writing attire.

I boot the laptop and open my latest blog file ready to post. Once I've checked what comments have come in since last night, I post the new file. Now it's time to slip off to bed. Monday is coming and it's Thanksgiving week.

Chapter Fourteen

Monday morning I'm back in the kennel room. The puppies are growing far too quickly for my liking. I wish I could stop it somehow. Bob is in his usual spot and lost to the world unless you take the bottle away. Andi has already finished with Mindy, and Lindy is going at it while we chat. Andi tells me how she's excited about going home for her break from school during Thanksgiving. We're closing the clinic on Friday and Saturday for the holiday. To offset this, we're open on Tuesday for in-clinic appointments.

With the long break ahead, Andi shares she's having difficulty concentrating on work. While we feed the puppies, I hear what her home is like. It sounds like a terrific place, and the plans she's made sound great. I haven't spent Thanksgiving with a family since my mother's death. After that, my father never did much to celebrate it. My foster family always went to visit Martha's parents and left me by myself. Then, while in school, I was busy studying and enjoying the quiet campus. Even when I was with what's-his-name, we did nothing special. I catch myself wondering what spending Thanksgiving with a family might be like, but dismiss the thought. This never provides positive feelings.

"How are the freeloaders doing?" Jason's amused voice carries from the doorway.

"Sucking it down like there's no tomorrow," Andi answers him.

The sound of a newcomer wakes Bob, who was asleep on my lap. Bob scowls at Jason, although Jason doesn't seem fazed. "Make sure Terri knows we want to start them on regular food during the break. If they tolerate it, we can find homes for them next week."

"We already discussed it. She's adjusting their feeding to twice a day. I think they're ready," she explains.

I don't think Bob sees it this way as he gives a tremendous huff, rolling on his back.

"Okay, sounds like you have it under control. Have a delightful time at home, but remember to come back. Oh, Jazmine, we need to talk over a few things. I'll check on the patients in the stalls, and if his royal highness can do without you for a few minutes, I'll meet you in your office."

"My office?"

"Yes. I know how much the disorganization in mine bothers you."

"Oh, okay. You could have sent me a text, or have you lost your phone in the pile on your desk?"

"No, I haven't even been to my office this morning. I came straight here because I knew you'd be here doing what I told you not to do. Anyway, give me a few minutes, and I'll meet you there."

Right then, Andi and I both hear Bob huff again, and we can't help but laugh at his timing. Jason shakes his head and walks away.

Andi's a little worried she might get in trouble. "He hasn't seen his office yet?"

I assure her I'll take any blame.

"I wish I could believe you, but I don't have the job security you have."

"What job security? You've been here longer than I have."

"True, but when the doc looks at me, he sees a veterinarian student. We're a dime a dozen. When he looks at you, he sees, well, he sees you. Not the norm for females around here."

"Andi! What are you saying? I'm no different from any of the other females here, and Jason sees me like he does all his employees."

Cindy comes in to take samples from a patient and overhears our conversation. "Sees who like all his employees?"

"Me. Andi seems to think Jason sees me differently from everyone else."

She stares at me. "Are you that oblivious to how he is with you? Is it even possible to be so clueless?"

"What? He's always professional around me, as I am with him. We relate like any boss and worker should. Nothing more, nothing less."

"That's what we mean. Always professional. Because you're both afraid to show your genuine feelings. It's not working though. Everyone sees right through both of you. By the way, who's the boss in this little scenario of yours?" She's giggling, but before I can form an answer, she moves on, "Now, if you'll excuse me, I have blood work to do. Andi, you want to help?"

"Thought you'd never ask." Andi follows Cindy, leaving me open-mouthed at what they said.

Is this true? Do I have feelings for Jason I'm suppressing? Better yet, does he have feelings for me? This can't be. They're making something out of nothing. We're professionals, and we treat each other as such.

To clear my head, I go through the lobby for coffee and stop to give Stanley something to drink. Yes, Mountain Dew—to prove I can, and will, go against Jason's wishes.

Coffee in hand, I head to my office and read through emails while waiting for Jason. What could he want to discuss?

"I'll be back in a sec. Need to get something from my office," he says, standing in my open doorway. I listen as he crosses to his office, waiting for it. "What? Where's? What happened to my office?"

The utter confusion in his voice is priceless. I move to stand behind him as several others appear. Most know what we did this weekend and stayed close to witness his discovery.

"What do you mean? Seems like a normal office to me." I'm peering over his shoulder at his now organized office.

"Wow, Jason, did you work on this all weekend? I can even see the floor," Doc Carson says.

Jason glares at me. "Where did you put my stuff?"

"Stuff? Junk is more appropriate."

"I know you're little miss organized, and we let you organize the files, the front office, and the supply room. Even let you get new systems and tablets, but why my office? I knew where everything was. Why did you have to mess with my office?"

"I'm not sure 'mess' is the correct word, Jason," Doc Carson says. "Looks to me like straighten—no, that's not sufficient. Maybe cleaned up? No, doesn't seem to fit either. I know. Resurrected. That's what she did. She resurrected your office. I didn't know there was an extra chair in here."

"He disguised it as a pile of old torn, useless overalls and stained work shirts," I say.

"Where are my books? They were on my desk. I knew where each one was." Jason's voice drips with sheer panic.

"Well, if you glimpse around the corner, you'll see they're in something most call a bookcase, which contained more junk than I thought was possible. Don't worry. They're in the same order they were in, but on shelves." I'm trying hard not to laugh.

"I have a bookcase?" It is a genuine question. It must have been so long since he'd seen it, he'd forgotten it was ever there. "Hey, what's this in the corner? Where did it come from?"

"Yes, you have a bookcase, and the object in the corner has always been there. It, believe it or not, is a small refrigerator. It took forever to get it open thanks to all the frost, but now it's clean and ready for use. I will confess, everything in there went in the dumpster. I'm thrilled EPA never saw it. That stuff was gross."

He's standing in the center of his office, no doubt searching for something to complain about. He'll find nothing as it's perfect. "Where are my files and the paperwork on the desk? Where did you put those?"

"In the drawers of your desk. There was plenty of room after I threw out the half-empty bags of stale chips and empty soda cans. Is throwing things away against your religion or something?"

"Hold it now. Where's my toolbox? My red metal toolbox?"

"Toolbox? That's a laugh. There were no tools, nothing but old wrappers and empty Ho Ho's and Ding Dong boxes. I couldn't believe how many were in there."

Doc Carson bursts out laughing. "So that's where you were putting them. I knew you were stashing them somewhere. I told Carin, but we couldn't figure out where you were hiding them."

"Well, it's still a useful toolbox," Jason mutters. "Where is it?"

"It's right beside the bookcase and the nine pairs of work boots which were scattered around."

"Nine? There were nine pairs of boots in here?"

"Yes, and a few took a long time to clean with the junk caked on them. I don't even want to know what it was. It's done, and I'm glad."

"You did this? All of this? When did you have the time?"

"Yesterday, after you left. I had help, but I'm not saying who. You owe the entire clinic donuts or rolls in the morning. It's your decision, but it's the least you can do." Considering this a job well done, I head back to my office.

Across the hall, Jason is still checking out the new layout of his office. He comes over a few minutes later. "We still need to talk."

"Sure. About what?"

"I think you know."

"Know what?" I'm confused.

"About the Fall Fling."

"Fall Fling? What's a Fall Fling?" I'm even more confused.

"You know. Don't try to fool me."

I don't understand his tone. Is he accusing me of something? "I can assure you I don't know what you mean. Please, what is a Fall Fling?"

"The dinner dance this Saturday night. You know all about it.

You can't fool me."

His answer astounds me. "Again, I don't know to what you're referring. This is the first I've heard of anything concerning a Fall Fling, or a dinner dance this Saturday or any Saturday."

"If you never heard of it, why did you go shopping for a dress for it? Care to explain?" His disdainful air causes even more disbelief.

"I never went shopping..." Then it hits me. "You mean when we were at the movies?"

"Movies. Yeah right, you were at the movies. I heard you bought several items, one being a dress for the dance."

Since he's being ridiculous, I give him a scathing scowl. "Yes, I bought something, but not for any fling thing or any dance."

"You didn't buy a sexy dress for the Fall Fling? It's not a nightclub gathering, you know."

"I bought a dress, but I can assure you it wasn't for this Fall Fling. I saw it and liked it and treated myself. Besides, I need not explain myself to you. What business is it of yours anyway, and how did you even know?" I can't believe his audacity in accusing me.

"It's a small town. Everyone knows you bought a dress and are now waiting for an invitation to the occasion to wear it. If not, why did you buy it?"

Staring at him for several moments, my blood boiling at his asinine attitude, I want the coldness in my voice to show my feelings. "It may be a small town, but your information couldn't be more wrong. Go back and check your sources. I didn't buy a dress for any Fall Fling. Is there anything else you need me to clarify, Doctor Withers?"

"This will not work. It will never work. You should forget it. From now on, my office is off limits." He leaves, slamming the door shut behind him.

In total disbelief, I replay the conversation. I'm sure no one mentioned a Fall Fling to me. I start to follow him to his office to continue this but stop. He's being an idiot and irrational. What business is it of his what I buy or don't buy? Who does he think he is?

The rest of the day I rehash the tiff with Jason. How could he have gotten such an idea? Who could have said something? It couldn't be Cindy or Terri. They wouldn't do that to me. Who would?

This is ridiculous. Shaking my head, I go to feed Bob. Terri is getting the bottles ready when I walk in, so I lift Bob and take my regular seat.

"Are you okay?" She seems concerned.

"Yes, why?"

"Well, Doc Withers doesn't yell when he's mad by any stretch of the imagination, but everyone knows there was a—I guess heated is a suitable word—a heated discussion after he saw his office."

"Oh, that? It didn't concern his office. Does everyone know? Did others hear us?"

"Well, no one could hear what you were saying, but it was obvious he was distressed. When he came out, he headed straight to the parking lot and drove off without Richard, who was to go with him on the call."

"He was that mad?"

"Yes. Kind of reminded me of the old days when Doc Carin would push his buttons. Like I said, he doesn't yell—ever. He used to storm out, like he did this morning, after an altercation with her too. Once, he even left a mare in the middle of a delivery. Had to turn around and come back when he remembered. Please don't tell him, I told you. He thinks most don't know."

"I won't, and I doubt our argument this morning was anything like that. He got wrong information and came to a ludicrous conclusion is all. I'm sure he'll cool off once he realizes how brainless and imbecilic he was."

She switches Lindy for Mindy. "What kind?"

"What kind of what?"

"Information. You said he got wrong information. What did he get?"

"Seems he heard I bought the dress on Friday. You didn't tell him, did you? Or Cindy—she wouldn't, would she?"

"I know I didn't and doubt Cindy would. What's the big deal with you buying a dress?"

"My thought as well. He thinks I did it so he'll ask me to some fling thing on Saturday."

"The Fall Fling? How crazy is that? Who buys a dress for something no one's invited them to?"

"I know. I assured him his information is wrong, and he's jumping to preposterous conclusions."

"I agree, but…"

"But what?"

"Oh, nothing," she says, taking Bob's bottle from me and heading for the sink.

"Nothing? No, you were thinking something."

"Well, you did buy the dress. Plus, the fling is the perfect occasion. I can see how he might arrive at his conclusion. You know men don't enjoy feeling cornered."

"What? I didn't even know this thing existed until he mentioned it this morning."

"I didn't say he was right, but when you examine the facts, I can see where his thoughts might've been heading. That's all I'm saying."

"Oh, okay, I guess, but I liked the dress and treated myself. That's all. Plus, you and Cindy were the ones bugging me to buy it. Telling me how perfect it was and how everyone would react when they saw it. I wasn't planning on buying it, but you kept going on and on about how I owed it to myself."

"Right, we twisted your arm. Sure, okay. I'll go along with that," she says, snickering.

"It's the truth, and you know it. We're not discussing this anymore. I never want to hear any mention of this fling thing again, okay?"

"Okay, but something tells me it might be out of your control," she says.

Cindy arrives and walks around to where we're sitting. "What's out of her control?"

"Someone told Doc Withers about Jazmine buying the dress Friday, and now he thinks she did it to get an invitation to the Fall Fling."

Cindy smiles and raises her eyebrows. "Interesting. I wonder how he arrived at that?"

"That's what I'd like to know. You didn't say anything, did you?"

"No, but anyone there on Friday could have."

She knows something. "Do you know who told him?"

"Well, nothing for sure, but I did see someone in the store when you were trying on the dress."

"You did? Was it someone from here? Someone from town?"

"Yes, they are from our town."

"And? Come on, tell me."

"Yeah, you better tell her. Doc Withers stormed out of here after discussing it. Man, was he upset. Even left Richard behind," Terri says.

"I heard he was outside chopping wood earlier, but didn't hear why."

This baffles me. "What do you mean chopping wood?"

"It's what he does when something has him riled. He takes his frustrations out on the woodpile. It's an excellent idea when you consider it. He gets to cool off, then has something to keep him warm," Cindy says.

"You still haven't said who was at the mall on Friday!"

"No, I haven't. Are you sure you want to know? There's already friction between the two of you. Maybe it's best you don't know."

I can't believe this. "Jill? Jill saw me buy the dress?"

"Saw you try it on too." Cindy can't conceal her grin.

"Why would she care if I try on a dress?"

"Because it's mega-perfect on you," Terri answers.

"I heard she tried the larger size on after you left but couldn't even zip it up," Cindy adds.

"Wow. That would have driven her over the edge. It must've shorted several wires in her brain or something," Terri says.

"Because of this, she told Jason I bought the dress, which made him think I'm trying to get him to ask me to this fling thing? How ridiculous is this?"

"Oh, I'm positive she told him, but he's not the one who thought about it being for the Fall Fling. His mind doesn't work that way. I'm confident Jill led him there. She's known for that," Cindy answers.

"Why would she do something like that? What have I ever done to her?"

"Two obvious reasons come to mind," Terri says. "One, well, you're you, and two, she saw you in the dress—the same one she couldn't fit into."

"I can't believe this. We're talking about a simple dress. Nothing more."

"No one would ever describe that dress as simple, and I doubt it was the dress itself. More how devastating you were in it," Cindy says.

"Well, I don't see it. Anyway, I need to get going. You both have a pleasant evening." I grab my things and head for Boris. I can't believe any of this. Maybe they're making things up to poke fun at me. That's it. They're having fun is all.

At home, after changing into my usual oversized shirt and with my hair tied back, I chuckle seeing myself in the mirror. Now there is one hot lady. What a catch. No wonder all the men are breaking down my door. Not!

Chapter Fifteen

Tuesday, I lie in bed waiting for the alarm to go off, fighting to hold it together. My stomach is edgy, and I can't decide what to wear. I have to redo my makeup several times, and don't get me started on my hair. Since there are no Women's Auxiliary meetings in December, Sadie's fund-raising committee is meeting today, which means a possible altercation with Jill. Then there's Jason. We didn't part on the best of terms yesterday when he stormed out and never came back. I hope he's worked through his deranged idea and realizes I'd never try to corner him. I'm not looking for a relationship.

All these thoughts fill my mind while I get ready. Maybe I shouldn't wear one of my new suits. Don't want to cause more problems. No, that's ridiculous. I bought them for work. I pick the gray one with the slight burgundy stripe and the matching slacks. To this, I add my new burgundy blouse and a gold and pearl necklace. The necklace was my mother's. I don't remember her wearing it, but it—along with several jewelry pieces—was in my suitcase, wrapped in my clothes, when I got to the children's home.

My nanny must have put them there. Several are valuable, and all are precious because they were hers. I kept them hidden for years, which was difficult. In fact, I don't think what's-his-name even knew of them. The two sets I cherish most are from my parents' wedding. First is the wedding set, my mother's engagement ring and their wedding bands. Second was her wedding jewelry, a necklace and earrings her father gave her. My dream was I'd someday be able to wear them at my wedding. That's becoming less plausible by the day.

To this I add the matching dangling gold and pearl earrings, and I'm set. I finish my coffee, check I have everything, and I'm ready for whatever today brings. At least I hope I am.

At the office, the first thing waiting for me is Bob. I get there quickly after dropping my things off and getting coffee started. When I get to the kennel room, I'm startled to find Andi. "I thought you were heading home?"

"I am. Needed to do the morning feedings. Plus, Doc Withers said I could take Lindy home for my mom. I'll start her on regular food while there. If she has problems, he said to bring her back."

"Amazed he didn't have you take all three of what he calls the freeloaders."

"I doubt I could get far taking a certain one. I saved Bob's feeding for you."

"That's why I'm here. Now you have a great visit and drive careful. We want to see you back here in one piece."

"I will. They report the roads are clear. I hope you have a fantastic Thanksgiving too. I'll see you on Monday."

After taking care of Bob, I get my coffee and replenish Stanley's saucer with fresh water—for which I receive a dirty glare—and settle in my office.

The morning goes by quickly, thanks to everything I need to do earlier than usual because of the short week. Cindy sticks her head in to say good morning, as do Terri, Cassie, and Georgia when they arrive. At about eleven, I get a refill of coffee and realize Jason isn't in yet. I check the schedule and see he's out on a call most of the day at a ranch west of here.

With one confrontation avoided, I'm feeling better. I go to help with the next feed and find Terri preparing things. Once Bob's settled on my lap, she hands me a bottle. It doesn't take Bob long to start. "Are you stuck here taking care of them during the break?"

"Sort of. My parents live in Casper, so I'll go there on Thursday. By then they should be on two meals a day. Jake said his guys will take the early feedings, so I only have the evening one when I check in on them. It's not too bad."

"Yeah, sounds like it will work. They'll be starting solid food soon then?"

"Yes, I'll give them a little kibble with milk this afternoon and see how they do. Then I'll increase the kibble and decrease the milk. By Thursday morning they should be on the two-meal plan." We both hear a disgruntled huff from Bob.

"I don't think he likes the reduction in meals," I say.

"He'll get used to it. That is if I can keep you from slipping him food. He has you so wrapped around his little paw. I may have to put a lock on here to keep you out."

"How can you say no to this face? He's so cute." I turn Bob toward her. This disturbs him since it causes his bottle to slip away. I rectify this, and he's again lost to the world.

"See. You are too bad. Anyway, this time next week, we can start considering homes for them." She acts like it's a marvelous thing.

"Well, no reason to rush. We need to make sure they're going to suitable homes with people who love them like they deserve. You will inspect the prospective homes, right? Before you let them go?"

"Oh, brother. You're not going to make this easy. Should we have a background check run on prospective owners too? Criminal history checks, perhaps?"

"Stop it. I only want to make sure they get the best place. Nothing wrong with that."

"Sure you do," she says, giggling. "I'm supposed to help Doc Carson with the sheep in the stalls. Are you okay here by yourself?"

"Yes. I won't be long, I have things to do before I get Sadie."

"Ah, that's right. It's Tuesday. That means you'll be seeing Jill, doesn't it?"

"Not sure. Since the clinic's open, I might drop Sadie off and come back here until she's done."

"Chicken."

"I'm not chicken. I don't want to cause any problems is all."

"Right, no problems. Which is why you told her how cozy you and the doc were the night you spent together in Guernsey," she says as she leaves.

"Cozy was your word, not mine," I call out, even though I doubt it will matter. I sit with Bob awhile, but know I must put him back. He doesn't mind. He's been asleep since he finished his bottle.

In my office, I get busy trying to accomplish what I can. When it's time to pick up Sadie, I gather my bags and go out through the lobby to let Jennifer know I'm leaving and when I'll be back.

Seeing me, she smiles. "I hear you got a new dress for the Fall Fling?"

"What? No, I did not." Does everyone know everything about me? I can't help but give a dramatic sigh. "Yes, I bought a dress, but it's not for this fling thing. I never even heard about it until yesterday. How did you know about the dress?"

"My mother asked if I'd seen it. Her friend told her you bought it to get the doc to ask you to the fling. Mom doesn't believe it. She said you'd never need to do something so drastic, but she hopes he asks you. She thinks you're a cute couple."

"We're not a couple. Why would she say we're a couple?" I say, shaking my head. "However, I'm glad she doesn't believe the gossip. How could anyone think I'd do something so underhanded?"

"Mom says with your looks and intelligence, you'd never need to trick any man into anything."

"Well, that's nice of your mother and tell her thank you, although I'm not sure of her reasoning."

"She said most men would trample over each other to go out with you anyway. She also said all the single women can't wait until you get hitched—maybe most of the married ones too."

"Why would anyone care if I was single or not?"

"Are you joking? You've got it all. Beauty, intelligence, sophistication, and you graduated from Harvard with multiple degrees. Mom says no one around here can compare to you. I'm hoping it rubs off on me."

"Well, thanks, but you're exaggerating things. Besides, it won't be long before you have the boys at Harvard fighting over who gets to walk you to class."

"Harvard? Me, go to Harvard? Are you nuts? There's no way."

"Why not? Someone has to. Your grades are excellent. I don't see why you shouldn't apply for any of the Ivy League schools. It depends on what you want, but if you're interested in an MBA, Harvard is an excellent place to start."

"You are nuts, the tuition is like crazy high. My parents are planning on helping, but there's no way I can afford to go there."

"Well, you'll never know where you can go unless you apply. I'd try it. All they can do is accept you or pass on you. Either way, it won't end your life."

"You think I'd have a chance?"

"It's a possibility. I'd look into it. Now, I have to get Sadie. Call if you need me."

"Okay, I'll hold the fort."

"You take care. See you soon."

Sadie is waiting when I arrive. I feel guilty since I've spent little time with her since Thursday evening. I turn Boris around so the passenger side is facing her, and watch her walk down the steps and along the sidewalk. Knowing better than to get out and help, I stay put. She wouldn't like it one bit and would take great pleasure in letting me know.

"This is such a beautiful day God's given us," she says, getting into her seat.

"To tell you the truth, I hadn't even noticed. I've been inside since I got to work," I let the comment of her god go unchecked. It's

Sadie being Sadie.

"Well, stop and appreciate it. This week reminds me how thankful I am for all the blessings He's given me. It's one of my favorite weeks."

"I'm glad for you." There's been so much tragedy in her life, it's amazing how she can concentrate on the blessings.

"I read your blog yesterday. You are a gifted writer. I can't wait for the next section, and here you are, sitting right next to me. Care to share?"

"Well, thank you, but you must wait like everyone else. The next section will be posted tomorrow."

"I could proofread it for you. I have time."

"I'm sure you do, but I'm fine. You can wait."

She chuckles. "Did anyone ever tell you how mean you can be?"

"Funny you should mention that. I hear all kinds of rumors are going around concerning me. You can add another one to the list."

"Rumors about you? What are they?"

"I'll not help in their spreading. Besides, I'm sure you'll hear everything at your meeting. I bet several of the women are dying to share the dirt on me."

"You sound offended. Is any of it true?"

"No. Not in the least, but since when does the truth matter to anyone?"

"It matters to those who know and care about you."

"Well, if you say so. I'm not comfortable having lies spread concerning me."

"Dear, people will talk, and you have little control over what anyone says. One can only control what one does. You can't live to please others; you never will. Knowing you did the best you could, that's what matters."

"You think so?"

"I know so. We're each given one life to live and are responsible for what we accomplish while living it. No one else. You need only to answer to God and yourself. Nobody else."

I must admit, there's logic to this. We're getting close to the community center, so I don't respond and contemplate our conversation. She's a wise person.

I stop where I can drop her off, having decided it's best for me to avoid meeting Jill. I fear what I might say to her. For a long time, I've been the sole one to stick up for myself. No one ever had my back, so I got effective at dealing with it. Kids can be mean when they want to be, and adults can be too. I don't want to be like that here, and besides, I'm the outsider. I stop by the door and wait for her to get out.

"Why are you stopping here? Aren't you going to park?"

"I thought I'd drop you off and go back to the office. The clinic's open today, so they might need me. Besides, I'm not a real member of the group. You go on in and call me when you're ready for me to come get you."

"I don't think so. You are a member of the group. Now park this thing so we can see what trouble we can cause."

"But the office—"

"Will be fine. You're not a vet, anyway. It will be good for them to manage without you for a few hours. Besides, they can call you if they get desperate. Go park this thing."

I follow her orders, since that's what they are, and we make our way inside the building. Quite a few ladies are here today. Perfect. We walk along the hall and into the room they use for the meeting. Is this what walking on death row feels like? As we enter the room, all I can do is take a deep breath and hope for the best.

To my amazement, Jill isn't here because of a conflict in her schedule. She needed to be in Casper today. Once I hear this, it's remarkable how much lighter the atmosphere seems and how everyone appears so much happier.

The meeting starts, and everything goes well. We're doing a cookbook for a fundraiser, and we're targeting it to go on sale late April. I'm appointed to head the group, putting it together and handling the marketing, with Stacy and five others helping. They cover several other topics, and I sit wondering how all of this will work out. It better, or Jill will make sure they roast me in the town square, if they have one here. If not, she'll have them build one.

After forty-five minutes, the meeting ends, and we stay for another thirty minutes and mingle with several groups. I wonder if any of these discussions going on are about my dress and Jason. There are glances my way, but I can't tell for sure. I stay near Sadie, trying not to draw attention to myself. To be honest, what's going on at the clinic is more on my mind, but something catches my full attention.

"A Rich Girl's Poor Life," is all I hear at first, so I listen closer. A lady is talking about a blog she's reading. Several others say they're reading it too and discuss what they've read so far. I can't believe they're talking about my blog. Most comments seem positive, but there are a few negative ones. I hear Sadie offering her opinion, even though she knows I'm the writer. What is she doing? I realize she's pointing things out to contradict the negative comments. All I can do is drink my coffee and shake my head. The conversation ends with several ladies offering their thoughts on what they think might happen next. A few question whether it's a genuine story. I give Sadie a glare when this comes up, hoping she refrains from saying anything. She does, and I hope my secret is safe—for now, at least.

The group thins out, and Sadie and I help clear the empty mugs and plates and say our goodbyes. After putting our coats on, we walk outside to Boris. I try to help her get in, but she'll have none of it, so I go around to my side. Finding I never locked the doors when I got out shakes me. This is the first time I ever remember leaving them unlocked. Maybe there's hope for me yet.

Sadie glances my way as I start Boris. "A productive meeting, don't you think?"

"Yes, it was."

"I think the cookbook has everyone excited. I know I am."

"Seems so. I hope it turns out okay."

"It will. It's why I made sure Deb put you forward for the head of the project."

A glance in her direction confirms she's wearing her innocent expression. "I have you to thank for this?"

"You didn't think I'd let anyone else handle it. It would be a travesty. No, you're the best choice, and Stacy will make sure everyone cooperates with you. Don't worry, she and I have your back."

"I hope so. I'm not sure I'm popular with these women, judging by the things I hear."

"Are you on that again? I told you what matters is to be true to yourself."

I'm not able to stop myself. "Isn't it against the Christian way to only think of yourself?"

"I never said think only of yourself, but to be true to yourself. There's a difference. As the Bible reports about the woman who anointed Jesus with expensive oil days before they crucified him. It upset the disciples because they saw it as a waste, but Jesus told them she did a good thing. He said she'd be remembered for all eternity because 'She did what she could.' This is what Christians should do. We are to do what we can. If you see someone who needs help and you can help, you help. It's that simple. So many try to put so much more into it with so many requirements and controls, or thinking a task is beneath them and such. It comes down to a simple question: did you do what you could? If the answer is yes, then you were a success. That's it."

"Interesting, and I understand your point. If everyone would do what they could when they see a need, things would go much better. Is that the way to heaven then?" Why did I ask this?

"No, not the way to heaven. That is how you should live your life on earth. What many might call the Christian life. Getting to heaven? That's something different, and that comes only through faith."

"Faith? You mean, if you have faith you're going to heaven, you will?" I'm trying to understand what she's saying. I thought those who believe in heaven thought you had to do many things to earn your way there.

"No, not faith in yourself. Faith in Jesus Christ. You can't get there on what you do. There's no working or earning your way into heaven. Paul explains this in Galatians. 'If righteousness comes through the law, then Christ died in vain.' This means if you could earn it yourself, there was no need for Christ to die. You must accept, by faith alone, that Jesus died and rose again. This is how you know you're going to heaven."

"Because of your faith, you're sure when you die you're going to heaven?"

"Yes, because of my faith in Him! You got it. Now, stop at the clinic. I need to talk with Jason."

"I'm not sure he'll be there. He was out on a call," I answer while my mind digests what she said. It can't be that simple, can it?

"We might as well check."

Chapter Sixteen

Once we arrive, I'm amazed Jason's truck is in its usual spot.

"See, I told you he'd be here. Why do you ever doubt me?" Sadie says while getting out.

I must admit, she's right. Why do I?

Inside, we head for the lobby, but I'm hoping we don't find Jason. My hopes rise when we reach the lobby and I still don't see him. I ask Jennifer if she knows where he is, and of course she does. He's in his office and Sadie is already heading there.

As I enter the hallway, I stop to keep from running into her, frozen in Jason's office doorway. After several moments, she's able to speak. "What happened to your office? I can even see the floor, and you have a desk?"

"You're overreacting, Sadie," Jason says.

Sadie takes a few tentative steps inside, gazing in awe. Her expression would fool anyone into thinking she was taking a tour of the Sistine Chapel or something.

"It's organized, and the books...they're on shelves. This is amazing. Did a certain place freeze? I hadn't heard, but it must have. A person could even function in here."

"That's enough. Yes, it's organized, and yes, I can find things, but I could before too. I managed for a lot of years. There was no reason for anyone to change it," he says, glaring at me. "It's done now, so we'll leave it. Can I do something for you?"

"I have to sit. Oh, my gosh, you have a second chair. Was this always here?"

"I said that's enough. Now, you're here because...?"

"I need you to pick up the turkeys this evening. I'm cooking two for the shelter tomorrow and then ours for Thursday. Carl soaked them in the brine for two days, and now they're bagged and ready. You need to get them tonight, and I don't want any excuses."

"I know. I told you I'd go after work. You didn't have to come remind me."

"Maybe not, since you can now find your desk. Still, it's best to play it safe. You can take Jazmine with you. She'll enjoy getting out."

This catches me off guard. "What?" Is she doing this again?

"You can go with him. Make sure he comes right back. Otherwise, he and Carl will get talking, and I'll be awake till all hours waiting. Take care of what you need to here, then you can take me home and Jason will pick you up at my place when he brings Tyler."

"Why do I need to go?" I remember what happened the last time she sent him on a similar task and I tagged along.

"Someone needs to make sure he gets back at a decent hour. You can do it, right, or do you have something important to do? Something for yourself, maybe? Something which keeps you from helping others?"

"Well, no, I don't." She's referring to our earlier discussion. She's excellent. "Isn't it a long drive, though? Like several hours each way? I doubt we'll be back before midnight." Jason had mentioned before it was a distance.

"No. It's on the other side of Casper. Shouldn't take more than an hour."

"Yeah, the Vickers retired, so now we get them from Carl," Jason says. "Not much of a drive. Still, no need for you to come. I'll manage fine. You might need to go shopping or something. Never know what occasion might be right around the corner." He's smirking.

"Why would she need to go shopping? She'll go with you. Now, both of you, move it. You're wasting time. Jazmine, I'll meet you outside." With this, she's gone, not leaving us with much of a choice.

"I'll get my things and take her home. What time will you be there?"

"You don't need to go."

"No, I wouldn't want you worrying what I might buy to tempt you with. I'll meet you at Sadie's." I storm off to my office across the hall.

"You don't need to go," he says again as my door closes behind me.

Fuming, I rummage around, grabbing what I need to take with me. Who does he think he is? "You might need to go shopping...never know what might be right around the corner." Is he serious? I can't believe he still thinks I bought a dress to make him take me out. How enormous is his ego?

Each thought gets me more distraught, but I don't want to give him the pleasure of feeling he's worth being distressed over. I put it out of my mind, walk out the back, and climb into Boris, the heat inflaming my cheeks as I head for Sadie's. Why is he acting like an imbecile? Besides being a male, I mean. Again, who does—

Sadie interrupts my thoughts. "Is there something going on between you two?"

"Believe me, nothing is going on between us."

"I'm glad to hear that. Can we slow down? I'd like to make it to my next birthday if possible."

I check and notice I'm almost doing ninety in a forty-five zone, but it matters little since we're close anyway. I let off the gas, and Boris slows as I turn into her driveway.

"Park in the rear, we'll use the back door."

"You sure? Making the loop is not a problem."

"Yeah, like the problem you're not having with Jason. No, park on the other side of my truck. It will leave room for Jason's."

"You mean the beast? It's good it's so massive with the ego he's carrying around," I mutter.

"What did you say?"

"Nothing. Nothing at all."

"A whole lot of nothing going on around here," Sadie says while getting out of Boris. I follow her into the house. "I'll start the coffee, dear. Take off your jacket and get an apron," she says while walking through the kitchen.

"Why do I need an apron?"

"You don't want to get your outfit dirty, and we need to start the pies."

"Pies? What pies?"

"The pumpkin and pecan pies for Thursday. Plus, the ones to take to the shelter. The stove can handle six, so we can get them all in before Jason gets here."

"We're making pies? Now?"

"Didn't I say so? What is it with you today? It will be fun. You'll see."

Knowing I have little choice, I remove my suit jacket and slip on an apron. First is the dough for the crust. Sadie has me chop pecans while she mixes other ingredients in a bowl. How will this make a dough? I thought you had to use flour and roll it out. I follow instructions anyway.

After thirty minutes, much to my disbelief, we have six pie pans containing crusts made with flour, butter, spices and, chopped pecans. Once mixed, we pressed the crust into shape in the pans. No rolling required.

Next, we start on the filling. I didn't expect these pies to be so easy to make. Fifteen minutes later, the mixtures are in the shells, and we retire to the dining room while we wait for the oven to reach the correct temperature. "What are you going to do with all these pies?"

"There are only six. Two for us, and four for the shelter. Not many at all. I remember times when I'd make six for us alone, but now it's only the four of us."

"Four? You, Jason, and Tyler. Who's the fourth?" I'm sure she'd never invite Jill, so who else is there?

She stares at me, staggered. "You. Don't tell me you're going somewhere else for Thanksgiving?"

"No, I'm not, but wasn't planning on coming here. You need to celebrate as a family. I'll be fine at my place."

"Where's this coming from? Of course you're coming here. There's no way you're sitting alone right down the street when there's plenty of food here. I won't allow it."

"I appreciate it, but it would be better if I didn't come. Don't worry, I'll be fine. I'm used to it."

"Hogwash. That was your old life. This is your life now, and you have people who care for you. You'll spend the day with us, and we'll have a marvelous time."

"I'd ask Jason first. He might need a break from me," I say, but realizing it was out loud I add, "I mean he might have plans with Tyler or something."

"I heard what you said. Don't worry. There's enough room here for both you and his ego." She cackles and heads to the mudroom. "I'll get the coolers for the turkeys."

"Sadie, maybe it would be best for me to take a pass," I call after her but get no reaction. She doesn't hear me, or more to the truth, chooses not to hear me.

Right then, Tyler runs full speed into the dining room where I'm sitting with my coffee. He stops mere inches before running into me. "Jazmine. Look what I made today!" He's holding out something made of construction paper as Jason arrives behind him.

"I told you, no running in the house. Now leave Jazmine alone."

I give Jason a frosty scowl. "He's showing me something, if you don't mind." Smiling, I turn to Tyler. "What is it, Tyler?"

"It's a turkey. See? I made it by drawing around my hand and adding other paper I cut out for the feathers." He's super proud of his creation. Scrawled across the turkey's body in young scrawl is *Happy Thanksgiving Jazmine!*

"It has my name on it?"

"Yes, Miss Dottie told me how to spell it, but I wrote it myself. Do you like it?"

"Yes, it's magnificent. I don't think anyone has ever given me anything nicer."

"Grandma said you didn't have any decorations, so I made it for you to put on your refrigerator. I made one for Dad too."

"How sweet of you!" I give him a hug and he holds on tight for some time. Tears sting my eyes. I enjoy holding him until someone interrupts the moment.

"That's enough, Tyler. Put away your coat and hat. I'm sure Jazmine has something she needs to do, so we can leave."

"He doesn't have to hurry. I doubt he's threatened by a woman helping him," I say, helping Tyler remove his coat.

"Great, you're here," Sadie says, arriving from the kitchen. "Now, you two don't dawdle. I want you back at a decent time. Go out the back, the coolers are on the steps. Go on then, get. Tyler and I have things to do," she says, setting a box of construction paper on the dining table.

"I'll keep your turkey here, Jazmine, for when you get back," Tyler says with a gigantic smile.

"Thank you. Don't let anything happen to it. I have a special place for it." I put my coat on and double check I have everything I'll need. Can't risk delaying Jason, or worse, make him return to the house for any forgotten items. I'd never hear the end of it.

"Now, Tyler, listen to your grandmother. You know the rules. No running or jumping in the house," Jason says, giving Tyler a stern gaze.

Sadie rolls her eyes in Jason's direction. "Would you get out of here? This house made it through you growing up, and I doubt he could even come close to the havoc you caused."

He lifts a brow. "What? I never did anything bad."

"Need I remind you of the sled incident?"

This gets my attention. "Sled incident? This sounds like something I need to hear." It's obvious Tyler is interested too.

Jason shakes his head. "Nothing to hear. Nothing at all. Are you ready?"

"Yes, but I still want to know about this sled thing. Sadie, you can tell me when we return," I call out while following Jason to the back door. "Tyler, you have fun."

When we get outside, Jason grabs the two coolers and continues toward the truck. I follow behind and climb into the beast. I chuckle at the memory of my thought concerning his ego. He glances at me while getting situated. "Something funny?"

"Not at all. You have enough room?" I'm unable to stop the laugh accompanying my question.

"Yes, why wouldn't I?"

"Thought I'd check. Wouldn't want you to feel crowded or trapped."

He snaps his head around to glare at me. "What's gotten into you?"

"Me? You're asking what got into me? You? The person who accused me of trying to manipulate him. Now you have the gall to ask what got into me?"

"Look, if it's about the dress thing, I'm sorry. I kept hearing about you buying a dress, and everyone kept asking if I was taking you to the dance. I mean, everywhere I went. I didn't intend to confront you the way I did. When I saw my office, it all came back. I don't know what got into me. You can buy anything you want. I'm sorry."

"Well, okay. I couldn't believe you'd think I'd do something so underhanded. Do you think I'm after you?"

"No, I know you're not after me. It's just that—"

"Let me be clear. I don't need a man, any man. I'm fine the way things are."

"Okay. I get it, and I'm sorry. Everyone is always trying to fix me up with someone, and I bunched you all together."

"You're saying I'm like all the other women around here?"

"No, it's…never mind. It doesn't matter."

"How many are we talking, anyway? Five? Ten? A dozen maybe? Come on. I'd like to know."

"I don't know. Several? I know you're not like the others, but I had a terrible stretch is all, and then the office thing happened, and it piled up on me."

"We were trying to help. Don't you think it's better now?"

"I guess, but I'm still trying to find things. Before, I knew where everything was."

"Right, somewhere in the gigantic pile of junk," I say with a smile, sensing the tension has eased a little. "I should apologize too. I let my anger at someone else come out against you."

"Anger? Who are you angry with?"

"It doesn't matter, but I want you to know I never even heard of this Fall Fling until you mentioned it. Didn't even know what it was, let alone when."

"I know, I know. I let it get to me."

We ride in silence for several minutes while I debate asking the question blaring in my mind to the point I blurt it out. "Are you escorting Jill to the dance?" Not sure why, but I'm dreading the answer.

"No, I'm taking Sadie."

Wasn't expecting this. "Sadie? She's going? She hasn't mentioned anything."

"Well, she has to go. The women's group is in charge."

"They are? There's been no discussion at our meetings."

"The Fling Committee meets on the other Tuesdays."

"Okay, yeah, makes sense. Is this an enormous thing, then? Does everyone go?"

"Not everyone, but it's big. It's been going on a long time. Ever since my family settled here. There were few families around at first, and they'd get together for Thanksgiving. It grew from there. They started having it on the Saturday after because the town grew, and people were spending Thursday with their families. When they started calling it the Fall Fling, they added the dancing. Now it's one of the biggest events of the year."

We drive on, and he explains further. It seems like a nice, sociable event. I can tell we're close to being through Casper and hope it's not much longer. Jason drives for another fifteen minutes and says the road we need is the next left.

When he makes the turn, there's a restaurant on the right with trucks and SUVs parked in the lot. No cars, mind you. We continue to drive for another ten minutes. It's sparse around here, with few buildings.

A single light appears ahead, shining on a driveway of sorts. I'm glad for its welcoming glow. Otherwise, we could have driven right by it. Jason makes the turn and continues along the drive to a house in the distance. He parks next to three trucks, which look like they've seen better days. "Well, shall we get our turkeys?"

"Lead the way."

We walk together to the front door with Jason carrying the coolers. He raps on the frame. After a brief pause, he knocks again, and we continue to wait. After a third unsuccessful knock, he opens the storm door and knocks on the door behind it. Still nothing, and he shakes his head. "Where can Carl be? Sadie said he was expecting us. You stay here while I check."

"Please be careful. It's dark."

"I'll try around the side." He heads around the corner.

All I can do is wait and rub my hands, trying to stay warm. I love my suit, but it's not made for being outside for long.

After what seems like an eternity, Jason reappears. "No one's here. A few lights on, but I don't see anyone, and Carl's truck's gone."

"What should we do?"

"I can't go back empty-handed or Sadie will roast me. We'll wait and see if anyone shows."

"You mean wait in the truck?"

"Yeah, where else? Don't worry. I have plenty of diesel this time," he says, chuckling as we walk back. He even helps me climb into the beast. I'm thrilled to feel heat coming out of the vents once he starts it. "You know, I haven't eaten, and now we'll be getting back even later. You hungry?"

"A little. Why? Did Sadie pack us a basket of food?" This better not be another one of her tricks.

"No, but there's a decent restaurant back by the main road. We can get something to eat while we wait, if you like?"

"What if we miss them?"

"Not a problem. I'll recognize Carl's truck when he goes past. Shall we?"

"Sure, beats sitting here. Let's go."

He turns the beast around, and we make our way back to the restaurant. Several people are here, most of whom Jason seems to know. He introduces me to a few before we find a table where he can watch for Carl's truck.

The menu is more appetizing than expected. After a quick browse, I decide on the house special, chicken fried steak. The server taking our order asks if I want the regular, medium, or large order.

"She'll have the small, and I'll have the regular, Katie," Jason answers.

"Coming right up," she says in a chirpy voice.

"You know, I am hungry," I tell him with a grin.

"Don't worry, it will be fine," he says.

We have an enjoyable time talking, and it reminds me of our trip to Guernsey. When the food arrives, my eyes open wide in disbelief. The steak is so big it's hanging off the edges of the plate, and the sides are on a separate plate of their own. Jason has two steaks on what has to be a platter in front of him.

"I told you the small would be okay. Don't forget to save room for dessert, though. They have unreal cinnamon rolls, but don't tell Sadie I said so."

"We'll have to see. This is more than I eat in a week," I tell him and take a bite. I don't know what they do to the gravy, but oh, is it tasty. The steak, along with everything else, is fantastic. Realizing I finished my dinner amazes me more than Jason.

"Looks like you managed well. You ready for dessert?"

"Not sure I have room, but those rolls sound tempting." I hope they aren't similar in size to the steaks.

He motions to the server, and she comes to take our plates. She stacks everything on his platter—that's how big it is. "I'll be right back with coffee and rolls for you. Anything else I can get you?"

"No, Katie, coffee and rolls will be fine. Tell your dad the dinner was great."

"I will. He said to tell you he'll try to come out to see you, but he's shorthanded tonight."

"Tell him not to worry. I'll catch him another time."

With this, she goes off and we sit for a while, concentrating on digesting our food. Soon, she's back with two plates of delicious smelling rolls and mugs of coffee. The rolls are not small by any stretch of the imagination, and they're as tasty as they are large.

Jason keeps a close eye on the road through the window. I'm sure he's getting concerned, so I try to distract him. "You know Katie's dad?"

"Yeah, he was best friends with my dad."

"Do you get out this way often?"

"A few times a month. Try to bring Tyler out on a Saturday. He enjoys visiting here, plus they give him all the soda he wants," he says, laughing. He has a delightful laugh.

As I devour the last bite of my roll, a man comes out from the kitchen area and heads our way. He appears to be limping, and I realize he has a crutch and only one leg.

"Jason, what you doing out this way?" He pauses, smiling at me. "And with such a pretty lady? Hello, miss, welcome to my establishment." He does a slight, shaky bow.

"This is Jazmine. She's my office manager. Jazmine, meet Jim, the chief cook and bottle washer for this establishment."

"Nice to meet you, Jim, and thank you. The food was perfect. I could eat it all over again."

"Thank you. We try our best." He turns to Jason. "How's Sadie doing?"

"Oh, you know Sadie. Ornery as ever. Still complaining about my not letting her drive. But it doesn't seem to stop her getting around. She has her four-wheeler for around the ranch when the weather's decent. You can't keep her inside."

"I'm sure you can't. She is one fine lady, though. I boxed a few cinnamon rolls for her," he says, setting a box on the table. "I know how she likes them."

"You trying to get me in trouble? If she saw me with your rolls, she'd tan my hide." The two men burst out laughing. Must be a family joke.

"Then take them to Tyler. I know he'll enjoy them. Ma'am, it sure was special meeting you. You brighten up this place. Now, you two have a fantastic evening, and I'll see you next time."

"Same to you, Jim. Take care," Jason says as Jim makes his way back to the kitchen. I notice he stops and talks with folks along the way.

Once he's gone, Jason resumes his quiet watching of the road outside. After a few minutes, he speaks. "He lost it in Iraq during Desert Storm. Went to help a person lying on the road, but it turned out to be a booby trap. Shredded his leg and cut him up pretty bad otherwise. He would have died except for the person with him."

"The other person knew first aid?"

"In a way. It was my dad. He stopped the bleeding and took care of the other wounds. Then carried him on his back until they met up with other troops in a Humvee and got a ride to the nearest aid station. The doctors couldn't believe what Dad had done. They said he saved Jim's life."

"Wow, I didn't know your dad was in the military?"

"Yeah, I was born while he was deployed. The army wanted him to be a vet, but he wouldn't hear of it and went to Iraq instead. He and Jim were on the way back from a village close to the checkpoint they were manning when it all happened. They were on break when my dad spotted several animals at a house nearby and wanted to check on them. I think he felt Jim's injury was his fault since he insisted on going. But Jim wouldn't hear it. Said he wanted to go too. Jim came home a month later, and Dad got back the next year. He felt he had done his duty and came back to the clinic."

"I had no idea. No wonder Jim's a great friend."

"Yeah. He was even best man at my parents' wedding, and Dad was his too. After Dad finished school, they both went off to Iraq."

Jason seems to be deep in thought. I'm sure he's thinking about his dad. His expression changes as he bolts upright in his seat. "There's Carl. You finished?"

"Sure, I doubt I could eat another bite," I say, grabbing my purse and rising. Jason helps me with my coat and ushers me through the door and toward the beast. "Don't you need to pay?"

"Jim won't let me. Believe me, I've tried, but he won't hear of it. I've left a large tip—if I can get away with it—but we must hurry before he comes out and tries to give it back." He opens my door and then rushes around to his.

He has the truck started before I even have my door closed and is pulling out while I'm still fastening my seat belt. I see Jim standing in the doorway, holding up what looks like money, and yelling something. Jason waves and smiles at him as we pull out of the parking lot.

Soon we're parked outside the house again. He's turning the engine off when a gigantic man exits the house, walking toward us. Jason gets out, so I follow suit.

"Jason, I saw your truck at Jim's. Did you stop by earlier?"

"Yeah, Carl, we did, but it's not a problem. We ate dinner while we waited."

"Well, Sadie said you wouldn't be here till after seven. We needed things from town and knew we'd be back by then. Sorry to make you wait." I snicker at the mention of Sadie and her message. I can't believe she did it again. "This must be the charming Jazmine I've heard so much about. My, you are the prettiest girl I've seen around these parts."

Where would he have heard about me? "Well, I'm not sure about that, but yes, I'm Jazmine. Nice to meet you, Carl." I shake his outstretched hand. It's enormous, yet his handshake is so gentle.

"I disagree. You are one fine lady. Too much so to be hanging around the likes of him. You're not a hostage, are you?" He gives me a knowing wink.

"I think we're both hostages of Sadie's," Jason says, and we share a knowing laugh. "She forgot to mention not arriving until seven to us. I'll need to have a talk with her."

"Better you than me. She scares the bejeezus out of me," Carl says while grabbing the larger cooler. Despite his size compared to Sadie's, he has every reason to be thankful he's leaving it to Jason. "Follow me, and we'll get the turkeys. They were in the brine for two days. Should be perfect."

"They always are," Jason says, walking with Carl around the side of the house. There's a small barn, and he opens the door and walks across to a giant cooler of sorts. From this, he removes three bagged turkeys and places two in one cooler and one in the other.

"They still have a little brine in them. Sadie knows what to do. I also have two smoked ones here she said she'd take to the shelter for me."

"Sure, no problem. Got plenty of room," Jason says while Carl opens a large door. A distinct aroma fills the barn, making it obvious this is the smoke room. He comes back carrying two grocery bags with smoked turkeys in them. He sets these on the larger cooler and lifts it all with no noticeable strain. Jason grabs the cooler with the single bird, and we head to the beast.

Once they stow the coolers, we're ready to go. "You drive careful now. Want nothing happening to this beautiful young lady so willing to accompany you all the way out here," Carl tells him, then turns to me. "Miss, you're welcome here anytime. I mean any time at all." He gives a slight bow.

"Well, thank you. I hope we meet again." I don't know what else to say.

"We better go before her head gets any bigger. It won't fit in the truck if you keep carrying on," Jason says, winking at Carl.

"Well, yours fits no problem. I'm sure I have nothing to be concerned about," I say, opening my door.

"Ouch. Sadie's right, she can handle you," Carl says while he and Jason walk to the other side. They talk a few moments and shake hands before Carl heads for the house and Jason gets in the beast.

It's not long until we're back on the main road. The ride back is quiet. It's been such a pleasant evening, I can almost forgive Sadie for meddling, again. I did say almost. Needing to ask one question which has been bugging me, I break the silence. "Now what is this sled incident Sadie mentioned?"

"Nothing, nothing at all. She was being Sadie."

"Why do I suspect you're not being honest with me?"

"Believe me, it was nothing." I stare at him with an expectant gaze. "Okay, okay, but it was nothing. When I was young, and after she moved back here, we'd stay at the ranch on Christmas Eve and, in the morning, we'd open the gifts from Santa. One year, I got a new sled. You know, like a toboggan. A friend got one earlier, and I wanted one. The problem was temperatures had been warm and there was rain. Meaning, no snow for sledding."

"And?"

"And nothing. I wanted to try it out is all."

"And?"

"Well, like I said, there was no snow, and it was raining, so going outside wasn't an option."

Sighing in exasperation, I glare at him. "Do I need to drag this out of you? What did you do?"

"Nothing." If he says that again, I'll pull the beast over and shake it out of him. After several glances my way, he has a sly smile. "I took it to the top of the stairs and slid down them. That's all. Nothing else. Not a big deal."

Is he serious? "Wait, the stairs? The ones in the house between the living and dining rooms? Those stairs? You slid down the flight of stairs inside the house?"

"Well, yeah. There was a runner, so I thought it'd slide well enough."

"Oh, my gosh, the hardwood floors? Don't tell me you scratched the floor?"

"No, I moved the rugs to be at the bottom, so I'd slide across them instead."

"No one stopped you? Your parents and grandparents let you do this?"

"Well, in all honesty, they were asleep." His mischievous grin reminds me of Tyler.

"You're kidding? You did this before they were even awake?"

"Well, yeah. It was Christmas morning, and I wanted to try it. What else was I to do?"

"I can think of several things, but it's obvious you were incapable of any logical thought process. So, what happened? There had to be something for Sadie to call it an incident."

"If you must know, I was going fast when I reached the bottom and couldn't stop, and the rugs didn't slow me down."

"You mean you kept going?"

"Yep, I did. Straight into the wall. The front of the toboggan hit first and made a huge dent, while I flew forward, driving my head into the wall. I was lucky and missed the stud. It knocked me out for several minutes. When I came to, my parents, Sadie, and Grandpa were there, and Mom was holding a bloody towel. Sadie needed to give me stitches. The cut was above the hairline, so the scar doesn't show."

"You gashed the wall and your head? Who would do something so idiotic?"

"Hey, that's enough. It would have been fine if Sadie didn't keep those floors so slick. I keep telling her someone will slip and fall one of these days."

"Right, the floors were too slick. That's why you got hurt. Had nothing to do with being an imbecile. Did you think any of this through? You had to know you wouldn't stop before hitting the wall."

"I thought I'd stop, but I was moving," he says, chuckling.

"No wonder you watch Tyler like a hawk. No telling what he'll do, being your son. Does he know of this little escapade of yours?"

"No, and I hope he never will. Don't worry. He's more than capable of concocting things on his own. Quite capable."

"Like father like son, I guess."

After Jason's story, the journey home passes by much quicker, and he is pulling into the driveway before I know it. He parks in the back by Boris.

As I climb out, Sadie is waiting for Jason to bring the coolers. I carry the two smoked ones, which are a load by themselves, and he brings the large cooler before going back for the smaller one.

"Carl sent two smoked ones for the shelter. Said the others still have brine in the bags to keep them moist," he explains, setting the coolers on the back porch. "They should be fine out here tonight, but I'll take the smoked ones into the house." He takes the two bags from me, for which I'm glad.

"Should work," she replies. "Now get in the house, it's cold out here."

"It's time for me to head home, Sadie. It's late, and tomorrow is a workday," I say.

"You don't want to come in for coffee? I'm sure your boss will understand."

"Thought she was the boss," Jason says, snickering.

I ignore him. "No, I have things I need to do, and I'm sure Jason needs to get Tyler home, and you need to get to bed. Goodnight for now. See you tomorrow, Jason." I turn to walk to Boris.

Jason hurries to catch me. "Thanks for coming with me tonight. It was fun."

"It was, although, I doubt I'll be able to eat soon. Thanks for letting me ride along and for sharing about the sled incident."

"Doubt there was a choice for either of us going," he says, nodding toward the back door.

"I understand. Tell Tyler goodnight for me."

He opens my door and waits for me to get seated. Right then, Sadie comes out holding a paper sack and says something about Tyler's decorations. The turkey Tyler made me! How could I forget it? Jason trots across and brings the bag back to me.

"Goodnight and be careful."

After starting Boris, I back out facing the driveway. At the end, I check the mirror one last time. Jason's still standing there, watching me drive away, and he gives a brief wave. Even though I doubt he can see, I wave back, realizing I'm smiling. What a night.

Chapter Seventeen

Wednesday is here and, after starting the coffee, I bathe in my grandiose washbowl of a tub. I'm wearing my other new slack suit today. It's deep maroon and is perfect with my new gray silk blouse. Once the coffee's done, I fill my travel mug and head for the office. It being the last day of work this week, I have several things I need to do.

After parking in my spot, I jump out and make my way across the drive. When I reach the door, it bursts open from the other side. Jake stops dead in his tracks, appearing as alarmed to see me as I am him. "Mornin', Miss Jazmine," he says in his usual slow drawl. "Didn't expect someone on the other side of the door. How are you this fine mornin'?"

"I'm doing well, Jake, but if you don't quit calling me Miss Jazmine, I'll start calling you Sir Jake. Also, it's single digits out here. How is this a fine morning?"

"Might be single digits, but least they positive ones. Please let Terri know I fed them two puppies, will you? Man, can they eat. I put their bowls of kibble down and turned for the milk. When I turned back, them bowls was empty. Had to check to make sure I'd given them any. It was mazin', I poured them milk, and it was gone in no time too. They started whimperin' like they hadn't seen food in days. True to form, they were still raisin' a ruckus when I left. That Bob might be small, but he can sure make noise."

"I know all too well about Bob. Thank you for feeding them, and I'll let Terri know. What's next for you?"

"We headin' out to repair fences."

"In this weather?"

"Yes, ma'am. Cowboys work in all weather. Cows don't mind, we can't mind. You have a pleasant day, Miss Jazmine," he says with a tip of his hat.

"You too, Sir Jake. Be careful now."

After setting my things on my desk, I head off to check on the puppies. As I go through the lobby, Stanley is by his water dish, appearing hopeful. I pour him fresh water, for which he doesn't seem pleased, and go on to the kennel room, already hearing Bob's cries.

Once there, I find him trying to climb out of the box. His front legs are over the edge, and he's moving his rear ones in a pedaling motion, trying to push himself over the lip. "What do you think you're doing?" I grab him, holding him in front of me. "Where do you think you're going, huh? Where?"

He doesn't answer, and now Mindy is also trying to get out. I grab the box with her in it and carry the lot back to my office. Maybe now we can have peace. I hang my jacket and sit at my desk to start on work, but first Bob wants on my lap, and then Mindy cries too, so I do the same with her. It's great they're still small, or I wouldn't be able to use my keyboard.

They're soon asleep, so I busy myself with the work in front of me. I'm stunned when Cindy comes and mentions lunch. I didn't even realize it was time. I let her know I'll skip it today. Thanks to last night's "small" serving, I'm still not the least bit hungry. But she doesn't leave and when I glance at her, she has a sly expression. "What?"

"Are you going to share the details of your big night or not?" She has an expectant grin.

"What? I didn't have a big night. What are you talking about?"

"Wasn't it your first actual date with Doc Withers?" She's beaming. "Come on, I'm an old married lady, I need a little romance in my life. Even if it is someone else's."

Here we go again. I should know news like this travels fast. After motioning her in, I have her close the door. "We didn't go on a date."

"Not what I heard. Word is you took a long evening drive and stopped at a romantic out-of-the-way restaurant."

"What? It wasn't a date. We did an errand for Sadie, that's all."

"Using the old errand excuse again. Not buying it. You didn't go to a restaurant?"

"Well, yeah, we needed to wait for Carl to return, so we stopped for dinner. Still, not a date. We ran a simple errand. I doubt anyone would consider Jim's a romantic restaurant."

"Let's see. A lengthy evening drive in the countryside. Dinner at a remote restaurant, followed by a marvelous drive in the moonlight. All with the two of you, alone, together. Sounds like a date to me."

"An errand, that's all. We did an errand for Sadie," I call after her as she waltzes out of my office, but all I see is a wave. What can I do but shake my head? I'm sure Cindy was trying to get a rise out of me. Seems it worked. As I maneuver myself toward the door to close it, Jason arrives. He glares at me, seeing the puppies on my lap as I try to walk while in the chair so I don't disturb them. "What? They're comfortable. They don't enjoy staying in that nasty old box."

"Their box is fine. The blankets are changed daily. They'd be fine if you'd let them be."

"They don't seem to agree with you." I'm stroking Bob's back and smile when I hear his muffled contentment. "Is there something you wanted?"

"No, I was coming down the hall and heard you call out. Was wondering what it was," he says, turning for his office.

"Cindy was trying to be funny. She was asking about our date last night," I say without thinking.

He spins back. "Date? We didn't go on a date. You didn't tell her we were on a date, did you?" The worry in his voice is paramount.

"No. I told her we were not on a date. We were doing an errand for Sadie. That's all."

"Does anyone else know?"

"Know what?"

"About our, um, our so-called date. Do you think others think this too?"

"You know this town better than me, but I wouldn't doubt it. Could even be the headline of this morning's paper. You know, I miss Boston and no one knowing anything about me."

"What should we do?"

"Don't ask me. I'm the new one here."

"Maybe I should go talk to Cindy. Let her know she shouldn't say anything to anyone?"

"Might be too late for that since it's already out there. If we make too much of it, everyone might think there's something to hide."

"But there isn't," he says with a desperate expression.

"Of course not. We were doing an errand for Sadie."

"Right. An errand. I guess we're lucky it's Thanksgiving tomorrow. This should be quick to blow over. I'm sorry, but now you know why I get so frustrated."

"If you go through this all the time, I guess so. It is frustrating."

Right then, my door opens, and Jason has to move forward to avoid being hit by it. "Sorry." Georgia says. "Jazmine, Mrs. Gregory is in the lobby asking for you."

"I don't know a Mrs. Gregory," I say, trying to recall who she might be.

"We take care of her cat," Jason says.

"Yes, she brought Tubby in for his shots but asked to speak with you," Georgia explains.

"Okay, I'll be right out." I have to put Bob and Mindy in their box, which they disagree with.

"Here, I'll take them back to their room," Jason says, grabbing the box.

"They can stay here. I shouldn't be long." He's already out the door. I get my suit jacket and follow Georgia to the lobby. "Mrs. Gregory? You wanted to see me?"

"Oh, yes, dear. I've wanted to meet you for the longest time. I've heard such delightful things 'bout you and what with Tubby's 'pointment, it worked good. Now seeing you with my own eyes, you're even purdier then everyone said."

"Well, thank you. It's nice meeting you too," I say, not sure what's going on. "Is Tubby okay?"

"Fair, but mind ya he don like goin' to the v e t," she says, spelling out the last bit in a whisper.

"We get that a lot. Is there anything else you need?"

"Well, I hate to be blunt, but I heard you was single and lookin'. Brung my Shelly in to meet ya." Georgia is struggling to stifle a laugh. "Get over here, Shelly, and meet Miss Jazmine," she calls out. Three people are sitting in the waiting area: an older couple and a boy who looks like he's thirteen years old. What is she thinking? "Shelly, get over here. Do you hear me? Don't make me come get you." Her voice has escalated to a volume the whole county could hear. It doesn't even faze the boy.

Then a movement behind the partition off to the side catches my eye. The partition stands over six feet high, and a cap on top of a head is visible, moving along behind it. This mountain of a boy appears around the end. He's enormous, but he can't be much over twenty years old. Even with his stooped-over posture, he's at least six and a half feet tall.

"Oh, Ma, I heard ya. Can't I go back to the truck?" this monster of a boy asks in such a quiet voice. He never raises his head and continues staring at the floor.

"No, I want you to meet Miss Jazmine. Now come here and say a proper greetin'," she says, and he lumbers closer. He has to weigh over three hundred pounds, but not because he's fat. He's huge.

"Hello, ma'am," he whispers.

"Hello, Shelly. Nice to meet you," I respond and realize he's holding a cat in his hands. It's not a small cat, but somehow, it's swallowed by the enormous arms holding it.

"This is my youngest, my baby. I wanted him to meet ya. He a good boy. Hard worker, and smart as a whip like his daddy. Almost finished the tenth grade."

"Your youngest? How many sons do you have?" I still can't believe what she's trying to do. It's like I'm on the worst dating show ever.

"Seven, but two got hitched, and another died when the tractor drove over him. Now, I only have the four with me. Shelly's my favorite, though. He loves his mamma. Don't you, Shelly?"

"Ma, I told you not to say that no more. Tubby needs his shot."

I turn to face Georgia, wanting to hide my expression of disbelief. "Georgia, would you call Terri to come get Tubby for us?"

"I'll get her," she answers, rushing for the door to the back, trying to hold back laughter. This leaves me facing a now empty reception desk.

Terri soon arrives, also trying not to laugh. Georgia must have mentioned my current predicament. "Terri, Mrs. Gregory and Shelly brought Tubby in for his shots. Would you mind taking them back to one of the exam rooms?" I'm hoping she gets the hint.

"No, not a problem at all. Here, I can take Tubby," Terri says, holding out her hands, grinning from ear to ear. Even Tubby, who is squirming and hissing, seems reluctant to go along with this plan.

"I'll take him. He's mighty partic'lar 'bout who holds him," Shelly says.

Again, I'm astonished at how soft spoken he is.

"You go with her. I'll chat wit' Miss Jazmine," his mother says, and he follows Terri to the exam room. "I heard you come from back east?"

"Ah, yes, from New York, but went to school in Boston."

"Never been to neither. Don't get to the big city much. Every few months for supplies or when Tubby needs his shots."

"You mean Casper?"

"Mercy, no. I mean Glenrock. I wouldn't know what to do in Casper, what with all those vehicles running every which way and those enormous buildings. Have you seen them?"

"Ah, yes—yes, I have. Do you live far from here?"

"'Bout an hour. What d'you think of my Shelly?" I realize my lower jaw is hanging loose from its upper counterpart. "You know, any of my boys would make a good husband. They ain't shy of work, and I teached them to treat a woman right. They be good and kind men," she says, as Jason times his return well and strolls into the waiting room.

"Mrs. Gregory, how nice to see you. How are things out your way?"

"Fine, Doc. Brung Tubby in for his shots and for Shelly to meet Miss Jazmine here."

"Well, isn't that nice? I'm sure she enjoyed meeting him. How are the boys doing?"

"Oh, you know them boys. Always out doin' somethin'. Them others went out huntin' before we left. How's Sadie?"

"She's fine, ma'am, and I'll tell her you asked after her," he says. I'm hoping he came out to help me escape. "Oh, Jazmine, the form you needed signed is on your desk. I know you need to take care of it right away, with tomorrow being a holiday."

"Oh, yes. Thank you. I'll take care of it. Mrs. Gregory, it was a pleasure meeting you and Shelly. You tell him I said goodbye, will you?"

"I will. You ever get out our ways, you stop a spell. We'll have us coffee and let you see the place. Mighty purdy out 'round our way."

"I'm sure and thank you for the invitation. Now, if you'll excuse me, I'll take care of this issue," I say and scurry to my office.

In utter frustration I collapse in my chair. I try to think through what happened. Did she in fact bring this boy to meet me hoping we might date? I remember her saying she heard I was single and looking. Oh no! Is that going around? I'm on the verge of a serious panic attack when Cindy pops her head around the door.

"I hear you have a new beau," she says, snickering.

"Did you hear what she said? She heard I was single and looking. Can you believe it?"

"Well, Shelly is one fine boy. He treats his momma gooood. Can't go wrong with a man like him. Do you prefer a long courtship or want to make it quick and get to the pleasurable parts?"

"You're no help. Now be serious. Does everyone think I'm looking for a husband?"

"I doubt everyone does," she says, although she's still chuckling.

"I hope not."

"A lot are out of town for Thanksgiving and won't hear until they get back."

"What? Cindy, please be serious! Did you see the boy she brought in to meet me? I mean, there's no way on this earth. I'm way older than him, for starters."

"He is a nice boy, but don't worry. She's done this with all her boys. They are big boys too."

"I don't think big covers it."

"Agreed, but they're also the kindest people you could ever

imagine. Would do anything for you. All you have to do is ask. Don't worry though, they don't come into town often. Kind of loners and live a distance out," she says. Jason arrives and Cindy heads back to the lab, but I guess she can't help but make one last comment. "Now you let me know about the arrangements. I'm sure the mayor can do the ceremony if we give him enough notice."

"Cindy!" I call out as she ducks around the corner.

Jason is still standing in the doorway, trying his best to keep a straight face. "Mrs. Gregory and Shelly left. She wanted to talk to you more, but I explained you were tied up with this being the end of the week for us. She said to tell you goodbye, and you're welcome to come see her anytime." He's putting on a calm act, but the corners of his mouth quiver into a grin.

"Well, thank you for helping me. I didn't know what to say."

"I understand. To have your pick of her boys and all. It's a tough decision to make."

"Ha! You're so funny. I thought you were trying to help."

"Hey, I got you out of there, didn't I?"

"Yes, you did, and thank you. I don't know what...did you see...I mean...he's...he's a boy."

"I believe he's twenty-one. Don't you like a younger man?" He's no longer fighting not to laugh.

"Twenty-one? What was she thinking? What are you thinking? I'd never date a twenty-one-year-old."

"Well, her other sons are older. I think the oldest is close to thirty. I could drive you out to meet them," he says in a calm voice while struggling to keep from laughing.

"Are you crazy? Did you hear what she said concerning my being single and looking? Who would spread something like that? Why would anyone even think it?"

"Well, you did buy the party dress. A few might see that as you being available and on the prowl," he says.

"What? I'm not on the prowl and it's a simple dress! Are all of you crazy?" I'm close to screaming in frustration. "Who would spread something like this? Do you think it was Jill?" Too late, I realize it was out loud.

"Believe me, the rumor mill works well with or without Jill. I doubt you could even single out one person for this. Don't worry. It will blow over."

"Easy for you to say. You don't have mothers dragging in their sons for you to meet."

"No, they hand me pictures of their daughters, nieces, sisters, cousins, you name it. Even pictures of their mothers with phone numbers on the back."

"What? How often?"

"Often. They stop me in stores, at church, in restaurants. Anywhere I go."

"What do you do? How do you handle it?"

"I thank them, pocket the picture and toss it when I can. There isn't anything else to do. Understand they're trying to help, even if you don't want it."

"Okay, but this has never happened to me."

"Relax, in a few more hours you'll have a long weekend to get over it. By Monday, you won't even remember any of this."

"I don't care how much relaxing I do, it's seared into my memory."

"Just try. Anyway, I have things to do. Oh, Tyler asked if we could come see the decorations he made for you. I told him I'd check because I didn't know your schedule."

"Oh, are you going to Sadie's tonight for dinner? You could stop by then, but I'll need to put the turkey on the fridge. Didn't have time last night."

"We will, but don't worry, I'll give you time. I understand there're more things in the bag."

"I never checked. I'll hang them when I get to my place. Come by anytime."

"Okay, and I won't tell him his turkey was still in the sack." He winks. "But in all seriousness, I want you to know I appreciate how nice you are to him."

"I enjoy being with him. I'm not doing it to be nice. He's a great kid. A proper gentleman."

"I know. Unlike his father," he says, chuckling.

"I never said that. There are times you behave. Other times, well, we'll let them go."

"That's mighty nice of you, ma'am. I appreciate you tolerating this poor boy's moments of weakness."

"Who said they were only moments?" I can't help snickering.

"Funny. Not. Now, I need to go. You take care, and I'll bring Tyler by later."

"Looking forward to it," I call after him. Just as I'm getting back to work, Jennifer, the afternoon receptionist, enters.

"I hear your afternoon has been productive," she says.

"What?" I glance at her, and she's grinning. "No, it hasn't. I keep getting interrupted," I say with a sarcastic smile.

"Well, you're managing well. I mean, first the doc, and now Shelly Gregory. Are you going to leave any for the rest of us?"

"Jennifer!"

"Oh, calm down, Shelly's a pleasant boy. I'm sure you'll learn to like him."

"Right, that's it. Get out. There's work for you to do. If not, I'll find some. Now get."

"Okay, okay. I'm going. Man, are you touchy!" she says, giggling.

I sit and concentrate on steadying my breathing. My afternoon goes by fast. I make sure it does by not leaving my office for anything. It's safer this way. At about five, I gather everything and head for the kennel room, hoping I go unnoticed. Skipping the lobby—to avoid Stanley giving me away—I take my chance going by the stalls instead.

I make it seeing no one and, better yet, no one seeing me. Once inside, my luck runs out. Cassie is checking on the patients. "Terri said you might stop by. I fed them, and they love the kibble. I mean *love* the kibble."

"I wanted to see them before I left," I say, taking a seat, thrilled she doesn't mention what happened earlier.

"They sure knew you were coming. Both started yelping and jumping. I didn't know what was happening. Then you arrived, and it made sense. I hear there was a little excitement for you earlier."

My thrill dissipates. "Yes, in a way."

"I understand. My folks live out by them, and those Gregory boys are something. We all attended the same school—well, when they went to school. They were a handful. One of the older boys showed up at our house one Valentine's. Had flowers for my sister. I thought dad would have a fit. He thought a strange man was calling on his teenage daughter. My sister calmed him down and let him know the boy was sixteen. They are friendly boys. Big, but friendly. They're also talented," she says while I pet Bob and scoop Mindy into my lap too.

"Talented? How?"

"They all play a bunch of instruments. It's how they entertain themselves. They have a band and play at dances and such. They're quite good. It's something the first time you hear them. Believe me, a genuine shock."

"I can see how it might be. Not the type you'd expect for musicians. I guess size doesn't matter when you're playing an instrument."

"No, it doesn't, and they sure have the size," she says, giggling.

I think it's best to change the subject. "Are you going to your parents' for Thanksgiving?"

"Yeah. I'll go there in the morning and come back Saturday to relieve Terri. Two days is all I can take of my mother. She pesters me about if I'm dating and if it's serious. It drives me crazy."

"I'm sure she wants to be part of your life."

"I know, but it drives me nuts," Cassie says with an eye-roll. "Are you going to Doc Withers' for Thanksgiving?"

"I'm going to his grandmother's who lives near me. Jason and Tyler will be there too."

"Sounds like fun. Do they have an enormous meal?"

"This will be my first time. But if I know Sadie, she'll go all out." I give a slight giggle. "She already made pies and mentioned a cake and asked me to bring cookies. I'm sure there'll be plenty. Might even have to skip meals for the rest of the weekend."

"I know what you mean. Well, we're done with these critters. Guess I'll see you Monday or maybe Saturday if you come see your fella?" she says with a cheeky grin.

"Jason's not my fella."

"I meant Bob," she says, winking.

"Oh, of course. You have a fantastic visit, and I might see you Saturday. Take care." I can't help but kick myself. Why did I assume she meant Jason? What an idiot.

Now it's me and "my fella." Oh, and Mindy, I guess. We can't forget Mindy. I sit with them a while but have to go. If Jason and Tyler are stopping by, I need to display Tyler's decorations. After laying the puppies back in their box, I head home.

Once there, I put my bag and purse in their normal spot. Checking Tyler's bag of decorations, I'm flabbergasted to find a chain of paper loops, along with other Thanksgiving-themed items like Pilgrim's hats in addition to the turkey. There's even a roll of scotch tape. Sadie thought of everything.

I tape the turkey to the refrigerator door along with two of the hats. The rest I place around the mirror above the small TV. As I stand back to admire the pretty decorations, there's a knock at my door. They're earlier than planned.

"Perfect timing," I say, opening the door. A figure huddles in the cold outside the porch door. As I take the few strides toward the outer door, I notice the vehicle out front isn't the beast. I can't decide if I'm curious or nervous. My confusion increases when I realize it's a young lady.

"Come in, come in," I say, opening the door. She wastes no time in hurrying past me. "Go on through where it's warmer." As I follow behind her, I notice she's wearing a designer wool and cashmere pleated skirt coat. Is that a Balenciaga? Those over-the-knee boots have to be Amina Muaddi Olivia. They alone cost over a thousand dollars. I could never afford either. Once we're inside, I ask to take her coat.

"Oh, I can't stay long. I hope I'm in the right place. Are you Jackie?"

"Ah, no. I'm Jazmine." She must have the wrong house. Hard to do around here, though.

"I mean, Jazmine," she says while scrutinizing the room. "I'm a little flustered. Michael said the house was basic and out of the way. Didn't expect this basic."

"Michael?" Wait. She can't be Felicia. What would she be doing here?

"Yes, we have an apartment in L.A. Oh, I'm sorry, I'm Felicia." She's holding out her right hand. Several bracelets and a large diamond ring twinkle in the dim light, all screaming how expensive they are. Saying Michael traded up may be an understatement.

"Oh, you share an apartment with Michael?" I can't remember the last time I said his name out loud, but I'm thrilled to sense nothing when it leaves my lips, hitting my ears.

"Well, we started out sharing like you two. Now it's more living together. I don't know how you never fell for him. He's such a sweet guy. He explained how he let you share his apartment to help you afford your tuition. How he arranged for you to move here, after you begged him to help you get out of Boston. His giving never stops. I'm impressed you came out here alone and started fresh. You must be an amazing person. Anyway, I'm visiting my folks for Thanksgiving, and Michael wanted me to check if a bag of his clothes may still be here. It's a blue hanging bag, and he thought it might be in the spare bedroom closet?"

Dumfounded, I stare at this woman standing before me. She knows nothing concerning my relationship with Michael.

"If you could look, that'd be great. I don't enjoy driving these back roads at night. You never know what you might run into." She gives a nervous laugh while surveying the room, her top lip slightly curled, as she takes in my pitiful furnishings and decor.

"I'll have to check. I haven't done much with the spare room."

She remains standing by the door as I walk away. She seems terrified to enter. Must not want to get her posh boots dirty or something.

"Michael said you enjoy living minimally. This place must suit you," she says as I walk away.

"It's working for now," I say from the spare room. Sure enough, there's a blue suit bag hanging in the closet. The tops of multiple hangers are visible, and from the weight I can tell it contains several items. I head back to the front.

"Oh, great, you found it. It has his tux, and we need it for the Holiday Gala in December. I hope it's presentable. You remember how his clothes were. I've seen better at garage sales. Can you believe he wore a cheap off-the-rack suit for his graduation? I'd have been horrified. Anyway, I've been able to replace a few, and I'm working on the rest. I appreciate you finding this," she says, reaching for the bag. "Oh wait, I almost forgot." She rummages through her Gucci shoulder bag. "I know I have it here somewhere. Michael thought you might want this," she says, holding out a medium-sized envelope. I take it and she takes the clothing bag. "Now I'll get out of your hair. I'd love to stay longer and share Michael stories, he's such a character. But I need to get back to the city. You take care. I'll show myself out."

I walk behind her while she totters across the porch. My inner voice screams to put her straight concerning Michael, but when I start to speak, she says, "You have a nice evening, Janice."

I watch her tiptoe to her vehicle, like she's afraid she'll step in something nasty. The Mercedes Benz SUV she's driving seems fitting. Leaning against my porch door, I watch her maneuver her expensive vehicle back and forth multiple times with intrigue. It seems like forever before she's pointing in the right direction and drives off.

I shut the door, shaking my head. I wonder what she'll do when she learns I bought his tux used from a rental place.

Still in amazement and holding the envelope, I mull over the visit while walking back into the house. I don't think I could ever have imagined something like that happening. Not even Hollywood could conjure up something so absurd. Maybe they could, but it would end in a cat fight or worse. At the table, where my well-worn knock-off Gucci bag is, I examine the envelope. I'm not sure how to feel, it being from him. Maybe it's another letter explaining his actions and begging for my forgiveness. Before I can open it, another knock brings me out of my musings. Did she get lost? There are two ways to go when leaving my place. It's understandable how a girl like her would be confused.

I stuff the envelope into my bag, then open the door expecting to go out to the other like before, but Sadie is standing right here. I move back to let her pass. Tyler is right behind her then Jason, carrying several bags. Now I'm the confused one.

Tyler runs to the TV pointing out the decorations. "Look, Dad, she hung them like she promised."

"I did. They're too pretty to leave in the sack," I tell him. "I wasn't expecting you, Sadie, but I'm glad you're here. Tyler, go check

196

out the kitchen."

"Tyler begged me to come, and I wanted to see, anyway. Jason, put the food in the kitchen. We can eat once Tyler settles."

Did I hear right? "Eat?"

Jason rolls his eyes at me. "Yes, but it's not much. Barbecue ribs, rolls, beans, and fries."

"Barbecue? I wasn't expecting this," I say while he hauls the bags to the kitchen.

"Barbecue is our tradition the night before Thanksgiving," Sadie says.

"Grandma, come see the turkey! It's right in the center," Tyler calls from the kitchen.

"I'm being summoned. If you'll excuse me," she says.

"I'm sorry I didn't call," Jason says. "Didn't realize she was planning on coming here until we got to her place."

Does he think I'm upset? "No, it's fine. No problem. A minor surprise is all."

"Sadie told me you made changes. I like what you've done. It gives the place color."

She and Tyler are back and sit on the small couch. "Sit down, both of you. It hurts my neck having to glance up at you," she says, chuckling.

Jason and I sit at the dinette table. Why am I so nervous?

"I thought I saw someone driving off when we left Sadie's," he says.

"You're not my first visitors this evening."

"Someone came to visit?" Sadie sounds astonished.

"I know, staggering," I say, giggling. "I've been here for several months with no one coming by, then in one night, it's like Grand Central Station."

"Who was it?" Jason asks.

"Well, to my utter disbelief, it was Felicia." I wait for their reaction.

"Who?" Sadie asks.

"Felicia, the lady who is sharing an apartment with Michael in L.A. She let me know it's more living together now. It seems they're an item."

"What did she want?" Jason asks.

"He left a hanging bag in the spare room. I didn't even know it was there. Anyway, he wanted her to check if it was here when she came to visit her parents during the holiday. I guess he needs his tux for a gala the hospital is having."

"Boy, that takes nerve. Must be one expensive tux," Sadie says.

"No, it wasn't. I wish I could be there when she realizes we got it used from a tux rental place. Everyone will think he's a waiter." I can't help but smile at this. "Now, let me get plates, and we'll have these delicious smelling ribs. Jason, can you move the table out so we can get the four chairs around it?"

Getting out the four dinner plates I have, I hand them to Jason, who came in to help. I take out forks, spoons, and knives, not knowing what we'll need, and glasses.

After asking what they want to drink, I fill the glasses. The smoky aroma of the ribs fills the room as he sets the two open containers on the table. He returns with the string fries and baked beans. As I take my seat, I notice Tyler is sitting on his knees to reach the table. "Let me get him something."

"He's fine. Stay in your seat," Jason says. After he says the prayer, we dish out the food.

I eat little, and it's not because it's not the best BBQ; in fact I doubt I've eaten better. It's because I'm enjoying sitting here spending time with them. Tyler shares what happened at preschool today. We talk about different things, like we do when we eat at Sadie's. It's the first time I've felt comfortable here.

Too soon, it's time for them to leave. It's almost Tyler's bed time, and Sadie says it's hers too since she has cooking to do tomorrow. She then mentions I do too.

"What? I'm cooking tomorrow?" Not again.

"It will be brilliant. We'll have turkey, green bean casserole, mashed potatoes, giblet gravy, cranberry sauce, deviled eggs, corn, rolls, and whatever else we can find. Plus, the pies and the cake, and don't forget your cookies," she says like it's an average day's meal.

"Don't worry, Jazmine, Sadie can make it in her sleep," Jason says.

"If we don't get out of here, I might have to." She shoos her boys toward the door.

I thank each of them for coming, and Sadie and Tyler give me enormous hugs. "Daddy said we can see Bob tomorrow. Will you come with us?"

"Maybe I'll meet you there. We'll see tomorrow."

"It's a date," he says with a giggle, surprising us, and takes off for the truck.

Jason shakes his head, and Sadie and I chuckle, making our way out. He makes sure Sadie doesn't trip or fall, and she tells him to help me since she's been taking care of herself for years. He helps her anyway. Once all are in, I stand by the porch as Jason drives out. He doesn't have any problem at all. Interesting. Wonder why it was so difficult for Felicia?

I wave and see Tyler waving back through the rear window. I'm amazed how I feel watching them drive away. A few months ago, I didn't even know who they were. Now I feel bad they're leaving, even knowing I'll be with them tomorrow. I don't think I've ever felt this way. Not even with Michael.

Back inside, I store the leftovers in the fridge and get started on the cookies. While they're in the oven, I'll do my blog and check my group.

When the cookies are done and I've finished editing, I hit the button to post "Mr. Right!" That's it for now, so I disconnect and shut off the laptop. I retire to my bedroom after making sure the oven is off, twice.

Lying in bed, I'm not sure I even remember getting in. I turn off the light, ready for sleep. Tomorrow, I'm celebrating Thanksgiving with a family and exceptional friends. I can't stop smiling.

Chapter Eighteen

The wailing of my alarm reminds me I didn't switch it off last night to prepare for my late morning. Not needing to be at work, I lie in bed, but I can't get back to sleep. I'm excited, but don't understand why. It's a simple meal, right? Nothing special. Many people put so much effort into this day, but it's like any other day. The difference is...well...I guess there isn't any difference.

I slip on my thick socks, deciding to check out the broken-hearted group. Passing through the kitchen, I start the coffee on my way. The table is still away from the wall, with the four chairs placed around it. Thoughts of last night and how much I enjoyed it flood my mind. Maybe there's something to this family stuff. They seem to have filled a void I didn't realize I had.

This sounds like crazy talk, and I put it out of my mind. They're not my family. I get the chairs back in place. My laptop is still on the table. After connecting my phone, I hit the power button. While it boots, I pour coffee but skip eating anything because I'm sure Sadie will have enough food to feed a small army.

Back at the table, I check out the group and the recent posts. As I read through them, I click the usual "like" and "love" buttons and make a few comments. I try to keep my comments positive and steer women away from enclosing themselves in their misery and hatred of who they feel caused it. This is hard, I know, but I hope my comments encourage them, like many have helped me.

This motivates me to get moving, so I shut off my laptop and finish my coffee, feeling ready for this glorious day. It strikes me this is what Sadie would say. After starting the water to fill my expansive lavado of a tub, I pick out my clothes. Jeans and a casual shirt are an option, but I decide to go upscale instead. Maybe I could wear my new party dress? On second thought, no. Jason might take it the wrong way. I sort through the few dresses I have and select the perfect one. It's a simple black dress I'm sure couldn't be threatening or enticing. To this, I add my mother's simple pearl necklace and matching bracelet. I'll carry a pair of cute heels with me to wear once I'm in the house.

Taking my time washing my hair, I'm sure to give it an extra rinse in hopes it cooperates today. My thoughts turn to the size of the bathroom. One could even dry their hair while in the bath. Knowing an electric hair dryer and a tub of water wouldn't mix well, I finish rinsing my hair and pull the plug to drain the tub.

For now, I don my lingerie and favorite oversized shirt. I apply enough makeup to appear fresh and blemish-free while highlighting my eyes, then blow dry my hair and add a few loose curls. My hair works out the way I want this morning, which brings a smile to my face. Often, it has a mind of its own.

While checking myself in the mirror, I remember the first time I saw my reflection glaring back at me from this same wall. What a change.

For the finishing touches, I put on my dress and jewelry. While the dress is conservative, it flatters my figure. My chosen attire, along with hair and makeup, should be perfect. I grab my coat and the cookies Sadie requested and start Boris. Sadie wanted me to be there this morning around ten, which seems early to me, but what do I know about cooking Thanksgiving dinner, or even most dinners?

I park Boris in the normal spot, and Sadie is waiting at the door.

"Wow. You are a vision," she says.

"Well, thank you, but it's nothing special. This was the dress I wore under my gown for graduations. You could say it's my lucky dress."

"Don't know about you, but any man who goes out with you would consider himself more than lucky."

"Sadie, I can't believe you said that."

"It's true, all you need to do is snap your fingers and they'll be lining up like steers for the slaughter. Go ahead, snap your fingers and watch what happens."

"Sadie, I don't want any man, and you know it." I need to change the subject. "Anyway, you said you need my help cooking, so what can I do?"

"Okay, I get the message. Guess you've already cut your steer from the herd," she mutters under her breath.

"What did you say?"

"I said you need to peel and cut the eggs. They're cooling in the pan by the sink."

This wasn't what she said, but I know better than to argue. Time to get to work. With apron in place, I start making my first-ever Thanksgiving dinner. The morning goes well, and Sadie assures me everything is on schedule.

A commotion comes from the direction of the front door, and I hear Tyler calling out my name as he hurries through the house. He reaches the kitchen and, seeing me sitting at the table, rushes across.

"Jazmine, look." He's holding a box. "It's Bob and Mindy. Daddy let me bring them for the day." He's beyond excited by the extra guests he's brought. Bob is trying to climb out of the box, so I grab him before he falls. Tyler sets the box on the floor and lifts Mindy before sitting in the chair beside me.

"There he is," Jason says, striding into the kitchen. "What did I tell you about running in the house? Now remember, the dogs need to stay in their box or with you. Don't let them run around Grandma's house. That goes for both of you," he says directing his gaze at me. I also hear a well-timed huff from both puppies.

Tyler is quick to correct him. "They're not dogs, they're Dachshunds! Isn't that right, Jazmine?"

"You are correct," I say while letting Bob lick my nose.

"This was a mistake," Jason says.

"No, the mistake was counting on you to cook the turkey. We're eating at three, you know," Sadie reminds him.

"I know. Is the bird ready to go?"

"Yes, I've put the seasoned butter under the skin, and it, like the rest of us, is waiting for you," she says, handing him a metal cone-like thing. He inserts it in one end of the turkey and stands it on the base. There's a section like a loop coming out the top. I thought they cooked turkeys in a roasting pan?

"I'll be out by the grill," he says while heading for the back porch. "Coming, Tyler?"

"Can I bring the puppies?"

"Yes, but they stay in their box. That's if you can get the moocher away from Jazmine," Jason answers in a serious voice, although the corners of his mouth are curling into a smile. I lower Bob back into his box next to his sister.

Tyler runs after him, box in arms. "His name's Bob," he calls.

I'm stunned they're going outside. "Don't they need coats?"

"You'd think so," Sadie says. "But they're men and not known for common sense. They're only going to the shed. It's not far. Now, you get started on the carrots. Peel a little of the outside off with the potato peeler."

After I chop everything Sadie has for me, she walks me through mixing it all to make the dressing, followed by the casserole and candied carrots. After this, Sadie says we can wait for the rest for now. Assuring me it will all be done on time, she refreshes our drinks and takes a seat opposite me. As if on cue, Tyler returns with the puppies, saying he's found a ball for them to play with. As he heads for the front room, he asks me to join him.

"Go ahead, we're done with the difficult work," Sadie says.

In the brief time it takes me to join Tyler, he already has the puppies out of their box and is watching them check out every inch of their new surroundings.

"Dad says to keep a close eye on them so they don't wet on Grandma's rug," Tyler says, rolling the small ball across the floor. Both puppies take a quick glance at the so-called toy and go back to their exploring. Tyler tries a few more times to get their attention, but this isn't their thing.

He calls out for Bob to fetch it, but Bob gives him a "you tossed it, you get it" expression, causing me to laugh. After a while, the puppies find their way toward the warmth of the raised hearth and stretch themselves out in front of the fire. I'm not sure Tyler gets the message, but this means it's time for their nap, and they want to be left alone.

With the puppies down, Tyler sits next to me on the sofa and asks if I'll read him a story. This takes me by surprise, but I agree. He hurries to his backpack and removes several books before hurrying back to me. "You can take your pick."

Several are the ones I read to the girls I cared for so long ago. I pick one of my favorites and start reading while Tyler lifts my arm so he can get closer and see the pages better.

I've read the first few pages when Jason pops his head around the corner. "I thought you were playing with the dogs?" This elicits a huff from near the fireplace.

"They're sleeping, so Jazmine is reading me a story. You want to listen?" Tyler asks.

"Sleeping, huh? About all they're useful for."

I don't understand his disdain for the puppies. "I thought vets like animals?"

"Oh, I like animals. All kinds. Not thrilled with freeloaders though, in particular ones with attitudes." This gets another huff in response. "I came to check on the firewood. Looks like we're set for now."

"Come listen. We're at the good part, and she reads it better than you. She does the voices different," Tyler says, which causes me to giggle.

"I'll see if your grandma needs anything. Keep an eye on those…" I give him a stern scowl. "Puppies," he says, rolling his eyes, and leaves while we go back to the book.

We lose track of time and read through several books, only stopping when Jason calls out, "Tyler, get cleaned up and make sure the puppies are in their box."

At least he called them puppies. I set the current book with the others while Tyler rounds up the puppies. They don't seem thrilled at being moved away from the warmth of the fire, so he puts the box in front of the hearth and they settle down.

I follow Tyler out, and he heads for the bathroom to wash while I go to the kitchen. As I pass, I notice the dining room table is set and ready for dinner. Must have gotten lost in a world of my own while reading. In the kitchen, I wash my hands and ask what I can do.

"You can stir the gravy," Sadie tells me.

As she transfers the food from pans to bowls ready to be moved to the dinner table, Jason comes in with the turkey on a platter. It smells delicious. A beautiful smoky aroma trails behind him as he walks past going to the counter. After slicing the turkey, he places the cut meat on a fresh platter and sets it in the middle of the table.

Everyone helps bring the various other bowls and platters and arranges them around the turkey, using it as a centerpiece. Once everything is set, Sadie pours the iced tea while we make ourselves comfortable. The spread appears magnificent, not to mention the beautiful china, crystal, and silver cutlery.

Since it's time for prayer, I hold back from digging into the food. We join hands as Jason says the blessing. It's longer than usual, but then it's Thanksgiving. I remain silent, with my head bowed until he finishes. When he does, I'm amazed to hear Tyler add, "Thank you God, for bringing Jazmine to us."

Then Sadie and Jason both say, "Amen."

Not knowing what to do or say, I'm close to tears. Tyler's words have filled me with all kinds of emotions: happiness, love, gratitude. I try to compose myself.

He gazes at me with concern. "Are you all right?"

"Ah, yes, I'm fine," I say, taking the bowl Jason is holding out.

The rest of the meal plays out like a dream. The food is delicious, but the conversation and laughter are even more delightful. I never want this to end, but know it must.

After clearing the plates from the main meal, we have our

dessert. I'm certain I won't be able to eat for at least a week, but it's all so delicious, I can't stop myself from trying a little of everything.

Once we finish eating, we clear and wash the rest of the plates. "Oh, Jason," I say in a panic, "did you let Terri know you brought the puppies?"

"Yes, I sent a text telling her, but that means we need to feed them ourselves. Tyler, get their food and bowls, and I'll get the puppies."

Tyler does as he's told, and I hear Bob's whimpers even before he reaches the room. His grumbles continue as Jason carries the box into the kitchen. I follow him to find Tyler measuring out the kibble and putting it in two tiny bowls for the puppies. He adds water to a third bowl and sets all three on the floor. Once Jason lifts the puppies from their box, they spot their bowls and are off across the kitchen at speed.

Less than a minute later, their bowls are empty, and the puppies have their noses in the water to wash it down. Although they seem well fed, their heads soon turn toward each person in the kitchen, hoping for the next helping. They check their bowls again to be certain and seem disappointed to find them still empty. "Are you positive we're feeding them enough?" I ask.

"They're getting plenty. These breeds will eat if there's food."

With no luck getting more, the puppies walk away from their empty bowls and start sniffing around the kitchen instead, maybe hoping to find crumbs. When Bob bumps into my leg and tries to climb up, I grab him and settle him on my lap. Tyler gets Mindy, and both seem content. On Sadie's suggestion we make our way to the front room.

We spend the rest of the evening sharing stories and chatting while watching Tyler try to play with the puppies. They never seem to get intrigued by the ball, but when he drags a string across the floor, it gets their attention. They play like this for some time, even after Tyler stops. We laugh when Bob grabs it and runs off, only to have Mindy pulling it the other direction. It turns into a game of puppy tug of war.

Way before I want it to be, I know it's time to leave. Words can't describe how much I've enjoyed my time with them. This is one of the best days I've ever had. I get a long hug from Tyler, which threatens to bring tears to my eyes, and one from Sadie too. Jason helps me with my coat, and after switching to my boots for walking in the snow, I'm ready to go.

"Jason, walk her out so she doesn't fall," Sadie insists, while handing me a bagful of food to take home. Seems she didn't get the memo announcing my not eating for a week.

"I can manage by myself, you know."

"Did I ask a question? Now, Jason, you go with her and don't forget to help her with her door."

With this, I guess we're resigned to our fate, and he walks beside me out to Boris. It's a quiet walk, and he opens the door and helps me get seated. Before closing the door, he says, "I'm glad you came today…ah, Tyler liked you being here…I did too, so thank you."

"It's not me you should thank. Sadie did most of the work. Plus, she insisted I come."

"Well, however you came to be here, we enjoyed your company," he says while gazing at me. He moves closer, and I feel there might be something else, but after a moment, he steps back and closes the door. "Drive careful," is all he adds.

I start Boris, but remain where I am for a few moments longer. What is happening to me? As I drive away I notice he's watching and waving. I wave back, trying to make sense of the feelings I have right now.

At my place, I get changed into my lounging clothes, deciding to watch movies. There are brilliant ones on this time of year. I make myself comfortable on the couch, not bothering with any food as I'm still stuffed to the point of bursting. I find a promising movie and settle in to watch.

After watching two, I force myself to turn off the TV and make my way to the bedroom while wiping the tears from my cheeks and eyes. Glad they're joyful tears.

In bed, I turn off the light, remembering the magnificent events of the day. My first Thanksgiving where I felt like I knew what it meant to be thankful. With this thought, I close my eyes. The dream of tomorrow is waiting.

~ * ~

With my day free, I didn't set my alarm. My eyes opening to the light shining through the window proves I slept later than expected. I think about how much fun I had yesterday. This puts me in an excellent mood, and it's not even diminished when I lie back in my opulent oversized bowl of a tub. Well, lie may be a stretch.

Once I finish, I dress in my normal writing ensemble. With coffee in hand, I head for the front room, avoiding even thinking of food. I'm still stuffed. Will I ever eat again? There are things I need to do for work, and I do these first. When I'm through, it's time for my broken-hearted group. It seems a few had a rough day yesterday and several try to comfort them. I know I'm avoiding the obvious, and procrastination has never been my thing. I need to do my blog and can't put it off any longer.

With fresh coffee poured, I'm ready to start on the next section.

In all likelihood, this will be my last, since I don't know what I'll write after this part. I better make it good.

The Rich Girl's Poor Life
My life, the ending

Our plan coming together thrills us, and the time until he needs to leave flies by. Once he's gone, I bury myself in work to keep from thinking how much I miss him. Weekends are the worst since the office is closed, and I wander around the apartment.

The need to move out of the apartment a month before leaving to join him allows me to send our things ahead to be there when I arrive. There's a small hotel I find to rent by the week, and I'm set. Except he's several thousand miles away. Plus, his schedule has gotten to where we can't Skype anymore. Now we exchange emails. Seems he's working long hours and is tied up even on the weekends.

My last day comes, and the office has a small farewell party in the morning since my flight leaves at noon. It was nice of them to do something. When it's time, I gather the last of my belongings and tell everyone goodbye. Now I'm ready to start our new life together. Can it get any better than this?

I explain how the orderly drove me to the house and my first impression of it. How I knew this was temporary and at least we were together. Then I mention the envelope and what I feared it contained.

Including the letter verbatim causes the depression to envelop me again. Even with changing the names and not including the locations, I can't escape that it's my reality.

As I sit, staring at the words of the letter on the screen, tears fill my eyes, and a few tumble down my cheeks. Then I remember the envelope Felicia gave me. Hurrying to the bedroom for my bag, I remember my thoughts of what it might be. A letter explaining his actions. Maybe even admitting how rotten he treated me and begging for my forgiveness.

My bag is beside the bed, and I grab the envelope from it. Not wanting to wait, I open it to find a sheet of paper folded around a picture. It's the picture I took at his graduation from medical school. He's in his gown and the new suit I bought him. The memory of that day floods my mind, and I remember how ecstatic we were. I read the note. *"Jazmine, thought you might like this to remember my big day."*

I get no further. My knees weaken, and I fall, sliding down the edge of the bed until I'm flopped on the floor. As I stare at the picture, the tears in my eyes blur my vision. I can't believe this. My heart is racing with the memory of his first note. The pain in my chest is unbearable. I struggle to breathe. From deep in my mind comes the memory of the frame I used for the picture. It was on my father's desk with my mother's picture in it. One of the few things I could take with me.

The frame was metal with gold beading around the edge. I knew it would be perfect hanging on the office wall or on the desk of a successful doctor. When I was at the children's home, one girl took it and tore out my mother's picture before I could get it back. She flushed the picture down the toilet while the others laughed at me. Then she tossed the frame at me, but I couldn't catch it. It hit the floor, shattering the glass.

I kept the frame under my pillow and every time I saw it, I tried to remember my mother's picture, but over time, the image in my memory faded. When we got the picture of his graduation, I felt it would be perfect for the frame.

Then it hits me. Only the picture is here. What happened to the frame? Maybe he explains it in the note? It's on the floor where it fell, and there is more written here:

Felicia liked the frame and replaced the picture
with one of her to keep on my desk. It's perfect.
M.

I sit in disbelief as the picture and note fall from my hand. The picture lands facing up, and seeing him staring at me sends chills through my body. I used to love his grin so much. Now it's a dagger to my heart. I even hear the laugh he used when he corrected something I said. The laugh now running through my brain with the words that followed it: "You're such a foolish little girl. How did you ever get through Harvard?" He said it was his little joke with me, but now I wonder, was it ever a joke?

After a while, I force myself up, sitting on the edge of the bed. Then I struggle to stand and stumble to the other room, leaving the picture and note behind. Plopping in the chair by my laptop, I sit in a daze staring at the screen. Dejection once again overwhelms me. I don't know how long I sit here, but I need to finish the blog. Taking a deep breath, I start where I left off, as tears wet my cheeks.

I have feelings of utter loss and failure, of being alone and knowing my life is over. How could he do this to me? To someone he loved? Did he ever love me? We were together for so many years, and it was always us. I was certain it always would be.

I add how I spent the next several days. How devastated I felt, how lost, how useless and unlovable. How alone.

The story is demoralizing, but needs to be true to my feelings. I knew my life was ending, but was it ever much of a life? My mother abandoned me, my father left me, I lost my house, my clothes, my school, my friends, and now, the person I thought never would had left me too. I have no one and know I'll have no one ever again. Something is wrong with me. Something makes me unlovable. Something drives people away. I know now that for the rest of my years, it will be nothing more than me going through the motions of life without having an actual life. How could I? Everyone has left me. I'm alone.

I finish, knowing there isn't any more to write. I'll review it tomorrow or Sunday since I have little else to do. With these depressing thoughts, I make my way to bed. I try to remember my feelings from yesterday, but that was a different girl. Not the real me, but the one the world likes to trick. The one the world let's get a glimpse of happiness until she believes it's near, then rips back the curtain to show her it was all a ruse, never to be a reality.

Staring at nothing in the dark, I listen to the sounds of the night, admitting to myself I have no life, I'm nothing but an existence. I will always be alone. With this, I close my tear-filled eyes and hope sleep comes soon. It's the only time I might find peace.

Chapter Nineteen

Saturday, the light shining through the thin sheers of my bedroom window wakes me. It's late, but what reason do I have to get up? The clinic is closed, and the puppies don't require help with meals anymore. Even they don't need me. All I can do is wait for Monday so my existence can continue. At least then I might provide a little use. It's all I have now. I need to accept this.

The tears come, and I can't stop them. Not even sure I care. It's not like there's anyone here they'll bother. I drift in and out of sleep for most of the morning. My phone rings, but I don't bother answering. It will be the world with another attempt to trick me into thinking I have a right to be happy. After the third call, I turn the ringer off, but my mind won't shut down, and I struggle for I don't know how long.

I'm not hungry, and coffee is too much of a bother. I could get online, but I have little to offer. I do need to review the blog section, though. I owe this to the few who might read it. I'm sure they think it's nothing but a story and question how anyone could be so useless in real life. If this were an actual person, why wouldn't they have ended their life by now? The joke's on them. I have no life to end. It ended the second Rick handed me the envelope. All that's left is to bury my corpse someday when my physical body discovers the truth.

It's an effort to drag myself from bed, but I make my way to the main room and the table with my laptop. Once in my chair, I wait for the laptop to be ready. After opening the file, I start my review.

At first, it's obvious I was feeling positive, what with still having the memory of my day with Sadie, Jason, and Tyler. As I continued to write, reality was setting in, and I was coming back to the truth I escaped for a brief time. When I reach the part covering the envelope, I again remember the one Felicia gave me. My insides quiver as my heart races, and I fight the dizziness threatening to overtake me. Dazed, I stare at the screen unable to focus on the words in front of me. I don't know how long I sit here. From somewhere in my fogged brain comes the realization I need to finish the blog. Taking a deep breath, I start where I left off, feeling the tears running down my cheeks.

I don't add anything or change much, concluding it explains things well. I also know there isn't any more story to tell. This was the end. The end of my life, so what else could I write? I hope maybe someday, someone may read this and wonder whatever happened to this foolish girl. Maybe they can lie to themselves and imagine she found happiness, but I know the truth: she never will.

No one cares or will ever care for this unlovable excuse of a person. I'll leave it like this and let my unfortunate readers have their fantasy.

I'll post it tomorrow. The one thing on my to-do list. I also notice there's been more calls. It's not like it matters. For all I know, Felicia called to see if I have any more of Michael's stuff, but I don't. He made a clean escape from me. He got away with everything he wanted and left this hollow shell of a person.

I shut off the laptop and get up, thinking I'll go back to bed. What else is there to do? But I don't have the energy and flop on the small couch. The tears are coming, but I don't want to cry anymore. Don't have the strength. Knowing I'm drifting off, I close my eyes. Sleep is the best thing for me now.

~ * ~

A pounding sound off in the distance wakes me. Not knocking, mind you, but heavy pummeling. I hear it again through the daze, and it's closer this time. It's coming from the front of the house. Before I can get up, it comes again, even louder, and the realization it's my front door breaks through my fog. Guess I need to answer it. With my luck, it's the property management company telling me I must move. I'm so pathetic I don't even deserve a dump like this.

While trudging my way there, I try to focus but a mist shrouds everything. The pounding comes again while I fumble with the lock. My fingers aren't functioning well, but I get the lock undone and turn the handle. The door bursts open, knocking me back, and I stumble, banging against the metal wardrobe, struggling to catch myself.

Sadie is standing in the doorway surrounded by the haze, and she doesn't appear cheerful. What is she doing here? How did she even get here?

"Why aren't you answering your phone? I called, but it keeps going to voicemail."

I struggle to find my way through the mist back to the couch. I can't put on the cheerful façade today. She must follow because when I glance up, she's standing in front of me.

"Is your phone broken? Jason even tried. He says he gets the same thing," she says, her voice echoing from a distance.

"I turned it off while I was sleeping. Why are you here?"

"You have to ask? Because you wouldn't answer your phone. What is wrong?"

"Nothing, I'm a little depressed. I'll go back to bed and should feel better tomorrow. Thanks for coming by, but I'm fine."

"No, you're not fine. Let's go. Get your things. You're coming with me."

"What? No. Why would I come with you? Where would we go? I'm good. I'll go back to bed."

"Again, you're not fine, and we don't have time to argue. Get your things and let's go."

I can't summon the energy to move. I can't play the happy-go-lucky girl the world likes me to pretend I am. Not today. What's the use? "What's the rush? It's not like I have anything planned or anywhere to go. You go, I'm fine."

"Is she okay?" It's another voice in the distance. Peering through the parting mist, I see Terri is standing by the door. That explains how Sadie got here.

"Did you bring her?" I demand.

"Yes, she called because Doc Withers wasn't available. I got her, and we drove here. Are you okay?" Terri seems to glide toward where I'm sitting.

"You watch her while I pack her things. She can change at my house," Sadie tells Terri, and is swallowed by the mist as she heads toward my bedroom.

"Sadie, no need to pack anything. You both can go. I'm fine," I say again, trying to put more effort behind it.

"Jazmine, this isn't like you. Don't you feel well?"

"Not a good day. I need to sleep. I'll be okay by Monday. You'll see."

Sadie appears with one of my suitcases and a hanging bag. "Get her purse and phone from the table. I'll get her boots and coat on and help her out to your truck," she says, setting the suitcase and hanging bag by the door.

While Terri gets my things, Sadie tells me to put my boots on, setting them in front of me. I try to argue, but she won't listen. Everyone is against me. Why won't they leave me alone and let me continue my miserable existence? Not sure why, but I slip on my boots. I have no place to go and no one who wants to be with me, so why leave the house? This depressing, run down, thimble-size house.

"Now let's go. We're leaving," Sadie says. "Terri, take the bag and suitcase out with her purse then come back and help me."

"Okay, I'll be right back."

Still confused, I stand and let Sadie slip on my coat. After zipping it, she turns me and pushes me toward the door. We meet Terri coming back, and she takes one arm while Sadie takes the other and they walk me into the mist.

"She's not wearing any pants," Terri whispers to Sadie.

"Of course not. I don't wear pants when I sleep," I point out.

"Doesn't matter. She won't need them for now. Open the door, and we'll get her in the back seat."

I realize I'm by a truck. Terri has the door open, and Sadie helps me in, telling me to fasten my seat belt. They get in the front seat, and Terri drives out. I'm not sure where we're going, but it doesn't matter. I try gazing out the windows, but the fog is too thick.

Off in the distance, Sadie tells Terri to drive around to the back where it will be easier. The fog thins when Terri stops by the steps leading to the house. Sadie appears at my open door, and both drag me out of the truck and to the steps. I still don't know why they're doing any of this.

"Get her things while I get her inside the house," Sadie says to Terri. "Come on, Jazmine, you need to walk."

In an instant, I'm standing in a bedroom. This must be Sadie's, but I don't remember ever being here. She leads me to a chair and lets me fall into it.

As I slouch in the chair, Terri arrives and sets my things on the bed. "What can I do now?" She seems concerned.

"We're okay now. You get ready, and we'll see you at the center," Sadie says. I don't know what Sadie means, but notice she's removed my coat and boots. When did she do that?

"Do you think she'll be ready in time for Jason to get you for the Fall Fling?" Terri whispers. Her question seems to come from hundreds of miles away, but it catches my attention. From somewhere, I summon enough energy to get to my feet and glare at both of them.

"I am not going to any fling with or without Jason. Is that what this is about? You're trying to trick me into going to this fling thing? Get out of my way. I'm going back to my place," I say, my anger causing me to sound gruff.

"How? You don't have a vehicle, aren't wearing any pants or

boots, and it's ten degrees outside. Are you walking home?" Sadie stares at me.

"I said I'm not going to any fling."

"Well, not the way you're dressed. Now, come and get in the shower. It will revive you enough so we can discuss it. Terri, you can go. I have it from here."

"Okay, if you're sure. Call me if you need anything. Jazmine, I hope you're feeling better soon. I'll see you at the center," she says as she leaves.

"Oh no, you won't. I told you, I am not going anywhere."

"Whatever you say, dear. Now get undressed so you can take a shower, and I'll show Terri out."

"I'm not taking a shower, and I'm not going to any fling, that's for sure." I turn their way, but struggle to make them out in the bright light around them. I hear their voices echo from the mist surrounding them.

Terri turns to Sadie. "What do you think happened? She's not acting like herself at all."

"She's depressed. I think she wrote the section on her blog last night of when she first got here."

"What blog? You mean she's writing about her breakup? Oh, my gosh. Is she Tiffany?"

"Yes. It's the pen name she's using. Don't worry, I'll take care of her. You get yourself all gussied up for your beau. It will be fine. You'll see."

After waving Terri off, Sadie returns, appearing full of authority.

"I'm not going to any fling, and I'm not depressed."

"Of course not, dear. Now let's get you in the shower. I brought your shampoo and conditioner, so we have everything we need." She leads me to the bathroom.

"Why do I need to take a shower? I told you I'm not going anywhere."

"I understand, dear. Let's take off your shirt." She undoes the few buttons I have fastened.

This is all I'm wearing apart from my panties. I don't sleep in a bra. Once the shirt is unbuttoned, she takes my arm and walks me to the shower. This makes no sense because I'm not taking a shower. There's no reason to. I'm not going anywhere.

The next thing I know, she's opened the shower door and helped me enter. Realizing I'm standing in the shower, I drop to the floor like an errant child. "I told you I'm not taking a shower. I'll sit here, but I'm not taking a shower."

"Suit yourself, dear," she says in her oh-so-sweet voice. The one where I know she's not listening to anything I'm saying. I watch while she turns the shower handle on full. To my horror, it's set for cold. "You do what you want. I'll be in the bedroom getting ready."

It's a struggle to stand while being blasted by icy water, and it seems like an eternity until I'm upright and can point the shower head away from me. Adjusting the temperature to hot, I crowd into the corner, waiting for the water to heat while I shiver. Why would she do this? The bathroom door opens, followed by the shower door. She tosses me a bottle of shampoo and conditioner and closes the door.

"Feeling better, dear? You need to get a move on. Still need to do makeup and style your hair. Don't doddle." The bathroom door closes behind her.

With the water warming, I decide a shower is not a bad idea. Since my hair is already wet, I'll wash it too. My shirt is soaking wet and I wring it out the best I can, tossing it over the shower wall. It lands on the floor with a wet thud. Serves her right. Slipping off my panties, they soon follow. After redirecting the shower head, I slip under the stream of now hot water.

"I'm still not going anywhere," I yell out again so she knows for sure. Who does she think she is, anyway?

This is my first shower in months, and I can't help but enjoy it. It's miles better than the thimble of a tub I have. I can even rinse my hair with ease. It feels outstanding, but I refuse to admit I'm feeling better. "I'm still not going!" I call out again, so she knows I haven't changed my mind.

"What, dear?"

"I said I'm still not going to any fling. Even if I took a shower. I'm not going."

"Whatever you say, dear. Now hurry along, we have little time and lots to do."

With the enjoyment of the warm water massaging my skin and relaxing my muscles, I'm taking my time. I've nothing to hurry for anyway. Unsure how long it's been, I feel somewhat refreshed, and turn off the water and squeeze the excess out of my hair. On the counter is a stack of towels for me.

I grab one and dry my hair the best I can. Its long length doesn't help the drying process. This doesn't concern me. I like my hair this way and no one else gets any say. With one towel wrapped around my head and another around my body, I make my way to the bedroom.

Sadie seems ready to go. I didn't realize how long I was in there. I let her know she's pretty, but I'm careful not to sound too enthusiastic.

"Where are my clothes?"

"You need to do your hair and makeup first, don't you think?"

"If I was going somewhere, yes, but I'm not, so no."

"Suit yourself," she says.

"Where are my clothes? You know many would consider this kidnapping and restraining someone without their permission?"

"How so, dear? You're free to go anytime you want. You know where the doors are."

"All right, then. Where are my clothes so I can leave?" I don't even see my boots.

"I don't have the slightest idea. If you're leaving, I guess you'll go as you are." She smiles at me.

"I can't go out like this. What do I have to do to get my clothes back?"

"I told you. Do your hair and makeup, and you'll get your clothes. You can't go out in a towel."

"I'll get even with you for this. You mark my words."

"Of course, dear. Now move along. We're wasting time," she says, leaving the bedroom.

All I can do is take a seat at the vanity and survey the makeup she's already laid out for me. This lady is something else. How did my makeup get here? I apply my usual foundation, powder and eye-shadow, but take my time and make sure I do it right. No sense in making myself appear worse. I do the best job I can, and the results are decent, even if no one will see it.

My brushes and hair dryer are set out on the bed. How did they get here? They weren't here earlier. At the vanity, I style my hair how I like it. In what seems like mere minutes and a handful of mousse later, it's terrific. Perfect, in fact. Not that it matters—for the same reason the makeup doesn't matter.

I turn to find my lingerie laid out on the bed. Where did it come from? It seems it's all here, along with my new black high heels. I never even heard Sadie enter. Still not knowing what's going on, I slip everything on, wondering all the while what's coming next. In the middle of the room, I stand in lingerie and shoes, appearing to be ready except for one minor detail. I'm missing something to put over it all.

My clothes bag is hanging on a stand in the corner. I totter across to it, careful not to cockle over in my heels, unzip the bag and stare in astonishment. How can this be? The one dress she brought, the dress that's hanging in this bag right in front of me, is the new cocktail dress I bought last week. The one that caused all the problems with Jason.

"I see you found it," Sadie says. She's standing right next to me, even though I never heard the door open. "Put it on and let me see. It's so stylish, even on the hanger. I can't wait to see it on you."

"There is no way I'm wearing this dress. This is the one that started all the gossip of me wanting Jason to ask me to this fling thing. No chance. I'm not wearing it."

"How can a simple dress cause so many problems? Even such a stunning one as this. I bet it's perfect on you. Now, let's get it on you."

"I told you I'm not wearing this dress. Jason will think I'm trying to trap him or something. I'm not putting this dress on, end of story."

"Suit yourself, dear, but you need not bother," she says, standing back after zipping it.

"What? How…when…how did you get this dress on me?"

"I don't know what you mean, dear. I held it out, and you stepped into it. Oh my, it's such an exquisite dress, and on you, it will take people's breath away," she says pointing at my reflection in the mirror.

The dress is perfect. Who am I kidding? I look fantastic. Too bad no one else will see me.

"Here, try these," she says, putting something in my hand.

In my palm is a set of earrings. They were my mother's favorite, her prized possessions. They came with a matching necklace. How did Sadie even know where I kept them? I realize she's holding out the necklace too.

"Turn around, I'll put it on you."

Desperate to see how it looks on, I follow her instructions and bend so she can reach my neck. When I look to the mirror, a burning lump fills the back of my throat and tears fill my eyes. The necklace is perfect, like it was meant for this dress. Delicate white gold flowers, each with a diamond in the center, catch the light and sparkle against my chest. I fix the earrings in place and check again. I haven't seen them in such a long time. They match the same floral design of the necklace, but each earring has a cascade of diamonds trailing down several inches.

This exquisite jewelry set was my mother's wedding gift from my grandfather. I don't know what happened to the dress, but I'm thrilled I could keep these. They were valuable when she got them. Who cares what they're worth now? To me, they're priceless.

"Oh, you are a goddess. This dress was meant for you to wear with this jewelry. You are a vision."

"Thank you. The dress is beautiful, but the necklace and earrings take it to a whole extra level."

"Yes, they do, dear. Remember though, they're simply objects. It's you who's the vision. Your beauty is what's so stunning. It's all you. Not them," she says and slips a mink stole across my bare shoulders.

"It's a little cool outside. This will help for the drive. You can't take your big purse, so I put what you need in this small clutch. I think it goes well with the dress and the silver highlights."

I turn her way. "Hold it, why do I need the stole and a smaller purse?"

"For going out, of course."

Right then, Jason calls out, seeming to walk toward us. "Are you ready yet? I've been waiting outside. This isn't one of your lady things of wanting to make an entran—" He stops dead in his tracks, seeing me standing in the bedroom. Sadie is hidden behind the door.

"Jazmine?"

It hits me. It's all a dream. This explains how things keep appearing and all. I'm dreaming, and it's all a fantasy. Might as well let myself enjoy it.

"What? You don't recognize me?" I say, while taking the small clutch Sadie is holding out from behind the door.

"Ah, yes, I mean no, I mean…well, you…I don't know…you're so different!"

"Don't you give the sweetest compliments. Magnificent you work with animals. You have such a problem with people." This dream is fun.

"I mean, you're even more beautiful than normal, and I didn't think it was possible."

"Nice comeback, son," Sadie says, stepping out from her hiding place with an enormous grin. "Anyway, we need to go." She takes hold of my arm and ushers me out.

"I'm parked out front," he says. As Sadie and I walk past him and head for the front of the house, his eyes remain glued on me like he's in a trance. I like this dream.

"Put your tongue back in your mouth, Jason. Get up here and open the door for us," Sadie calls over her shoulder. I am so enjoying this.

He seems to snap out of his stupor and rushes ahead to open the front door. Once we're through, he hurries to open the porch door. I suppress my laughter, watching him fumbling with the handles. Still flustered, he holds out a trembling hand to help each of us down the steps before scurrying ahead to the car.

I can't believe my eyes. There's an actual car parked on the drive. Now I know I'm dreaming. It's my father's white Cadillac Fleetwood Limited, the last model year they made them. I forgot all about it. Guess anything is possible in a dream.

"Jazmine, you sit in front with Jason. I'll take the back," Sadie says while Jason holds the door open and helps her get seated. Once she's set, he closes her door and opens mine.

"Thank you, sir. Seems you can be a gentleman."

He hurries around to the driver's side, jumps in, and starts the engine. "We'll be a few minutes late, but I guess this means you can make your entrance."

Without thinking, I glance at him. "Be late for what?"

"The Fall Fling. What did you think?" His questioning glance toward me causes the car to cut the corner as he turns onto Cole Creek Road. The car jolts as the tire goes off the pavement, startling me, and reality hits. This isn't a dream. It's happening! Jason struggles to wrestle the car onto the road.

"Excuse me, I never said I was going to this Fall Fling," I say, giving him a scowl for good measure. How did I get here? How did she do this? I said I wasn't going, I wasn't taking a shower, I wasn't doing my makeup, I wasn't doing my hair. I definitely said I wasn't putting on this dress, yet here I sit. This lady is evil, I tell you, evil. "Where did you get my father's car?"

"It's okay, Jason. Drive on and be careful," Sadie says in the voice I've learned to be wary of. "This was my husband's last car, dear. He loved it so much. Jason keeps it for special occasions, like tonight."

"You are evil, Conswella Sandra Stephenson. Evil, I tell you," I say, scowling back at her.

Jason glances my way. "What did you say?"

"Never mind, Jason. Keep your eyes on the road. You can gawk at Jazmine when we get to the center."

All I can do is shake my head. I still don't know how she managed this. Then again, how does she manage anything?

Jason fixes his eyes on the snow-covered road, driving with the caution Sadie requested. We stop at the front entrance of the community center. There's a grand circular drive leading to the main doors. The trees lining both sides of the driveway sparkle with thousands of twinkling lights whose light shimmers off the lawn's blanket of snow. Fancy ribbons drape around the entrance doors, giving it a regal appearance. They've spent a lot of time and money transforming this bland building into a breathtaking venue. I'm here. Might as well make the most of it.

Chapter Twenty

There's a valet to open mine and Sadie's doors, and another is holding Jason's. After passing the valet the keys, Jason comes around to walk with us.

Someone is manning the doors, and they open as we approach them. We make our way to what Sadie calls the ballroom. Before reaching the doors, she motions for the person there to wait a minute and looks at Jason. "I'll go in first and you can escort Jazmine. Remember, you're escorting a vision." She nods for the door to open.

While she's stepping forward, he comes beside me. I've never been so nervous in my life. "Relax. She's right. You are a vision," he says. Right then, the doors open, and we move forward.

I try to act natural, but it's hard when everyone in the room stops talking and turns to scrutinize you. I'm not even sure I'm breathing, but I continue to walk with him. He leads me to the side and stops. Sadie is handing across her mink jacket, so I realize it's the coatroom. Several people have resumed their conversations, but most are still gazing our way. When Jason slips the mink stole from my shoulders, the place gets quiet once again. The hush is deafening.

While I wait for him to check the stole, the mayor is walking toward us. "Sadie, you look divine. We are so glad you could make it. You too, Jason. Miss Jazmine, you are an angel. I checked my pulse to make sure I hadn't died and gone to heaven. Welcome to our Fall Fling. With you here, it's a blessed event."

"Thank you, Mayor. The center is amazing. They did a spectacular job on it."

"I'll mention it. But it pales compared to you. May I escort you to our table?"

"Why, yes. I didn't realize we were sitting at your table," I say, glancing at Sadie.

"Sadie and Jason must sit at the head table. It's tradition. Their family started all of this. It's the town's way of saying thank you," he says, holding his arm out. I hook my arm through his while Sadie and Jason walk behind.

As we make our way through the rows of tables, everyone's gaze follows our movement. There is whispering, but I can't make it out. We pass Terri's table, and she gives me a brief wave with an enormous smile. As I try my best to hide my nerves, I mouth "thank you." She nods, and I know she understands.

I recognize many of the people, all of whom seem to watch my every move. Is this happening for real? We reach the head table, which has the salad and a piece of cake at each place. Seated in one chair is the mayor's wife, and standing beside her is another gentleman. Judging by his uncanny resemblance to the mayor, he must be their son. There's another lady seated with her husband standing beside her. He's the sheriff, and I'm assuming she's his wife.

By now, Sadie and Jason have arrived, and Jason holds her chair out while she sits. The mayor does the same for me. He introduces everyone at the table, but I'm sure most already know each other. Then he excuses himself, saying he needs to earn his keep.

He goes to a podium on one side of the stage, and I sense an eerie sensation descending on me. I spot Jill, a few tables over, and her dagger stare and sour expression perhaps explains the eeriness. Not being able to do anything about it, I listen to the mayor.

"Ladies and gentlemen, thank you for coming to this year's Fall Fling. Glenrock has a fine history, and this evening's tradition is an enormous part of it. You do Glenrock proud. Let me introduce the people seated at our head table. There is my beautiful bride, Mrs. Sarah Donaldson; my son and our district attorney, Mr. Aaron Donaldson; our sheriff, Carson Cassidy, and his beautiful wife, Althea. Then, representing one of our original families, Mrs. Conswella Stephenson, known by all as Sadie, and her grandson, Jason Withers." There is polite applause after each one. "Also seated here is our newest resident, the charming and most beautiful Miss Jazmine Strake." The applause I get, not to mention the whistles, amazes me. Please let me crawl under the table and hide before I die of embarrassment. "Well, it sounds like our Miss Jazmine has made quite an impression on folks around here." I know I'm turning red. "I'd also like to thank the Women's Auxiliary for decorating the hall for this evening, led by their chairperson, Mrs. Jillian Carmine. You ladies did a fine job."

Even though no one else did, Jill stands and waves. There's a splattering of applause, but it's quick to pass, and she takes her seat.

"Now, since we're not in an election year, I'll be brief and close with this prayer. We are thankful for all the good Lord has blessed us with over the years. May He continue, and may we continue to be thankful," he says with head bowed. Afterward, he makes his way back to our table.

The dinner starts, and several servers arrive to refill drinks. Everything is so formal. Not like what I was expecting. All the men are in suits and the women in gorgeous dresses. The older women are wearing longer evening gowns. The ones my age, I'm glad to see, are wearing dresses similar in style to mine.

This entire evening is so fabulous I struggle to eat my salad. Despite this, the staff bring out the main course, and they didn't skimp on the menu. It's prime rib with fluffy potatoes and asparagus wrapped in bacon. The food tastes fantastic. The conversation is light while we eat. Once they clear the plates from the main course, everyone starts with their dessert. Jason swaps his for mine, which was a pinkish cake with bits of strawberry and what appeared to be strawberry icing. He switches it for what turns out to be Devil's Food cake with fudge icing.

Now we're talking. I whisper, "Thank you."

"Don't mention it. I doubt I could eat anything so rich," he says, chuckling.

We continue enjoying our desserts and conversation while the servers make their way around filling glasses for anyone who needs a top-up. A little while later, the servers bring out tea and coffee. I have coffee and notice Sadie does too. Jason doesn't appear ecstatic with this, but I'm not sure there's anything he can do about it. At least the servings are in small cups.

Once most tables are clear of plates and cutlery, the mayor again rises and goes to the podium. "That was a superb meal, don't you think? Let's give a round of applause to those who prepared and served it, the kitchen and wait staff of our own Paisley Shawl." A hearty applause thunders around the area while the group in question gathers across the front. "Thank you again for such a spectacular meal. Now, ladies and gentlemen, let the musical portion of our evening begin. I give you one of our favorite local bands, The Gregory Boys." Another deafening applause fills the room and several large men take their places on stage. I recognize Carl right away, but the most shocking sight is seeing Shelly at the keyboard.

The lead singer thanks everyone and says they're glad to be here. They start off with what I guess is a favorite around here, *Mammas, Don't Let Your Babies Grow Up to Be Cowboys*. Out of the corner of my eye, I notice Sadie say something to Jason.

He turns to me. "Would you like to dance?"

"I'd love to, but I'm not any good."

He assures me I only need to follow his lead and stands, holding my chair out for me. The other men follow suit, reminding me gentlemen still exist in this world. Jason walks me to the dance floor in time for the next song. He takes my hand in his and places his other one on my hip as I set my free hand on his shoulder. Here goes nothing. Not only is he an outstanding dancer, he is also correct; all I need do is follow him.

The band plays around twenty songs, a pleasant mix of popular and country. Jason and I dance to a few, but several others also ask me to dance. When the first man asks, I smile at Jason while answering yes. He's not the only fish in the sea. I dance to most of the songs and spend others watching. Several folks here are brilliant dancers. There's one group who are partial to line dancing and are something to watch.

Jason and I dance to the last number before the band exits the stage for a break, saying they will be back. As we return to our table, soft background music plays. At least the lower volume will make it easier to talk. This is my first chance to ask him what Sadie told him earlier.

He chuckles at first and says he won't tell me, but I continue to pester him until he spills. "She said I better ask you before you snap your fingers and the line forms."

"You're kidding?"

"No. Looks like she was right too, what with all those who've been asking you to dance."

"I hope you don't mind."

"No, it's fine. It's not like we're a couple or anything. You enjoy yourself."

I have to agree and excuse myself to find the ladies' room. Several ladies are in line. While I'm waiting, Terri and Cindy rush to me and comment on my dress and how amazing I look. The compliments, I'm sure, are because of how I was when Terri came to get me with Sadie. I'm glad she doesn't mention it.

With the visit to the ladies' room accomplished, I walk with Terri and Cindy back to the tables. We're halfway there when Jill steps out in front of me, making a point of blocking my way. She's standing, arms crossed, one foot out front, tapping the floor with an intimidating glare. Those near us take a step back, and the hubbub of conversation hushes.

Not knowing what else to do, I smile at her. "Evening, Jill. Are you enjoying the event?"

"Strake, huh? Jazmine Strake," she says. Venom fills her voice, and I'm not sure what she's getting at.

"Yes. Is there a problem?"

"Problem?" She looks around the room. "She has the nerve to ask me if there's a problem," she says and turns back to me. "Yes, there's a problem. The people here need to know the truth about you," she says, waving her arm around the room.

I'm frozen, not knowing what problem she could mean.

"Jill, this isn't the place," Jason says, rushing to us. I'm appreciative for his well-timed entrance. "Maybe you should cool off a little."

"No, Jason, you need to hear the entire truth concerning this supposed esteemed little lady here. See, your Miss Jazmine not only goes by the name of Jazmine Strake, but also Tiffany Waldensmyth. The writer of 'The Rich Girl's Poor Life' read by many of us. However, that's not the best part. She's also the daughter of the man who almost ruined this town." She pauses for effect.

I know what's coming next, but I don't understand why this would matter to these people. Then the words Sadie shared concerning Jill and her family come to mind. How investments went bad and cost her family everything. Now I understand. Once again, the world is yanking back the curtain to show my reality. Happiness for me is nothing but an unreachable dream. This is my fate. Why did I ever think this time would be different?

"Yes, everyone, let me introduce the daughter of Theodore A. Strake. The man who ruined my father and others, and caused the near collapse of the bank. Yes, the same man who went to prison for his part in the Ponzi scheme costing my father and others everything." She sticks her chin in the air, glancing around, appearing pleased with herself.

Jason clears his throat. "Now, Jill, you know it was not your father's sole investment that failed. There were many even, and it was years before he lost everything. Yes, Jazmine's father went to jail, even though he wasn't one of the primary people involved. He liquidated everything to return as much of the money as he could, then went to jail rather than running and hiding from his responsibilities." Not a single person in the room isn't listening to every word being exchanged.

"It doesn't matter," Jill says. "He caused it, and yet she dares to show her face here with her fancy clothes and all," she says, waving a hand at me. "I bet she spends her nights laughing at the gullibility of you pathetic people and how you fawn over her. Even thinks everyone is beneath her and not worth the time of day." From behind Jill, the mayor is trying to negotiate his way through the maze of tables and chairs to get to us.

I must stop this. I should say something, but it won't help. People will believe what they want. The facts don't matter. Not even the fact I was twelve years old when my father went to jail and even younger when the investment scheme started. None of this will make any difference.

Pushing through the crowd, I rush out of the room. There's nothing I can do but leave. Let them say what they want. I can't defend my father, nor can I make them understand I wasn't part of it. It ruined my family too. I hurry outside while wiping the tears running down my face. Why did I ever come? Tonight only gave life another chance to slap me. I'm sure everyone is laughing at me as the doors close behind me.

I hear Jason call out behind me, but I don't care. I can't face him. Not now. Not after this. Leaving the building, I have no idea where to go. Plus, it's cold and there's no one around. The parking valets must be elsewhere since the event isn't over. Spotting the car we came in, I dash to it. It's unlocked, and I get in the driver's seat. I check the ignition, but the keys aren't here. They're not in the visor either. What a time for someone to not leave the keys. Is everything stacked against me?

With no ability to escape, the tears come. I thought this was behind me. Why did I ever write that stupid blog? Then it hits me: I'll have to move. Where? Where can you go when you're kicked out of a town of fewer than three thousand people? The tears cascade down my cheeks as I lean forward against the steering wheel.

After a few minutes, the passenger door opens, and someone enters. "Jazmine?" It's Jason.

"I'm sorry, I didn't know where to go. Please let me think for a minute, and I'll leave."

"You don't have to leave. Where would you go? I came out to see if you were okay."

"If you're not kicking me out of your car, can you take me home? I promise I won't bother you again. I'll drop Boris off with your keys tomorrow and clear my things out of the office. You'll never hear from me again," I mumble through my tears. I still can't believe this happened.

"Why would you do any of that?"

"Do what?"

"Drop off Boris and clear out your office, not to mention me not seeing you again. I'm sorry, but none of that will happen."

"Why not? Don't you want me out of your life? Didn't you hear what Jill said?"

"Yes, I heard."

"Well, it's all true, every bit. My father was part of a deal that swindled millions of dollars from people and ruined their lives." I can't bring myself to look his way. I feel him hold me by the shoulders, turning me to face him. I can't look.

"Jazmine? Jazmine, look at me," he says. "Please look at me."

I lift my face until our eyes meet. Why is he gazing at me with such concern?

"If you'd have waited a few moments, you'd have heard me tell Jill and everyone there your father died in prison while trying to help a defenseless man. You would have heard me remind them you were twelve years old when they took your sole living parent away and how you lost everything too. They made you move to a children's home and then into foster care."

I try to let his words get through. Did he say all that? Did he defend me?

He dips his head so it's level with mine, looks me in the eye, and continues, "You'd have heard several women share what they learned from your blog. How you cared for the two young daughters of the foster family you lived with. How you studied hard and worked part-time jobs to save money for college. How you couldn't go to Yale because of your father's scandal. While your grandfather made it possible for you to attend Harvard, it was your grades that got you accepted. How you worked hard and got your degrees with honors while still being under the shadow of your father. You'd have heard me tell everyone I knew who your father was, what he was part of, and what happened in jail. That you were not part of it and thus didn't carry the blame."

I want to believe, but remember the night in the truck.

"Of course, you knew. I told you the night we spent in the beast—at least a little—and you put it all together. It changes nothing," I tell him. Why won't he let me leave and go somewhere no one knows who I am?

"No, I knew before then. Sadie and I both knew when we heard who was moving in across the way. I've known everything concerning your father, and so do many people here. No one thinks you have anything to pay for, and no one blames you. They care for you and want the best for you."

"Jill doesn't. She's been gunning for me since the first day we met."

"When it comes down to it, I doubt even Jill holds a real grudge against you. She saw you as a threat to what she wanted and struck out the only way she knows how. Don't be mad at Jill. You should feel sorry for her. If anyone can understand what she's gone through, it's you. It goes the other way too. Instead of letting it consume you, causing you to use people to get what you think should be yours, you put it behind you. You worked hard to accomplish something on your own. The first weekend you were here, you took a plate of cookies to someone you didn't even know and visited with her. You took her shopping and spent time with her. Those are not the actions of a terrible person. Those are the actions of someone I want to get to know. Someone I admire."

I can barely breathe, but somehow say, "You knew? Even when you hired me? You knew about my father?"

"Yes. None of this was a secret to me or most of the people in town. I don't know why Jill didn't know or why she thought she'd wait for tonight to share it like this. After you left, people told her she was wrong to confront you like she did and to make it sound like they agreed with her. They're on your side. They want you to come back so they can show you. You're one of them. One of us. They care for you. They're hurting, knowing you're hurting."

"I can't go back in there. Not after what she said, not after they saw me run away. I could never face them again." I'm staring at my hands twisting in my lap.

He lifts my chin with his finger. "You're facing me now. You have nothing to be ashamed of because you did nothing wrong. You walked away from an unpleasant situation instead of making it worse. You did what the Bible tells us to do. You turned the other cheek instead of striking back. I know you could have said something that would have stabbed Jill. You have a quick mind for barbs, and I could give many examples of the ones I've witnessed. However, none were in fear or hatred. They're done in fun and with love—which is why you said nothing to Jill. Instead, you left. You walked away with your dignity intact, leaving Jill's in shreds, and you never said a word. I know you would never say a word to hurt anyone on purpose. Not you."

"How do you know? I've said nasty things to Jill. I'm no different from her."

"You might have said things, but they weren't so bad, and none were to inflict pain. They were more to apply humor to a situation you didn't understand. What amazes me is, since the first time you met her, you've worried what she thought and what might hurt her. Not yourself, but her. It's one thing I love about you. From the first moment I saw you standing in your doorway trying to hold your coat closed, I knew you were someone special. Even then, I knew who your father was, but after meeting his daughter, I needed to know her."

"From the first time we met. You mean when I was dressed like a big city hussy? That first time?"

"Yes, that first time. It wasn't so bad though, and I knew you weren't expecting company. Who cares what you were wearing? You made cookies and took them to a neighbor. Even though all you knew about her was she couldn't get out like she did in the past. You got dressed and walked out in the cold, not even knowing where you were going or who you were meeting. That's the Jazmine I needed to get to know. That's the Jazmine I'm falling in love with."

For the first time since he got in the car, I sit bolt upright and look him straight in the eye. "What? You're falling in love with me? You know little about me. We met not even three months ago. I aggravate you in so many ways. I put gasoline in your diesel truck. I pamper the puppies. I give Stanley Mountain Dew when I shouldn't. I cleaned and organized your office without asking, and I'm sure there are many more things I've done you don't like. Yet, you're falling in love with me?"

"Yes, I am. I've tried not to. Believe me, I tried. I've thought for a long time it was only ever going to be Tyler and me. He was to be the center of my life. I'd already enjoyed the love of my life, but she needed to leave. There was nothing to make me think I could have another shot at love. Then you came into my life. Into our lives—Sadie's, Tyler's, and mine. I watched how you spent time with them, how you were around them. How they came to love you. I don't know what the future holds for us, but I want to find out. Yes, we've known each other less than three months, and in another few months we might find we can't tolerate each other. I'd rather risk that than not take the time to see if we're meant to be together. Jazmine, I want to spend time with you. I want to get to know you even better and want you to get to know Tyler and him to know you."

He cups my face in his hands. The warmth of his touch makes me accept this isn't a dream. This is happening.

"You mean that? You want us to get to know each other? Be a couple? Is that what you're saying?"

"Yes, we owe it to ourselves, and to each other, to find out what we can have together. I'm willing to take the risk. Are you?"

"Well, I don't know. You can be a little hard to get along with. You're mean to the puppies and strict with Tyler. Then there's the not liking mayonnaise thing and the way you treat Stanley. I must give this serious thought." I enjoy every second of watching his expression change from one of hope to one of despair.

"You're serious? You'll have to think. Is this what you're telling me?"

"I thought you liked it when I fired my barbs at you. Isn't that what you said?"

"I don't believe this. After I pour my heart out, you come back making a joke?"

"I thought you said, and I quote, 'It's one thing I love about you?' Weren't those your words? Did I get it wrong?" I'm unable to hold back a giggle.

"No, you got it right, and now I'll pay for saying it for a long time. I don't care. I'll take it if it comes with the rest of you. Shall we? What do you think?"

"I think you're crazy, but that's one thing I love about you. Yes. I want to get to know you more too. You've got me whether or not you want me, and you might live to regret it."

"Okay then. Now, I need two things from you, so I know you're with me in full." His expression shows how serious he is.

"Okay, two things; what are they?"

"I need you to get out of this car and walk with me back into the center with your head held high. You need to show everyone what a formidable woman you are. I think you need to do it for yourself and for those people in there who care for you."

"You want me to walk in there, back to where I ran away in humiliation. Is that what you're asking?"

"Yes, that's what I'm asking. Don't worry. I'll be with you. Right beside you. You have nothing to fear. Nothing at all."

"Okay, I'll try if you promise to stay close."

"I promise. I never want to be anywhere else."

"Right, okay, but you said two things." I'm not sure I can even do the first.

"I need you to kiss me. Right here, right now. I don't think you have ever been more beautiful, and I want to kiss you more than I've wanted to kiss anyone in a long time."

"What are you waiting for, big guy? An engraved invitation?"

He pulls me close, and our lips meet for the first time. It's like no kiss I've ever had. Please don't let it end. Seems he doesn't want it to either. We let it last and enjoy the moment while he holds me tight. I've never felt so secure in my life. We separate, and it's so quiet in the car, neither of us appears to be breathing. I can't stop looking in his eyes, and he keeps his gaze locked on me as well, smiling. My heart is pounding as my body tingles and my mind races. I can't gather any thoughts. Is this what it's like to be in love? I've never felt this way about anyone or anything, ever.

"Are you ready?" he asks.

"I'm game if you are. It's not like I have anything to lose."

"I think they'll surprise you. Let's go show them the new couple in town," he says, then opens his door. I'm not convinced it's the right thing to do, but my door opens, and Jason is standing with his hand held out for me.

His expression shows he's not only willing, but ready to help, and my fears fade away. I now know I no longer need to go it alone. People will help, and I need to let them. I need to grasp the outstretched hand so I'm no longer on my own.

I place my hand in his. In an instant, I'm assured I'm where I should be. He helps me to stand and we walk toward the front doors. The frosty night air bites at my bare skin, reminding me I never stopped to get Sadie's stole. He realizes I'm shivering and slips his suit jacket off, placing it around me along with his arm, holding me tight against him.

At the front doors, he holds one open for me. After a few steps toward the doors of the ballroom, I freeze on the spot. "I can't go in there—"

"Don't worry. I'm here, remember?" he says, gazing at me. "We'll go through this together."

While I appreciate the thought, I realize he's a man and has misread the situation.

"It's not about going in there." Slipping his jacket off, I hold it out. "I can't go in there like this. I need to fix my makeup. Wait here. I won't be long." I enter the small bathroom off the entryway. I can't believe the sorry sight in the mirror. My mascara and makeup have smeared and left black streaks down the length of my face. I'm atrocious.

I don't know if I love the fact Jason never mentioned it or if I'm mad because he was letting me go in there like this. Maybe a little of both.

I get wipes from Sadie's small clutch. It takes work, but I clean most of the mess. I redo what I can before staring at my reflection for a few moments. Satisfactory.

I know what I've endured in my past and the inner strength I've somehow drawn from throughout my life. I can do this—not because of me, but because Jason believes in me. He believes I can do this. If he didn't, I know he'd never let me try.

With my resolve set, I turn and walk back to Jason, who is smiling while he watches me come toward him. "You are amazing!"

"Well, I don't know if amazing is accurate, but it's the best I can do, so it will have to be enough."

"One thing before we enter."

"What?"

"A kiss for courage." Our lips meet again. With him holding me in his arms while we kiss, I can't think of a better, more comforting place to be. Pulling away, he gazes into my eyes. "You ready?"

"With you by my side, always."

I take his arm and know I'm squeezing it hard. He leads me into the room. At first, no one sees us. Then, those closest turn in our direction. As we move, more turn to watch and the chatter stops, causing a hush to fall across the place while Jason and I walk arm in arm to our table.

I stare straight ahead and try to hold my head high. He said I have nothing to be ashamed of, so I'm trying to present this image. Inside, I want nothing more than to get to our table. Around me I hear soft music playing while the band is on break. My luck we'd come in now, but it's too late to go back. I continue to walk.

Sadie meets us halfway to the table, taking the position on my side opposite Jason. The three of us continue to the table, and the men there stand. "Miss Jazmine, I am honored you have returned and graced us once again with your presence," the mayor says.

"Thank you, Mayor. I apologize for disturbing this delightful evening. I hope all can forgive me," I say, taking my seat in the chair Jason is holding out for me.

"No forgiveness needed because you have nothing to apologize for," he says. Everyone takes their seats; everyone except for Jason. I watch while he goes to the stage toward the podium. Oh no, what is he thinking? Relief floods through me seeing him motion to Shelly. They speak, and Jason comes back to our table. Again, he doesn't take his seat.

He stops near me, holding out his hand. "May I have this dance?"

Despite the surge of emotion washing over me, I manage to smile and say, "Yes, always." I take his hand and follow him to the dance floor.

He turns me to face him, places my arms around his neck, and nods to Shelly. As the music plays, he pulls my body against his. Then I hear Shelly's sweet voice sing *You Light Up My Life.* I don't think any song could ever be more appropriate, but it improves as I rest my cheek on Jason's chest and feel his arms around me.

The song ends, but I don't want to let go of Jason. I don't want him to let go of me either. I lift my head and gaze into his eyes, seeing nothing but kindness, tenderness, and love. He leans his head down, and we kiss once more. Right then, I know I'm right where I need to be. In his arms.

Several people clap and call out words of encouragement. They make their way onto the dance floor and surround us. What should I do? Jason is smiling, and I'm brought back to the here and now, realizing I'm blushing.

The band prepares to play their next song, and I hear, "Ladies and gentlemen, Miss Jazmine Strake. She's got it all." I recognize the first few bars of the song they're playing. It's the intro to *She's Got It*

All, and while Jason holds me in his arms, I hear the phrase "She's got it all, my heart, my soul, my wishes."

When the song ends, he escorts me back to our table. Terri and Cindy rush to meet us. Try as I might, I cannot stop the tears, which causes them to cry. We embrace in a three-way hug and laugh through our tears of joy. I've never known what it was like to have genuine friends like these two. We don't even speak any words; we need none. After this, I need to redo my makeup again, I hope for the last time. I let Jason know I'll be in the ladies' room.

Several ladies offer a warmer greeting than I expect and share how glad they are Jason and I are together. This doesn't help the makeup situation, but at least I'm not smearing it this time.

With so many thoughts running through my head, I decide not to go back to the ballroom right away. There's a room lit by moonlight, and I find a chair behind a partition. I sit for a few minutes to think about what has gone on tonight and what this means. I need a few moments to collect my thoughts before I'll be ready to return. I'm sitting in the dark, thinking, when I hear Sadie's voice.

"Thank you for what you did," she says. "I couldn't have done a better job."

"Thank me? For what?" a second voice replies. "Making a fool of myself in front of the entire town?"

I'd know that voice anywhere. It's Jill.

"Not at all. You gave Jason the push he needed. He can be a slow mover, and nothing I was doing was yielding any results. You gave him the perfect shove."

What on earth is she referring to?

"Shove? I did no such thing. I was trying to split them up, drive them apart, not push them together," Jill says with the usual dose of contempt in her voice.

"Those may have been your intentions, but God has a way of using our actions to accomplish what He wants. From this day forward, we'll both know God used you to bring them together. He works in mysterious ways," Sadie says.

I smile upon hearing her say this. Sadie must walk away because I hear Jill call out louder.

"Well, we'll see. Who cares about a stupid dance and a paltry kiss? This doesn't mean they're getting married or anything," she says, her voice trailing off after she passes the open door, marching off along the hallway.

I wait a few minutes to make sure Jill has left before making my way back to our table. When I get there, I lean down and kiss Sadie on the cheek. "Thank you," I whisper.

"Thank me for what?"

"I think you know. I think you always knew and always will. You are one special lady." I kiss her cheek again, and she pulls me into a hug.

Never one to let me have the last word, she whispers, "If I'm so special, why don't they dedicate a song to me? Besides, I thought I was evil?" She pouts her lips and tries her best to appear wounded.

What can I say? She's Sadie.

The rest of the night is a dream. People let me know how glad they are I returned, telling me again and again I have no reason to apologize. I dance to several more songs, but only with Jason. I think the other men got the message because no one even bothers to ask. It's a magical night.

But, like all magnificent things do, it ends. We stay until most people have left, and we know it's time for us to leave. We collect our belongings, and once outside, Jason signals a valet, who retrieves the car.

The valet holds the door for Sadie while Jason holds mine, and I slide into my seat. As he drives us away from the community center, I know we are leaving, but a part of tonight will stay with me. We ride in silence, lost in our thoughts. I can't believe the number of stars out tonight, shining so bright. Everything seems like I'm seeing it for the first time, like I'm experiencing this glorious world through a fresh pair of eyes. Maybe I'm learning to appreciate it.

Jason turns to me when we reach Sadie's driveway. "Wait here. I won't be long," he says and gets out.

He opens Sadie's door, helping her out and to the house. I'm not sure what he's doing in there, but it's a long time before he reappears at the front door. When I notice he's carrying the suitcase Sadie brought my things in, it makes sense. He puts it in the back and walks around to the driver's door.

We wave goodbye to her before making our way back to my place. For the first time since I got here, I'm disappointed by how short the drive is. He stops beside Boris. After helping me out, he grabs my suitcase from the backseat.

He takes my hand, walking me across the porch to my front door. The suitcase hits the ground, and I feel his arms wrap around my waist as he pulls me in for another kiss. If I thought our previous kisses were passionate and meaningful, I was wrong. The feel of his body being so close to mine and the way he holds me is like nothing I've ever experienced. I sure don't want tonight to end.

"Do you want to come in?" I ask between kisses.

"More than anything in the world, but it wouldn't be right, so I'd better say goodnight." His arms still hold me close.

His answer throws me for a loop, and I pull back. "Why not?"

"Have you forgotten where we live? If I go in there, it will be all over town before the door even closes. I'll say goodnight so I don't give the tongues anything to wag about."

"I think it's too late, but I understand. I don't like it, but I understand. Wouldn't want this big city hussy ruining your reputation," I say, nestling my cheek against his chest.

"I'm not concerned with my reputation, but I better go before I can't," he says and kisses me once again. He stands back while pushing my door open.

"I still don't like it," I say as he sets my suitcase inside the doorway. "You can bring it on back?"

"Again, I better leave. We'll talk tomorrow."

With reluctance, I watch him walk across the porch and down the steps. He gets to the car and turns back with a wave and a sweet smile. I watch him drive out of my driveway, but not out of my life. I don't think he could ever, or would ever, leave me.

I close the door and carry the suitcase back to my bedroom. It contains the clothes I wore to Sadie's. This brings to mind my harrowing time in the shower, and I'm stupefied to find the clothes are dry. I don't know how, but that's Sadie.

I'm still in a dream world emptying my suitcase and putting my jewelry away. While undressing, I replay most of the night. I'm not ready for it to end. If I go to bed, I'll go to sleep and wake to a new day. I'm not ready for that. I slip on my shirt, get my laptop, and climb into bed, waiting for the computer to boot while I reminisce over tonight's events.

Once the desktop screen appears, I click the icon for the last section of my blog. It opens, and I scroll to the bottom, making sure I don't read any of it. That is not why I'm here. I need to do justice to the end of this blog.

The Rich Girl's Poor Life
The Epilogue

While writing this last section, I became more and more convinced this was indeed the end of my life. My mother left me, my father left me, my life as a princess vanished, and now, the love of my life had left me too. What's left? Only the empty shell of a girl and her unfulfilled dreams.

Since then, I've learned I was correct. Without dreams, our lives may as well be over. When I first moved here, a person told me, 'In less than a year, you won't even recognize your old life.' I didn't believe her, but I know now this is the end of this rich girl's poor life. Because, I realize, my old life needed an ending before my new life could have its beginning.

This was my journey, from ending to beginning!
Pray for me and be on the lookout for:
This Poor Girl's Rich Life!
Coming soon!

Epilogue

I can't believe it's almost Christmas. The time since Thanksgiving has flown by, but it's been great. While it's been an adjustment, the new man in my life has made things even more interesting. It's no longer just me, but I have to say he can be a bit of a bed hog. Then there's his moodiness, and he's also a little over-protective of me at the office, which I wasn't prepared for. But those there have adjusted to the new arrangement, and it's getting better. Of course, Jason still refers to him as the Master Freeloader, but Bob and I ignore him. I think Jason's jealous.

At first, I think Bob missed Mindy after she left, but he's gotten better. Not long after Thanksgiving, a family brought in their Dachshund, who was very old with multiple health issues, and the decision was made to put her down. This devastated their young daughter, and it was almost as if Bob and Mindy knew this. They were in my office when they heard her crying and her mother talking to her. I didn't even notice the two of them left at first, and when I went looking, they were with the little girl, as if they were comforting her. Mindy went home with her forever family that afternoon.

On the other front, the relationship with Jason is going well. We keep it somewhat professional in the office, but outside he is so caring and loving it scares me a little at times. I've only had the one serious relationship before in my life, and it was nothing like this. I've started attending church with Sadie and him, and they help to answer my questions. I'm learning a lot, but seeing their faith in action is having the greatest effect on me. There's more to this God of theirs then I thought possible.

Tyler has spent a few Saturdays with me while Jason worked, and I'm learning how active a four-year-old can be. I thought it was a male thing, but when I helped with a birthday party for a girl in his Sunday School class, I found out its more a four-year-old thing. They never stop.

While it's only been three months, it seems like a lifetime ago I was slumped on my musty couch thinking I had nothing and no one. Now I have Jason, Tyler, and Sadie, the friends at work, the ladies' group, the church, and the community. There are so many I can't even name them all, and even Jill is coming around. But then that was a lifetime ago. That was my old life and now I have the beginning of my new one. I can't wait to see what this brings.

Acknowledgements

I would like to acknowledge all the people who helped this dream become a reality. There are my two editors, Lisa Bambrick and Cat Chester. My many beta-readers and fellow writers and members of the P2P Facebook group who provided wonderful comments, suggestions, and over the top support. This would have never happened if it wasn't for all of them.

About the Author

Born and raised in Muncie, IN, Craig is about as typical middle-America as they come. He was young when his parents divorced and his grandmother came to live with him, his mother, and two sisters. Seeing his grandmother's faith in God on a regular basis led him to accept and know everything is okay, God's in charge.

Craig served 20 years in the U.S. Air Force and followed this as a Department of Defense contractor where he had multiple tours overseas and around the U.S. While there were events in his life that tested his faith in God, nothing compared to when his first son was born with major medical issues. As a twenty-one-year-old father with a young devastated wife, his faith had never been tested more. After enduring several surgeries, some considered experimental, his son passed away at six months and two weeks. But even in his short life, he had a huge impact on Craig and others.

Since then, God has blessed Craig with two more sons and has been a constant guidance in his life. Craig's time in the military and as a contractor afterward included over 20 years overseas where he was part of local mission churches. On their last return to the states, God led Craig and his wife to Oklahoma where he teaches Bible studies and serves as a deacon in a local church.

Craig loves to hear from his readers. You can find and connect with him at the links below.

Website/Blog: http://www.authorcraighastings.com
Website: http://www.mooseridgeendingtobeginning.com
Facebook: https://www.facebook.com/authorcraighastings
Twitter: http://www.twitter.com/ch875299_craig

~ * ~

Thank you for taking the time to read *Moose Ridge: Ending to Beginning*. We hope you enjoyed this delightful story as much as we did. If you did, please tell your friends, and leave a review. Reviews support authors and ensure they continue to bring readers books to love and enjoy.

Turn the page for a peek inside *Flaherty's Crossing*, where a successful yet emotionally stifled artist's life takes an unexpected turn after her father passes.

Flaherty's Crossing
Kaylin McFarren

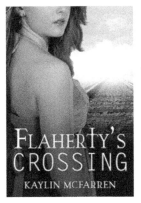

From the Pacific Northwest's award-winning author, Kaylin McFarren, comes a powerful novel about love, loss, and the power of forgiveness ...

Successful yet emotionally stifled artist Kate Flaherty stands at the deathbed of her estranged father, conflicted by his morphine-induced confession of his part in her mother's death.

While racing home, Kate's car mishap leads her to a soul-searching discussion with a lone diner employee, prompting Kate to confront the true reasons her marriage hangs in the balance.

When her night takes an unexpected turn, however, she flees for her life, a life desperate for faith that can only be found through her ability to forgive.

EXCERPT

Kate's lungs burned as her boots pounded the bumpy dirt road. Musty dampness condensed the air. It hurt to breathe, yet she couldn't stop. She had to run. Far and fast. Before Mick realized she wasn't coming back.

Where could she go?

She needed a guide now more than ever. She glanced up and searched for the moon. Clouds had eclipsed the light, and the drizzle was nearly blinding her. Moisture filled her eyes. Raindrops, tears—she wasn't sure which.

Suddenly something latched onto her toe. She screamed as she flew forward. The heels of her hands hit first, bulldozing two paths in the mud like fleshy garden hoes. The mystery trap released her foot and her knee slammed against material more unforgiving than dirt. The pain burst through her adrenaline wall, curled her body into a cannonball with no swimming pool to catch her landing. The rain pelted down, faster and faster, streaking over her face. She was drowning with fear, drowning like that day at the lake.

But now her father wasn't here to save her.

A tree branch cracked behind her. She snapped her head up from the mud and dared to look back. Patches of fog. Tar-black darkness. The shadow of the Reaper reaching for her soul.

Don't make me come lookin' for ya. Mick's words clawed at her mind.

With the ball of her foot, she pushed against the railroad track that had taken her down and scrambled to her feet. A nauseating headache erupted, beating into her neck and grating on the backs of her eyes. Inside, she was screaming for help. The muted screaming of Edward Munch's terrifying painting.

She had reached the highway. Now where to?

Her window of opportunity was slipping away.

To her left, only a wall of blackness. She'd have to take her chances with the lit house she'd passed a few miles back and just hope someone was home.

She turned right and made her way down the middle of the slick pavement, hindered by her limp. Strands of her wet hair swung at her eyes and adhered to her cheeks with mud as thick as rubber cement.

The bridge was no more than thirty feet away when she spotted a light flickering through the trees. She increased her speed, ignoring the flare in her lungs. With every aching step, she hoped the glow wasn't merely a street lamp.

Please...please be a house...

She heard the hum of a motor growing louder and nearer. She grabbed her knee and wheeled about. The approaching headlights blinded her. She raised her hand to flag the vehicle down, its white orbs prancing on her pupils. As the car slowed, she exhaled her greatest thoughts of doom.

She squinted against the glare, thankful to be saved from a lunatic's grasp. Yet no sooner had her mind found relief than a ghastly theory pillaged her hope. She knew he'd been lying to her, keeping her there deliberately. What if Mick's truck had been parked in back all the time?

A newfound horror streaked through her, riding her veins as her heart pumped painfully. She spun around, begging for her feet to cooperate. Yet her pleas failed to reach her legs, which softened like jelly.

Somehow she pushed on. Head for the bridge. Cross the river.

Get to safety on the other side.

Tires crunched over gravel. The engine quieted.

"Kate!"

A man's voice. She knew it was him.

"Kate, stop!"

She stumbled, her feet searching for traction on pebbles as round as marbles.

A door smacked closed.

Her footing regained, she stumbled along the shoulder of the road. Away from his car. Away from him.

"Kate! Hold on!"

She forced a glance over her shoulder. Just as the outline of his body took shape, the ground below her gave way. Down she slid, the muddy bank taking her. Her arms flailed as she reached for a rope that wasn't there.

Her arms yanked, and she stopped. She'd found a tree root. She held on with both hands, as the relentless rain pelted her face. Fear was everywhere: above her, below her, behind her. She looked down, white spots still blocking her vision, and heard the sound of water. The river. If only she could see how far the drop was.

"Oh, God," she implored, "please, please help me."

A hand clamped over her forearm. "I've got you!"

"No!" she shrieked.

He was going to kill her. Right here. Right now. She tried to pry his fingers loose, but mud coated her hands like oil.

"Kate, stop it! It's me!"

She pounded on his wrist twice before registering the voice. "Drew?"

"It's okay," he said. "Give me your hand."

She raised her gaze. Indeed it was her husband, silhouetted by shining headlights, an angel coming to her rescue.

Out Now!

What's next on your reading list?

Champagne Book Group promises to bring to readers fiction at its finest.

Discover your next
fine read!
http://www.champagnebooks.com/

We are delighted to invite you to receive exclusive rewards. Join our Facebook group for VIP savings, bonus content, early access to new ideas we've cooked up, learn about special events for our readers, and sneak peeks at our fabulous titles.

Join now.
https://www.facebook.com/groups/ChampagneBookClub/

Made in the USA
Coppell, TX
21 November 2021

66118363R10134